The Republic of Night

By the same author

LYING CRYING DYING

The Republic of Night

Dominic Martell

An Otto Penzler Book

CARROLL & GRAF PUBLISHERS
NEW YORK

THE REPUBLIC OF NIGHT

An Otto Penzler Book
Carroll & Graf Publishers
An Imprint of Avalon Publishing Group Inc.
161 William St., 16th Floor
New York, NY 10038

First Carroll & Graf edition 2002

Library of Congress Cataloging-in-Publication Data is available.

ISBN: 0-7867-1123-X

Book design by Michael Walters
Printed in the United States of America
Distributed by Publishers Group West

Thanks are due to the kind officials of the Pressestelle of the Zurich Stadtpolizei and to Eric Maréchal in Paris. Any foolishness to be found in these pages is due solely to the author's poor understanding.

The Republic of Night

ONE

'They came just before midnight. We heard the lorries pull up in the square and all talk stopped, in an instant. We knew. The sound of feet hitting the earth, a lorry door slamming . . . I hear them in my nightmares, monsieur. The squeal of brakes in the night and I begin to tremble again.'

The *moro* cradles the coffee cup in both hands, his black eyes wide and arresting in the seamed face, the eyes of a dog lying in the street with its back broken. The collar of his worn suit jacket is turned up and everything he owns is in the plastic carrier bag at the foot of his barstool. His French is replete with the heavy trilled Arabic *r*. *'Je commence à trembler encore.'* Looking past him through the arched doorway of the bar Pascual can see sunlight on stone, a *moto* parked in the narrow street, two widows in black conferring on the curb.

The *moro* takes a sip of coffee; just now his hands are steady. 'There were five of us in the room that night, and I am the only one who lived. My brother Hocine sat there with a card in his hand, raised, the card he had been about to play, and we looked at each other for perhaps five seconds, hearing them pile out of the lorries and calculating the distance, the direction. I could see him thinking exactly what I was thinking. They were between us and our families.'

The *moro* sets the cup down on the bar, very gently. He says nothing for a time, staring at the zinc countertop, hands on his knees. 'Why didn't I stay with my family that night? Because you can only live so long with three hours of sleep a night, sitting up on the roof with a shotgun, a shovel, a kitchen knife. We had been through that, weeks before, when other villages were being attacked. Nothing happened and we got tired of staying up at night. We began to think it could never happen to us. We were too close to Algiers, the army would protect us, God would protect us. I don't know what we thought. I suppose we stopped thinking. And then we heard the trucks.

'We moved all at once, five men jumping up, knocking over chairs, spilling out of the house. We heard the first shots, the first scream, before we reached the square. They had already sent men down the lanes, they had men on the road at each end of the village. Hocine ran screaming at two of them and they cut him down with an axe. They had rifles, but they didn't have to use them much; nobody in the village had weapons because the army doesn't allow it. If you have weapons you are a guerrilla. So they don't have to waste much ammunition in a village like ours.

'Hocine was faster than I and that's what saved my life. When I saw him die, I turned and ran the other way. I wanted to circle around through the orchard on the edge of the village, try to come up on my house from behind. They were starting to pull people out of their houses and the wails were rising together like the sound of a siren, a strange sound. I was praying that my wife would have got the children out and into the fields. My house was not far from the end of the street. I thought if I could get there soon enough we could get into the fields and run. But they had put men in the orchard, too.

'There were two of them at least and they didn't waste bullets on me. It was dark and I was running, so they heard me before I heard them. I made them out in the dark and tried to dodge, but somebody must have hit me on the head. I don't know why they didn't cut my throat. Perhaps someone else came into the orchard and they went to deal with them. All I know is that when I came to I was a newborn, having to learn everything over again. I learned that I could walk, that there was blood on my face, that my head hurt. I learned that these were trees and those were houses. I learned that those were fires among the houses. I learned what those distant screams meant. You learn very quickly the second time you are born and soon I was running again.

'I wish they had cut my throat in the orchard. By the time I reached my house I knew what I was going to find inside. I could see that the door had been kicked in and my only hope was that they had got out of a back window and into the fields. I didn't want to go in, monsieur. I wanted to stand there in the street forever, until the world stopped turning. But the thought that they might have somehow survived, like me, made me go in finally.'

The *moro* swallows once, hard, and Pascual hopes that he

will not have to sit and listen to the bitter end. Stop now, friend, he thinks, but senses that the *moro* must tell it to the end; that, more than the hunger etched on his face, is why he followed Pascual into the bar.

Now he looks Pascual square in the face again. 'I cannot watch a lamb being slaughtered,' he says. 'On feast days I turn away when they put the knife to its throat. So imagine if you can, monsieur, what it was to find my children in there. I could see just what kind of shoes the killers wore, printed on the floor in the blood of my children.

'My wife had fought so hard they had had to kill her with an axe. She had tufts of hair clutched in her fingers. That saved her from being raped, I think. That is all the comfort I have. My children didn't have to see that. And they say that you die quickly of a cut throat. Lambs do. But the lamb also suffers; I've seen it.'

The *moro* has told the whole story in the voice of a man explaining a minor traffic accident to a *guardia urbana*. He gives the impression of having been drained of all horror, all life. Pascual wonders how many times he has told the story and how he manages to sleep at night. Perhaps he doesn't; it was in the wee hours that Pascual first spotted him, wandering in the Plaça Reial, plastic bag dangling from his fingers. Only the eyes set him off from the other Arab illegals who gravitate to the lower Gothic Quarter. For three days now Pascual has seen him here and there, with the gait of a waif and the face of a hundred-year-old man, too dazed even to beg, and this morning he has finally taken pity on him and brought him into this dark portside *tasca* to buy him some bread and coffee.

The *moro* finishes the coffee. 'You want more?' Pascual asks, breaking a silence.

'No, monsieur. I thank you.' The *moro* wipes his mouth delicately with the little square of paper that came with the bread. 'You have many questions,' he says.

'Questions?' Pascual blinks at him.

'Who were they? Who could do such a thing? Why do they wish to kill us?'

Faintly ashamed, Pascual says, 'Well, yes. One wonders.'

'I can answer only the first question.'

'And?'

Something new comes into the *moro*'s eyes now, almost a gleam, perhaps the first glint of madness. 'They were our own.'

'Your own?'

'At least two of them were from our village. Boys who had left to go into the *maquis,* a couple of years before. They were seen pointing out houses. This one has to die, that one can live.'

Pascual stares into the *moro*'s face, eyes narrowed. He has seen and even done many unpleasant things in his life but this is new to him. 'What is happening in your country?' he says quietly.

The *moro* eases off the barstool and bends to pick up his bag. '*Chez nous,* monsieur, we have finally done the impossible. We have tried God's patience too long, and He has turned us out into the night. *Adieu.*'

Santa Maria del Mar is a very long way from a village on

the Algerian Mitidja. Pascual loves the old church in spite
of his bitter atheism; the remote reaches of its high Gothic
vault can move him to tears. If there were a God, He
would haunt a place like this. Pascual comes here when
he needs silence and apartness. Here at least he can dream
of forgiveness.

He slips into a pew near the rear of the church, his face
lifted to the bright slashes of stained glass that march in
column down the side of the church. The *moro*'s story has
stirred his permanently uneasy heart. On one hand Pascual
can think *at least I never cut a child's throat,* but on the other
hand he knows that the difference between the man he was
and an Algerian *intégriste* killer is one of degree rather than
kind. He crosses his arms on the pew in front of him and
lowers his face to rest on them.

Footsteps come softly up the aisle behind him. The church
is seldom free of tourists and Pascual has learned to ignore
them. When the footsteps halt at his side, he waits for them
to move on, then looks up in irritation.

'*Voilà le bon Samaritain,*' says the man. Pascual cannot
make out his face, silhouetted as it is against the light from
the windows. He stares in confusion; who is talking French
at him now? 'Move over,' says the Frenchman.

'What do you want?'

'I want to talk to you. Reward you for your good deeds
maybe. You brought a tear to my eye, feeding that poor *boug-
noule* like that.'

'Go away.'

'*Pousse-toi.*' The familiarity would be intolerable from a

stranger, but the man gives Pascual a nudge on the arm as if he has known him all his life. Pascual slides over and the man sits next to him. He is solidly built with close-trimmed black hair greying at the temples. He has heavy brows over dark eyes that appraise Pascual with a hint of amusement. Pascual has never seen this man before but he knows that a simple mistake in identification is too much to hope for. The man smiles. 'Praying?'

'I don't know you.'

'Ah, but I know you.'

'I doubt it.' Pascual begins to rise. There is no class of people he fears more than strangers who claim to know him.

A hand descends on his arm. 'Pascual Rose.'

'No. You've made a mistake.'

'March, then. Pascual March. That's the new version, isn't it?' The Frenchman pronounces it *Marsh* rather than the correct Catalan *Mark*.

Pascual sinks back to the pew. He blinks at his new friend, who looks pleased at having scored a point. He hears feet hitting the earth, lorry doors slamming. 'Not here.'

'Ah, fine. Shall we take a walk, then?'

Outside, Pascual walks briskly toward the port, shaking out a cigarette. The Frenchman trails him by a meter. 'Why don't you just tell me where you'll be? I'll catch a taxi and meet you there.'

Pascual has in fact been running through schemes to lose the man: sprint down that lane, jump on a bus. He decides that only the most drastic measures would give him more than temporary relief and he is not prepared for drastic measures.

He gets the cigarette lit, tosses away the match, blows smoke over his shoulder. 'I like to walk fast.'

'Not from what I've seen. Dawdling from bar to bar seems more your style.'

'Very clever. Am I supposed to be impressed with your surveillance skills?'

'Oh, no. You made that part of it easy. If I were you I'd be more worried about how I knew you were in Barcelona.'

Pascual slows a little as he rounds the corner of the Llotja, the port opening out on his left, sea air in his face. As the Frenchman draws even Pascual says, 'Let me make some guesses. You're with somebody's intelligence service, probably the French because sometimes the obvious is true, most likely the DGSE. You knew I was here because you've always known it; you and the Spanish and the Americans have all used me as a commodity at one time or another. If I had any sense I'd disappear, go someplace else, but I don't. I like it here. So you didn't have too much trouble finding me.'

The Frenchman shrugs modestly. 'A little, all the same. You don't have much of a paper trail. You pay your rent in cash, you have no stable employment, no driver's license, you pay no taxes as far as we could tell. Don't worry, we won't tell the *fisc*.'

'So you sat outside the Café de la Opera and waited for me to walk down the Rambla.'

'Well, it wasn't quite that haphazard. There is a police detective up the Via Laietana who is very fond of you.'

'Ah, that must be Serrano. Fond of me would be stretching it.'

'Fascinated, then. He says he's been trying to decide if you're a scoundrel or a hero ever since you first crossed his path.'

'He buys me a drink sometimes. We talk about football and he tells me to stay out of trouble. If he told you where to look for me then he obviously didn't mean it.'

'I'm not here to bring you trouble. I am here to make you an offer.'

'I don't need anything.'

The Frenchman laughs. 'Ah, no? Where is your rent coming from this month?'

'That's my affair.'

'And that's just for starters. How are you ever going to buy one of those smart new laptops so you don't have to go on borrowing a computer every time you get a translating job? What are you going to do when your looks go and you can't get women to buy you dinner anymore?'

Pascual stops, pins the Frenchman against a wall with a hand on his chest. 'I don't need anything you can give me. And I don't have anything you need. Pascual Rose is dead.'

The Frenchman has a rugged face that some women would find handsome: a cleft chin that will require a lot of shaving, a finely curved upper lip perfect for the Gallic sneer, imperturbable eyes, very dark, under the black brows. Right now he has a look of unshakeable supercil-iousness that will not be dented by a hand on the chest. It will take a bullet, maybe two, to wipe that look off his face. 'Very well, he's dead. Perhaps you can establish psychic contact with him. He's the only man in Europe who has what I need. As for what I can give him, if he's not interested in a hundred thousand dollars in a nice safe tax-exempt account, well, I suppose he can always donate it to the poor. After he buys you a laptop, maybe.'

Pascual releases the Frenchman's jacket and lets his arm fall to his side. He has very bad memories of the last time somebody offered him a lot of money. He draws desperately on the cigarette and forces smoke out between his teeth. 'Who are you?'

'You know who I am. You just said it.'

'I suppose it would be too much to ask to see some sort of credentials?'

'My credentials are what I know about you and what I'm going to tell you. Do you think we carry around little plastic cards that say we are intelligence agents?'

'I thought you'd say something of the sort.'

'If I wanted to shoot you I'd have done it in the church. Rest assured I really do want to give you a hundred thousand dollars. Good yankee dollars, none of this euro nonsense.'

Pascual gives it two or three more puffs. People pass them on the pavement, uncurious. 'No,' he says.

'You're going to make me pull out the stick, aren't you?' The haughty look has faded to one of weary regret, the look of a long-suffering schoolmaster.

Pascual just stares at him, shoulders sagging; half the world has a stick to beat him with. He looks down at his cigarette, flicks ash onto the Frenchman's shoes. 'The *fisc*, for example?'

'Oh, we can do much better than that.'

Defeated, Pascual takes a last drag on the cigarette and flings it into the street. He looks the Frenchman in the eye and says, 'Why can't you leave me in peace?'

The Frenchman tugs at the tail of his jacket, straightening it. Icily, scathingly, he says, 'Now those are funny words to hear, coming from somebody with your history.' Finally taking pity on Pascual, he reaches out and slaps him on the shoulder. '*Écoute.* I'm not a woman, but I'm willing all the same to buy you lunch. The best lunch you've had in a long time, and if after that I still have to pull out the stick, at least you'll be well fortified.'

'Spare me,' says Pascual. 'Spare me the *bonhomie.*'

TWO

Once in his distant youth Pascual was taken to Can Culleretes by well-heeled relatives; as far as he can tell, nothing has changed. The dark wood paneling is still covered with photos and sketches of the famous, the beloved and the merely egotistical who have dined there through the years. If it is not the oldest restaurant in Spain, as claimed, it is certainly the one with the most self-esteem.

Morrel sits with his back to the wall. A careless twitch of his shoulder could dislodge a signed Picasso. Pascual wonders if Morrel is the Frenchman's real name and takes charge of the ordering. He is determined to take Morrel at his word and make him pay. He airily demands a *parrillada* and the most expensive Grand Cru on the menu. Morrel merely raises an eyebrow.

'How does a man as poor as you preserve such expensive tastes?'

Pascual has resolved not to let Morrel win the linguistic war with his continued *tutoiement*. He levels a finger at Morrel. '*Écoutez.* My friends I call *tu*. There are aged relatives whom

I call *vous* even though they use the familiar with me. You are neither. If we're going to have a professional relationship you're going to call me *vous. Vous comprenez?*'

'My apologies.' For the briefest moment Morrel looks genuinely sorry. His lips firm and he says, '*Sans blague,* how can you go on living the way you do?'

'And what do you really know about the way I live?'

'I know you live in a pension in the Calle Princesa and frequent the type of bistro where you could eat for a week on what I'm about to pay here. I know you give private language lessons for a handful of bills each time and you live out of petty cash. Occasionally you get a translation job that keeps you busy for a few days and puts you a little bit ahead. I know most of your disposable income goes on tobacco and alcohol. I know you have friends but I also know you're afraid.'

'Yes. Of people like you.'

'Not just me. You're vulnerable here. Extremely vulnerable. Paper trail or no paper trail, it wouldn't be all that hard for one of your old PFLP comrades to sit in the Café de la Opera and wait for you to come down the street.'

'I don't think anybody's left who cares that much. A lot of them are dead or in jail. Anyway, the last one who showed up, I killed.'

'And you're confident you could do it again.'

Pascual makes him wait for an answer, tracing circles on the white tablecloth with a fork. 'I'm not confident of anything. I make no claims, I have no ambitions. Now why don't you tell me what the hell you want?'

Morrel nods, looking thoughtful and not overly supercilious.

The wine arrives and they are silent through the fussy business of uncorking and tasting, a privilege Pascual cedes to the Frenchman.

When the waiter is gone Morrel says, 'As I said, I want to give you a lot of money.'

Pascual knows there is a ritual to be followed. If he overturns the table and flees, either his life in Barcelona is over or he will have to go through the whole thing again soon. He might as well enjoy his lunch. 'For services rendered?'

'For very important services rendered.'

'To whom?'

'To my government. To several others, for that matter.'

'That's conveniently vague.'

'Nothing involves just one country now. It's the age of globalization.'

'So they say. Can we be a little more specific? What do I have to do for my money?'

'You have to give a man the kiss of Judas.'

Pascual sits and listens to patter from neighboring tables, the clink of silverware and crockery. He takes a drink of wine. 'Again?'

'Again. You're the recognized expert in betrayal.'

'Who the hell is left? You've had nine years to catch them all.'

'We'll never get them all. What you gave the CIA and Mossad when you came over allowed them to gut one branch of the PFLP and roll up some loose networks in Europe, but as you well know there were a lot of very nasty types out there.'

'Still are, no doubt.'

'Precisely. Some of them have quit and are lying low, others have found themselves powerful friends. Some have even got quite rich.'

Pascual lets seconds tick off and says, 'Just who are we talking about?'

With the air of a history professor embarking on an account of the Trojan War, Morrel says, 'Do you remember Abu Yussef?'

Pascual has to think about it; he thinks while the *entre-mèsos* are placed before them, mushrooms, olives, slices of potato, *allioli*. As Morrel tucks in, making sounds of approval as he chews, Pascual is remembering another very different lunch: a dusty roadside terrace somewhere between Hama and Aleppo, a table under an awning, nothing stirring under the brutal midday sun. There are bottles of Coca-Cola on the table and plates with tomato and cucumber, Arab bread and hummus, a spit of roasted lamb slices. Across the table sits the man he was told to call Abu Yussef. 'I remember,' he says.

'You never knew his real name, of course.'

'They told me during the debriefing. But I don't remember it.'

'Daoud Najjar. That's been established for certain. From a minor branch of a prominent Baathist family in Aleppo.'

'*Najjar.* Carpenter.'

'Is that so? So he had an ancestor who did honest work with his hands.'

'I only met him a few times.'

'Well, that's more than any other living man can say.'

'Where is he now?'

'Ah, if we knew that . . . We have some sightings, that's all.'

'How am I supposed to find him?'

'You're not. You're supposed to identify him when he shows up.'

'Shows up where?'

'Paris.'

Pascual shakes his head. 'I'm not sure I could do it. I met him a handful of times between twelve and fifteen years ago. Could you identify, say, the manager of the bank you used to patronize fifteen years ago?'

'I could if we had conspired to embezzle funds together. Don't tell me you don't remember the man.'

Pascual works at his food; his argument is weakened by the great clarity with which he is seeing Abu Yussef in his mind's eye, in a hotel room in Sofia, in a squalid Hamburg *Kneipe:* across a table, a long Semitic nose above a mustache, very dark eyes with an expression of wary intensity. 'I remember him. But people change. I could walk by him on the street today and not recognize him.'

'But if you were told he was one of five or six people in a room, you could walk in and pick him out.'

'Pick him out of a lineup, eh?'

'In a manner of speaking.'

Pascual has no appetite but chews anyway, stalling, dreading. 'Why me?'

'Because, as I said, you're the only man alive who can do it.'

'I don't believe it. I've been out of the game for nine years. There must be several dozen people who could identify him and all of them more current than I.'

'You might think so. But Najjar has been out of the game as long as you have. He disappeared in eighty-nine, a few months after you defected, just before the Wall came down. Perhaps he saw which way the wind was blowing.'

Pascual takes a sip of wine. 'If he's been out of the game for so long, why do you still want him?'

'Because he killed sixteen citizens of the French republic.'

Pascual has to think for a moment. 'When?'

'Eighty-seven. The Paris bombings.'

'That was Abu Yussef?'

'He was behind it. He bought the plastic in Czecho-slovakia. That's been established.'

'I'm surprised he would get his hands that dirty. When I had dealings with him, he seemed more of a liaison officer.'

'Yes. That's what he was, essentially. The PFLP's direct link to the KGB.'

'So we thought, anyway. Nobody ever admitted it.'

'Oh, that's been established, too. When the Soviet files opened up, a lot of suspicions got confirmed.'

'I remember he spoke Russian. I think he'd studied in Moscow.'

'Yes, another of those Lumumba boys.'

'So you still want him for that. I'm surprised. French memory, in my experience, tends to be highly selective and linked to intrigues of the moment.'

'Well, it's not just us, as I said. A lot of people want him.

There's fairly good reason to believe he was involved in one of those bombings in Argentina a few years back. Somebody blew up a Jewish cultural center, remember? Some said the Iranians, but there seems to have been a good deal of local involvement. There's a Syrian community there and there were traces of one of Najjar's known aliases.'

'I thought you said he was out.'

'It would be more accurate to say he'd shed his old skin. What seems to have happened is that he became a sort of terrorist entrepreneur. There can be a fair amount of money in it and he does have skills to peddle. He seems to have gone the way of the rest of the Soviet establishment and put himself up for the highest bidder.'

Pascual muses, rolling some Grand Cru on his tongue. It tastes expensive but he finds less pleasure in the thought than he expected. 'You seem to have followed his career well enough without me. I can't possibly be worth a hundred thousand dollars to you.'

'Ah, but you are. You see, we don't have a face.'

'Come on. The Americans must have it. They had my face. They had everybody's.'

'Not Abu Yussef's. I told you he'd disappeared? He made a good job of it. They'd trained him well, the KGB, and they probably helped him go up in a puff of smoke, too. When I say he disappeared, I mean all of him disappeared. Photos, KGB records, everything. Even the files at Patrice Lumumba University were purged, sometime in nineteen ninety. Abu Yussef had friends in the right places.'

Pascual peers at Morrel across the table. 'But lots of

people knew him. We all knew him in Damascus. Go to Stammheim and talk to Schneider. He knew him.'

'Ah, well. Now we come to the best part. We'd love to talk to Schneider, but we can't.'

'Why not?'

'He's dead. He toppled over from a heart attack last year. Pity, he was only forty-eight. Must have been those drugs you all took. He looked like a man of sixty.'

'There must be others.'

'No, that's the really beautiful part.' Morrel smiles, a man enjoying himself. 'They're all dead.'

'Who?'

'Anybody who knew Abu Yussef.'

'Anybody?'

Morrel counts them off on his fingers. 'The Syrians. Khouri, shot to death in Athens in ninety-two. Abd-el Ghafour the same year in Beirut, no arrests ever made in either case. The Soviets. At least two former KGB officers who knew Abu Yussef have been killed since he went under. Arrests were made but they were murky gangland sorts of killings, you know how things are in Russia now.'

'You're saying he's had KGB people killed, just to cover his tracks?'

'Their clout didn't stack up to his, apparently. I told you, he's got the right kind of friends.'

'*Putain.*' Pascual is beginning to be impressed. Serious alarm, he senses, is just over the horizon.

'Let me continue. DiFiore, the old Red Brigade courier, in Bologna in ninety-three, supposedly a fight in a brothel, a

Libyan arrested but released for lack of evidence. Schneider, maybe a real heart attack, who knows? There were others. Everybody's gone. Everyone who ever worked with Daoud Najjar.'

Pascual waits for Morrel to say it but it never comes. Finally he drains his wine glass and as Morrel reaches for the bottle to refuel him, he says it. 'Except me.'

'Except you, *mon ami.*' Morrel pours him a generous measure. Pascual leans back on his chair, arms folded, sullenly resisting. Morrel works the bottle back into the ice bucket. 'So you see. You have a very high market value suddenly.'

There are other implications as well but Pascual is resisting them. 'Why suddenly? What's going on in Paris?'

'Interesting things. It appears that Mr. Najjar has a new career.'

'Let me guess. Doctor? Bookmaker? Priest?'

'Higher up the tree. He appears to have become a banker.'

A puff of ironic laughter escapes Pascual. 'Somehow that seems in character.'

'Yes. I think we're talking about one of the great Darwinian successes of the collapse of the USSR.'

'A Russian bank?'

'No, a French one.'

'How is that possible?'

'We're not sure. The bank in question has recently changed hands. It went on to a reef in the property crisis and was declared insolvent. What came next has not been entirely elucidated. These things don't always take place in the light of day in France. The Tribunal de Commerce rejected several plans for bailing out the bank; some of the major stockholders mysteriously balked at others. Finally the biggest stockholders sold out and a deal was cobbled together that put majority control in the hands of a company called Miracle.'

'Miracle.'

'That's M-I-R-A-K-L. Odd spelling. The deal was a bit controversial and there was some question as to whether it was legal. There was some muttering about bribery and so forth but the competent authorities seemed to be happy to see the bank rescued. There was a satisfactory influx of capital and business went on.'

'And who's behind Mirakl?'

'That's a very difficult question to answer. It's headquartered in the Channel Islands and has offices in Zurich, Vienna, Antwerp, Tel Aviv—and Moscow. Ultimately, it's Russian.'

'I see. The plot thickens.'

'Yes. Mirakl is one of those excrescences that have come out of the rubble of the Leninist state. It was originally based on oil but it seems to have a finger in everything—including a few things one doesn't mention in polite company. Russian girls in Milanese cathouses, the odd SAM missile here or there, that type of thing.'

'Good Christ, and they let them buy a French bank?'

'Well, after all, they're careful not to put the white slavery and the weapons deals in the prospectus. Mirakl runs plenty of legitimate enterprises. As I said, they've got one of the major Russian oil companies. They make cars in Volgograd and plastics in Kiev. The dirty stuff happens in subsidiaries and they've got so many of those that it's never obvious what belongs to whom. The board of directors they put together for the bank is perfectly respectable, as far as anyone can tell. They found an Italian with impeccable credentials and made him PDG. On the surface there's nothing to reproach anybody with. What I'm telling you is the fruit of some very tedious research. The type the average French judge or newspaper reporter is not in a position to do.'

'All right, where does Najjar come in?'

'Well, probably right at the top. He seems to have ridden the coattails of his good friend Colonel Kovalenko.'

'Don't know him.'

'I wouldn't expect you to. If you had, somebody in your outfit would have been guilty of some very serious breaches of security.'

'What is he, KGB?'

'Was, anyway. Former first deputy chief of the old First Directorate. A very well placed man. And one who sensed the winds of change early on. All that happened when the Soviet Union went under was that the communist *nomenklatura* transformed itself overnight into a bandit oligarchy. They had held everything in trust for the proletariat, of course, so once the idea of the dictatorship of the proletariat went down the drain they simply forgot about the trust part of it. They'd never got around to issuing the proletariat any deeds of ownership, it seems. Well. Evidently Kovalenko picked up enough of an idea of capitalist technique while lurking about Western capitals to get a pretty big jump on the competition. Now, he's one of the richest men in Russia. He's got homes in Switzerland and Spain and a private security force of a couple of hundred men, a good many of them former KGB. He's got more personal power than your average head of state. And he employs some very interesting people.'

'Like Najjar.'

'Apparently so.'

'Maybe it's time to tell me where Najjar comes in.'

'Ah. Here comes our food.' The *parrillada* arrives, mounds of seafood that was swimming this morning, grilled and heaped on a platter. Morrel makes a show of interest, poking through the feast with a fork, asking for names.

Pascual loses patience quickly. 'So, Najjar. He's in Paris?'

'Has been. Will be again soon, we hope.'

'How do you know?'

Morrel dissects a mussel, inserts the flesh carefully in his mouth. He chews, swallows and says, 'The Banque Villefort occupies an elegant old *hôtel* in the second arrondissement. Like any bank it needs security personnel. One of the security officers, a glorified doorman really, who was held over from the *ancien régime* when the bank changed hands was a former Algerian army officer who had emigrated to France in the late eighties after betting on the wrong side in all that turbulence they had back then, when they got rid of Chedli and put in some new fellows. A fellow named Mourad Mediane. He had been a member of military intelligence back in Algiers and he made use of certain contacts in our service to get his current position. A fairly sound man by all accounts. And last month he came to us with an intriguing bit of news.'

Pascual waits while Morrel eats, entirely conscious that he is watching a master dramatist and salesman at work but powerless to speed the story along. 'Which was?' he says finally.

Morrel takes in some wine and sighs, content. 'Which was that Abu Yussef had walked into the bank one day.'

'He knew him?'

'He had dealt with him in the course of some negotiations over a hijacked airliner that wound up in Algiers a few years ago. Apparently Najjar showed up as a sort of go-between, on behalf of somebody or other who was bankrolling the hijackers, probably the Syrians at several removes. But the point is, Mediane knew him. And he told us he was certain it was Abu Yussef.'

In spite of himself Pascual feels curiosity growing. 'And what was he doing there? More than just cashing in travelers' checks, I imagine.'

'It appears he is part of the new management team.'

'Remarkable.'

'Yes. He makes use of a private suite of offices and comes and goes as he pleases, usually as part of a team that stays for only a day or two. Mediane told us he had seen him twice in the last four months.'

'Well then, what's your problem? You wait until the next time he shows up and you arrest him.'

'It's not quite that simple, unfortunately. The new management is a slippery bunch. Emissaries from Mirakl tend to show up unannounced, closet themselves with the local manager and then vanish. The less privileged employees are a bit vague on who's who.'

'Well, for Christ's sake, you have Mediane dash to the phone the next time Najjar turns up and you hurry over with sirens flashing. You've already got your Judas.'

Morrel shrugs, his jaws working. He washes the bite down with the excellent wine and shakes his head, giving Pascual a rueful look. 'Believe me, that was my intention. I'd just as soon have avoided this little trip, though I have to say the lunch almost makes it worthwhile. But there's one problem.'

'Which is?'

'Mourad Mediane's dead, too. You may have read about it. The six Algerian exiles slaughtered in the basement of that restaurant up in the eighteenth arrondissement last week? Mourad Mediane was one of them.'

THREE

'No,' says Morrel, 'there's no reason to think it was anything but what it looked like. Six dead Algerians in a basement, blood all over the place, my money's on the *intégristes,* the GIA or whatever they call themselves. It's got everybody scared, that's for sure. Apart from the bombings in ninety-five there hadn't been much spillover from all that shit down in Algeria. Now it looks like it's starting to seep across the Mediterranean. This one had everything one hears about, all the nasty bits. Blood, severed limbs, the whole thing. They herded everybody into the basement and hacked them to death. They found the head of one of the victims in a pot on the stove.'

Twice in one day, thinks Pascual. He does not believe in omens but a theme is emerging and he does not like it. 'How the hell did they get away with it? Didn't anybody hear anything?'

Morrel shrugs. 'It all took place after closing time. There were a few gunshots but most of the killing was done by cold steel, *arme blanche.* They might have held them all at gunpoint, taken them down the steps one by one. Who knows? The police have a few leads but they're not talking about them.'

'There would be a good deal of blood. How do you slaughter six people and walk away without attracting notice?'

'Maybe you bring a change of clothes. Maybe you just jump in a van and speed away. Maybe they did attract some notice. I expect they'll catch them eventually.'

Pascual drinks, attempting to deal with unpleasant implications. 'And how does Mediane fit in?'

'He was probably just in the wrong place at the wrong time. He frequented the place, knew the owner. Some of the victims had apparently run afoul of the Islamists down there in Algeria. The police are still trying to sort all that out. The restaurant seems to have been a rendezvous for exiles of one sort or another. Dissidents, secularizers, hangers-on of the old regime, like Mediane.'

'So there's no reason to believe Mediane was the target, particularly.'

Morrel's smile is arctic. 'That's a very nasty thought, isn't it? No, as far as anyone can tell, it was just our bad luck that the man who alerted us to the presence of Daoud Najjar in Paris got himself killed in a politico-religious *règlement de comptes* a few days later.'

Pascual holds it up to the light and looks at it from every angle, and from every angle it looks ugly. 'As far as anyone can tell,' he repeats.

'Look, I don't think Mirakl took the trouble to mount a small military operation to mask a hit on a man who might or might not have recognized one of their operatives. Mediane never said Najjar recognized *him*.'

'Would he have known?'

'I couldn't tell you. But I think this is one of those times when it really is just coincidence. I think it was another aspect of his past that caught up with Mediane. Such things do happen.'

Pascual returns his stare across the table. 'Yes,' he says. 'I suppose they do.'

'It's time to pull out the stick,' says Pascual. He and Morrel have made their way through the narrow lanes to the Ramblas and are descending. Pascual is desperately fighting the feeling of well-being brought on by the wine and the massive meal. There has been talk of a *café y copa* in some congenial venue. The sunlight diffused through the plane trees dapples the broad promenade. Pretty girls walk arm in arm; old men dawdle at news kiosks; buskers and beggars and baffled tourists make eddies in the stream.

'I haven't convinced you?' says Morrel.

'You've convinced me I'm a regrettable oversight on the part of Abu Yussef. I'm not sure even a hundred thousand dollars is enough to make me walk into a room and shake his hand.'

'So you want to see how big the stick is.'

'Hit me with it and I'll see if I can take it.'

'I wouldn't like to do that. I'd much rather you gracefully accepted the money in exchange for carrying out your civic duty.'

'My civic duty?'

'Well, after all, you used to be one of his boys. I'd say you've got some atoning to do.'

'No doubt.' Pascual nods at an acquaintance, walks on, his pace growing slower as his weight seems to increase with every step. 'So what happens if I say no?'

Morrel halts, turns toward him. The look of humorous condescension is gone, replaced by a look Pascual was once very familiar with, the look of the professional intelligence officer about to exert leverage. *'Sans blague?'*

'Sans blague.'

'Well, I'd have a range of options to choose from. I don't think I'd even bother with the local tax man. You're just small fry. I could always try to stir up trouble with your old pals in Damascus—there must be *someone* there who still bears you a grudge. But all in all I think the best approach would be the most direct. I imagine it would be fairly simple to get word to Daoud Najjar that a man who can identify him is living in the Pension Oliver in the Calle Princesa in Barcelona.'

Pascual stares into Morrel's face as people brush by them. He is an expert on ruthlessness, and at this moment he is very conscious that the only people who approach utopian fanatics in ruthlessness are members of government security organs. 'You'd do that?' he says, for form's sake.

'Of course,' says Morrel. 'What do you take me for?'

Pascual resumes walking. 'I could run.'

'Sure. And I probably wouldn't bother to look for you. Of course, if you've stayed here this long, it means you've got a good reason for not running.'

'I like it here. And that's what you counted on, wasn't it?'

'That's what I counted on, yes. Can I give you a word of advice?'

'No.'

'The question was rhetorical. My advice is to give in to the inevitable and think about the money. It's sitting there waiting for you; I can show you a check if you like. The money's quite real, and it's a hell of a lot more than thirty pieces of silver. You can put it into one of those nice annuities the Swiss do so well and come back here and live off the interest. And once Najjar's caught, you'll be safer. Think of that as well.'

Pascual wonders if there isn't something wrong with that last point but he is too fogged by wine to put his finger on it. He has been hooked, played and gaffed by a master fisherman, he realizes.

'Paris,' he says. 'I used to know Paris quite well.'

The Tin Man sits staring at the television with a vacant gaze. He has taken the funnel off his head, revealing a patch of scraggly blond hair that contrasts oddly with his silvered face. His eyes are bloodshot. He looks up as Pascual enters and murmurs a greeting.

'What's the matter?' says Pascual. 'That nasty old witch been giving you a hard time again?'

'You can't imagine how tiring it is to stand immobile for ten hours every day,' says Bernabé, who earns his daily bread as a living statue on the Ramblas, a harsh and exacting craft. 'Perfectly immobile, with all manner of idiots gawking at you. The amount of muscular exertion—'

'I know. Is equivalent to swimming ten kilometers.'

'And the fucking costume itches as well.'

'You should have stayed in medical school,' says Pascual, stepping across the outstretched tin-clad legs. 'Is Enric in?'

'He's in there going over the books, scheming to nudge the rent up another few notches. But he's not going to get much more blood out of this turnip.'

Pascual raps on a door marked *Conserjería*. It opens and Enric stands there smoking, with unruly hair and Trotsky glasses. '*Hola*. What's up?'

'Can I talk to you for a moment?'

'Sure.' Enric makes no move to invite him into the office, and Pascual wonders if Bernabé is right about the scheming. He cannot quite see past Enric to the desktop. 'I have to leave the pension for a few weeks,' he says.

'You don't say.' For a moment there is surprise and per- haps a tinge of genuine regret but then Pascual can see Enric tumbling to the opportunity this affords him to jack up the rent. 'What a pity, we'll miss you.'

'I'm coming back. I just don't know when. I was won- dering if there was some way you could hold the room for me. Not keep it vacant, you know, just rent it out temporarily perhaps, make clear that as of, I don't know, September, the room has to be vacated again.' It might take a week, it might take two months, Morrel has told him.

Enric smokes, frowning at him. 'Man, that would be diffi- cult. I don't know, I don't think I can do it that way. Toss someone out after they've taken your place? I don't think I could do that.'

'You tell them it's only for a month when you rent it. I'll ring you before the end of the month to let you know if I'm coming back. If you don't hear from me, you can rent it out for another month.'

'That's a little problematic. All I can say is, if you want to pay a month or two in advance, I can hold it for you that way.'

And still rent it out while I'm gone and collect double, thinks Pascual. 'I don't have it in advance. But if things go well, I'll be in funds when I come back. Hold the room for me and I'll pay you one month extra when I come back.'

Enric considers this, the tip of his Ducado glowing dangerously close to his fingers. 'Done,' he says.

'At the same rate as I pay now.'

With the air of a man forced to concede his fortune at gunpoint, Enric nods. *'D'accord.'*

It occurs to Pascual that if things go well he will be able to afford a much better place to live. But poverty has conditioned him to cover his bets whenever possible and in any case there is much to be said for a pension where the owner winks at women slipping into one's room and is liberal with his cognac late at night. 'All right, then. I'll be leaving in a couple of days.'

'Where the hell are you going? Don't tell me somebody's given you a job.'

'Paris. And yes, somebody's found a use for me. I'm to tutor the son of an Omani sheikh in French and English.'

Enric looks at him with new respect. 'Fabulous. Your gift of tongues finally paid off.'

'So it seems.'

'Bastard,' says Bernabé behind him. 'How I envy you. I love Paris. People appreciate an artist there. The whole city's a theater. There's more life on a single Paris street than in all the talking shops in this whole city put together.'

Pascual spent much of his childhood in Paris and he knows streets there that reek of death and solitude. 'It's quite a town, all right.'

'Don't come back. If I were you I wouldn't come back.'

'Oh, I hope to be back,' says Pascual. 'I hope very much to come back.'

Morrel's hotel suite contains a sitting room with a desk. There is whisky on the desk and a comfortable chair for Pascual at one corner of it. Outside is the Rambla de Catalunya, a higher-rent district than those Pascual is accustomed to. Whatever its faults, the Direction Générale de Sécurité Extérieure appears to grant its minions a generous expense account. *'Santé,'* says Morrel, hoisting his glass.

'I don't get it,' says Pascual.

'What?'

'The plan. You say you don't even know when or if Najjar is planning to stop in again. What am I supposed to do, sit in the lobby all day pretending to do crossword puzzles?'

'Najjar will be back. A pattern's been established. If I had to guess, I'd say he's what the Americans call a bagman. He carries the money. Maybe not in a literal bag, but money all the same. Why do you think Mirakl needed a bank?'

'To launder their money, what else?'

'Exactly. And a setup like Mirakl's generates a lot of it.

So I think we can assume that Mr. Najjar will be making regular visits.'

'Fine. Still. What do I do, leave a phone number with the manager, ask him to contact me when the bagman comes?'

Morrel gives him an exasperated look over the rim of his glass. 'You're still not taking this quite seriously, are you?'

'The very good chance I'll go the way of all those ex-KGB heavies? Yes, actually I'm taking it quite seriously.'

'Then pay attention. You'll need somebody inside the bank to notify you when the envoys from headquarters drop in.'

'Ah, that simple, eh?'

'That simple.'

'And when I get the word I simply wander the corridors knocking on doors. Saying, "Excuse me, I'm looking for the man who used to work for the KGB." Is that it?'

'You'll have access to the bank. You'll have a pretext, a cover.'

'You've got it all arranged, have you?'

'Of course. I'll go over all that with you in Paris.'

Pascual sighs and drains his glass. 'Well then, I suppose the logistics are all that's left to discuss.'

'Yes, of course.' Morrel digs in a manila envelope and whisks out a plastic card. 'There's your *Carte Bleue*. I'm sorry it's not *blanche* but we have to have some limits. You've got a hundred thousand francs to draw on and that ought to suffice for the moment. If things drag on and you need more we can arrange it. We'll find a way to pay it out of next year's defense budget somehow. As from tomorrow you will be one Marcel Garnier, born in Saint-Cloud in nineteen sixty-two. We've got a little shop in the *sixième* not too far from the Luxembourg Gardens where we can take your photo and fix you up with a passport, driving license and *carte d'identité*. We've got a flat for you in the *dix-neuvième* and we've got reservations on the Air France flight to Paris tomorrow morning.'

Pascual's stomach takes flight; it is really going to happen. 'You mentioned something about a check,' he says.

Morrel smiles, the man who can afford the magnanimous gesture. He lifts a briefcase off the floor and reaches into it. 'I'll need this back, of course.' He hands Pascual a long rectangle of paper. 'When we have Najjar in custody you'll get this to keep and you can do whatever you want with it. I can recommend a very shrewd man in Geneva. He'd be happy to help you structure your investments.'

Pascual takes the slip of paper. It appears to be a certified check drawn on something called the International Caribbean Bank and Trust. The name Pascual March leaps out at him on the payee line and the words *One hundred thousand and no/100 Dollars* are typed neatly below. The signature is illegible. Pascual finds his heartbeat has accelerated. He stares at the check for a moment and then shakes his head once. Holding the check in his left hand, he slides his right into his jacket pocket. 'And what if I simply walk out of this room with it right now? Gave you the slip and strolled into the first bank I came to and opened an account?'

'I would, of course, immediately have payment stopped.'

'Presumably you would have to be alive to do so.'

It is only the briefest of freezes, the merest second of immobility, but Pascual senses that for the first time he has truly got Morrel's attention. The Frenchman smiles and says, 'Credibility. A threat has to have credibility.'

Pascual lays the check on the desktop. His right hand is still in his pocket. 'You considered everything, didn't you? Except the possibility that I might revert to form. That I might like it here so much that I'd kill to stay here. You didn't consider that. Did you?'

Morrel's smile is gone, leaving only a faint ironic light. 'Certainly I did. And I'll stand by my judgment. What have you got in there, your prayer beads?'

Pascual stares at him. 'You like Westerns? I always wanted to try an old-fashioned quick-draw. When I was underground we preferred not to give people a sporting chance, but I'll let you make the first move. I don't know where, but I know you've got a *flingue* here somewhere. Go on, I'm sure you're quite fast. And it's harder than it looks to pull a gun out of a pocket. I'd say your chances are pretty good.'

Morrel laughs, a single puff of disdain. 'Well, if I'm to make the first move, obviously the best policy is for me to sit here until you get tired and come to your senses.'

Pascual gives it a long second and then jerks his cigarettes out of his pocket. The way Morrel flinches as he does so gives him a certain satisfaction that lasts through the process of getting one lit. *'Sans blague,'* Pascual says. 'You're lucky I'm a changed man.'

Morrel is smiling, in control again. Reaching for the

check, he says, 'You must remind me not to patronize you in the future.'

Making his way home, Pascual has the stirring in his loins. He makes a pass through the Café de la Opera, trolls the arcade in the Plaça Reial, looking for someone, anyone. The little German blond in the Glaciar, what was her name? Elena the sculptress, supple and willing, cheerfully depraved. If he can catch her alone for a moment he can take her home again. Tomorrow he is going to Paris to look the devil in the eye and tonight he needs someone in his bed.

He spots the German girl at a table with four other people outside the Glaciar but walks on through to Carrer Ferran and stands smoking, restless and discontent. He cannot for the life of him remember the German girl's name. Two lovers pass, arm in arm, and Pascual looks after them with an unexpected pang. Sometimes you want only the act and sometimes you want the person. Pascual has wanted only the act for months now; the German blonds and the Elenas, he realizes, have had a strictly utilitarian role. Tonight he wants someone to lean on him, whisper to him the way that girl is whispering to her boy.

Sometimes you just want the act and sometimes, like tonight, you want the person. And if there is no person, there is no solace.

FOUR

Which Paris will it be this time? thinks Pascual. He has had relations with a number of them. Emerging from the Métro onto the Boulevard de Sébastopol he feels like a man meeting his ex-wife, torn between old grudges and melancholy regrets. First there is always the Paris of postcards and Hollywood musicals, a complete fantasy but inescapable, a skyline etched in human consciousness. After that, Pascual's Paris bifurcates: the Paris of his childhood and the Paris of his university years. The first is a pastiche of vivid detail on hazy background, this or that corner where a memorable scrape occurred, the shopkeepers who were friendly and those to be avoided at all costs, a storm riffling the surface of the river along the Quai de la Tournelle, a scolding from his mother for wet clothes. The second and later Paris was a cauldron of awakened sexuality and political fervor, a whirl of shabby flats with posters of Che on the wall and the *fac* and the *restau-U* and an intoxicating freedom. Sabine with hair under her arms and hard brown nipples; Teresa the Brazilian girl with those huge black eyes. And everything ended in death. Paris in the early eighties was the brink of the abyss for Pascual.

Now everything is different but nothing has changed; the tourists are still here, the same ones it seems, still peering at the menus posted in the restaurant windows with the same worried look. Sébastopol is still a bazaar with careening traffic; the pavements are still a maze to be negotiated, stepping around bins full of cheap cassettes and confabulations of Africans in robes. Pascual wanders away from the boulevard and here is Beaubourg, the architectural scandal that was *tout neuf* when Pascual was last here and is now just an immense plumbing catastrophe, the repair scaffolding blending imperceptibly with the original. The street artists are still here, the pavement Michelangelos and the skeletal saxophonists who play with their eyes closed, the jugglers of hatchets and the Arab boys spitting fire. Pascual returns to the boulevard. He walks all the way to the river and watches a *bateau-mouche* go by, captive Germans looking up at him through glass. He flicks a cigarette butt into the water and sees a meteor disappear into the atmosphere of a cold planet far below.

Pascual is afraid. He is afraid of spoiling the first Paris by finding some degraded trace of it in the light of day and he is afraid that the second Paris may not be dead enough.

Morrel brings another bottle of whisky along with Pascual's freshly minted documents. Pascual wonders if this is something they teach young officers at l'École Normale Supérieure d'Espionnage: keep the subject well-lubricated. Outside, the plebeian nineteenth arrondissement lies quiet in the night. This street is dead as a cemetery, with murmurs of traffic in far-off exotic quarters just reaching it on the night breeze. They have given him a sparsely furnished flat in a fabulously ugly building with a façade of raw brick framed in naked steel. Pascual stands at the window smoking, acknowledging Morrel's remarks with an occasional grunt. On a corner a hundred meters away he can see a cheerful-looking *brasserie;* he longs to be there.

'You are listening, aren't you?' says Morrel from the room's single chair. 'There's a good deal at stake here.'

'I'm listening. Who's my target?'

'Villefort,' says Morrel. 'You'll go right to the top.'

Pascual drifts to the small table where Morrel has put the whisky and two glasses. He pours and takes a sip. It is a good single malt that tastes of smoke and seaweed. Pascual swallows and grimaces. 'Villefort. Wasn't that the name of the young *procureur* who sent Edmond Dantès to the Château d'If?'

'Could be. I'm not too strong in history, to tell you the truth.'

Pascual does not buy the numbskull act for an instant. Morrel was the name of Edmond Dantès's employer and that is too much coincidence. 'The name of the bank at least is real, I assume.'

Morrel gives him a brief smile and looks down at the file on his lap. 'Oh, yes. Named after the founding family, now somewhat in decline. The surviving male of the dynasty is one Jean-Marie Hervé Charles de Villefort. Seventy-nine years old, now the owner of the bank only in name, though he still controls a few shares. Mirakl kept him on as a doorstop and table ornament. He still has the fancy office, spends a few hours a week there, rubber-stamps a few decisions now and again. He's reportedly still quite able but dissolute and losing interest fast. He spends a lot of money on horses and desperate measures to reverse the aging process. He's your man.'

'He's going to welcome me into his inner circle, is he?'

'He'll have no choice.'

Pascual nods slowly. 'What have you got on him?'

'What haven't we got on the old sod? I've never had so much fun compiling a dossier in my life. Mr. Villefort has led a rich and varied life.'

Pascual goes back to the window and leans against the frame, looking down into the street. 'You must find your work very rewarding.'

'It has its moments, I assure you.'

'So what am I using to club the poor bastard with?'

'I think we'll go with his war record.'

'Oh dear, not another one.'

'Yes, sad to say some of our greatest men were not as cool to the Nazis as one might have wished. Though so many of them managed to fiddle with the records afterward. If the Resistance had had as many men as later *claimed* to have belonged, we'd have rolled the Nazis back across the Rhine while Eisenhower was still choosing wallpaper for his flat in London.'

'So Villefort was a bit too chummy with the Nazis?'

'That's putting it mildly. The Villeforts were very rich and very Catholic and they were terrified of Bolshevism and its Jewish agents. Old Villefort, Jean-Marie's father, was a leading member of an organization called France-Allemagne and he was a close friend of Laval, the Vichy prime minister who wanted France in the German camp from the start. The Banque Villefort didn't do too badly out of the occupation, either. The old man decamped to Vichy to work with the government, but young Jean-Marie stayed in Paris, where he led a rather privileged existence looking after the family interests and pressing champagne on all those nice young Prussian officers billeted in Paris. Of course, that's what allowed him to claim later that he had secretly been involved with the Resistance—nobody could say with too much precision what had gone on after the Germans rolled in. And de Gaulle didn't feel like pressing the point after the war because he needed what was left of the establishment with him. So by the fifties Villefort the younger was a pillar of the community.'

Pascual frowns. 'Am I supposed to blackmail him with sixty-year-old gossip?'

Morrel pulls papers from a file and holds them out to Pascual. 'How about SS reports from nineteen forty-three citing young Mr. Villefort for his valuable services? These are photocopies, of course.'

Pascual skims the documents, shaking his head. 'You've got a bag full of tricks, haven't you?'

With a modest shrug Morrel says, 'Another bonus from the Wall coming down. The Stasi had them. You should have seen all the aces those fellows had up their sleeves.'

Pascual tosses the papers on the bed. 'So what's the idea? I wave these at Villefort and he agrees to phone me when the Russians come to town?'

'Something like that. My idea was that he takes you on as his secretary.'

Giving Morrel a sharp look Pascual says, 'You've cleared this with his current secretary?'

'His personal staff is always rather in flux. Don't worry, you won't cause much of a stir. His personal assistants tend to come and go. They're all highly presentable young men and the rumor is that they do more than just take dictation and book restaurant tables.'

Pascual sags against the window frame. 'That's the way it is, eh?'

'I told you we had fun with the dossier. It's the perfect cover. Delicacy will prevent people from asking too many questions. Of course, you'll need a shave and a haircut and a few nice suits.'

Pascual begins to laugh, shaking silently. In the street below, two men are talking quietly, cigarette tips glowing. 'Do I get to keep the suits?'

'If you really want to, I don't see why not. An operational budget can be a marvelously flexible thing.'

'Perhaps you can put one of them on me for my funeral.'

'I don't think you need be so pessimistic. We'll be ready for Najjar this time and we'll get him.'

'Presumably before I join Mourad Mediane in the unsolved slayings file.'

'If they get you we'll do our best to solve it, rest assured.'

Pascual gives him a withering look as he moves to the bed and sinks onto it, the springs creaking beneath him. He drinks more whisky. 'Tell me more about Mirakl. You said something about a private security force.'

'Yes. What precisely would you like to know?'

'I'd like to know if I'm likely to wind up dissected and strewn about the premises. If they did kill Mediane, it means they have impressive resources, not to mention a very unpleasant attitude. Supposing the recognition was mutual, Najjar must have passed the word to somebody who then mounted a fairly sophisticated operation to stalk Mediane and kill him. Is Mirakl capable of that kind of thing?'

'Capable? Probably. But I think your imagination is getting the best of you.'

'One hears remarkable tales coming out of Russia.'

'Yes, all right. It's pretty rough-and-tumble out there. You know they've got to be fairly muscular to operate in their own neighborhood, so it's fair to assume they've got some rough types on the payroll. But have they ever been caught doing anything naughty in the West? No. As far as the local operation is concerned, there aren't any thugs with Uzis hanging about the premises. It's an ordinary working bank. When the VIPs come in, they do tend to have some of those stiff young men in sunglasses, but so far everybody's behaved in exemplary fashion. As far as we can tell. We haven't found any bloody knives in the wastepaper baskets, in any case.'

'That's very comforting.' Pascual watches the gentle swirl of whisky in his cup. 'So where do I find Mr. Villefort?'

'Well, when he's at home he's in a big house on the Avenue Foch.'

'Ah, of course, where else?'

'But I doubt you'll get in there, to start with anyway. They don't answer the door for just anybody. You'd probably have better luck in the Tuileries late at night.'

'Marvelous.'

'Actually he doesn't need to do that, though one hears he's not above the occasional *rencontre éclair*. Seriously, there's a discreet little *boîte* in the rue Vieille-du-Temple that he's known to frequent. I'd try there first. You could start tonight. I can drop you there.'

The prospect fills Pascual with loathing. 'I think I'd like to turn in early tonight, thanks. Start fresh in the morning. Are we in a hurry?'

'I don't really know. We could have weeks to wait. Or Najjar could fly in and out tomorrow, who can say? In any event we can only push things so fast. Any work of this kind requires patience. As you know. You've stalked a few men in your time.'

Pascual drains the whisky and reaches for the bottle; he has a feeling he is going to need a good deal of this medicine. 'Yes,' he says. 'But patience was never my strong point.'

No, thinks Pascual, quick and dirty is going to be the watchword, all the way down the line. The house in the Avenue Foch sits back from the pavement behind a high iron grille. The house has three stories and a mansard roof, the classic Parisian abode of old French money, a survivor in a street largely given over to vulgar nouveaux riches. The monumental façade is dominated by high Corinthian columns and closed shutters behind ornate iron-railed balconies. The door is approached by steps curving up to a massive porch. The garden is compact but lush, full of flowers and small well-disciplined trees. There is an intercom set into one of the gateposts. There is no nameplate, only the number above it. Pascual leans on the button.

In an hour he is to meet Morrel to go shopping; Pascual has ventured out into the morning rush hour on the theory that the surest time to find an old *roué* at home is when he will be sleeping off the previous evening. A tinny and irritated voice sounds from the speaker. *'Oui?'*

'I must speak to Mr. Villefort.'

'Who are you?'

'Marcel. It is of the utmost urgency.'

'Marcel. Who is that, Marcel?'

'I am a friend of Mr. Villefort. I must communicate to him something very urgent.'

'Have you an appointment?'

'No, but this is an emergency.'

'Mr. Villefort is not receiving visitors.'

'He will want to see me. It concerns my condition.'

'Mr. Villefort has not yet risen. Go away.'

'You do not understand. I tell you, it concerns my condition. Mr. Villefort must know immediately.'

'What did you say? What condition?'

'That is for Mr. Villefort to know. You must give him the message. I'll wait.'

There is a pause of nearly half a minute and the voice comes back, peremptory: *'Attendez.'*

'Very good, I'll wait.' Pascual turns his back on the house and lights a Gauloise. Traffic eases past; on the broad parkway some Americans are sailing a plastic disk through the air. Two women in tight skirts loiter at the curbside further on; surely not *péripatéticiennes* at this early hour? Pascual turns and peers through the gate at the house. Is that a curtain moving?

'Écoutez,' erupts a voice from the speaker. 'Go around the corner to the door in the rue Pergolèse.'

Pascual throws his cigarette into the street and obeys. The diagonal side street cuts the house off at an angle; a terrace sails above like the prow of a ship. There is a small door in the blank side wall and Pascual rings the bell next to it. A man of middle age in a black suit opens the door. He looks at Pascual with open hostility. 'Follow me.'

Heels click on the tiles. These are the nether regions, devoid of architectural splendor. Pascual follows the man to an elevator hidden round a corner. Going up in the elevator the man scowls at the indicator above the door. Long hairs curl out of his nostrils and he is very annoyed at having to share this space with Pascual. The elevator creaks to a halt and they get out.

Here mirrors adorn the walls, chandeliers dangle from a ceiling high above. Light pours in through a window overlooking the street. The majordomo, if that is what he is, leads Pascual to a door and knocks. There is a murmur within and the man pushes the door open. He stands back to let Pascual enter.

This room surprises with its contemporary decoration; Pascual was expecting more gilt and rococo, more poor man's Versailles. Here is a room done up in cool metal-and-stone colors, with clean functional furniture, thick carpeting and a cluttered, lived-in look, magazines and empty glasses. A man in a blue satin robe stands with one hand on the back of an armchair, compressing the cushion with a fleshless claw. He is elderly if not quite decrepit; he has very recently risen and is none too happy about it. His eyes are red and alarmed. Sparse white hair springs upward from a mottled pate, skin sags off cheeks and throat. 'Bring coffee,' he snarls at the servant. As the door closes softly he looks at Pascual and rasps, 'Who are you?'

Pascual slips his hands into his trouser pockets, rocking on his heels. 'Marcel will do.'

'I've never seen you before in my life.'

'No. I apologize.'

'I wouldn't waste a second look on you.'

'Of course not. I fabricated the whole thing.'

Three seconds pass and the red eyes narrow. 'Then all that about your *condition*—'

'Was a pretext. I had to get in the door.'

A shudder passes through the old man; he rises briefly to his full height, inhaling, and subsides again. 'And what do you want?' he snarls, putting all the venom he can muster into it.

'I'm here to blackmail you,' says Pascual.

Villefort gapes at him, seems to totter, then begins to quiver. His shoulders shake, his face spreads into a rictus, yellow teeth showing. He comes around the chair and sinks onto it. His shins are sticks covered with a fine white down. Pascual realizes he is laughing. The laughter dissolves into a fit of coughing. Villefort pulls a handkerchief from a pocket of the robe and dabs at his lips, then his eyes. 'Please,' he says, replacing the handkerchief. 'Tell the world. Shout it from the mountaintop. Jean-Marie de Villefort is an old *pédé*. What can you possibly hope to gain? Do you think I care in the least? Do you think anybody cares? You are absurd. Leave my house at once.'

'You misunderstand me. You are quite right, no one has any interest in your taste in boys, least of all me.'

'What are you here for, then?'

Pascual pulls the photocopies from the pocket of his jacket, unfolds them, and steps across the carpet to hand them to Villefort. The old man takes them with a look of apprehension and a hand that trembles. He peers at them, holding them ten centimeters from his nose, for a very long time. 'That's German, for God's sake. What am I supposed to make of this? Never could read the filthy language.'

'You may notice your name there, about halfway down. Again near the bottom. There are a couple of other names you may recognize, too.'

The hand holding the papers drops to the old man's lap. 'What is this?'

'Proof that you sold your friends to the Nazis, that's all. I can do you a rough translation if you wish.'

Villefort stares at him with watery eyes, immobile. 'Petit was a communist,' he breathes, barely audible.

'No doubt. The others as well, probably. Nonetheless I

wonder what a *magistrat* would make of it all. Papon at least had the excuse of orders to follow.' Villefort refolds the papers slowly and holds them out for Pascual, who says, 'Keep them. I've got the originals.'

The old man tosses them onto a coffee table. 'You don't understand. Nobody can. We had to choose between two devils.'

'I'm not here to argue that.'

'What do you want?'

'I want you to take me on as your personal assistant.'

'Impossible.'

'I need access to the bank.'

'Ah, of course. Now we're getting to the point. I congratulate you on your resourcefulness. I've always admired a clever thief.'

'I don't want a single centime. What I need is information about the new owners.'

There is a silence. Pascual moves to a chair across the low table from Villefort and sits down. The old man watches him, his tongue flicking out briefly between dry lips. 'Who do you mean, Chiesa and that crowd?'

'No. I mean the Russians. Mirakl.'

'Ah. The Russians. That's what they are, is it?'

'Some of them.'

'I don't have anything to do with them. Chiesa runs the place now. Talk to him.'

'I don't need to. All I need to know is when they're coming back. I need to know the next time a delegation from Mirakl comes and I need to meet them. Get a look at them, at least, without rousing their suspicion. You can arrange that, can't you?'

'Good God, you think they tell me anything? They come and they go. I see them sneaking in and out of offices. They don't even talk to Chiesa.'

'Of course not. I'm sure he's careful not to pay too much attention to them.'

Villefort peers across the table at him, wheezing faintly. 'They're all crooks, aren't they?'

'I think that's a fair description.'

Villefort's head sags back and he closes his eyes. 'I knew they had to be, but I had no choice.'

'They're quite good at disguising it.'

'I couldn't hang on to the place. We were going under, you see. It was the *crise immobilière*. I got bad advice, things got out of hand. They made me the proverbial offer I couldn't refuse. Two hundred years my family took to build this bank and I took my patrimony and tipped it into the gutter. Christ, I'm tired.'

Seconds pass and Pascual is afraid the old man is going to expire there on the chair, his breath rattling in and out. Finally he stirs, exerts himself, sits up and rubs his face. 'So you're a policeman, then.'

'Of a sort.'

'I might have known, you have that look.'

Pascual grins. 'It's that obvious?'

'One can always tell.' Villefort shakes his head. 'I won't have any scandal. I'd be happy to help you shop the bastards, but I won't have our name dragged through the mud.

'We don't want a scandal any more than you do. If there's a scandal it means we haven't done our job.'

'I see. Well. So you're going to be my new assistant.'

'I can type and make dinner reservations in six languages.'

The old man gives a snort of disdain. 'That's more than I can say for any of the others.'

FIVE

The Banque Villefort stands in the rue du Quatre Septembre a stone's throw from Crédit Lyonnais, secure and imposing behind its grey stone façade. Above the entrance stand twin angels, draped in robes, pointing to the bank's coat of arms like game show hostesses posing with the grand prize. The massive black double doors have been swung open and Villefort's chauffeured Mercedes eases through into the courtyard. Pascual hops out and hastens around to open the door on Villefort's side, cutting off the chauffeur, who shrugs and leaves it to him. Villefort hauls himself out of the car with some effort but stands erect, straightening his tie of deep blue silk and smoothing the tails of his exquisitely tailored suit. Pascual's suit, picked off the rack at Costardo in the rue de Richelieu yesterday, would not stand a close comparison, but in it he is a different man from the rough trade that stormed the house in the Avenue Foch yesterday. Shaved and shorn, he shocked himself in the mirror this morning: this debonair stranger is the man he could have been. Villefort makes his way majestically over the cobblestones to the door that is already being held open by a smiling functionary. 'Good morning, Martin. This is Mr. Garnier, my assistant.' Pascual shakes hands with the doorman, who is not effusive; he has no doubt seen other assistants come and go.

Through the door and up one story, Villefort leads him through corridors carpeted in a plush that silences their steps. They are far from the public precincts of the bank here. There are dark wood paneling and windows that reach half a meter above a tall man's head. Villefort greets the few people they pass with lordly condescension. He halts at a door and pulls out a key.

'This is my office,' he says, ushering Pascual in. 'I can give you a key to this door but you'd have to talk to Desjardins to get the key for the building and I doubt he'd give you one. The new people seem to be particularly keen on security.' The office is vast, laid out and decorated to cow the suppli- cant. On a carpet of rich purple hue sits a massive desk carved from several tropical trees; behind it double windows open onto one of the balconies that give the façade its charming aspect. The walls are lined with bookshelves and portraits of Villeforts past. The green baize blotter on the desktop is as smooth and empty as a football pitch. Villefort sits behind the desk and glares at Pascual.

'My grandfather sat here and talked with Lesseps about financing the Suez Canal,' he says. 'History's been made in this room.'

'Impressive,' says Pascual, meandering, hands in his pocket.

'You can use that small desk. Open those doors there and you'll find a computer. They insisted on giving me one. I'm told it works; I don't even know how to turn it on.'

Pascual opens the doors and closes them again, scans the spines of books. 'I'll try not to interfere with your work too much.'

'There's not much to interfere with. Chiesa tolerates me the way one tolerates a senile uncle. He used to answer my questions quite courteously, but after a while I got tired of asking. Occasionally somebody rings up or stops in to interview me. Nobody ever consults me for anything more important than the choice of wine at luncheon. I suppose I've become a sort of public relations mascot. If you want to make yourself useful you can open that cabinet and pour me a whisky.'

'At ten o'clock in the morning?'

'I didn't hire you to argue with me.'

Pascual applies himself to his first official duty. 'I don't want to overplay the role, but a tour of the place and an introduction to the staff might be a good idea. Just so people get used to seeing me.' He sets the whisky on the desk. 'I won't need to be here every day, but I don't want to turn heads when I do show up.'

'Certainly. They'll get suspicious if you take any real interest in banking, you know.'

Pascual shrugs. 'Then I shall try to remain bored with it.'

The Italian Chiesa is thin and almost totally bald with gold wire-rimmed spectacles and a tie pulled so tight it must be choking him. He is in shirtsleeves at his desk with a highly efficient-looking middle-aged female secretary in attendance. He rises to shake hands with Pascual when Villefort introduces him but clearly has little time for either of them. 'Mr. Garnier will be handling the details of my personal and professional affairs,' says Villefort. Chiesa raises an eyebrow; Pascual takes pains to look vapid.

Desjardins has an office on the ground floor. He has the look of an old French soldier, a weathered and close-cropped look that clashes vaguely with his fine suit. He has white hair and intense blue eyes. His handshake is firm to the point of assault and in his eyes Pascual can see the suspicion that he is paid to cultivate. He repeats the name Marcel Garnier slowly and Pascual suspects there will be phone calls, perhaps a computer search soon; he must tell Morrel.

Pascual trails Villefort about the premises and nods at a dozen more people. The bank appears to be carrying on normal operations; the high-vaulted main lobby is impressive with its gilded tellers' cages and finely carved paneling. Back in Villefort's office the old man sits down with a sigh. 'Well, then, you've met the inmates and they've met you. You can begin your spying.'

Pascual stands facing the desk, hands in his pockets. He is uneasy, waiting to awaken from this peculiar dream. 'You're the one who'll be doing the spying. Just keep your ear to the ground. I'll only make the occasional token appearance here.'

Villefort spreads his hands, claps them down on the desktop. 'Splendid. *Eh bien*, we've put in a good morning's work here. If you'll be so kind as to phone Le Doyen and reserve a table, I believe we can go to lunch.'

'Well, it doesn't sound as if he's going to work you too hard,' says Morrel.

'No.' Pascual smokes, watching foot traffic in the street below. He has changed out of the suit and hung it over the back of a chair, a circus clown shedding his costume after the show. Morrel has brought the whisky but Pascual has refused. 'Desjardins worries me.'

'Marcel Garnier is as real as we can make him. He'll find him on the books. Remember, you're a plaything of Villefort's, not a bank employee, so he can't object too much. The old man is totally peripheral, so you're peripheral. He'll keep an eye on you for a while, make sure you're not peeking in keyholes and so forth. The important thing is to keep the old man to his side of the bargain, make sure he's paying attention.'

'He seems adequately tamed. I think the family name is his weak point. He doesn't care if it's tainted with a little vice, but he doesn't want to be remembered as a Nazi. Or a crook. If he thinks we're going to rake up a major scandal, he won't cooperate.'

'You made all the necessary promises?'

'I told him it would be a surgical operation. I don't know how far he trusts me.'

'Wave those SS reports at him again.'

Pascual comes away from the window. 'It's under control. The principal problem is going to be boredom.'

Morrel smiles, closing his briefcase. 'You're in Paris. How can boredom be a problem?'

Pascual walks, looking for a Paris he knows. It is there on every corner, in every bar, *brasserie* and *tabac;* the florist still flicks water onto the glorious eruption of blossoms at the door of her shop; the smells of fresh bread, stale beer and automobile exhaust still waft on the breeze. The traffic is atrocious, the population fabulously varied and unruly. At the same time the familiar is overlaid with things that baffle him. No more PTT and what the hell is a Minitel?

With the light beginning to go he finds one of his childhood homes, the favorite, the touchstone. Just off the Boulevard Saint-Germain, in the highest of high-rent districts, he and his mother shared a garret here, more than thirty years ago. Pascual remembers the dizzying stairs, his mother stooped under the sloping roof, pigeons outside the window. It was affordable only because of its squalor; they shivered together under multiple blankets in the winter. Pascual stands in the courtyard looking up, wondering what the same space goes for now.

He walks along the boulevard, cuts toward the river. This is the Paris of his earliest memories; later came the move north to the *quartiers populaires,* up in the *neuvième,* the *dixième,* the immigrant quarters where he thrived and his mother languished. Today they would call her a single mother and deplore his deprived upbringing; Pascual remembers being happy except in school. He remembers his mother's first grey hairs, her insistence on regular letters to his father in far-away mythical New York. How his mother supported him on violin lessons and language tutoring he cannot imagine. He remembers her counting change on a tabletop. He remembers crying when she told him they had to go back to Barcelona, defeat in her eyes.

Fifty meters from the Quai des Grands Augustins Pascual finds his mother. As close as he will come, at any rate; with a ghostly ripple through his heart he recognizes M. Gilbert's shop, the violins hanging in the window just as they did more than thirty years ago, the same ones perhaps, the same array of sheet music on display beneath them. His feet take him across the threshold before he can reflect. He pushes through the door into the long narrow shop. A bell tinkles above; Pascual stands uncertainly and looks at the ranks of violins and violas ranged along the walls, the rich reddish hues and exquisite curves the same, the long glass case with bows and boxes of rosin unchanged. This is where his mother toiled, patiently enduring the excruciating noises produced by children with no talent on rented fiddles, collecting her cut of the fees weekly from M. Gilbert and taking home just enough to feed herself and a boy who sometimes sat reading behind the glass case while she conducted a lesson in the back room. Pascual wonders how this memory has lain so long neglected in his psyche. M. Gilbert, he recalls, was distant and correct, kindly and tolerant, a thin and unhandsome man who always wore a suit. Is it his imagination, or does he remember his mother blushing as she alluded to mysterious changes in M. Gilbert's conduct, and was that related to their move?

'Monsieur?' Startled, Pascual turns to see the old man rising from a chair, closing a book. He recognizes M. Gilbert at once, still thin and now looking mottled and frail, thirty years on and not aging well. His hair has whitened and thinned, revealing a shiny scalp, but the suit is still clean and pressed. He regards Pascual with an air of dubious courtesy.

'Monsieur Gilbert.'

The old man nods. 'That is my name.'

'When I was a *gosse* I used to sit in here.' Pascual smiles, seeing Gilbert's brow knot in puzzlement. 'Amàlia Ferrer was my mother.'

The old man stiffens, eyebrows rising. A look of amazement takes possession of him. For a moment his mouth hangs open and then he says, '*Mon dieu.* You must be *le petit Pascual,* then.'

'I was. That was a long time ago.'

Gilbert comes around the table and advances on Pascual like a man in a daze, hands reaching for him. He clasps Pascual's hand in both of his and says, 'My God, you look like her. You have her eyes.'

'So I've been told.'

'You disappeared. Someone told me you'd gone back to Spain.' He releases Pascual's hands but squeezes his arm as if to prove he is real.

'We did. Later we came back. But she'd given up teaching by then.'

Gilbert nods, the light in his eyes fading. 'She's well, your mother?'

Pascual shakes his head. 'Dead for many years.'

'Ah. *Désolé.*' Gilbert's eyes are watery and he does not look healthy. He looks like an empty house with the wind whistling through. 'I was sorry to lose her. She was my best teacher. And a very fine violinist. She had a gift.'

'I remember.'

M. Gilbert turns back toward his chair, looking for support. 'She was beautiful, your mother was.' Pascual finds nothing to say. 'And did she make a violinist of you?' says Gilbert, sinking onto his chair and mustering a smile.

'I'm afraid not. I was more interested in football and cars.'

Gilbert nods, the smile going melancholy. 'And what have you made of your life?'

'Nothing much,' says Pascual. 'Nothing much at all.'

'Ah,' says the old man. 'Ah. I can't say I've done much better. I'm closing the shop next month, you know.'

'Really?'

Gilbert gestures with fine pale hands. 'I'm an old man. It's time to find a quiet place to die. I've sent the last few students elsewhere, found a buyer for my stock. I've sold the building and they're going to gut it and make luxury flats out of it. They've already chased out my last tenants.'

'I never knew you owned the building.'

'When one has no family, one can more easily amass capital. Instead of children I accumulated property.' A melancholy smile animates the bloodless lips. 'I hoped at one time that your mother might return the esteem I felt for her, but I'm afraid I was merely an irritation. Perhaps she mentioned it to you.'

Pascual shakes his head. 'You weren't the only one,' he says.

'No, I imagine not. Your mother was . . .' There is a moment of suspense and Pascual nearly winces as the look on the old man's face wavers and turns to one of sheer pain, long buried.

'Yes,' says Pascual. 'She was.'

Overwhelmed by the past, Pascual leans on a wall above the Seine and wishes he were anywhere but Paris.

'It's a fool's errand,' says Pascual. 'I'm losing my sanity.'

Morrel lashes out at a pigeon with his foot. 'Filthy beasts. Rats with wings.' For variety's sake they have met in the Jardin du Luxembourg today, the classic random encounter on a park bench, Pascual with his nose in *Le Canard Enchaîné* and Morrel chewing doggedly at a sandwich he has bought from a pushcart. 'I don't see what you can possibly complain about. It's not what I'd call a heavy workload. You spend more time in the *brasserie* across the street than you do with Villefort.'

'By mutual consent. We'd be at each other's throats otherwise. And what looks like leisure to you is mere tedium to me. How many hard-boiled eggs can a man eat?'

'Don't give me that. You're getting your share of free lunches in some very fine restaurants. I envy you.'

'Eating well is poor compensation for the company. He's complaining now that I'm forcing him to work too hard. It seems he had gotten used to putting in no more than a couple of three-hour days a week. I've insisted he check in every day this week, and he doesn't like it.'

'Don't push him too hard. We can't have him rousing

suspicions. A finger on the pulse, an ear to the ground, that's all we need.'

'His own pulse is the only one that concerns him. That and his precious family reputation. The next time he launches into one of his apologias I'm going to knock his dentures across the room, I assure you. The Nazis were misunderstood, did you know that? Not a bad bunch of fellows at all.'

'So I've heard.'

'I defy you to enjoy a meal with a steady diet of that as a side dish.'

'At least he hasn't asked you to pick up boys for him.'

'Not yet. I'm telling you, when he does, I'm gone.'

'I shouldn't have to remind you—'

'No. You don't. But I'm starting to wonder if you're wasting your time and mine. Najjar's not coming back, if he ever was here.'

'He'll turn up.'

Pascual whips over a page, savagely. 'And then what happens? What's the drill? I'm not quite clear on the plan. I pull a little silver whistle out of my pocket and run into the street blowing it? Commandos rappel down the face of the building and kick in the windows?'

'Well, no actually. We can't really storm the bank, much as we'd love to put on a show. Things don't happen that way here. What we had in mind was a discreet phone call, a couple of agents in a parked car, a quiet arrest on the street or perhaps in his hotel room. *Pas de scandale.*'

'I don't know how close I'll be able to get to him. Old Villefort, presuming he is actually able to detect the arrival of visiting firemen, is not likely to be in on the plotting. He says they may let him shake a few hands if they're in a tolerant mood that day.'

'Then make sure you're there to watch him shake hands.'

'I can't guarantee anything. I haven't exactly penetrated the inner councils.'

Morrel chews for a while, tears a crumb off his sandwich and throws it to the birds. 'You survived six years underground with all the police of Europe looking for you. You must be a fairly resourceful sort of person. I leave it to you to find a way.'

Pascual folds the paper, scowls out across the gardens. 'What if I get no advance notice?'

'Then you ring us as soon as you're aware he's there. We'll be in permanent contact from then on. You'll have a mobile phone and a number to ring. We get people into position while you find out where he's going to be and when. As soon as you can pin down his movements, or lack of movement, for anything more than, say, fifteen minutes into the future, we rendezvous—we'll be close. You take us to him and plant the kiss on his cheek and we pull out the handcuffs. We don't expect any shooting.' Morrel's casual tone makes it sound like a trip to the *boulangerie*.

'And if he resists? If he's got an army of Russian thugs with him?'

Morrel is losing patience; he screws the paper wrapping of his sandwich into a tight ball and flings it at a milling cluster of pigeons. 'Good intelligence work prevents nasty surprises. You do your job and we'll do ours.'

Pascual broods; knots of tourists mill, vying with the pigeons for space. 'Speaking of good intelligence work, am I to assume you have me under surveillance?'

'You could assume that. My trust in people is always provisional.'

'Then is he one of yours, the fellow with the black bag over there by the fountain, feeding your flying rats?'

Morrel goes very quiet for a while; Pascual looks in the other direction, feigning boredom. 'The North African?' says Morrel.

'Is that what he is? I wondered.'

'Seen him before, have you?'

'He took my picture the other day.'

'What?'

Pascual is pleased to have stung a reaction out of Morrel but beginning to feel uneasy at the implications. 'I just realized it. I came out of the *brasserie*, heading back to the bank to check in with the old degenerate, and he was just snapping off a shot. Not looking at me, you know, just a picture of the streetscape, or so I thought. I didn't think much of it because some fool's always taking a picture of something in this town, but the penny dropped, just now, when he hove to over there. It took me a minute but I knew I'd seen him before. I think it must have been my picture he was taking. He's not one of yours, then?'

Morrel says nothing for a long minute. 'He's gone off now. Are you quite sure it's the same bloke?'

'Reasonably. I do have an eye for people when I feel I might be shot down in the street at any moment. You don't suppose he could be a Central Asian, do you? One could easily mistake him for a North African.'

Morrel stands, brushing crumbs from his trousers. In the tone of a man working hard to be unconcerned he says, 'He could be one of ours. I can't claim to know them all. All the same, if you see him again, let me know, will you?'

'And you,' says Pascual. 'If you see him again, be sure to let me know.'

'Where the hell have you been?' says Villefort as Pascual eases into the office. The old man is behind his desk, picking his teeth. 'I could have used you at lunch.'

'Dropped your napkin, did you?'

'Very funny. Actually, I was accosted by a journalist.'

'I should have thought you'd enjoy that. What on earth did he want?'

'It was a woman. At least she claimed she was a journalist. The impudent slut barged right into the dining room at Lasserre and came up to my table. Before I could find my tongue she'd sat down and started asking questions. If you'd been there I'd have had you pitch her out.'

'Surely the restaurant personnel could have handled that.'

'One doesn't like to make a scene. Think of the figure I'd have cut, waving for assistance, spluttering in outrage. In the event I had to sit there and listen to her.'

'And what did she want?'

'The same sort of thing you want, apparently.'

'Oh?'

'Asked a lot of questions about the new management. Did

I know this, did I know that? Did I know who was holding meetings in my bank?'

Pascual chooses a chair. 'Did she mention any names?'

'Names? I suppose she did. Why?'

'Who did she mention?'

'How should I know? You think I was paying attention? I was trying to catch the waiter's eye, get him to bring more wine. Arabs, all of them.'

'Who, the waiters?'

'No, for God's sake. The people she mentioned. She asked me about a lot of Arabs.'

Pascual crosses one leg over the other, clasps his hands, unclasps them. 'She wanted to know about the Arabs who have been meeting here?'

'Yes, pay attention, can't you? She was Arab herself. Perfect French, mind you, but black as midnight, you can't change their color. She told me her name, too.'

'But you can't remember.'

'She said it so fast I didn't catch it. Not a French name anyway, how the hell am I supposed to retain it? And what does it matter?'

'Did she ask about a man named Najjar?'

'I tell you I can't remember. Is that the fellow you're waiting for?'

'What publication did she represent? Did she show you any credentials?'

'Yes, yes, she waved something at me. Algiers, it was. Some rag in Algiers.'

'Algiers.'

'Stop repeating things like a damned parrot. I tell you she was Algerian. All dressed up like a Christian and her French was perfect, but she was an Arab. No hiding it.'

'And she asked about Najjar.'

'I don't remember the name. Some grand vizier or something, I tell you I wasn't paying attention. I referred her to Chiesa—she said she'd already tried to interview him and he'd refused. She said nobody at the bank would talk to her and Thierry Fort had suggested she try me, but not during banking hours.'

'Who's that, Fort?'

'One of the ones they let go. Good type, very sharp. Appealed to me to save his job when they let him go. I had to tell him it was out of my hands. Anyway, she'd been on to him and he'd filled her head with all kinds of nonsense, dark forebodings and so on. Told her I was a prisoner or some such nonsense.'

Pascual stares across the desktop at Villefort. The old man's nostrils flare; he is scowling at his toothpick. 'What else did she say?' prompts Pascual, suppressing the urge to fling himself across the desk and wrap his fingers about Villefort's throat.

'She asked about that poor devil who got himself killed in that massacre up in the Goutte d'Or. What's-his-name, the fellow who worked here. Seemed to think there was something suspicious about it.' He sniffs. 'As if I'd know anything about it.'

As if you'd know your ass from a drainpipe, Pascual thinks,

clamping his lips shut. He takes a deep breath and says, 'Did she say where she could be reached?'

Villefort looks at him in surprise. 'At the paper in Algiers, I suppose. Now look here, you're not thinking of talking to the press about any of this, are you? You said you'd keep a lid on things.'

'She didn't leave you a card, a phone number?'

'She didn't have time. I finally managed to pluck at a waiter's sleeve and have her thrown out. At least she went quietly, I'll give her that much. And I'm afraid I didn't give her much to write about. Pretty much played dumb, to tell you the truth. You can't expect me to collaborate in spreading rumors.'

Pascual lets his homicidal impulses smolder as Villefort daintily disposes of the toothpick under the desk. 'No,' he says. 'You did the right thing. When in doubt, act naturally.'

SIX

'Good God, am I to have no peace?' Villefort glares over the top of *Le Figaro* as Pascual pulls out a chair. 'How on earth did you find me?'

'I asked your driver where he'd dropped you.' Pascual settles on to his chair and casts an eye about the somnolent recesses of the exclusive café. Here in the world of the 30-franc coffee and marble fixtures, he feels like a peasant soiling the manor house floor. 'If you'd managed the two hundred meters on foot I'd never have found you.'

'I'm too old and too damned rich to walk. What the hell do you want?'

A waiter as starched as his white jacket takes Pascual's order with an air of contempt. Pascual crosses his legs and gives Villefort a studied smile. 'Any news?'

'Of what?' Villefort takes a sip of his aperitif.

Pascual merely stares at him. 'If I were to get the impression that you're not taking your responsibilities seriously, you would be surprised at the speed with which certain historical documents might find their way to unsympathetic readers. I remind you.'

'And I remind you, my position at the Banque Villefort is not what it once was. I'm sure you wouldn't want me to arouse suspicion by insistent questioning on sensitive matters.'

'They must surely expect a little curiosity from you about what goes on in your own bank.'

Villefort smooths the crease in his newspaper lying on the table. 'Actually, I have very little at this point in my life. My only child died eight years ago in the stupidest fashion possible, driving his Porsche off a cliff in Switzerland. After that the bank collapsed, and I confess that it ceased to matter to me. I have no heir and my principal hopes at this point are to sate my physical desires and to die without pain. It was with that understanding that I was allowed to retain my position at the bank. I don't meddle and they let me come and go as I please. When I show the slightest interest in affairs, doors slam shut.'

Pascual's teeth are clenched; a panic seizes him as he realizes the futility of the whole lunatic scheme: the shabby room up in the nineteenth, the endless days, the hatred he can feel coursing across the table. 'I see,' he says.

Villefort inclines his head, a gracious gesture. 'Nevertheless.'

'Nevertheless?'

'I have certain sources.'

'Yes?'

'We have a kitchen at the bank, did you know that? The managers have a private room where they can take lunch if they desire. It is a small affair on most days, but when there are visitors Philippe exerts himself. I make it a point to visit Philippe occasionally; he has been with the bank for years. And of course he knows when a delegation is expected.'

Pascual realizes he is holding his breath. 'And?'

'And today he told me that he has been instructed to prepare a first-class production for next Wednesday, the fifteenth.'

'Next Wednesday.'

'Yes. He was holding forth today on varieties of caviar. You see, as he put it, the Russians are coming.'

'Why so fucking glum?' says Morrel. 'The curtain's about to go up and you're the star. Judas Iscariot, a reprise of the classic drama. It's the role of a lifetime and you get to retire when it's done.'

Pascual glares at him. 'It was the role of a lifetime for Mediane, too, wasn't it?'

'Don't worry, you've got us to baby-sit you,' says the man on Pascual's left. Pascual has always assumed that Morrel has colleagues but this is the first he has seen of them. The man introduced as Serge outweighs Morrel by ten kilos and Pascual by five. His shirt cannot quite close around his thick neck and his tie remains comfortably loose. He has lots of forehead and vast slabs of clean-shaven cheek above a jaw that turns abruptly from vertical to horizontal and makes for a small jutting chin that gives him a pugnacious look, framed by a drooping mustache. His hair has just begun to go grey and when he takes off his sunglasses his eyes are a disturbing hazel. He looks like a butcher dressed up for church.

'Serge is the tactician,' says Morrel, and Pascual translates that as muscle and nods. 'He doesn't want to do it in the bank if we can avoid it.'

Pascual picks up his glass; today it is a pedestrian *petit rouge* instead of whisky, served in dirty glasses in a cluttered room behind a *quincaillerie* just off Stalingrad, not too far from the safe house. Pascual had envisaged a spotless conference room in the Ministère de Défense, a long table and a scattering of uniforms around it, but apparently the official bodies are determined to keep him at arm's length. He drinks and says, 'Wouldn't it be easiest to grab him inside? I can pin down his location and lead you to him.'

'Probably. But it would also mean the maximum scandal.'

'I see. That's the main consideration, is it?'

'Just good public relations.'

In his rumbling bass Serge says, 'Arrest him in the bank and we make enemies. On the street or in the hotel there's no need to go into details about the reason for his being in Paris. Not at first anyway. People have time to prepare their statements while the journalists put two and two together. There's a certain etiquette to these things.'

'Why waste etiquette on these crooks? You've told me that the bank's basically a front for a bunch of Russian thugs. Why don't you storm in at the head of a special weapons brigade and denounce them all, get the headlines along with Najjar? I should think that would do good things for a career.'

Serge and Morrel trade a look and Morrel picks up the ball. 'Not at all. You misunderstand the nature of our work.

First of all, we're not policemen. Even if we had solid evidence that the bank was being used in criminal enterprises, it wouldn't be our job to arrest anybody for it. Secondly, an ambitious CRS lieutenant or a PJ *commissaire* might enjoy making headlines, but in our job headlines are death. We want a clean quiet arrest of Daoud Najjar and then a few handshakes and a maybe a bottle of champagne back at the office. We'll let the *procureur* get the headlines.'

'All right. So how's it going to work?'

'Simple,' says Serge. 'You'll need to identify him, and then you'll need a way to mark him.'

'Mark him. What the hell does that mean? Chalk an X on his back?'

'We've moved a little beyond that stage. We have electronics now.'

'I see. And how do I get him to hold still while I clip the transmitter on to his earlobe?'

Serge must have dealt with this brand of belligerent skepticism on many occasions. He shows no signs of annoyance but merely reaches inside his jacket and pulls out a black pen, which he slides across the table to Pascual. 'You give him that.'

Pascual picks up the pen. It is a thick heavy fountain pen with gold trim and a silvery nib, with a prestigious brand name inscribed on it. 'Lovely. Let me guess. The transmitter's inside.'

'That's right. We'll be able to triangulate on it and follow him wherever he goes.'

Pascual lays the pen gently on the tabletop. 'And you

don't think he's going to be a bit suspicious when I hand him this? What do I say? Can I please have your autograph and by the way you can keep the pen, it only cost a thousand francs?'

'No. They'll all be getting one. We bought ten of them. You'll be handing them out as gifts from your employer.'

'I see.'

'You'll need to pick the right time. I'd suggest lunch. Villefort will welcome the distinguished visitors, make a little speech perhaps and offer them each a small token of his esteem. You'll hand out the pens. If Najjar's there you slip him the special one. You'll have it set apart from the others in some way that we'll rehearse. It's basic sleight of hand.'

Pascual shakes his head. 'Villefort's agreed to this, has he?'

'That's your job, to organize it. Remember, he's taking orders from you.'

'Well, yes. But I'm not sure anybody at the bank is taking orders from him anymore. I'm not even sure he can get access to the meeting.'

'He won't need to be at the meeting. They've got to have lunch sometime. If not lunch, there will be drinks, at least a round of handshakes and ass-kissing. Bankers love that kind of thing. Villefort is your trump card. Make it look like his idea and you're in. You play the flunky while Villefort makes the speech, but you make sure Najjar gets the bugged pen. It's foolproof.'

In Pascual's experience the word *foolproof* is an infallible predictor of disaster. 'You're going to look damned silly staking out the café where he leaves the pen by the telephone.'

'No, with a pen like this people are careful. That's why we got the best.'

'Look,' says Morrel with irritation in his voice. 'The pen is just a backup. The basic idea is that we put airtight surveillance on him and arrest him the second he's vulnerable. The key is your identification.'

'So where's the phone you promised me? Or am I supposed to shout out of the window?'

Serge reaches into his jacket again; his pockets are bottomless. 'Once you've got a completely positive ID, whether or not you've managed to slip him the pen, you call us on this.' He sets a cellular phone and a small white card on the table. 'Memorize the number I've written there. Step out for a smoke, go to the gents', whatever. Call us and we'll tell you the next step. What you have to do is to give us as much information as you can in advance. Find out what name he's using, what hotel he's in, that sort of thing. The more we know, the better we can plan and the less can go wrong.'

Pascual chews all this over and washes it down with the plonk. 'If he's part of this delegation—if—I can almost certainly get a look at him but I can't guarantee you I'll get a name and address.'

'Use Villefort, let him do some of the work. Get us a name to go with the face—we'll need that if we lose him somehow.'

Pascual is beginning to feel like a six-year-old talked into criminal mischief by older lads. The looks he is getting across the table, however, do not invite reservations. 'I can't predict how it'll go,' he says. 'Desjardins has his eye on me.'

Morrel sighs, a faint disappointed sound. 'In nineteen

eighty-four you managed to dodge the police of three countries long enough to stage manage a clandestine meeting in Rome between representatives of four different terrorist groups. What we're asking you to do should require about a tenth of the resourcefulness you expended on that little affair.'

Pascual shrugs, reaches for his glass. 'Those were different days. I was a different man.'

The Cimetière Communal de Pantin was the best a poor immigrant woman could do after being run over by the 75 bus at the Place de la République; Pascual remembers the pitiful cluster of mourners, the few cheap flowers, the hasty words of condolence, the brief firm embraces. He remembers the anaesthetized feeling, the detached wonder at his lack of tears. He remembers his anger: stepping in front of a bus, *que burrada, mare, morir així estúpidament com una nena de tres anys.* He has never forgiven her.

Here is her name, graven in stone: Amàlia Ferrer March. Here she has lain for half his lifetime now, under the sun and the rain and the snow. Pascual empties his lungs of air and regrets. So much would have been different, had she not walked about Paris absorbed in her dreams. *'Hola mare,'* says Pascual quietly. The last time he was here he told her *adieu*, thinking he would never be back.

After a time Pascual stands, joints creaking, feeling for his cigarettes. He makes his way back to the main gate and leaves the cemetery. The sun has risen higher and the morning is warm. He wanders, musing. The streets are quiet, with little traffic; nonetheless it is not until he comes to rest at a bus stop that he becomes aware that his prejudices have confounded him; there is no reason to assume that only a man could be following him.

He has seen this woman already this morning, the one loitering at the corner, pretending to see something interesting in the trees. She was on the bus, he remembers; she descended with him in Le Pré Saint-Gervais. He noticed her dark eyes and shock of black hair and then forgot her; an Arab woman on a bus to the *banlieue* is nothing out of the ordinary. He is certain now, however, that hers were the steps he was half conscious of behind him on the descent from the cemetery. She is dressed in jeans and a loose-fitting shirt with sleeves rolled up to the elbows, a string bag for the market dangling from her fingers.

Pascual assumes there are no coincidences for a man in his position and he has had enough of being taken for a fool. He extracts a cigarette and steps slowly toward the woman, who looks over her shoulder at the sound of his steps and stiffens. 'Have you got a light?'

No simple request for a match should bring such alarm; Pascual can see that whatever his own worries, this woman is afraid of him. *'Désolée,'* she says, nearly shying like a frightened pony.

'You were following me,' Pascual says, stowing the cigarette. He is a meter away from her. She is very thin, dark of complexion, with luminous black eyes that elevate a distinctly Arab and somewhat severe face to something just short of beauty. 'Why?'

Her eyes flick a few meters along the pavement, where jocular male voices and banging noises come from the depths of a garage through an open overhead door. A man in a blue coverall has come to stand in the doorway and smoke. 'You are imagining things, monsieur.'

'No. You were on the bus, you followed me to the cemetery. I'd like to know why.'

In perfect unaccented French she says, 'I went to visit my father's grave. Does that concern you? Excuse me.' She moves past him, toward the shop.

'Wait.' Pascual grasps her arm, not too hard. She tugs and in reaction he tightens his grip.

'*Ça va pas, non?*' she says, louder.

Pascual is irritated by the heat and the accumulated tension of the past weeks and he jerks her back toward him. 'Where the hell are you going? *Merde.*'

She cries out. Pascual releases her, throwing her off balance. She totters away from him and begins to run. Pascual hesitates and starts after her but he is not going to get very far.

'*Eh, oh.*' A hand lands on his chest. The mechanic on his smoke break has moved into his path. 'That's not how it goes, *mon brave,*' he says.

'I'm not going to hurt her,' says Pascual. 'We're having a chat.'

'It doesn't look to me as if she wants to talk to you.'

Pascual can see her fleeing, just short of a trot, casting uncertain glances over her shoulder. 'Go fuck yourself,' he says, knocking the man's hand away from his chest. 'Wait,' he calls. 'I can tell you what Villefort wouldn't.' Pascual is focused on the woman but he is quickly forced to attend to matters closer at hand as he is spun and slammed into a wall. Suddenly the entire workforce is there, more blue coveralls spilling out of the shop.

'Pretty boy's got a dirty mouth, eh?'

'Funny, it doesn't quite go with the nice suit.'

Pascual's rational faculties are telling him to keep his mouth shut, cut his losses and flee, but they are losing to his Latin temperament. He shoves back, hard. 'Did your mother dress you boys this morning? Run away and play.'

'*Connard.*' Pascual slips the first punch and gets one of his own in, not very solidly, before he is grabbed from behind, rendering an effective boxing stance impossible. In short order a left hook catches him in the face. There are multiple lights, odd discontinuities and an unpleasant awareness of the bone structure of his face; hard surfaces come up to meet him. He is vaguely aware of a babble of voices, mostly male, and a milling of feet all about him.

On one knee, he probes gently at his face with his fingers, feeling for blood and misaligned features. He will have a shiner and a prize headache, but as far as he can tell, no plastic surgery will be needed. He looks up to see the woman, twenty meters away, giving him an appalled look with her hands to her face. The workmen are shuffling back into their shop with a slightly guilty air, trailing a few final observations. Pascual squeezes his eyes shut and waits for his head to stop hurting.

When he opens them again she is standing over him. 'How do you know who I am?' she says quietly.

Pascual gains his feet and totters only a little. 'Lucky guess. Where's your pal with the camera today?'

She gives him a long look and he can see her rapidly reassessing what passes for her tradecraft. 'Waiting for me to phone,' she says finally.

'Well,' says Pascual, brushing dirt off his suit, 'why shouldn't he be in on this? Let's make a party of it.'

SEVEN

The waiter in the *brasserie* across the street from the Banque Villefort gives Pascual a sympathetic grimace. '*Oh la-la,*' he says, 'somebody's got a wicked left.'

There is a mildly awkward silence when he leaves. The man and woman across from Pascual do not look as if they are enjoying themselves. '*Je m'excuse,*' the woman says finally. 'I shouldn't have run.'

'I don't think it would have made any difference,' says Pascual. 'It was my day to take a pounding.'

'I'm sorry. Are you badly hurt?'

'Nothing that aspirin and alcohol can't cure.' Pascual lights a cigarette and examines his new friends. The man has a high forehead, a sallow complexion over high-cheeked Maghrebi features, a mustache that accents a protruding lower lip, glittering black eyes that do not trust Pascual. 'What do you do, take turns?' says Pascual. 'The other day in the Luxembourg it was you.'

The scowl deepens. 'We're not professionals.'

'That's easy to see. Is this the way journalists usually work?'

The woman says, 'Only when nobody will talk to them.' She draws on her own cigarette. She has long bony wrists, a hollow in the throat. Her skin is a deep rich brown. 'And I assure you, nobody will talk to me.'

'But why the photo, why the tail? If you want to know who I am, the usual procedure would be to ask me, wouldn't it?'

'The usual procedure would be for people to answer our questions politely. But the Banque Villefort doesn't seem to operate that way. We decided to try something different.'

'Like getting everybody on film?'

A long look passes between them and Pascual can read it like a book; she wants to talk but her companion would rather cut out his tongue. She says, 'We're trying to establish who works there, who all those men in the chauffeured limousines are. Who comes and goes.'

'It sounds like a lot of work.'

'It is. But then, we have a lot of time on our hands.'

Pascual nods slowly. He looks again at the plastic-encased card lying on the table. In the photo her hair is longer and she has the rigid stunned look that ID photos too often capture. The name *L'Avenir* is emblazoned across the top and her name is typed in: YACINE Djemila. 'What sort of paper is that?' he says.

She flicks ash off the tip of her cigarette. 'It's an independent weekly in Algiers. As independent as anything can be in Algeria.'

Pascual slides the card back across the table. '*Djemila.* Beautiful.'

She holds his look for a second before slipping the card into her handbag. 'Yes, that's what it means.'

To her companion Pascual says, 'Rachid, eh? You work there too?'

'No. Before, I was a photographer at *El Moujahid*.'

'The official paper.'

'Yes.'

'But you don't work there anymore?'

His chin juts forward a centimeter or two. 'You have any idea what it's like to be a journalist in Algeria right now?'

'One hears disturbing things.'

'I'm a coward if you will, but I left.'

Djemila says, 'We're both in theory on leave from our jobs. Unpaid, and probably permanently, but we cherish the illusion there may be something to go back to someday. For the moment we're loosely associated with a small paper here called *La Voix du Maghreb*. We contribute the odd article or photo and they let us use the telephone.'

Pascual nods. 'And why are you interested in the Banque Villefort?'

Djemila says, 'I think before I answer that I would like to know just who you are.'

Pascual gives it a couple of seconds' thought. 'You can call me Pascual.' The decision to jettison his work name is hardly conscious. 'I work for Mr. Villefort.'

'That doesn't really answer my question,' says Djemila.

Pascual returns her gaze, recognizing the brains of the outfit. 'I am Mr. Villefort's personal assistant.'

She grasps an essential point. 'You don't work for the bank?'

'I have nothing to do with the bank. I am barely tolerated there.'

Rachid says, 'I told you. He's just the errand boy.'

Pascual watches Djemila's face and sees the light go out as she comes to the same conclusion. 'So it seems.' She smokes, exhales. 'My apologies, monsieur, for wasting your time.'

Pascual knows Morrel would crucify him but Morrel is not here. Who am I working for? Pascual asks himself, and decides the answer is *me*. 'Perhaps it's not a waste of time. You'd like to know what happened to Mourad Mediane. So would I.'

Pascual has found the magic word, he can see. 'You knew him?' says Djemila.

'Never met the man.'

'Then . . .'

'Cards on the table?'

'Cards on the table.'

'Tell me what you know about Mirakl and Daoud Najjar and I'll tell you what I know.'

There is a long silence. The waiter arrives with two coffees. Somebody at the bar laughs, a video game beeps, change clinks on the countertop. Djemila has not moved. 'I've never heard either of those names.'

'Villefort said you had asked about somebody he described as a "grand vizier." I assumed it was Najjar because that's who I'm interested in.'

She looks at Rachid, takes a deep breath. 'And why is Mr. Villefort's personal assistant interested in somebody named Najjar?'

Pascual drains his glass and sets it down. 'You can take it that my appointment as Villefort's assistant is temporary.'

On Djemila's face the look of a swimmer in unexpectedly deep waters is gradually replaced by the look of the journalist recognizing a gift-wrapped source. 'You are . . . Never mind. You're willing to talk?'

'Up to a point.'

'On the record?'

'Absolutely not. As far as I'm concerned there is no record. But if you've got something I need I'm willing to pay the market price.'

'You mean a trade.'

'Put the pieces together, see what we come up with. Except none of it came from me, in case anybody asks.'

She nods, intent. She turns to look at Rachid and he says something to her in Arabic, very softly. Pascual learned his Arabic at the other end of the Mediterranean but he can understand the word *careful*. Djemila's lips tense and she looks back at Pascual. 'All right, you've mentioned three names. I know one of them, Mourad Mediane.'

'Start with him. Is there a connection between his death and what he saw at the bank?'

She gives it a few seconds before she answers. 'Maybe.'

'And what did he see?'

'Whom did he see would be a better question.'

'Your "grand vizier"?'

'Yes.'

'And his name is not Daoud Najjar?'

'No.'

Pascual finds he needs another cigarette. He gets one going and tosses the match in the ashtray. 'You think Mediane and the others died because Mediane saw somebody he wasn't supposed to see?'

'I think it's possible.'

'That would mean it wasn't a gang of GIA fanatics who slaughtered all those people.'

'Yes, that's what it would mean.'

'And do you know of any evidence that it wasn't just what they're saying it was?'

'None whatsoever. Only the coincidence that Mediane died a week after I talked to him.'

'That would be rather . . . extravagant. To kill six people to silence one.'

'Where we come from, death has reached new heights of extravagance.'

Pascual smokes and tries to repress a desire to flee in panic. 'How did you get interested in Mediane?'

'I had information that the man I was interested in had visited the bank in secret. Mediane confirmed it. As a security officer he was well placed.'

'Funny, I've been assuming what got him killed was his recognizing my bloke.'

Djemila gives him a long look. 'And who's your bloke?'

Pascual can hear Morrel screaming at him. He says, 'Daoud Najjar. *Nom de guerre* Abu Yussef.'

She looks at Rachid, shakes her head slightly. To Pascual she says, 'And what would he be, Palestinian perhaps?'

'Syrian. Urgently sought by the French. Now apparently

working for Mirakl, the outfit that owns the Banque Villefort.'

Djemila leans back on her chair, looking dazed. *'Quel bordel.'*

'Yes, I'd say that puts it well. Now who's your man?'

Djemila gives Rachid a token look but Pascual can see that the decision is hers. 'A certain General Boucherif.'

Pascual smokes. 'Algerian?'

'What else?'

The deafening noise of three people thinking hard settles around the table. Pascual drains his beer and says, 'You think he could engineer something like what happened to Mediane? You think he would?'

'I think the GIA provides the perfect cover for just about any crime you can think of.'

Pascual nods. 'So. You've got an Algerian general visiting the bank in secret, I've got a Syrian terrorist working for the bank's holding company. And maybe we have a mass murder to cover the whole thing up. Sounds like we've got an interesting story.'

'If it's all related.'

'If they're using the same bank, they're related. I don't care if they've never met each other. That's a hell of an interesting bank.'

'Yes. And so far completely impenetrable.'

Pascual watches her smoke. 'You say you've got a source who tips you off when your general visits the bank?'

Rachid speaks, a growling torrent of Maghrebi Arabic too fast for Pascual to catch a word. Djemila nods, replies. She looks at Pascual and in her deep black eyes he can see that the question of whether she can trust him means more than whether he is a good source. Pascual says, 'All right, don't tell me. I'm just looking for ways we might help each other. If your source can spot a general he might be able to spot a terrorist.'

She considers for a moment and says, 'I don't think so.'

Pascual thinks. 'All right. You've got someone in Algiers, then. So we're interested in different parts of the picture. Maybe we can put them together.'

She considers. 'Maybe.'

'The only thing is, I don't have much time left. After next Wednesday, I'm gone.'

'Next Wednesday?'

'The man I'm interested in is supposed to turn up then. When he does, my business here is concluded.'

Djemila and Rachid exchange a long look. Rachid gives up with a shake of the head and a sigh. Djemila turns those black eyes on Pascual. 'Wednesday the fifteenth?'

'Yes.'

'You amaze me. The general's due in on the fifteenth as well.'

'Can you get a list from Chiesa?' Pascual says it again, a little louder. He has little stomach for it, but he sees that he is going to have to bully the old man.

'Why would Chiesa give me a list?' Villefort says petulantly, searching through the pill bottles that cover his dressing table. He is in dressing gown and slippers at five o'clock in the afternoon and his sitting room, windows shut tight, smells of age and infirmity.

'Because you asked him.'

'He'd want to know why.'

'You tell him you want to know who these people are. You're still the boss, aren't you?'

Villefort looks up sourly. 'We have long since abandoned that polite fiction. Open this, will you?'

Pascual gets the bottle open and hands it back. 'So tell him you've begun to take an interest again. Your pills have kicked in and you feel rejuvenated and you want to take an active interest again. Tell him anything you damn please. But get me a list of the people who are coming from Russia.'

Villefort pours water into a glass, pops the capsules into his mouth, drinks. 'I don't know where they're coming from. Philippe called them the Russians, that's all.'

'That's good enough for me. I need to know who they are.'

'Chiesa won't tell me. If I ask, he'll be suspicious.'

'Get on your high horse, make a stink. Tell him nothing happens in your bank you don't know about. Play the pompous old fool. But get me the names.'

Villefort stares up at him, red-eyed, hair in disarray. 'I detest you.'

Pascual sighs, slips his hands into his pockets. 'Pity, I've grown rather fond of you myself.'

'That's what I detest most, that type of sarcasm.'

'If I get what I want on Wednesday you'll be quit of me forever.'

Villefort's nostrils flare and the corners of his mouth are

drawn tight; for a moment Pascual thinks he is about to vomit. 'It won't be easy,' the old man says, and goes back to rooting among the bottles.

Serge is in the driver's seat, sunglasses in place, scanning the pavement, the mirrors. The traffic on the rue du Quatre Septembre moves briskly past them. Morrel talks over his shoulder to Pascual from the passenger seat. 'You're sure there's no other exit?'

'None that I've seen. There may be a way through the back of the courtyard into the street behind, but in my experience they come and go by this gate.'

'All right, I think we can assume he'll come out by car, through the main gate.'

'I suppose so.'

'It would be good if you could get a description and number of the car that brings him.'

'I'll put it on the list. You want the color of his socks as well?'

Morrel twists to give him the weary patient look he is so good at. 'We've made it too hard on you, have we? Asking too much? Let me tell you something. Serge here was once given twelve hours to find a way to bug a room in the George V where a foreign head of state was to stay. Twelve hours, and with the security cordon already in place. He managed. Didn't you, Serge?'

The roll of fat on the back of the thick neck creases as Serge shrugs. 'Cut it a bit close, but we got it in place. The things we heard, let me tell you.'

'I congratulate you,' says Pascual.

'Initiative, enterprise. Ingenuity.' Morrel's finger is raised, in didactic mode.

'Bribery,' says Serge. 'Threats.'

Pascual lets out a puff of laughter.

'What's funny?' says Morrel.

'Nothing. Nothing at all.' He watches a pretty girl glide by on the pavement. 'Do you know who the Russians are meeting on Wednesday?'

'No. Do you?'

'Yes, in fact I do. They're meeting an Algerian general named Boucherif. At least I assume that's who they're meeting—they're all coming on the same day.'

Silence. 'Is that so?' says Morrel. 'And how do you know that?'

Pascual has decided that certain cards need to be held in reserve. 'Villefort told me.'

A look passes between the two men on the front seat. Morrel says, 'That's interesting. But also completely irrelevant.'

'And that's also perhaps why you need to be discreet about arresting Najjar? After all, we wouldn't want to embarrass our Algerian friends, would we?'

Morrel gives him a sardonic look over the seat. 'We stick to tactics, *compris*? The strategy, that's made by better minds than ours.' He trades another look with Serge. 'First rule of intelligence work.'

'Absolutely,' says Serge. 'Rule number one.'

Pascual walks along the Boulevard des Italiens, thinking

hard and looking for a phone. He finds one and waits, smoking a cigarette, while a girl with wild blond hair and jeans bursting at the seams finishes shouting into it over the noise of the traffic. When she hangs up Pascual throws the butt away and steps to the phone. He dials the number Djemila gave him in the afternoon. A man answers. Pascual gives his name and waits, plugging his free ear with a finger. Over the line he can hear a child wailing, a faint clinking of plates and glasses.

'Yes?' says Djemila.

'If you're still interested in Wednesday we need to talk.'

A few seconds pass. 'I didn't think you'd call,' she says.

Pascual watches cars weave on the street, sees a man dash for the curb. 'Neither did I,' he says.

She gives him the name of a bar near Métro Pyrénées in Belleville, not entirely familiar territory for Pascual. When he steps out of the Métro he finds himself in a district that at least sets off certain resonances; this is the Paris of immigrants, the working poor and the upwardly mobile. The rue de Belleville winds down a steepish slope, giving a fine view of the distant Eiffel Tower silhouetted against the western sky going orange. On either side the shops have a foreign air: Egyptian *épiceries,* Turkish and Thai restaurants. An Arab youth yells insults up at a window and an old woman turns to glare at him.

The bar stands on a corner, under a blue awning, barely more than a counter with enough floor to stand on. There are three small tables on the pavement but with the glass doors slid all the way open there is little to choose between inside and out. A man at the curving zinc bar can flick ashes into the street. A large black dog sleeps on the floor. Most of the small crowd was born on the south side of the Mediterranean, Pascual judges. His face draws a look or two but they are only looks. He pays for a cognac at the bar and lights a cigarette and waits. People pass in the street; the merest breath of a breeze drifts through.

Conversation does not stop when Djemila appears in the doorway but heads turn. The looks she gets seem evenly split between lust and disapproval. Djemila wears a light jacket in the evening cool and her hair is a wild tangle around the dark angular face with the deep black eyes. 'I'm sorry to make you wait,' she says, joining him at the bar. 'But better you than me.'

Pascual nods. He meets a few of the gazes and chases them away. 'We could leave,' he says.

'No. Actually I'd love a drink. I don't often get the chance. And if I leave with you it will only start rumors that will get back to my brother.'

'That was your brother on the phone?'

'Yes. The last time he had to knock someone down in defense of my reputation was when I was sixteen and I'd hate to make him do it again.'

'I'll try to behave myself, then.'

With a cigarette going and her own cognac in front of her, only her coloring betrays that her ancestors were not Gauls. 'I had second thoughts about coming. Rachid was appalled that I would even consider it. I don't know who you are, who you work for.'

'But you're a journalist, so you had to do it.'

'Yes.'

Pascual shrugs. 'I don't work for anybody, not willingly. I'm a conscript.'

'You're not a *flic*?'

'No. Closer to the other side, actually.'

Her brow creases. 'Meaning?'

Pascual has lived with secrets for so long that it takes immense efforts even to approach them. He smokes, looking across the bar at bottles. 'What I am is a stool pigeon, an informer. A nark, a grass, a turncoat, a weasel. A *mouchard*.'

He glances at her to see her raise an eyebrow, 'All that?'

'And more.'

'So who's got their hooks in you?' says Djemila.

'The French. The DGSE, I think.'

'You don't know?'

'They don't explain much and they don't apologize. In my experience that's fairly typical of intelligence agencies. And my experience is fairly extensive.'

Pascual can see Djemila making calculations, and he can see that she knows how much is riding on them. 'So what's happening on Wednesday?' she says.

'What would you like to happen?'

'I'd like to sit down with General Boucherif and ask him why he's visiting the Banque Villefort in secret. But I don't expect that to happen. I'd be content to confirm that he was actually there. Catching sight of him would be a coup. Of all the officers on the junta, he's probably the most secretive.'

'Would it help if I could get you into the bank?'

There is a long pause while she studies his face. 'And why would you do that for me?'

'I don't know,' says Pascual. 'Maybe because I need allies.'

'I thought the French were your allies.'

'No. They're not allies. They're masters. They're running me.'

'Running you?'

'It's an intelligence operation. I'm breaking every rule there is by telling you about it.'

Her eyes narrow, maybe because of the smoke, maybe because of her skepticism. 'Then why are you telling me?'

'Because I don't like working blind. Because you might have knowledge I need and you'll want something in return.' Because you have such large black eyes, he thinks.

Djemila gives it some time, smoking and toying with her glass. She looks at him and says, 'All right. How can you get me into the bank?'

Pascual smiles. 'With your brains and my pretty face, it ought to be a cinch,' he says.

EIGHT

The sun rises pale and hazy over Paris, a weak creature nearly smothered at birth. In the street below Pascual's window the early light has the dim unreal quality of the bottom of an aquarium. The smell of exhaust, the rumble of traffic just finding its footing, the urgent scurrying on the pavement; Pascual remembers when these things quickened his pulse. Today they fill him with dread.

Leaning out of the window he can see the tops of heads, foreshortened humanity in grotesque perspective. I could jump, he thinks; there is no reason why I must go and look the devil in the eye today. Lean out a little further and after a brief exhilarating descent there is an end to all my cares.

He closes the window and goes to put on his clothes; Morrel is due in fifteen minutes and there are moves to review, lines to rehearse. Pascual drops his shirt on the floor and goes to lean over the toilet; with his stomach empty he can vomit only a thin viscous drool with a vile taste.

'Boring for you,' says Pascual.

The chauffeur looks up from his paper and shrugs. 'One gets used to it.'

Pascual stands in the side entrance to the Banque Villefort, lighting a cigarette. In the courtyard in front of him, two sleek black limousines are drawn up among the usual Mercedes and high-end domestic makes. One driver has disappeared but the other leans against the bumper reading *Le Figaro*. Pascual offers him a cigarette.

'No thanks. I'm quitting again this month.'

'Well, I can go you one better. I quit every single night.' The chauffeur vents a polite puff of laughter and turns over a page. Pascual comes down the steps. 'So who are you hauling today?'

Without looking up the chauffeur says, 'The usual lot. The Ritz crowd, you know.'

'Mm. They give you the Russians or the other fellow?'

Seconds go by. 'They don't confide in me,' the chauffeur says, eyes on the paper.

And even if they did, thinks Pascual, any man whom the Banque Villefort would trust to drive its clients would never tell. He grunts and wanders toward the street. He stands in the open gateway smoking. He watches the traffic while he finishes the cigarette and then grinds out the butt with his foot and turns back toward the door. He walks slowly, hands in his pockets, memorizing the numbers on the two limousines. He checks his watch and finds it is nearly eleven. If Daoud Najjar is in the building at all, he has been here for nearly two hours.

'You didn't get a list?' Pascual's voice rises and Villefort reacts by stiffening, battening the hatches and preparing for battle behind the fortress-desk.

'Of course I didn't get a list. What, you thought Chiesa would politely jot down the names for me? He was suspicious enough when I insisted on meeting them.'

'Somewhere in this building there's got to be a list of who these people are. And you've got to be able to get your hands on it. Can you try Chiesa's secretary, for example?'

'Marguerite? Not bloody likely. You'd have to tear out her nails before she'd tell you what time he got in this morning.'

Pascual rubs at the bridge of his nose, trying to extirpate the vicious headache he can feel brewing. 'All right. Can you remember any of the names?'

'I told you, he rattled them off too fast. Can you remember names when you're introduced to a group of people? I'd like to see you do it.'

'You didn't catch a single one of them?'

'They were Russian, for God's sake. The first one started with *K* I think, Kropotkin, Kremlin, something like that. And there were the usual *vitches* and *koffs* and things at the end.'

Pascual strives to keep his hands off the old man's throat. 'Did any of the names sound Arabic at all?'

'Arabic? How should I know? I'm not a bloody ethnologist. I told you, they sounded Russian to me.'

'The man I'm interested in is not Russian, though he speaks it. He'll be about fifty years old. Darkish, mustache, glasses. Did one of them look like that?'

'My dear fellow, they all looked like that. Except for the little fat one.'

Pascual clenches his fists, deep in his pockets. 'All right. Where are they now?'

'In the conference room upstairs. They've been there all morning.'

Pascual paces over the thick carpet, finding places on his jaw where his shave was less than perfect this morning. So far he has drawn an utter blank and Morrel is camped somewhere nearby, waiting for a call. 'All right. We'll just have to see what happens at lunch. You've got your little speech ready?'

'Hang on. Who says I'm going to be there?'

'I told you. You're giving a welcoming message and I'm handing out the pens.'

'I've already made my welcoming message. You can't ask me to sit through lunch with them. I detest those working lunches.'

'You agreed. You said you'd at least get to enjoy one of Philippe's productions.'

'Well, I've changed my mind. I'm going to the Pré Catalan today.'

'Listen, you rotting old cadaver. You're having lunch here just as we agreed. And if the speech doesn't go well your face will be on TF1 news with a swastika beside it tonight.'

'They're not expecting me. It's too late to add another place.'

'It can't be too late.'

Villefort sighs. 'You can't expect Philippe just to throw another steak on the fire. He's not a fast-food cook.'

'You've got to try.'

Villefort gives him a toss of the head and snarls at him. 'You go and talk to him. You're my personal assistant. What the hell do you think I hired you for?'

Pascual descends to the kitchen; Philippe is not pleased. Pascual anticipated a cartoon chef, corpulent and comical in the toque, but the real Philippe is gaunt and intense, a technician. His kitchen is small but gleaming with the usual copper, stainless steel and starched white linen. 'The food's ordered and half of it's cooked. What does he want, the miracle of the loaves and fishes?' His two helpers glance up from their labors as their master becomes exercised.

'One more place. Can't you manage that?' Pascual has assumed the air of complete vacuity that the personnel of the Banque Villefort have come to expect of him. He stands with hands in his pockets, impervious.

'Manage? Of course I can *manage*. It's not a question of managing. It's a question of respect. I don't barge in and ask him to throw in an extra million for me on his financial deals and I don't see why he should expect me to snap my fingers and pull an extra *émietté de crabe* out of the air at an hour's notice.'

Philippe has reached the stage of extravagant gesture and Pascual knows he has his work cut out for him. 'How much is it worth to you?'

Philippe looks down a long thin nose at Pascual. 'It's not a question of money,' he says.

'Is there a problem?' says a voice in the doorway. Pascual turns and sees Desjardins.

'Not at all. Merely arranging a place for Mr. Villefort at lunch,' he says.

Desjardins comes three paces into the kitchen, slowly. 'Mr. Villefort is not expected at lunch.' Desjardins has on his no-nonsense look.

Pascual tries out his disarming smile. 'Nonetheless, he has expressed a desire to be present. He wishes to become acquainted with our guests. And of course to benefit from Philippe's extraordinary talents.'

'Ah.' The chef is unmoved. 'He has no conception of the difficulties.'

Desjardins has not taken his eyes off Pascual. 'It will be a business luncheon. The matters under discussion do not concern Mr. Villefort. He would certainly prefer to dine elsewhere.'

'Surely that is for him to decide.'

'It has already been decided.'

'But he has just told me to arrange it. He wishes to dine with the others. I understood that Mr. Villefort was the president of this establishment.'

There is a faint smile on Desjardins's face that says clearly *you understood wrong*. 'You will convey the chef's regrets to Mr. Villefort. It is not possible.'

Pascual looks from one to the other, blankly. He shrugs. 'If you say so. He's not going to be pleased.'

'Well, then. We all have our jobs to do, don't we? Yours as I understood it is to ease Mr. Villefort's displeasure.'

Pascual holds the stony look for three seconds. 'And a thankless task it is,' he says, and leaves the kitchen.

Pascual nods at the men as he passes. If there is any sign that something more than business loans to weavers from Tourcoing is being discussed in the Banque Villefort, this is it: two gorillas in dark suits decorating the passage outside the conference room. They eye Pascual as he shuffles along the carpeted passage, trying hard to look as if he has a destination. They return his nod with all the warmth of coiled vipers. They have a generic look of trained hard men and they look as if they hail from somewhere beyond the bounds of the Western European gene pool. Pascual goes down to the end of the corridor and through a door to the stairway. As the door closes behind him he is seized by an urge to flee. He checks his watch. Until this instant he has nurtured the illusion that something will happen to spare him the need to leap into the ring and grab the bull by his wicked curving horns.

'All right, we're going to lunch,' he announces as he enters Villefort's office. 'I've called for the car.'

Villefort swivels his chair away from the window. He holds a drink in his hand and he is clearly still enjoying his victory in the struggle over lunch. 'About time, too. Will you need me this afternoon?'

From its place in the corner Pascual takes the leather document folder containing ten Mont Blanc fountain pens still packed in their boxes. 'With any luck you'll be quit of me this afternoon. Let's go, the car will be waiting.'

In the courtyard Pascual sees the old man into the car and goes round to get in on the other side. The limousines are still there but neither driver is in sight. The Mercedes eases out onto the street. Villefort is slumped in his corner of the seat, his eyes closed. The driver makes a turn into the rue de Richelieu and Pascual calls to him. 'Pull over here—I'm getting out.' To Villefort he says, 'Enjoy your lunch. I won't say it's been a pleasure serving you, but you've earned a word of thanks from a grateful nation.'

'Wait,' the old man calls, but Pascual has slammed the door and gained the pavement. Striding away, he tugs at his tie and tries to fight down a sense of panic. He turns into the next street and looks for the café he scouted out last night. He makes no attempt to spot counterintelligence officers spilling out of cars behind him or murmuring into handheld radios; he assumes that Morrel's team must be watching but sees no reason why they should interfere.

Djemila is sitting just inside the door of the café, smoking. When Pascual darkens the doorway she stabs out the cigarette and rises immediately. She scoops the paper-wrapped bouquet of roses off the table and follows him out onto the pavement. 'I was starting to worry,' she says.

'Save it.' Today Djemila has followed his instructions and put on a skirt; she has slender dark legs and in makeup and the feminine oufit she looks like a different person. Pascual is walking briskly; he would run if he thought she could keep up. 'They'll be going to lunch in ten minutes,' he says. 'It would be best to catch them in transition. Once they're seated they may have the gorillas on the door again.'

'Gorillas?'

'At least two of them. The kind you don't argue with.'

They turn a corner. Djemila grabs his sleeve. 'Slow down. You don't want to look like you've just finished a marathon.'

At a saner pace they turn into the rue du Quatre Septembre. Pascual has decided that a frontal assault is the best bet; in through the lobby and look for somebody to admit them to the inner regions. If Desjardins is there it will be a tough sell but the flowers are real. Pascual leads Djemila through the high ornate portal into the bank.

Desjardins is nowhere in sight. They pad across the lobby toward the locked door. 'Flowers for the gentlemen up on the second floor,' Pascual says to the green-jacketed doorman who wanders up to them. The doorman takes in Djemila's legs and gives the flowers a skeptical look, but he is already reaching for his keys. Pascual beams at him as they pass through the door.

There is nobody outside the second-floor meeting room and the door is locked. Pascual swears quietly. 'Missed them. They'll be in the dining room.'

'Where's that?' Djemila's eyes are huge in the dim passage.

'Downstairs. We'll have to hope they've thrown the gorillas some meat, too.'

They take the stairs. Just before he opens the door, Pascual looks Djemila in the eye and says, 'All right? Breathe deep, bright smile.'

'You're sweating.' If she has any doubts she is concealing them; she looks exactly like the flower-shop assistant Pascual wants her to be.

Pascual fishes for a handkerchief and mops his brow. He takes one look into the document folder and says, 'Let's go then.' Approaching the dining room, Pascual can see that if the gorillas are eating they are doing it in shifts. There are two of them on guard, heads close together gossiping, different from the two he saw before but equally imposing. Pascual finds to his amazement that he is calm now; he has survived far more perilous things than talking his way into a room full of financiers having lunch. The gorillas look up as Pascual and Djemila approach.

'The flowers,' Pascual says. 'For the gentlemen.'

The gorillas stare as if flowers are new to them.

'What flowers?' one says. He is tall and broad and visibly North African with his close-cropped wiry hair and black mustache.

'The roses. From Mr. Villefort.' Djemila rustles the paper helpfully, exposing the blossoms to view. 'And the gifts from the president,' says Pascual, holding the folder open for their inspection. 'A token of welcome and esteem.' He beams at them.

The gorillas exchange a look. The second man must be Slavic; he has the blunt heavy-lidded features of a Cossack or a Spetsnaz non-com. In accented French the Arab says, 'Nobody said anything about gifts.'

'They're from Mr. Villefort. For the delegation.'

'Who's that, Mr. Villefort?'

'The president of the bank, I told you.'

'Nobody said anything about him to us.'

'Well, you can see they're flowers. And pens. Look.' He takes one of the boxes out of the case.

The Arab pokes at the roses and sees that there are no weapons concealed under the paper. He spreads the folder open and says, 'Very well. I'll take them in.' He tugs at the folder.

Pascual draws it back and says, 'Ah, no. I was told to deliver them personally, with a message from Mr. Villefort.'

Another look passes between the two men and this time it is the Slav who speaks. *'Pas possible,'* he says. The North African gives Pascual a shrug.

Pascual inclines his head politely. 'Very well. I'll be back. With Mr. Villefort himself.' Striving to look affronted, he wheels and goes, trailed by Djemila, who is giving a convincing portrayal of baffled innocence. They return to the door at the end of the corridor.

'The kitchen,' breathes Pascual as the door closes behind them. He leads Djemila down the steps, hoping his guess is correct. 'The waiters will have a separate entrance to the room.'

In the corridor below he can see no one. If there are guards here as well, it is over. He forces himself to slow down and saunters into the kitchen, Djemila trailing. The two guards he saw outside the conference room earlier are here, at a table in the corner, hunched over plates. Brazen, thinks Pascual. No one doubts the brazen. Philippe is at the stove, furiously whipping something in a saucepan; he shoots them a look. Pascual is already making for the door in the corner, pointing. 'Is this the way to the dining room? Desjardins said to take the back way.'

Philippe is an artist plagued by the pettiness of worldly concerns; he does not deign to answer. Pascual leads Djemila toward the door. A chair scrapes on the floor. *'Attendez.'*

One of the gorillas has risen and is motioning to them,

wiping his mouth with a napkin. He looks like a Turkish wrestler with his handlebar mustache and oft-boxed ears. Pascual gives him a who-me look, eyebrows raised.

'What have you got there?'

Pascual understands, gives him the smile. 'Flowers. For the gentlemen upstairs. And some small gifts. Courtesy of the management.' In a confidential tone he adds, 'From Mr. Villefort, the old man. He likes to keep his hand in, you know? Pretend he's still the boss.'

Pascual grins into the small suspicious eyes, hoping that Philippe's cooking will tip the balance away from the call of duty. The wrestler probes the wrapping of the flowers and looks into the folder, just as his colleague upstairs did. He gives Pascual an annoyed look and Djemila a curious one. Pascual is thinking about escape tactics when the wrestler mutters, 'I'll have to come with you.'

They pass a waiter on the stairs, trotting down with an empty tray and a feverish look. Up one flight, the old steps creaking, and then there is a doorway and suddenly they are in and Pascual is stricken with stage fright. The room opens out before them, a long room lit by high windows giving onto the street, a table down the middle covered in white, six men around it captured *en plein déjeuner*, forks suspended. Six dark men in dark suits, and all of Morrel's scheming has got Pascual into this absurd fix, an inane grin on his face as he prepares to hand out flowers and trinkets to six men he has never before seen in his life.

The men are peering at him with varying degrees of bafflement and Pascual's mouth is hanging open, no words emerging. The wrestler stands to one side, frowning. 'Gentlemen,' Pascual manages. 'Compliments of your host, Mr. Villefort. He would like each of you to have a small memento of the occasion.' Pascual puts a hand on Djemila's arm and approaches the table. He is no longer thinking; now the words come in an effortless flow. 'My employer could not be with you today but he wishes you to know that you are welcome in Paris and in the Banque Villefort.' Pascual reaches into the folder and takes out one of the pens. He lays it at the head of the table, looking its occupant in the eye. This is a Russian; Pascual has seen faces like this in Damascus, in Sofia, in South Yemen. Djemila lays a rose beside the pen. The Russian glowers at them. 'The Banque Villefort is one of the oldest in France. In this very building Lesseps discussed the financing of the Suez Canal.' Pascual lays a pen at the next place, Djemila trailing. The man here is older, round, bald, bespectacled, of no obvious prove-nance. 'Inside these walls the intrigues of the Second Empire were carried out. Fortunes were made.' At the third place Pascual finds himself looking into the eyes of a casbah cutthroat; if this hatchet-faced killer isn't Djemila's general there are no certainties. 'Zola banked his royalties here, Marcel Proust politely disputed overdrafts with Mr. Villefort's grandfather.' Free-associating, inventing desper-ately, Pascual rounds the far end of the table. The man at this head is an imposing specimen, all shoulders and eye-brow. Pascual plops a pen on to the table by the salad plate and moves on. 'The Banque Villefort underwrote the con-struction of the Eiffel Tower and the first two lines of the

Métropolitain. Baron Haussmann had to talk to a Villefort before he could knock down a single tenement.' Pascual is on the home stretch now and warming to his subject; he can see the door ahead of him and if the bullshit holds out he and Djemila will be on the stairs in ten seconds, but things come to an abrupt halt because Pascual suddenly finds himself looking into the face of Abu Yussef.

He has wondered if he could possibly recognize him but now he wonders how he could ever have missed him. The man who passed him money, papers and orders over tables from Damascus to Lisbon has not aged a day, it seems. There is the same wavy hair touched with grey, brushed back off the high forehead and spilling onto the collar of the suit, the gently hooked nose above the full mustache, the graceful curve of the jaw; the unobtrusive wire-rimmed glasses. The Latin intellectual look, Pascual remembers calling it: he has known Argentines in Barcelona and Milanese in Rome with the same general aspect. The eyes, however, are those of Abu Yussef; he remembers them. 'It was the Banque Villefort that bankrolled the brothers Montgolfier,' he says after a breathless pause, smiling at Abu Yussef and reaching into the second compartment of the folder, which holds a single pen. He lays it by Abu Yussef's plate.

The sixth man could be Jacques Chirac and Pascual would not notice; he plucks another pen from the folder and fairly throws it on the table. 'In short, gentlemen, you could not have chosen a more fitting, a more respectable place in which to do your business.' He is backing toward the door, ducking and bowing in classic MC style, Djemila at his side, smiling prettily. 'On behalf of Mr. Villefort let me wish you a memorable and profitable stay in the City of Light and assure you that if there is anything he can do to make your visit more comfortable you have only to ask. Thank you, *messieurs*.' With a final bow he turns to the door, his eyes sweeping past the impenetrable gaze of the Turkish wrestler. As he leads Djemila out, someone at the table says *merci* uncertainly; a snort of laughter sounds as they go down the stairs. The closing of the door cuts off further comment.

The descent to the kitchen is the longest walk of Pascual's life. He hauls on the reins with all his might, trying not to break into a run. In the kitchen the wrestler makes a beeline for his lunch, ignoring Pascual's cheerful word of thanks. The second gorilla has disappeared. Pascual nods at the personnel; Philippe gives him a black look as he passes, ushering Djemila out of the kitchen. They say nothing as they walk the thousand miles to the end of the corridor. Round the corner to the right is the door to the courtyard.

They must first pass the elevator; the doors open as they approach and Desjardins strides purposefully out, along with the second gorilla from the kitchen. Surprise is mutual as the two parties nearly collide. Desjardins pulls up short, smiles and says, 'Ah, the flowers. How thoughtful of Mr. Villefort. I do hope there's one left for me.'

NINE

Desjardins's office is on the first floor. It is small and the single window overlooks the courtyard. Behind his desk Desjardins sits stiff and straight like a para colonel dressing down an insubordinate *soldat de deuxième classe*. Behind Pascual and Djemila the two gorillas from the kitchen stand with their backs to the door. 'What's all this nonsense, then?' says Desjardins.

'Mr. Villefort thought it was a nice gesture.' Pascual is feeling for the tone of injured rectitude that Frenchmen do so well but grasping it only imperfectly. The remaining roses and pens are spread on the desktop and Djemila stands with her arms folded, looking frightened.

Desjardins' eyes flick back and forth between them. 'Where's Villefort?'

'He's gone to lunch.'

Desjardins searches Pascual's face and in the pale eyes Pascual can see that he has no credit left there. 'Where?'

'The Pré Catalan, I believe.'

'Why didn't you go with him?'

'He told me to stay and make the presentation. For Christ's sake, what's eating you? You're worried I slipped a couple of spoons into my pocket, is that it?'

Desjardins has cold blue eyes. 'That's an idea. Search him.' Before Pascual can object, the gorillas shove him against the wall. Quickly and expertly he is probed from neck to ankles.

'There's this.' One of the gorillas tosses Morrel's cellular phone to Desjardins. 'No weapons.' He lays Pascual's wallet, cigarettes and matches on the desk.

'Of course I don't have any fucking weapons. Who do you think I am, Carlos the Jackal?' Pascual adjusts his jacket with much indignant flapping of arms.

Desjardins examines the wallet. 'You haven't got a lot of stuff here, have you? My wallet's a mess, all the things I shove into it. Not much of a life this Garnier has, one might say.' He looks at Djemila and says, 'Now her.'

'Hang on,' says Pascual. 'You can't do that.'

'I can, in fact. See what she's got in those pockets.'

The gorillas handle Djemila a little more gently; there is no actual groping but the pockets of her jacket and the waistband of her skirt are efficiently examined. Djemila stares at Desjardins throughout the indignity.

'Nothing,' says a gorilla.

'Nothing? No purse?'

'Nothing.'

If Desjardins finds this odd, his face does not show it. 'And where do you carry your *carte d'identité,* mademoiselle?'

'I keep it at the shop,' says Djemila.

'And what is the name of the shop?'

She stares at him and finally says, 'Are you a police officer?'

'I am the director of security for this bank.'

'I will talk to a police officer but I will not talk to you. I demand to be released immediately.'

Desjardins makes a very slight bow of the head. 'I will try to arrange one of those two options as soon as possible.' Rising, he scoops Morrel's cellular phone off the desk and slips it into his pocket. He points to one of the gorillas. 'You, keep them here. You, come with me. I'll be back.'

'You can't hold us against our will,' says Pascual.

'We'll see.'

'What about my phone?'

'You'll get it back.' The door swings shut.

Pascual trades a look with Djemila and spreads his hands, throwing himself on the mercy of his captor, the Turkish wrestler as it happens. 'What have we done?'

'You be quiet now.' The gorilla's French is slow and labored, overlaid with a thick accent. He has stationed himself with his back to the door. He folds his arms and looks at them with a complete lack of human interest.

'May we sit?'

'Sit.'

Djemila takes the chair in front of the desk. Pascual sighs, kicks a wastepaper basket, goes to the window. Below is the courtyard, the limousines still parked there. He cannot see the exit to the street. He wonders if Morrel can muster a team of commandos to storm the gate. He sinks onto the chair behind the desk. He is already thinking of notes in empty cigarette packages tossed out of the window, desperation leaps, ruses from juvenile thrillers. If Morrel does not receive his phone call soon he will take action; he must. He looks at Djemila; she is watching him intently but he cannot make out what she is saying with those huge dark eyes. He wants to tell her he is sorry.

Minutes pass. His guard has not moved from his station on the door. There is a knock. The guard opens it. Desjardins is in the doorway, to one side; beyond him is Abu Yussef, a.k.a. Daoud Najjar, standing back in the passage, looking directly at Pascual.

The eyes he has never forgotten; Abu Yussef had a quiet concentrated way of looking at you that made you think of a boy pulling the wings off flies. Now he is looking directly at Pascual, not curiously, not with recognition, just a man in a corridor looking at a stranger through a doorway. Desjardins turns his head from Pascual to Najjar and back again, and then closes the door. Pascual opens his mouth, too late, and is left gaping.

The footsteps die away outside. Pascual finds that he is making decisions rapidly. He is rediscovering a feeling he recalls from his operational days, a liberating awareness that no possible inhibitions make any sense in the current state of affairs. He pushes away from the desk and stands up. He walks around the desk and stands in front of the gorilla, trying to look dignified. In his best Levantine Arabic he says, 'I need to piss.'

The wrestler's brow wrinkles. In French he says, 'What? What's that you're talking? I'm no Arab.'

Pascual shakes his head in a show of irritation and repeats it in French. The wrestler shows very faint signs of amusement. He juts his chin at the wastepaper basket. 'Piss there,' he says.

Pascual looks at him coldly, a man suffering indignities at the hands of his social inferiors. He turns and walks back to the desk. He sits down. Djemila is staring at him. Pascual lets thirty seconds go by and turns to her. In Arabic he says, 'Can you understand me?'

She blinks and says, 'Of course.'

'Good. Then here's what we'll do. In a few seconds Godzilla there is going to come running over here and that's when you go for the door. I'll try to keep him busy long enough for you to get out. I don't think they've got anybody in the corridor. If they do, you'll just have to take your chances. Go for the eyes would be my advice.'

'*Ah, oh, non, non,*' says the gorilla. 'You talk French or you talk nothing.'

Pascual takes his cigarettes and matches off the desktop and holds them up in inquiry. The wrestler grunts. Pascual fishes out a cigarette, offers the pack to Djemila and says, 'Avoid the elevator, try to find the lobby and go out the front. Understood?'

For all the response Djemila makes, he might have been speaking Chinese. 'I'm not sure I can do it,' she says finally in a weak voice.

Pascual lights the cigarette. 'They're going to kill us,' he says.

'*Je vous dis, fermez la gueule.*' The wrestler is not used to being disobeyed. Pascual makes an appeasing gesture and reaches for a sheet of paper lying on Desjardins's desk. It is a memo of some sort but he does not bother to read it. With the still-burning match he carefully sets fire to a corner of it.

'What are you doing, imbecile?' The wrestler crosses the office in three steps, his French dissolving into a growl of abuse in what might be Russian. Pascual shoves away from the desk on Desjardins's high-tech ergonomically designed chair. The wrestler comes around the corner of the desk, reaching for the paper, which is just beginning to burn in earnest. Pascual drops the match on the carpet, his fingers singed.

As the gorilla swipes at the paper, Pascual catches hold of his tie with his free hand, up near the knot. The bulging eyes half a meter from his suddenly take on the classic panicked expression of a man caught in a trap. Planting his feet, Pascual wrenches sideways with all his might and rams the man's head into the wall behind the desk. There is a dull crack and Pascual is falling backward, the chair scooting out from under him and a hundred kilos or so of lightly stunned Turkish wrestler coming down on top of him. Pascual lands hard but that is nothing compared to the impact of his opponent's forearm on his chest. The wrestler bucks upward but quickly reaches the limit of Pascual's grip on his tie. This is a problem quickly solved; Pascual does not even see the punch. His face has barely recovered from the last beating he received and by the time the *son et lumière* show inside his traumatized skull subsides, the wrestler is already in the corridor, shouting.

Fear is a wondrous motivator and Pascual finds himself on

his feet and making for the window despite the shaky condition of his vision and his legs. He wrenches at the handle and the casement swings inward; he has one knee up on the sill when his guard reappears in the doorway.

Pascual has time to see the roof of the limousine three meters below him and make the judgment that three meters is a mere step. There is a rush behind him but the hand clutching at the tail of his jacket fails to stop him. The leap is extremely brief but stimulating and Pascual manages to land more or less properly on the forgiving surface of the roof, hitting feet first and rolling. He makes an enormous boom.

Someone is shouting as Pascual slides off onto the cobbles via windshield and hood. Through the glass he glimpses the shocked face of the chauffeur behind the wheel with the look of a man abruptly awakened. Above him in the window the wrestler is spluttering and pointing. The second chauffeur is frozen on the steps to the bank entrance but the door is opening. Pascual does not wait to see who will emerge; he is out of the gate in a second.

Klaxons and curses trail him as he runs.

Serge comes back along the pavement, hands in his pockets, sunglasses on, a man lollygagging at the airport, killing time. Overhead a jet screams into the sky, clawing for altitude. A hundred meters ahead Pascual can see the two limos parked in front of the Air France terminal. Serge slides back into the car. 'They're empty,' he says. 'The drivers are whistling at girls and looking at their watches. Nobody inside, never was. We followed two empty limousines.' He and Morrel trade a long smoldering look. 'I have to hand it to you, it worked,' says Serge.

'Don't start.' Morrel raises a finger.

In the back seat, Pascual says nothing. This is one he is going to be happy to watch.

Serge turns the key in the ignition. 'You said it, people take care of a nice expensive pen like that.'

'I'm telling you, don't start. It wasn't me that fucked it up.'

'He liked it so much he gave it to the fucking chauffeur.'

'*Merde*. All right, let's think. Where are they?'

Like a schoolteacher with a slow pupil Serge says, 'Well, since we're here at Roissy, I'd bet they're at Orly, getting on a plane.'

Morrel gnaws on a fingernail. 'The hotel. There's still a chance.'

'Presuming they were ever really at the Ritz.'

'You have a better idea?'

Wearily cranking the wheel, Serge says, 'You're the idea man.'

On the highway back into the city Morrel is intent again, speaking rapidly above the noise of the engine as Serge weaves from lane to lane, leaving mortal drivers in the dust. 'The old briefcase-in-the-taxi thing. The gentleman left his briefcase, you dropped him off there, you think he was Russian. If they're still there, they'll make an effort to match the case up with a guest. It could work.'

'And if they've left?'

'Just drive, *merde*.'

An hour later, Serge crosses the opulent lobby of the Ritz,

his feet making no sound on the deep, yielding carpet. 'Gone, eh?' says Morrel.

Serge nods. 'Half an hour ago. They were in a hurry, the concierge says. He wasn't surprised one of them left his briefcase in a taxi. They'll hold the case and wait for an inquiry. He agreed with me that they sounded Russian.'

Pascual can feel Morrel seething beside him. After a moment Morrel says, 'Well, then. Let's get the hell out of here.'

Morrel's cell phone goes off as they are stalking morosely back to the car. Morrel drags it out of his pocket, listens, snarls into it and puts it away. Serge gives him a look but Morrel says nothing until they are back in the car. His voice under tight control, he says, 'One of the limo drivers just unloaded six new Mont Blanc fountain pens on a small-time Corsican fence down near Montparnasse. Jacky wanted to know if he should go on following him.'

Serge grunts and says, 'Why not? As long as we've lost the Russians we might as well see what we can pick up in the way of Gypsy pickpockets.' He turns the key in the ignition.

The atmosphere in the dusty room behind the *quincaillerie* is not cheerful and there is no wine this time. Morrel paces, runs a hand through his hair, avoids looking at Pascual. 'A total failure, *merde*. You didn't even get a name. And you scared him off.'

Pascual's head hurts. He has no cigarettes and a drink would be an act of mercy. 'If you had done what I said, surrounded the place and been ready to go in the moment I rang you, you could have had the whole lot.'

'We don't want the whole lot. You still don't get it? All we want is Najjar.' He gives a whiff of laughter. 'Are you serious? Surrounded the place, kicked in the doors? If we'd done that, we'd be picking up cigarette butts in Martinique tomorrow.'

Pascual shrugs. 'You lost him. Not me.'

Morrel halts, jabs a finger at him. 'They wouldn't have pulled the stunt with the limousines if you hadn't roiled the waters.'

'Look, he recognized me. That was always a risk. And once he'd spotted me, he knew there was something bogus about the pens. If you'd kept people on the gate you still could have—'

'Shut it.' This is evidently a sore point with Morrel. 'You try running an operation like this with the resources they give us. Not to mention an informant who doesn't bother to ring us until he's set off a stampede to the exits.'

Pascual probes gently at the fresh swelling around his left eye. 'Easy for you to criticize, but I'm the one with my head on the block.'

Morrel has already forgotten him, conferring with Serge. 'We can work on the hotel angle, get a list of names.'

There is a silence and then Serge says in his deep rumble, 'Who was the girl?'

Pascual has been waiting for this. 'She came with the flowers. A little extra touch I thought up at the last minute. I thought she might provide a useful distraction. If Najjar's looking at her, he's not looking at me.'

Morrel snorts. 'Worked like a charm, didn't it?'

Serge has a talent for speaking volumes with a mere lowering of the eyelids. 'It would have been nice to clear that with us. We don't much like wild cards popping up in the middle of a hand. She didn't look as if she'd enjoyed her little visit to the bank. She came out the front and broke into a run. Who's she going to talk to and what's she going to tell them?'

This is the first indication Pascual has had that Djemila managed to get out; his relief is immense. 'As far as I'm concerned, that's your problem. I got you your identification.'

'You didn't get us a damn thing,' says Morrel. 'We don't know any more than what Mediane had already told us. We needed a name. Or a chance to tail him. Instead you sent him running for cover.'

'*Merde!*' Pascual has had enough; the light deal table between him and Morrel is not much of an obstacle. Morrel fends off the flying table with his foot and Serge jerks Pascual up short with a hand on his collar. A brief struggle, a wild swing and Pascual is pinned to the wall with Serge's forearm across his throat.

'Easy there, friend.' Serge has the mass of a bull and the eyes of the man who slaughters it. Pascual sags and raises his hands in surrender as Morrel rights the table. When Serge sees that there is no more fight in Pascual he takes his arm away. 'Calm, eh? Nice and easy.'

Morrel heaves a sigh. 'Got that out of your system now? Feel better?'

'He's had a hell of a day,' says Serge. 'Got to understand.'

'He has. I can see that. Sorry if I pushed a little hard.'

'Get the man a drink, for God's sake.'

'Of course, what am I thinking? Where's that damn bottle?'

Serge sets a chair upright. 'Hard on all of us, most of all you. Sit down, take a load off.'

Morrel is foraging in a cabinet. 'I get wrapped up in things, I forget. You've had a tough role to play. I don't mean to make light of it. Here. Where's a glass, *merde?*'

'You did a hell of a job, should have made that clear. Cigarette?'

Pascual drops onto the chair like a bag of cement. He takes a cigarette and Serge lights it for him. Morrel splashes wine in the glass and sets it in front of him. 'I'm through,' says Pascual.

A silence ensues while the two Frenchmen take their seats, blink at each other. 'I'm afraid not,' says Morrel.

'I'm not going to follow them to Russia.'

'If we ask you to, you will,' says Morrel. 'But it shouldn't be necessary. And you'll be compensated, remember.'

'You can't possibly need me anymore. I've spotted him, given you a confirmed sighting. You know who he works for, who he associates with. Now you go after Mirakl. I can't believe they have that much political cover, that they can go on protecting him.'

'They haven't. But then they'll never admit it's him. Daoud Najjar? Never heard of him. And if we press, they'll keep throwing phony identities at us until we get tired and give up. They'll give us two or three dozen Syrians and none of them will be Najjar. He'll be working on his next passport, still out there. Our only chance is to catch him somewhere and for that we still need the only man who can spot his face.'

'He's seen me now, recognized me. How long do you think I'll last if he sees me again?'

'There are security problems, it's true. But you have an advantage Mediane didn't have. You don't have a fixed address, you don't have roots. We can hide you.'

'I'm going home.'

'Ah, that wouldn't be hiding, I'm afraid. Not for long.'

That is the threat that Pascual cannot trump; he smokes and looks at nothing until the dimensions of his prison become clear. 'So what next?' he says.

'Us, we go at it from the hotel angle, maybe other angles. Maybe it's time to come at Mirakl from a direction they're not expecting. We've got other cards up our sleeve. You, for a start, you go back to Villefort. You tell him to get you whatever he can about this delegation. Names, contact addresses, the lot. Above all, names. Push him a bit.'

'He won't stand for it. He'll break first.'

'No, he won't. He values the good life too much. Tell him how long he might live yet, in prison.'

'I'm telling you, there's no more there. Nobody at the bank trusts him anyway. That vein's worked out.'

Morrel's look hardens. 'If you want to catch him before he goes out for the evening, I'd suggest you phone him now.'

The majordomo is distant and *très correct;* he conducts Pascual to Villefort's private apartments and leaves him in the sitting room. What he thinks of Pascual's comings and goings over the past weeks is not apparent in his face or his manner. Pascual flops in an armchair with his legs flung out, exhausted. The room is lit by a single lamp and in the gloom Pascual begins to nod. He is awakened by the murmur of voices and the sound of a door opening.

Villefort stands before him, nattily turned out in a grey silk suit, rigid with anger. Behind him is a young man in jeans, eyes scanning the room, full of wonder. The young man has the fresh face of a Normandy cowherd. 'What are you doing here?' Villefort forces out between clenched jaws.

Pascual is groggy with sleep but grasps the situation immediately. 'We must talk,' he says. 'It will only take a minute.'

'Get out of my house.'

Pascual rises, takes a deep breath, meets the youth's amused, insolent look and leans toward Villefort, intimidating. 'Tell him to go and powder his nose. Five minutes and I'm gone.'

Villefort's mouth works and for an instant Pascual thinks the old man is going to spit in his face. The moment passes and Villefort turns and says to the youth, 'Go through that door and wait for me, please.' The young man shrugs, makes his way across the room while giving the furniture an appraising eye. When the door shuts on him Villefort snarls at Pascual. 'You told me you were through with me.'

'I thought I was. But I never got a name. You have to get it for me.'

'Impossible.'

'Nothing's impossible. I need the name of the Syrian who

came with the Russians. Get it somehow. I'm out of patience.'

Villefort also is out of patience; he is actually quivering. His moist brown eyes under the overgrown brows are the purest expression of hatred Pascual can remember seeing. 'One moment,' he says. He wheels, moving with remarkable decision for a man of his age, and stalks to a desk in the shadows. There is a rustle of clothing, a clinking of keys and a drawer opens. Pascual peers at him, wondering. Villefort takes something from the drawer and comes stalking back.

The revolver is large and black. Villefort holds it steadily enough to do immense damage at this range. Pascual has missed his chance to run and he knows it; now he might make it to the door but not without considerable damage. 'There's no need for that,' he says.

'I ought to have done this the very first time you stood in this room,' says Villefort. 'But it's never too late.'

Pascual is calculating chances: a sudden enough move might avoid a crippling shot; is an old man's grip strong enough for the stiff trigger pull of a weapon like this? He is afraid to move. 'With a witness in the next room? You'll go to prison faster this way than if they find out you were a Nazi.'

'I was never a Nazi,' snarls the old man. 'I have never been anything but a patriot.'

'I'm not going to argue with you. I'm going to turn around and walk out that door and you're going to put that thing away and go entertain your guest there.'

The pistol wavers; it is a heavy thing for an old man to hold at arm's length for more than a few seconds. Something in Villefort's eyes changes and Pascual feels a jolt of panic. He is rocking on his heels, ready to jump, roll, scream, when the old man moves.

Villefort puts the revolver to his right temple and grimaces with the effort of squeezing the trigger; there is an atrociously loud noise and the left side of his head lands halfway across the room. He crumples like a suit sliding off a hanger, the revolver falling softly on the carpet.

Pascual stands in shock until the door to the bedroom creaks open. The boy's face appears in the gap, eyes wide. 'He killed himself,' says Pascual in wonder. Villefort's eyes are open but very, very empty; never has a man looked so dead so fast. The boy creeps out of the bedroom and then starts to pick up speed, giving the heap on the floor a wide berth.

'*Salut les gars,*' he says, brushing past Pascual. Pascual listens as he runs into the majordomo on the stairs. Voices are raised, blows are struck, panic is abroad in the land. Pascual finds himself making for the bedroom; there is a window there giving onto the garden, and it will not be the first time today he has eschewed the stairs.

Djemila answers the phone after a single ring. 'I hope I'm not waking you,' says Pascual.

Over the line comes the sound of an exhalation, a laugh perhaps, or a sigh of relief, maybe just an easing of tension. 'Where are you?' she says. Her *tutoiement* surprises him and he realizes that he himself has instinctively dropped the *vous*.

'On the street. Safe. More or less.' Pascual is still seeing

Villefort's brains going sideways; it has been a day full of extreme sensory stimuli. 'What about you? You sure nobody followed you?'

'I don't think so. But I'm not sure I'd know.'

'If you made it home you're probably all right.'

There is a silence. 'So what happens next?' says Djemila.

Pascual gives it some thought, watching the late-night traffic on the boulevard. 'I don't know. I was rather hoping to be far away by this time.'

'So why are you still here?'

'That's a very good question. Can we talk tomorrow?'

'I think we should,' she says.

TEN

'I congratulate you,' says Morrel. 'You've managed to render the Marcel Garnier identity entirely useless. Every policeman in Paris is looking for you today.' Morrel lets the curtain fall back, turns away from the window. 'God knows what that little *pédé* is telling them, but they seem to believe it's a love triangle gone sour.'

Pascual spits toothpaste into the sink. 'I told you he'd break. You didn't listen.'

'You simply didn't know how to handle him. Serves me right, sending a butcher to do the work of a surgeon. I over-estimated your diplomatic skills.'

'You've overestimated everything about me from the start. I have nothing to offer you. Keep your suits and your money and let me go.'

'I'm afraid I can't do that.'

Pascual stuffs toiletries into his bag; today there is no reason to shave. 'He's gone. I fucked it up and he's gone. Try something else.'

'Oh, we'll try something else. But we'll still need you.'

'You'll know where to find me, then. Try the Café de la Opera late in the afternoon. I'm usually awake by then.'

'You really think I'm going to let you go at this point?'

'You really think I'm going to hang about? You'll have to handcuff me to the bed.'

'I don't think so. I think with your face on the front page of every newspaper and on the wall of every police station in France you're going to find it a little hard to make your way home. Or wherever you're planning to go. Don't make me release the photo.'

Pascual goes through the motions for half a minute or so, gathering socks. Then he slams his bag against the wall in fury. '*Merde!* What am I supposed to do, sit in the Tuileries and feed pigeons while you search the globe for Najjar? I've got a life to live.'

'We'll pick up his track again before too long. In the meantime you'll be fed and housed, though perhaps not in the style you became accustomed to with Villefort. And while you're feeding the pigeons you might give a moment's thought now and again to that bank account in Switzerland. I should think that would keep you going for a while.'

Pascual slumps on the bed. 'How long?'

'I can't tell you. Not forever. I'm afraid we'll have to take back all your Garnier papers, including the money card. But we'll rig you up a new identity as soon as we can. In the meantime, here's something to be going on with.' He produces a fold of banknotes from a wallet. Pascual takes them and counts ten one-hundred franc notes at a glance. 'No more lunch at Fouquet's, but you won't starve. Try to make that last a couple of weeks, all right? The budget isn't infinitely elastic. I'd like you to check in each morning at the number I've written down by the phone there. If I don't hear from you I'll have to contact the inspector in charge of the Villefort inquiry. And the minute we have a lead on Najjar we'll be in touch. All right?'

Pascual says nothing. He refolds the banknotes and slips them into a pocket. He stares at the floor and does not respond to Morrel's good-bye. When the door closes Pascual sits motionless for another minute and then reaches for the telephone. He is surprised to find that he knows Djemila's number by heart.

They meet at Métro Buttes Chaumont, near the entrance to the park. Djemila is in casual mode again, in a print shirt and jeans. A necklace of blue beads caresses her throat. She is thin and graceful, all bones and nerves but under careful control. She does not look like a happy woman. She greets him warily, no doubt reading the signals in his face. 'Rachid's busy today, is he?' Pascual says.

She gives him a puzzled look and says, 'He works. Just a few hours a week, taking pictures of children in a photographer's studio.' A faint wry smile touches her lips. 'He was one of the best news photographers in Algeria, before he left. He hates himself for being a coward but he would almost certainly be dead if he had stayed. They'd made his paper a special target.'

'Tell him a coward's a more effective reporter than a dead man.'

'I have, or words to that effect. He doesn't trust you, you know.'

'That's easy to see. I don't think I would either, in his place.'

'We had a serious talk about it. He thinks I was insane to go into the bank with you.'

'It's hard to fault his judgment, at this point.'

'He still thinks you could be a spy, set on us by Mirakl.'

'Just out of curiosity, what makes you so sure I'm not?'

'Seeing you slam that man's head into the wall. Until then, I had my doubts.'

'And you came in with me anyway?'

Djemila gazes into the distance. 'Sometimes you have to take a risk.'

Pascual nods. 'Let's walk,' he says.

They descend through trees; beside the path water cascades gently toward the lake. 'What would have happened if I'd run to the police yesterday?' says Djemila. 'I almost did.'

'Probably nothing. You would have spent the rest of the day telling the story over and over, and at some point you'd have had to face Desjardins again. He would have described how we crashed the meeting and denied everything we said with a condescending smile. He might have insisted on bringing charges for trespassing, and the story of Mirakl and Mourad Mediane would have died a quiet death. Like us maybe, sometime soon.'

'That's about what I decided.'

They have gained the lake with its steep wooded crag rising in the middle. A pack of joggers straggles by, devoting more breath to talk than to running. 'We're not finished, are we?' says Pascual.

She sits on a vacant bench, lets him light her cigarette. 'I don't know about you. I'm certainly not,' she says.

Pascual smokes and watches ducks riot and splash on the water. 'If I had anything to say about it, I'd be on the next train home. But I don't.'

He can see her in the corner of his eye, studying him. 'Where's home?'

'Barcelona.'

'You're Spanish?'

'I don't know what I am. Catalan? Maybe, whatever that means now. I spent part of my childhood here in Paris. Other parts of it in New York. I can pass for American as easily as French.'

'And you've spent a lot of time in Lebanon, judging from the Arabic you came out with yesterday.'

'Syria, mostly.'

'Ah. You've led an interesting life.'

Pascual lets a dry little laugh escape. 'Mostly, I've wasted it.'

From one of the bridges to the island high above some boys are heaving rocks at the ducks, without notable accuracy. 'So. What did we accomplish yesterday?' says Djemila.

'We established that an Algerian general is meeting, in considerable secrecy, with representatives of a Russian consortium with a reputation for skulduggery. What does that mean to you?'

'It adds to a pattern I've been trying to track for about three

months. I've got a source in the office in Algiers that—'
Djemila halts suddenly.

'Don't tell me. Whether you trust me or not, don't tell me. You've got a source, I understand.'

Shaken, she takes a few seconds to recover. 'I've got a source who can tell me when he leaves the country and where he's going. This is his third trip to Paris in three months, all in secret. The second time, Rachid and I were able to trace him to the Banque Villefort. Until yesterday we had no idea whom he was meeting there.'

'All right. What does a rogue Russian multinational want with an Algerian general?'

'The mind reels. My question is, what do we do next?'

Pascual heaves a sigh, shakes his head. 'Well, my handlers say they're going to go after Mirakl. Maybe we let them do some of the work. And maybe you keep your ear to the ground for signals from Algiers. I think we rousted them before they were quite through yesterday. That may mean that there'll be another meeting soon. Probably somewhere else. If you can get wind of it, we'll go. Where Boucherif is, we'll likely find Najjar.'

'So we share the same interest, do we?'

He cocks his head at her. 'Of course.'

'I wondered. You see, I want to find out what's going on and tell the world about it. But as I understand it, you want to help the French arrest a man, without making much of a stir. I'm not sure those two objectives are compatible.'

'The objective we share is to find them.'

'And do your handlers know about me?'

'They saw you. I told them you came from the flower shop.'

'Why didn't you tell them the truth?'

'You think they'd appreciate having a journalist in on things?'

She acknowledges the point with a raised eyebrow. 'Did they believe you?'

'I don't know.'

When they finish their cigarettes they walk. It is the height of summer, a splendid day. Children and tourists, the idle and the aimless, litter the grassy slopes. Through the trees they catch glimpses of the city, never far away. Djemila walks with her eyes on the ground. 'I wasn't raised for this, I wasn't trained for it. I never wanted to be a detective or a spy.'

'Why pursue it, then?'

A hiss of bitter laughter escapes her. 'What else am I going to do? In the past year I've lost a husband, a job and a country. I'm living off a brother who can ill afford it, and every newspaper and magazine in France has told me regretfully there are no positions open. I can either do what I was trained to do or go slowly mad watching my nieces draw on the walls. If I get the story it means money and maybe a job. It means I have a life again. Unless, of course, somebody kills me.' She shuffles a few steps further, stops, turns to face him. 'I haven't thanked you.'

'For what?'

'For helping me get out yesterday.'

With a shrug Pascual says, 'Considering it was me who got you in there in the first place, I'm not sure you owe me any thanks. But then maybe all yesterday proves is that we've got complementary skills. You've got the brains and I've got . . . I don't know. I'm not sure what my contribution is.'

Djemila seems to give it some thought. 'The courage?'

'If you only knew,' says Pascual. 'If you only knew.'

'I'd stay out of public places if I were you,' says Morrel over the telephone. 'I don't think they've got any leads, but I wouldn't give them any help. Keep your head down.'

'They know it was suicide,' says Pascual. 'The papers said so.'

'They may be coming around to that. But they still want to talk to you. And if they pick you up, you're on your own. Nobody here has ever heard of you. You'll be released eventually, but there will be cameras in your face, whatever story you tell them.'

'I'm running low on money.'

'You get another allowance on Monday, not before.'

'So what's the news? Where's Najjar?'

'Nobody knows. We got a list of names from the hotel but they're all Russian. Which one was Najjar, we don't know. He's probably got half a dozen Russian passports to choose from. But we're working on him. There are avenues we haven't gone down yet. We'll find him.'

'Doesn't anybody have the authority to go after Mirakl? Interpol, NATO, the United Nations, I don't know. Somebody's got to be able to hold these people accountable.'

'It's not that simple, *mon vieux*. In the first place they've dispersed authority so well that it's difficult to say who really is responsible for any part of the structure. Kovalenko? He's already got out of more than a few scrapes by simply denying that he has anything to do with the operation in question. The KGB invented deniability. "Running drugs? How shocking, but I'm afraid we sold that company months ago. Prostitution? You can see that this nightclub is owned by so-and-so, not me." And so-and-so takes the fall, a risk he's been well paid to take. You can be assured that we'll never prove Kovalenko employs Najjar. Secondly, Najjar himself will be buried behind three or four layers of protection, identities he can shake off like a snake slipping out of its skin. He's lived that way for years. That's why we need you, for the face-to-face. We need another break like Mourad Mediane's sighting, and we need you.'

'Mourad Mediane, yes. I seem to recall hearing he came to a bad end.'

'Well, old man, as for the risk, that's what *you're* being well paid to take.'

La Voix du Maghreb occupies a cramped office reached via a narrow flight of stairs in one corner of a courtyard in an old and not especially well-kept building just up the rue Seveste, *dix-huitième*. From the window of the office Pascual can see the tumult on the Boulevard de Rochechouart, a crowd that could have been rented *en masse* from Algiers or Tunis milling on the wide promenade. 'They let us use this desk,' says Djemila. 'As long as nobody needs it urgently.'

The desk in question is one of four in the office, leaving little room for chairs or indeed those who prefer to stand. A fax machine and a filing cabinet further increase the demands on space. 'It's the newest and smallest of the Arab papers in Paris,' says Djemila. 'An old colleague of Rachid's from Algiers puts the thing out every week with the help of two part-time assistants. He can't afford to hire us but he gave us a key and lets us use the computer and the phone. It helps us pretend we're still journalists.'

Rachid brews tea with water boiled on a hotplate and serves it to them with sugar piled thick in the bottom of the glass. 'Like we make it back home,' he says. '*Là-bas, chez nous*. In our dear martyred homeland.' He says it with the required touch of irony but there is a brief dip in the temperature, a second of embarrassment or distaste, as at the mention of a disreputable relative. Djemila's eyes meet Pascual's for an instant and flit away. 'So far we've been able to play journalist without the distractions that would accompany the exercise of our profession back home,' says Rachid. 'Though we're careful to keep the door locked, particularly since the massacre. That happened two hundred meters from here.' He settles onto a chair and gives Pascual a challenging look. 'Do your handlers know about us?'

'They've seen you. They don't know who you are.'

'Are you going to tell them?'

'Not unless I have to.'

Rachid takes a drink of tea and then looks at Djemila. 'So now everybody's on to us, the French, the Russians and our own dear General Boucherif.'

She bristles, just visibly. 'I got what you couldn't get with your camera. I got proof he was there.'

'I don't want anybody to get hurt. We didn't leave Algeria to get our throats cut in Paris.'

'No. But we're in the wrong profession if we want security. We're from the wrong country for that.'

A silence follows. Pascual watches as the temperature cools, two people stifling a family quarrel before an outsider. Djemila lights a cigarette and leans back on her chair. 'We've learned a good deal, actually. I'm working the telephone, trying to track down people who have dealt with Mirakl. Thierry Fort has put me on to a man in the Ministry of the Interior who's agreed to meet me and I'm waiting for a callback from an Italian revenue agent who I was told went after one of their front companies in Milan. I'm starting to find people who know things about Mirakl. Nobody seems to have much good to say about them. But it's slow work, old-fashioned footwork. Rachid's had a go at the Internet and found some interesting things.'

Rachid shakes his head. 'Nothing to get excited about.' He pulls a folder full of papers across the desk. 'There are a lot of references to Mirakl, but nothing really useful is going to be out there on the net. As for Najjar, not a bloody thing.'

'He had shed that name by eighty-nine,' says Pascual. 'He saw what was coming.'

Rachid nods. He sifts papers, passes some across to Pascual. 'These are for you. My English is just good enough to spot them but I don't read it that well.'

'I'll have a look at them.'

'Mirakl's left a lot of tracks, anyway. Kovalenko is the nominal head but there seem to be a lot of partners. All former military or security types. And they all seem to have got very rich fairly suddenly. If you were well connected you could get money from the state at very low interest rates to buy up privatized enterprises through shell companies. The bids were rigged, of course. In other words they just took what they wanted. Kovalenko is one of the three or four richest men in Russia and he helped get Yeltsin elected president.'

'Where does the money come from?' says Djemila. 'Oil?'

'Some of it. Oil, cars, chemicals, construction materials. They've taken a lot of the cream of Soviet industry and made it more or less competitive. That's the legitimate part. They can point to any number of real, working firms that make up Mirakl. But to get there they stole the country blind. Kovalenko made a fortune early on by borrowing rubles and buying up everything from titanium to timber and selling it for dollars. In nineteen ninety-two he bought four million tons of oil at fifty rubles a ton, which was about five dollars. Then he sold it on the world market for a hundred and forty dollars a ton. That's where a lot of Russia's natural wealth went.'

Djemila shakes her head. 'And meanwhile the old pensioners live on potatoes,' she says.

'What about the really dirty stuff?' says Pascual. 'I don't suppose you found any of that on the Mirakl home page.'

'You mean the smuggling, the drugs, the women? There's a lot of speculation but that's all it is, at least in the sites I can get to. There's a lot of talk about the alliances between old organized crime groups and the new Russian ones. The Mafia, the Colombians, those types, laundering money in Russia, buying weapons there. I'd guess Mirakl gets its share of that kind of deal. But I don't have any proof. We're going to have to do our own digging.'

They let that hang in the air for a moment before Pascual says, 'So what does Mirakl do that might appeal to an Algerian general?'

Rachid closes the folder. 'You want me to make a guess? I'd say guns. That would be my first guess for Boucherif. But that's Djemila's area of expertise.'

She frowns, considering. 'I wouldn't say Boucherif's interested in women or drugs or any of that—he's got a reputation for probity. Austerity, even. He's a natural hardliner. He spent the war of independence in the *bled* fighting the French and he's always been the man they turn to when the dirty work needs doing. He was in on the coup against Chedli and they put him in charge of putting down the riots in eighty-seven. Now he's generally regarded as the leader of the *éradicateurs,* the ones who will accept no compromise with the Islamists. And as far as anyone knows he hasn't stuffed his pockets or helped his relatives stuff theirs. He lives in a modest villa up in Hydra above Algiers and his sons have gone into the army just like him. He's reputedly quite devout and that may be why he's an eradicator. He considers the guerrillas to have disgraced Islam. If he wants anything from Russia, Rachid's probably right. It would be guns.'

'Why would he need guns? He runs the army, doesn't he?'

Rachid and Djemila exchange a look that says *the poor naïf.* 'They always need more guns,' says Rachid. 'A private army is never a bad thing to have in Algeria. Your back is never safe, and if you can train and equip a few hundred troops whose loyalty is to you and your family, so much the better. You form a special unit, nominally part of the army, but maybe you put your sons in the key command positions. And you might want to stockpile a few second-hand Soviet artillery pieces while you're at it. That way, when the regime breaks down you've got your power base.'

'Is that a danger? The regime breaking down?'

'Who knows?' Djemila says. 'It can happen fast. The regime's held together so far but they're under incredible stress. There's the opposition between eradicators and negotiators. There's a Western-oriented faction and an Arabist faction. There's a pro-French clique and a pro-American one and a good many who wish the Soviets were still around. There are those who favor privatization and those who think they've gone too far from socialism already. The only thing that holds them all together is the oil.'

Rachid makes a noise of disgust. 'The safest place in the world right now is an oil field in Algeria. That's where the troops are, guarding the oil. Let the civilians die, just keep the oil flowing. That's the regime's *raison d'être*. As long as the oil is safe, the royalties coming in, they can hold out against the world.'

'But not against each other,' says Djemila. 'When the disposition of power comes into question, the colonel sitting across the table from you is more dangerous than a thousand guerrillas in the *bled*. And I would bet that's why Boucherif is talking to the Russians.'

In the silence that follows, Pascual sips tea and feels

fervently grateful for the geographical accident of his birth. 'You don't have to pursue this, you know,' he says. 'Millions of people will go to bed happy tonight without knowing the first thing about General Boucherif and his intrigues. You could give up journalism and open a couscous joint.'

'Don't think I don't consider it,' says Djemila. 'Every single day.'

ELEVEN

'I'm afraid we have to insist on knowing who your Arab girl is,' says Morrel with the air of mild regret that Pascual has learned masks his firmest diktats. Morrel makes himself at home on the chair by the window while Pascual sits on the edge of the bed, still dazed from his sudden awakening. 'You didn't really expect us to buy that about the flower shop, did you?'

Pascual shakes his head and gropes for a shirt. 'You've been following me around. And here I thought you trusted me.'

'Trust you? You insult me.'

Pascual pulls on his trousers, shambles toward the bath-room. 'She's an old friend. I looked her up when I got here because I knew I'd need help.' He shuts the bathroom door and proceeds to pee, striving to put together a story.

When he emerges, Morrel is examining his fingernails. 'And the *mec*? The fellow you spotted in the Luxembourg that day? Is he an old friend, too? He knows her, anyway. They're thick as thieves, in fact.'

Pascual collapses on the bed. He has wondered how long

he can keep the two parties apart and what would happen when the wall between them was breached. The one principle he has to go on is to keep the word *journalist* out of the conversation. 'All right, they approached me. They're interested in the Algerian general, Boucherif.'

Morrel sniffs. 'Ah yes, I wondered about that. I didn't think old Villefort could possibly be the source of that little item. What are they, journalists?'

Pascual contrives to look startled. 'No. They work for a human rights organization.'

'Human rights? In Algeria? That's like working for chastity in a brothel. No wonder they're here and not over there. What's the name of the organization?'

'I don't know. League for something or other, the rights of man or something like that.'

'Find out. And I'll need her name.'

'It won't help you. She told me they have to treat membership records as top secret. They won't confirm or deny that she belongs.'

Morrel seems amused. 'She told you that, did she?'

'Look, she showed me credentials. She's what she says she is.'

Morrel does not seem inclined to press the point. 'What the hell do they want with you?'

'They've been tracking the general and he led them to the bank. They wondered who I was, I wondered who they were. We decided to compare notes. They knew there was something fishy about Mourad Mediane's murder but they thought it was seeing Boucherif that got him killed.'

Morrel gives him a long heavy-lidded look. 'And what did you tell them?'

'I told them I was a journalist.'

Morrel must know he is dealing with a professional liar, but after a long moment he allows himself a smile. 'I must give you credit for inventiveness. And what was a journalist supposed to be doing posing as Villefort's assistant?'

Loftily Pascual says, 'I am carrying out an inquiry into Russian crime groups and their infiltration of Western European institutions.'

'I suppose that's plausible.'

'They seemed to buy it.'

Morrel nods, taps his lips with a finger. 'And now you're squiring her about the city.'

'Squiring her about? Hardly. We had lunch yesterday, it's true.'

'And the day before. What do you talk about?'

'We have decided to put our heads together and see where our separate paths might converge. They've intersected once at the Banque Villefort. If they intersect again we could both learn something.'

Morrel does not like it, Pascual can see, but for the moment there is nothing he can do about it. 'I am assuming you know better than to breathe one single word of your true objective to these two good people,' Morrel says.

Pascual blinks at him. 'You insult me.'

'The name of Daoud Najjar, for example, has not been spoken. So I assume.'

'Frankly, I doubt they would be interested. All they want to know is why their leaders are going to the bank in Paris while people are being slaughtered back home.'

'And if the answer should involve Najjar?'

'I don't see why it should. They trailed Boucherif to Paris hoping to find him working out secret deals with the Islamists. That's what they're interested in—politics, not money. But Boucherif's obviously just working out some deal to salt away money for his retirement. They're about to lose interest.'

Morrel rises from the chair. 'Good. Well, then. There won't be any further reason for you to consort with this woman or her friend, will there? Unless you're hoping to get her in bed. In which case I must warn you—that's a very touchy proposition with Arab women, even these *évoluées*. I hope she doesn't have any brothers around, at least.'

'Why don't you mind your own fucking business?'

'Oh, dear, I seem to have touched a sore spot. You're not really considering it, are you? Give it up. We'll spot you the money to take a ramble up the rue Saint-Denis one of these evenings if you're that desperate.'

Pascual resists an absurd impulse to defend his intentions toward Djemila and a slightly less absurd one to split Morrel's lip. 'You needn't concern yourself with my private life, such as it is.'

'Oh, yes, it's very much my concern, I'm afraid. And I don't want any more dalliance with this woman or her companion, is that clear?'

Calmly Pascual says, 'Let me point out one thing.'

'What?'

'If, as she claims, she has a way to track Boucherif's move-ments, she could help us. If we disrupted his meeting with Mirakl before it was completed, then Boucherif's next port of call might also be Najjar's.'

Morrel stands halfway to the door, hands in his pockets. It takes him some time, but Pascual can see him working his way round to conceding the point. 'That's a lot of ifs. But *if* they all hold, and *if* you can keep your mouth shut, then you have permission to cultivate her. As a source, you under-stand. Nothing more.'

Pascual sinks back on to the pillow, rubbing his eyes. 'Nothing more. Good Christ, what do you take me for?'

They walk until they reach the Seine at the Quai de la Mégisserie, where they stand watching the water. The sky is clouding over, promising a shower. The Île de la Cité shim-mers in the darkening river. 'We walked a lot,' Djemila says. 'Five or six of us, strength in numbers. Down Sébastopol, along the *quais*. You never knew where it was safe to go in and ask for an Orangina but the streets were for everyone. We'd watch the buskers, look at boys, stare into the shop win-dows, giggle. I was never allowed to go out alone, but with a couple of friends I could conquer the city. We'd walk till our feet blistered, maybe take the Métro home if we had the money. My brother would accuse me of meeting boys but if any boys ever talked to us we'd turn tail and run. God, we were innocent. In that way, anyway. In other ways we had to be as tough as nails. There was always somebody giving you the look, snarling about *petites salopes,* jostling you off the pavement. Not to mention slipping a hand in where it shouldn't be, rubbing up against you on the Métro. It was an adventure, every time. A little band of Arab girls, us against the world. Half of us had lost fathers in the war, we'd all been tossed into school here to sink or swim with our ten words of French and somehow managed. We just wanted to fit in. I don't know where any of them are now. Married and living in an HLM probably. Me, just as I was starting to feel French I went back to Algiers. My uncle sent me back because he was afraid I'd lose my virtue.'

Pascual smiles. 'Any regrets?'

She gives it some thought, head inclined to one side, hair tossing in the freshening breeze. 'In Algiers my virtue was safe, but I'd lost the boulevards. Funny, I still couldn't go out alone and I was still an outsider because I'd lived over here, I spoke like a *parigote*. With my Arab face and my French clothes I seemed to have a particularly inflammatory effect on the type of man who has nothing better to do than cluster with his mates on a street corner and there are a lot of those in Algiers. It was enough to make me think about taking the veil. Besides all that, I was poor again. My mother and I shared a room in the Casbah, very picturesque I'm sure you'd find it, but that's just another word for squalid. A widow with three years of schooling didn't have a lot of earning power, which was why she'd sent us all to Paris to begin with. She worked like a horse to feed me and pay for books, and I cried myself to sleep at night. I'd missed her brutally but once I was with her all I could think about was getting away again. That's what it is to be Algerian. Wherever you go, half of you is somewhere else.'

Pascual is familiar with the phenomenon. He blows smoke and says, 'I'd say this half of you here is better off right now.'

'No doubt. And I still cry for Algiers. I did make a life there, after all. I left a husband there.'

Pascual studies ripples on the river. 'What happened?'

Djemila shakes her head, slowly. 'He got tired.'

'Tired of what?'

'He got tired of taking precautions that added an hour a day to the simplest routines. He made the ghastly error of walking directly to his car from the newspaper office one day. They killed him at the first red light.'

Pascual does not move for a long time. He watches the river and senses her movements beside him, languid and controlled. She smokes, shifts position, drops the fag end to the pavement and grinds it out with her heel. 'I heard it,' she says. 'From my desk. I heard it and I knew.'

'I'm sorry.'

'Saleh had almost managed to make me into a good Algerian. Almost. With him I felt as if I had a stake in the place, anyway. They got rid of two of us when they killed him.'

Pascual tries to interpret the note in her voice. 'Who could blame you?'

'Me. Every waking minute. Why am I here, a parasite, when I should be there, with my colleagues, carrying on?'

'It's not as if you're idle.'

'No, that's true. And yet. I can't help feeling—it's my country, and I've cut and run.'

Pascual straightens, flips his cigarette over the rail, stuffs his hands in his pockets. The first light droplets of rain are touching his face. 'If you ask me,' he says, 'the idea of belonging to a country is highly overrated. None of us is allowed to pick the spot where we're born and the best we can do is build a decent life for ourselves. When they make that impossible, you have the right to go. Take it from one who has toyed with and spurned a variety of nationalities.'

Sheltering under an awning as the rain begins to drum in earnest, they stand shoulder to shoulder. Pascual watches the city dissolve, grey and insubstantial, and feels his spirits plummet in a long slow arc. 'Someday,' says Djemila, 'you must tell me the story of your life.'

'Someday,' says Pascual, 'I will.'

Rachid has been living on tea and stale bread, to judge by the debris that is crowding his files off the desktop. 'It was just a matter of correlating things I ran across on the Internet,' he says, disheveled and haggard, intent on his notes. 'You find a reference and you follow it up. A lot of what I found was in German and I had to get somebody to translate it for me.'

'I could have done that,' says Pascual. 'My German's pretty good.'

Rachid gives him a look. 'Next time I'll know.' He frowns at the papers in front of him. 'I'd made a list of companies that were possibly Mirakl subsidiaries, and one of them turned up in a piece in *Die Welt* on a former KGB officer who sells arms from an office in Vienna. He supposedly runs several front companies, and one of them has the same name as a Mirakl subsidiary I found mentioned elsewhere.'

'Curious.' Djemila peers over his shoulder.

'Yes. I would say it's got to be the same company, given the Russian connection. According to this piece, it's headquartered in Udine, Italy, and it's one of the main conduits for arms and radioactive material out of the former Soviet Union. Urichko is the name of the fellow in Vienna and according to the article he can get you just about anything you want if you've got the money.'

They digest this for a moment and Djemila says, 'Any connection with Kovalenko?'

'Just the old KGB credentials. They certainly could have known each other. Urichko is supposedly independent but from what I've learned I wouldn't be surprised if he's got some kind of working agreement with Mirakl. Whether he's a wholly owned subsidiary or just a licensee of some kind, who can say? But it raises interesting questions.'

'Yes. Radioactive material, you said?'

'Plutonium 239, strontium 90, caesium 137. Take your pick, they've got the best selection in town. Of course, you have to supply your own physicists. Unless you can afford one of the ready-mades. There are plenty of stories about warheads gone missing and that sort of thing.'

'Good God, isn't anybody tracking this stuff?'

'Well, the article's a year old and there's been a bit of a crackdown recently. Whether they're still in business, in the same form anyway, I don't know. But Mirakl's still there, and if they've got people like Urichko on their corporate roster, then you can bet they can still get you whatever you want. As long as you've got the money.'

'So maybe Boucherif is on an official mission after all. It

doesn't sound as if artillery pieces are the only thing Mirakl can offer him.'

Rachid nods. 'The Soviets had rules about what they would send a client regime. I imagine with Mirakl the customer is always right. If you've always wanted a few ICBMs with multiple warheads to give your country a little instant credibility, I would think now is a good time to pick up a couple on the sly.'

In the lamplit gloom the three of them listen to the rain, which has settled into a steady soothing murmur outside. Pascual wonders why he is here; none of this is his affair. He wonders if Morrel has had him followed here. He wonders what would happen if Rachid were not here, if it were only he and Djemila listening to the rain.

'Credibility with whom?' says Djemila in an appalled voice. 'What possible use could they be?'

'One wonders,' says Rachid.

'You've got very sly, haven't you?' says Morrel. 'Ducking in and out of Métro stations, acting like a secret agent in a bad film. Is it the police or me you're worried about?'

'I don't know what you're talking about,' says Pascual. He has returned to the bed after rising to let Morrel into the flat. The Frenchman is groomed and shaven, brisk and definite, an affront to Pascual's lie-abed sensibilities. Pascual watches him move about the room, shifting newspapers on the table, peeking into the wardrobe.

'I can't blame you, I suppose,' says Morrel. 'It can't be too pleasant knowing you're on a short leash.'

'You're afraid I've fallen in with bad companions, are you?'

Morrel comes to rest at the foot of the bed, looking down at Pascual with what might be amusement. 'She told you she worked for a human rights organization, eh?'

Pascual rubs at his face and strives to catch up. 'That's what she said.'

'Well, she lied to you. She's a journalist.'

'A journalist.' Pascual takes his hands away from his face. 'You amaze me.'

'She works for a rag in Algiers.'

'How on earth do you know that?'

'We followed her, of course. She's been pestering busy functionaries in various ministries. Asking about Mirakl, we're told. Her partner we're not sure about yet. Perhaps you can fill us in.'

Pascual senses it is time to put feet on the floor and look Morrel in the eye. He rises and struggles into his jeans. 'I had no idea.'

Morrel stands shaking his head, a craftsman looking at a bad piece of work. 'Look, maybe you're right. Maybe she can help us. But don't lie to me. You and me, we have to have our cards on the table to get along. What have you told her?'

Pascual pulls on a shirt, gets a cigarette going and sags onto the edge of the bed. 'Everything. What do you expect? She had part of the picture and I had another. We had to put them together.'

'So she knows about Najjar?'

Pascual nods. 'She doesn't give a damn. All she's interested in is what Boucherif's up to.'

Morrel goes to the window and muses, looking out at the street. 'How do you think she knows about his movements?'

'I'd guess she has a source close to him, inside his office maybe. The person who makes the airline reservations or something like that. She won't tell me, which I can hardly blame her for.'

'No. Why do you think she worries me?'

With a shrug Pascual says, 'Because you don't want Daoud Najjar to read about himself in the paper.'

'It's not him I'm worried about, actually. He already knows we're after him. It's the politicians and other high-minded types I'm worried about. Nothing shoots down a covert operation faster than a minister anxious to take the credit. Before you know it we'll be answerable to six different committees, and that'll be the end of our freedom of action. If any of this hits the papers the whole thing is blown to hell.'

'That's possibly the cleverest rationale for complete lack of accountability I've ever heard. But don't worry, it won't hit the papers. She didn't know who Najjar was, had never heard the name. As far as she's concerned he's just another crook in a bank full of crooks. Her interests are elsewhere.'

Morrel gives him a long look. 'I certainly hope you're right.'

'As long as we're putting cards on the table, why don't you talk to her? Bring her onto the team. Stop all the cloak-and-dagger nonsense. We could all sit down around a table and plan out a campaign.'

Morrel takes a few steps toward him, hands in pockets, his face going from incredulity to contempt. 'Oh, yes, just deputize her perhaps. Pin a little star to her chest. She's a journalist, you imbecile.'

Pascual blows smoke at him. 'And potentially a very good source.'

Morrel nods. 'Yes. Potentially. And that, my friend, is the only reason we're not whisking you out of Paris within the hour and having her shipped back to Algiers tonight. But I'll tell you one thing.'

'What?'

'She'd better deliver. Something. Soon. Or the party's over.'

'Some party,' says Pascual, rising and heading for the bathroom. 'I've had more fun at funerals.'

'Zurich,' says Djemila. Her voice at the other end of the wire is disembodied but startlingly close, hushed and intimate in his ear.

'Zurich? Zurich what? What the hell is Zurich?' The ring of the telephone has torn him from sleep and Pascual is still groping for clarity.

'It's a city in Switzerland.' Djemila could be talking to a five-year-old, infinitely patient.

'I know that. What's going on? What's with Zurich?' He thrashes at the sheets, manages to sit up. It is dark and outside the city is only a murmur.

'Boucherif, remember him?'

'Of course. What about him?'

'I've just had a call from Algiers,' Djemila says. 'Boucherif's going to Zurich next week.'

TWELVE

In all his wanderings during the dark years underground, Pascual somehow managed never to set foot in Zurich. He has shivered in mist from the *jet d'eau* in Geneva and spat off a high bridge into the Aare in Bern, but for him Zurich has remained the mythical city of gnomes and numbered accounts. Waiting for a taxi at Kloten, luggage at his feet, he feels a faint thrill of anticipation expire under a pall of naked dread.

There are green hills all about but these are the outskirts of a sizeable city, the eczema of urbanization creeping up the pastoral slopes. The taxi descends through ranks of grey apartment blocks and suddenly they are in the city proper; after Paris even this conglomeration seems small. There are cobbled streets plied by rumbling trams and needle-thin steeples crowning clocks; here is a glimpse of the river, complete with swans. Pascual slouches in the back of the taxi, not quite able to believe this place is real.

The Baur au Lac stands at the convergence of the Talstrasse and the Bahnhofstrasse, perched on the bank of a canal, a stone's throw from the lake. This is the type of hotel

Pascual has always sneered at; in hotels like these Pascual's monthly rent would barely last till dinner. He is afraid that they can smell his poverty here, but he slides the credit card given him by Morrel across the reception desk with a casual air. He lodges his sunglasses on top of his head and glances about the discreet, unassuming lobby. He is now called Hugo Berger and has a French passport to prove it; he is slovenly in a monied way, with a week-old beard and carefully faded designer jeans and a cotton shirt that cost three hundred francs open halfway down his chest. 'You are rich and idle,' Morrel told him in Paris last night. 'You were born with money and have devoted your life to spending it. Places like the Baur au Lac are only background for you. Don't forget to tip generously.'

Pascual's room is on the third floor; his steps in the corridor are soundless on the forgiving carpet. He fumbles over the tip but the superbly disciplined bellboy manages to occupy himself with curtains and other details until it is time to feign pleased surprise at the bills slipped into his hand. Pascual explores the suite like a child sneaking about a forbidden wing of the house, afraid to touch anything. There is enough furniture and enough liquor in the minibar to host a party but Pascual would be terrified of spilling his drink on this red satin. The bathroom is shimmering white, clad in marble and featuring enough plumbing for a sizeable family to wash without too much jostling. There is a telephone within arm's reach of the bath.

Pascual stands at the window, parting the filmy gauze and looking down at water; he could perform a swan dive off his balcony into the canal. The feeling has overtaken him again, the feeling of being thrust into an absurd dream where he has no business but to strive to awake. There is only one reason why he is here and that is that this is where Boucherif will be tomorrow, and with him just possibly Daoud Najjar. Pascual feels like a man shoved into the reptile house at the zoo and told to find the escaped cobra. He must spot Najjar before Najjar or any of the hard-eyed men who were with him in Paris spot him. He must replay what he did in Paris without the advantages of anonymity and surprise. He must deceive men who are trained to detect deception and escape with his life.

He must have a drink. He downs a scotch from the minibar, hesitates over a second. He decides it is fresh air he needs most. In an hour he will meet Morrel. Summoning his courage Pascual leaves the suite and descends to the public precincts of the hotel. He wanders, spotting landmarks: a deterringly elegant restaurant, the American bar. He feels safe until he reflects that Boucherif or Mirakl could well have sent security personnel ahead to prepare the ground. The sunglasses come down over his eyes. He leaves the hotel and walks to the end of the Talstrasse, where the lake opens out before him under a sky innocent of clouds. A tour boat docks gently, holiday-makers crowding the rail. A cool breeze comes off the water; green shores recede into the distance and sailing boats play across the opaline surface of the lake.

I could swim, thinks Pascual. I could leap into the water and swim toward those hills with slow steady strokes. I could probably last until sunset and then sink deep down into the clear cold depths, fatigue numbing the pain of extinction. The last thing I would see in the world of men would be stars, peaceful and remote.

Morrel's safe house lies just off the Langstrasse, in the more plebeian quarters behind the Hauptbahnhof. Here Pascual feels strangely reassured; there are people in these streets for whom next month's rent is plainly a concern. Many of them seem to have come from south of the Alps, Pascual notes, searching for the address Morrel gave him. He has heard Spanish, Serbo-Croatian and Turkish in the last five minutes. Here men lean on high tables on the pavement, drinking beer; from a doorway a whore flashes him a warm if thoroughly meretricious smile. Here is a greengrocer's sporting a Spanish flag; there is a strip club, *Geöffnet ab 20.00.* Recovering from his last wrong turn, Pascual locates the building, a mustard-colored apartment house across from a schoolyard where boys are playing football on concrete. He finds the name Morrel gave him and rings the bell.

How security services rig up safe houses at short notice Pascual has no idea. Presumably something can always be arranged if price is no object, and Morrel's standards are not exacting, to judge by this flat. It is empty of furniture and the wooden floor is battered and without luster. The paint on the walls shows where posters were tacked and then removed. Windows in the front room look down on the street.

Someone has brought in camp chairs and air mattresses; open suitcases lie in the corners and screws of greasy paper litter the counter in the cramped kitchen. A telephone, plugged into a jack, sits on the floor. Morrel shoves a garden chair toward Pascual while Serge stands at the window. A third man, introduced as Jacky, leans in the doorway to the kitchen, sipping coffee from a paper cup. He is lean, pale and intense, with a hairline in full retreat and watchful grey eyes. 'Here we are, roughing it while you wallow in luxury at the Baur au Lac,' says Morrel. 'You can't complain about your treatment now.'

'It's a beautiful place to die,' says Pascual. He is looking at more cases stacked in the corner, gleaming steel ones, flat black ones, canvas duffel bags. Communications equipment? Automatic weapons? Serge's toys, evidently.

'Nobody's going to die,' says Morrel. 'Your sense of melodrama is running away with you again.'

'Maybe so. I'll try to take it in my stride when they shoot me.'

'Are you certain nobody followed you?' says Serge from the window.

'I did all the recommended dawdling and doubling back. But I'm not an expert and never was.'

'I'd be surprised if anybody spotted you,' says Morrel. 'I'd be surprised if anybody's in place yet.'

'I am burning with anticipation to hear about your new plan.'

'Not much to it, actually. We've thought a good deal about what went wrong in Paris and decided that simpler is better. This time we'll be in there with you. Once you spot him, we'll take over.'

'The trick will be spotting him without getting spotted right back.'

'I don't think it will be a problem,' says Serge. 'Your role will be entirely passive this time. A hotel's a lot more public than a bank, which makes it all a lot easier. We'll be right on top of you and you won't have to take any risks. You won't have to lift a finger, in fact. All you're going to do is watch, and we'll be right there watching with you. When Najjar shows up all you have to do is point him out to us and your job's over.'

Pascual drags his cigarettes out of his pocket. 'My goodness, that easy? Imagine the look on Najjar's face. Why, they'll all be caught flat-footed, won't they? The advance security teams, the phalanxes of bodyguards. I'll just stand there at the reception desk innocently peering into faces and they won't even notice me, will they?' He lights the cigarette, giving Morrel a withering look.

There is a moment of heavy silence and Jacky speaks from the doorway. 'Maybe he'd like to hear the details.'

Serge folds his arms and rests his considerable buttocks on the windowsill. 'All right. Look. It's a simple matter of surveillance. We know when Boucherif is coming, and on the assumption that he's coming to talk to Najjar, we know more or less when he's coming, too. That is, sometime tomorrow afternoon probably. There's a fairly narrow window of time, considering they're probably planning a quick meeting, a day or two at most. Fly in, fly out, and if the general's coming tomorrow then Najjar's probably coming then, too.'

'Assuming he's coming at all,' says Morrel. 'Assuming your

lady friend has given us reliable information and assuming this is a continuation of the Paris meeting.'

Serge shrugs. 'That's a lot of assuming, but it's probably sound and in any event it's all we've got. Now the big advantage we have is that there's only one place to check in. They may sneak the occasional film star or royal personage in the rear entrance, but somebody's still got to register at the desk, pick up keys and whatnot. And generals and Russian gangsters probably won't rate film-star treatment. So sometime tomorrow Daoud Najjar is going to walk up to that desk.'

'All right. But he won't be coming by himself. He'll come with the whole crew of arm breakers he had in Paris. And they're going to see me.'

'Possibly. If they're very good, they may even recognize you. But it will be too late. By the time they've spotted you, we'll have taken over and you can cut and run. We'll have people standing by to get you out and away.'

Pascual smokes. 'I'm a little unclear on the mechanics. What am I going to do, lurk at the desk all day making small talk with the concierge?'

'No. There are always idlers hanging about a hotel lobby. There's any number of nooks and crannies where you can keep the desk in sight while you read your paper or thumb through your guidebook. If you get tired of that there's the Pavilion outside, across from the entrance. You can sit there and drink tea and watch.'

'All day?'

'As long as it takes.'

'You don't think I'll be a little conspicuous sitting there hour after hour? How much tea can a man drink? And what if I have to piss?'

'For God's sake, you'll have some freedom of movement. First of all we'll have men on the approaches, outside. As soon as a likely looking taxi pulls into the forecourt, we'll be alerted. If you're in the toilet, we'll get you back there in a flash. You'll have a pager, one of the silent ones that vibrate. You can get up, stretch your legs, take a stroll in the park. You get tired of the lobby, you can camp in the bar even. As long as you're within a minute or so of the front desk.'

'And what happens when I see him?'

'As soon as you have a solid ID, you find me. Me or Morrel here. We'll be close by, you'll always know where we are. You point him out or you give us a description and you're off. Jacky here will take you under his wing. We'll set up a ren-dezvous point. You want to go back to your room, pack up your things, that's fine. If you're that scared, you can just cut and run. Find Jacky and give him the word and he'll have you back here in ten minutes.'

'With six Russian gunmen on our tail.'

'Nonsense. Jacky's a pro, we all are. We'll go over the ground this afternoon and you'll see.'

Pascual blows a smoke ring, musing. 'Why can't you use the hotel's own security? Surely the management would cooperate with you. And don't they have all manner of secu-rity devices, cameras and one-way mirrors and things, that would allow me to spot Najjar without sitting out in the open? There's got to be a room behind the desk somewhere where I could sit and wait for him to show up.'

'Christ, he's scared out of his wits,' says Serge, looking at Jacky.

Pascual flicks ash in his direction. 'I tell you, Najjar recognized me in Paris and he'll be looking for me.'

Morrel sighs. 'Forget the cameras and the mirrors. Can you guarantee me a good identification on one of those little black-and-white screens? Look, it will be easier this time. You've seen him once and you'll spot him across the room. And if he's looking for you, what good will it do him? He sees you and you're gone, and by that time we've got him.'

'You're going to nab him right there in the lobby?'

'We'll see. I couldn't tell you right now. It will all depend on who's with him, how they're disposed, things like that. But yes, we're planning to take him in the hotel. Or the environs.'

'I see. Fewer toes to step on here in Switzerland, eh?'

'That's one way to put it.'

'Do the Swiss even know you're here?'

'What do you care?'

'Just curious. I wouldn't want you to wind up like those Israelis in Bern did awhile back, all red-faced and shuffling their feet in front of a judge.'

Morrel smiles. 'Why don't you let me worry about things like that?'

'Fine. None of my business, I suppose.'

'Not really, no. One more thing.'

'What?'

'Your friend. The Arab bint.'

'What about her?'

'She's clear on the arrangement is she? As we discussed?'

Pascual examines the tip of his cigarette. 'I told her,

whatever I might find out about why Boucherif is here, I pass on to her.'

'Whatever you find out? That's not exactly what we agreed to.'

'I thought that was reasonable in view of the fact that it's her information that got us here. It's called a *quid pro quo*. Don't tell me you've never heard of that. I know how the intelligence business works.'

'If you know how the business works, you know I can't let you just pass on *whatever you find out*. I thought we had hashed all this out in Paris.'

'I'm aware of the constraints. Whatever I say, I'll clear with you.'

Serge says, 'She wouldn't by any chance be planning to join us here in Zurich, would she?'

Innocently, Pascual says, 'Not as far as I know. She doesn't have the budget you do. I promised her a full report back in Paris. Frankly, I don't think she wants to get anywhere near Boucherif, after what happened to Mediane.'

Morrel swaps a look with Serge and takes aim at Pascual's chest with an index finger. 'There's to be a wall around this, do you understand? A firewall. Airtight, hermetic. Nothing gets out to her or anybody else until we've got Daoud Najjar under sedation ten thousand meters above the Alps, flying west. Is that clear?'

Pascual sucks the last life out of his cigarette. 'Oh, yes,' he says. 'You've made yourself quite clear.'

THIRTEEN

When the telephone purrs Pascual is stretched out on the bed, working on the last of the scotches from the minibar and wondering if he is going to have to submit an expense report to Morrel. Djemila's voice brings him up to a sitting position. 'Where are you?'

'In a hotel, across the river from the station. The cheapest I could find and I'm still going to run through my money in two nights. I hope you're planning to work fast.'

'Don't worry about the money. I'll come over tomorrow and put your room on my credit card.'

'You could do that?'

'It seemed to work here. If there are problems later they can take it up with the French secret services.'

There is a pause and Djemila says, 'I thought everyone would speak French here but it seems I was wrong.'

Something in her voice gives Pascual a clear vision of her, sitting in her room with her knuckles going white around the phone receiver. 'Look here,' he says. 'Have you eaten?'

'Not yet. I had a look at a menu or two and I'm not sure I can afford it.'

'Give me an address. I'll come and get you.'

It occurs to him to wonder if Morrel mistrusts him enough to put a watch on him; he has spotted nothing that smacks of surveillance in his tentative probing about the hotel, but hotels are full of idle people to provide camouflage. Pascual decides that a simple taxi ride will put anyone who cares to follow him to the test.

He stands in the forecourt in the cool of the evening as the doorman whistles up a cab, idly looking about. Nobody comes plunging out of the hotel after him and there are no cars in the Talstrasse lurking at the curb with idling motors. He watches through the back window as the taxi pulls away and decides that he is most likely free. Nonetheless he pays off the taxi in the Bahnhofplatz and smokes a cigarette just inside the entrance to the station, watching cars and people in the broad square before him. A ramble about the interior of the echoing station proves nothing but increases his confidence, and when he finally crosses the Bahnhofbrücke on foot, fifteen minutes later, it is with an untroubled step.

The Niederdorfstrasse snakes down through the old town parallel to the lake, closed to vehicles, five hundred meters or so of bars, bistros and dance clubs looming over the cobbles, leavened by the occasional sex shop or strip joint. Pascual finds Djemila's hotel in a side street, marked by an ill-lit sign. Djemila is seated in the cramped lobby, paging through a magazine under the indifferent eye of a man behind the desk whose face is only a shade off the fiery red of his hair. Out on the street she shows no signs of intimidation or discomfort. Pascual has begun to feel sheepish about his protective impulses, remembering that she is a Parisian and a journalist. They make their way slowly through the early-evening crowd. Italian restaurants are a persistent theme, their outside tables causing eddies in the flow; the bars have wide windows flung open to the street, music throbbing as they pass. They come to a Spanish *bodega* and Pascual touches her arm, but after a look inside he shakes his head; too much smoke, too little room and no food in sight. A little further along they slip into a *trattoria* with a slightly upscale look, linen tablecloths and a long, well-stocked bar.

'You've raised my standard of living abruptly,' says Djemila, looking at the prices on the menu. As Djemila has neither German nor Italian, Pascual translates and handles the ordering with aplomb. When the wine arrives Djemila sips and allows herself to sag back against the wall with a smile. 'I have yet to discover a language you don't speak,' she says.

'Six of them in all. Out of several thousand in existence. That's not so many.'

'German, French, Spanish, Arabic . . . what else? Oh, yes. English.'

'American, anyway. Brooklynese to be precise. And Catalan.'

'Well, you're four ahead of me. How does one learn both Brooklynese and Syrian *'ammiyya* in one lifetime?'

'One has a fractured and chaotic life. I don't recommend it.'

'You said you'd tell me your life story sometime.'

'Is this the time?'

'It might as well be.'

Soup arrives. Pascual takes up his spoon, brow furrowed. 'I am the product of a failed international marriage and a misguided sense of adventure. My father was American, a poet and a socialist. My mother was Catalan, a musician and a lapsed Catholic. I was raised with a romantic belief in rebellion and a totally unrealistic view of modern industrial society. Also with a deep unfulfilled yearning for security and a fairly broad experience of bohemian life on two continents. When I was twenty-three I became a terrorist.'

Djemila stares at him for a while. 'That's a very flexible term. And not one that people apply to themselves, generally.'

'It fits. I thought there were people who deserved killing.'

She swallows and says, 'Who, for example?'

'Members of certain classes, certain nationalities. I had adopted the simple calculus of the collectivist.' Pascual meets her gaze. 'You want details? I was recruited by the Popular Front for the Liberation of Palestine, based in Damascus. Because of my languages I was made a sort of liaison officer and spent my time promoting links with other groups, mostly in Europe. I participated in only three active operations in my six years underground, two of which were total failures. The third I will have on my conscience until I die. I supplied the getaway car for the assassination of an Israeli diplomat and his wife in Bonn. Myself, I never fired a shot in anger. In nineteen eighty-nine I defected to the CIA, thus adding betrayal to my list of sins.'

Djemila has given up on eating and is blinking at him with enormous black eyes. 'What changed your mind?'

'I'm not sure. There are days when I take credit for a change of heart and others when I think it was only cowardice. I had been shunted into a more active role and life spans tended to be short for people like me.'

For a time there is only the gentle babel of others' talk and the clink of silver on crockery. 'At least you have a conscience,' says Djemila. 'That's more than some can say.'

Pascual finishes his soup and lays down the spoon. 'A little late, perhaps.'

After the meal, night having fallen, they make their way to the quay and stand looking at the Limmat, light shimmering on a restless opacity. Disembodied voices come across the water; a tram lurches by behind them. 'What happens if your man doesn't show up tomorrow?' says Djemila.

'Then I'll have had a holiday in Zurich.'

'At others' expense, at least. If I come up empty on this little jaunt I'll have gone further into debt for nothing.'

Pascual muses. 'I'm not exactly sure why you're here.'

'Because you're my source and this is where you are. It's that simple, really. On a story like this you just try to stay close to the action.'

'I don't know how much I can give you. If things go well I'm going to flee the instant I spot Najjar. We'll have to work out a rendezvous.'

'Fair enough. But you're not the only possibility. There's a man at UBS here who Thierry Fort says can fill me in on the Russians. Besides, Mirakl has an office here, and Boucherif's coming.'

'I wouldn't make myself too conspicuous if I were you.'

She shrugs. 'I don't expect anybody to sit down for a heart-to-heart chat. It's more a matter of documenting the small things—he was here on this date under a false name, for example. Get the name if possible. A phone call to Mirakl to see if they'll admit they know him. Even denials can be illuminating. You amass facts and start listing questions. Why he's in Zurich, for a start. What's here that's not available in Paris?'

'Banks? They have a lot of banks here.'

'He's got a bank in Paris.'

'Well, you've got me stumped, then. I'm not supposed to be here with you, by the way. They've generously agreed to let me talk to you after Najjar's in custody.'

He can feel her looking at him. 'You don't care much for rules, do you?'

A motorboat speeds up the river, leaving a ghostly wake in the dark. Water laps at stone beneath them. 'Not theirs.'

He walks her back to her hotel. 'Tomorrow, then,' she says.

'I'll ring you if I'm still alive.'

It is past midnight and human flotsam drifts in the streets. Pascual plods along the Limmatquai and crosses the Münsterbrücke, churches looming above. He takes an occasional look but he is not worried about pursuit; the game begins tomorrow.

The park across from the entrance to the Baur au Lac is dark and filled with the rustling of night air through trees. Pascual hesitates; he would rather sleep on the grass than in the vast overstuffed bed upstairs. Upstairs, however, he can lock his door.

The lobby is empty. Pascual rounds the corner and heaves

to in front of the elevators just as doors ease open and a man he knows emerges: one of the Algerian heavies he last saw in the corridors of the Banque Villefort in Paris.

'Of course he recognized me,' says Pascual, slopping coffee on to the carpet. 'He brushed past me coming out of the elevator.'

'But he made no move, showed no sign.' Morrel leans forward on the edge of the sofa, intent; Serge, as usual prowls, hands in his pockets.

Pascual has slept little since his first panicked call to the safe house roused an irritable Morrel, and at the beastly hour of seven-thirty in the morning the coffee is proving ineffective against hangover mixed with fear of mayhem. He sets the cup down on the saucer with a clatter. 'He lingered there, looking at me. I took a sudden interest in the floor of the elevator and rubbed my brow, trying to hide my face, but I could see his feet and he paused, watching me. I thought the fucking doors would never close.'

Morrel sighs. 'Well, you're still alive.'

'So is the man with a noose around his neck, right up until the rope snaps taut.'

'Ever the dramatist. Look, what are you afraid of? They're not going to shoot you in broad daylight.'

'What's to stop them?'

'You can't even be sure he recognized you. And if he did? It's the Russians we have to worry about, not the Algerians.'

'You think they don't communicate? That looked like a team effort in Paris.'

'They probably do. But the most likely outcome if they're

worried about you is that they'd cancel the meeting. It's not your worthless hide we should worry about, it's the operation. I'm the one who ought to be steamed if you've blown our cover again.'

'Why didn't you stay in your room?' says Serge from the window. 'What were you doing out cruising the streets in the middle of the night? You told us you were planning to stay here, make an early night of it.'

'I needed fresh air. This place suffocates me.'

'Why we're wasting good money putting you up here is beyond me.'

Morrel raises a hand. 'Easy. Tell us where you went.'

Pascual shrugs. 'I walked up the Bahnhofstrasse, crossed the bridge, came down through their nightlife district there. I had a bite to eat, something to drink.'

'And it took you till nearly midnight?'

Pascual assumes a petulant expression and stabs at a croissant with a knife. 'I went to a sex shop.'

Serge puffs in contempt. 'Christ. And how much of the tax-payers' money did you drop on dirty pictures?'

'Is this actually relevant?'

'Not really,' says Morrel as Serge turns back to the window. 'What's relevant is whether you've got the nerve to do what you're supposed to today. Najjar may be here already. Which means we're going to be aggressive, not let him go to ground in some conference room or suite. We'll have to keep an eye on the restaurants, the bar, all that. It's going to complicate things a little.'

'I'll be right here. You've got the number.'

'We may need you to help, as we've got limited manpower. We'll try to give you an assignment you can handle, like camping in the bar.'

'Look, I'll stick out a mile if I go roaming about the place. When you really think you've got him I'll come and plant a kiss on his cheek. Until then I'm not leaving this room.'

There is a stiff silence until Serge says, 'Actually I think he may have a point. We don't want him blundering about the place any more than we absolutely need.'

Morrel looks at his colleague for a moment and shrugs. 'If you say so.' He turns to Pascual. 'All right. We were going to give you a pager, but I don't think that's the way to go now. If Najjar's already in the hotel we might need to give you precise instructions on where to go. You'll be next to a phone, so you wait for a call.'

'And Jacky will be waiting with the car? Once I've tagged Najjar for you, I can cut and run?'

'Jacky will be watching out for you. I can't guarantee how the choreography will go, but there won't be more than a couple of minutes to wait. If you can make it to the front door, he'll bring the car right up. But listen. We'll need something very definite, something more than a hesitant pass and a jerk of the thumb. We'll pick you up when you get out of the elevator. If you spot him, you find one of us and ask for a light. You've got cigarettes? We won't let you go until we're certain we're on the same page. If I have to ask you to go and spill coffee on him, I will. Understood?'

'Yes, I got it the first time. Just make sure Jacky's where I can find him.'

Morrel leans back on his chair, regarding him with distaste. 'We might not get him on the first try, you understand. There's bound to be more than one swarthy middle-aged guest in the hotel today and we might have a few false alarms.'

'Understood. Just don't rush to the phone every time a Greek on his honeymoon strolls in. Look for the receding hairline, the curving nose. And remember he's tall, at least six foot two in height. And look for the gorillas. He'll be surrounded by them.'

'I think you can trust our judgment, you know. The question is, can we trust your nerve?'

Pascual sips coffee, not inclined to answer, until he sees they are both quite still, looking at him. 'Of course,' he says. 'My nerve? Never better.'

Pascual shaves off all but the mustache. It is just enough of a mustache to register and he hopes that it changes his aspect just enough for a scanning pair of eyes to pass over him. This is closer to his Paris look but if they are looking for a beard after last night it may delay identification for the second or two that may get him in range.

He fiddles with the radio until he finds somebody playing Mozart; this may be the best he can do. He yearns for the order and serenity of the baroque, Bach by preference, but his is a disappearing taste in a decadent world. He lies on his back on the bed, eyes closed, reviewing the self-deceptions, misjudgments and fatal weaknesses that have brought him to this pass. Perhaps alone among his fellows, Pascual blames none of his misfortunes on others; having spent the best years of his manhood organizing murder in the service of a failed tyranny, he must concede that he deserves whatever befalls him. He finds a strange peace in the notion.

With few safe havens in his memory, Pascual tends to live for the moment and before long he is thinking of Djemila, who has the saddest eyes in the world. He rolls off his bed and dials the number of her hotel. A man answers and tells him that she has gone out. Pascual declines to leave a message. Thirty seconds after he hangs up the telephone sounds.

Morrel is breathless. 'Get down here to the lobby. A messenger just came through the hall calling for a Mr. Rakhmonov.'

'Who the hell is that?'

'That's one of the names we got from the Ritz, *merde*. Don't you see? Ten to one it's Najjar. They're calling him to the desk for some reason. Now stop wagging your jaw and get down here.' The phone cuts off with a loud clack in Pascual's ear.

Pascual stands, takes a deep breath, and tells himself that Switzerland is a civilized country where not even Russian gangsters can kill a man brazenly in the lobby of a hotel. He remembers Najjar looking at him from the corridor in Paris and for a moment his knees go weak. The thought that he might be free and speeding away in a Mercedes with the competent Jacky at the wheel in under five minutes finally tips the scales and takes him to the door. He takes only what he has on his back; if Morrel cannot have his luggage collected later, the chambermaid can have it.

In the elevator Pascual is already looking ahead. Lie low in the safe house until Morrel confirms that Najjar is taken; then no doubt endless debriefings and much burning of telephone wires between Zurich and Paris. Finally there will be some sort of modest ceremony perhaps, the presentation of the check, an escort to one of the banks just up the Bahnhofstrasse. Until now Pascual has not allowed himself to think about the money. He imagines it in a box nestled safely on a shelf next to Marcos's or Mobutu's. He will be able to take Djemila to fine restaurants on his own account now. The elevator doors open.

Pascual smiles as he swings into the corridor. Like a swimmer coming up after the plunge he is finding that the water is not so cold. All he has to do is saunter through a crowd of idle rich much like himself, his peers, and find a familiar face. For Pascual the good life is about to begin.

There is the usual scattering of idlers in the lobby, the usual opulent somnolence. Pascual trolls by the reception desk but there is no Najjar there. He stands looking out through the revolving door for a moment and then meanders back into the hall with a prickling at his hairline. He scans but fails to find anyone he recognizes, friend or foe, Russian or Algerian. He stalls for a moment and comes to his senses: watch the desk. He finds a vacant couch directly opposite reception. Where the hell is Morrel?

Pascual leans back on the couch, feeling perilously exposed. If the mysterious Rakhmonov is indeed Najjar, he will no doubt appear with his usual escort. Pascual fishes his sunglasses out of his pocket, debates whether to put them on, finally lodges them on top of his head, deciding that a man wearing sunglasses in the muted light of a hotel lobby will only attract attention. He curses silently and scans for Morrel, for Serge, for Jacky with the car keys.

Minutes pass and nothing happens but the fleeting appearance of Serge, who ambles by without looking at Pascual. Serge appears to be dressed for the golf links, looking like a football pools winner trying on expensive new clothes. Pascual is comforted but beginning to grow impatient; clearly he is on a fool's errand here. Najjar or not, Rakhmonov is not coming. Pascual has just decided to move, find Morrel or Serge and cadge that light, when Daoud Najjar strides purposefully into the lobby from the direction of the elevators and makes for the exit.

For a moment Pascual cannot believe his eyes. It is unmistakably Najjar; he passes by, five steps away, without looking at Pascual. He is alone and he looks as if he has urgent business outside. Pascual hesitates for three seconds and then rises. This was not in the script. He tries not to hurry as he steps toward the exit, tries not to swivel his head too frantically as he scans for support. Najjar has disappeared out of the revolving door and Pascual picks up the pace; if a car is waiting all is lost.

Outside it is a splendid summer morning and a doorman is cheerfully proposing to summon him a taxi. Pascual waves him off; he has spotted Najjar, disappearing out of the gate into the Talstrasse. Hoping desperately that somebody on Morrel's team is paying attention, Pascual sets out after him. He remembers other operations that went wrong, other spanners flung into the works, cock-ups and fiascos and sundry disasters. Nothing ever works as it is supposed to. What the hell is Najjar doing? Coming out of the gate, Pascual glimpses his heels as they disappear into the Börsenstrasse.

He hustles up to the corner and curses; there is no Najjar in sight. He has crossed the road, perhaps; Pascual scans. Or ducked into one of these shops; he is going to meet Boucherif over *Mandelgipfel* and meringues in this coffee house ahead. Here is a man stepping from the back seat of a Mercedes onto the pavement; here is another looming at Pascual's elbow, sticking something hard in his ribs. It is happening so fast that Pascual barely has time to register it; this is one operation that is going like clockwork. He opens his mouth to draw breath for a shout, a frantic appeal to these good Swiss burghers passing on the pavement, but his head is rammed against the roof of the car as he is forced on to the back seat, stunning him. Rallying, Pascual manages a hoarse cry but then the muzzle of the automatic is jammed into his mouth, quite effectively silencing him. He is man-handled to the middle of the back seat and bracketed on either side; the gun comes out of his mouth, the sight on the barrel painfully clipping a tooth. Doors slam and the Mercedes pulls away from the curb and nobody has seen a thing. In the rearview mirror the Turkish wrestler, whose head he lately rammed into a wall in Paris, smiles at him.

FOURTEEN

On the drive Pascual has time to rue his naïveté and Morrel's; in this match they are outclassed. All of this was engineered, the message for Rakhmonov, Najjar's pass through the lobby, everything. He has been gulled by experts, flushed from cover and neatly bagged. Somewhere behind him the useless Serge will be looking puzzled in his lime-green cardigan.

Such thoughts divert Pascual from the contemplation of his prospects. He has no loyalties at stake, and will tell them whatever they wish to know; even so, he has no illusions. A bullet in the head is the best-case outcome. For a time he tries to keep track of direction; they have crossed the canal and sped into the badlands behind the Hauptbahnhof. He is quickly disoriented and gives up, closing his eyes and letting his head loll back. He will not let them shoot him without a fight. In Syria he has seen men executed at close range and wondered at their docility. Torture is another kettle of fish entirely; he knows that willingness to talk is no guarantee of gentle treatment and he wonders if one can really commit suicide by swallowing one's tongue. He folds his tongue back experimentally; would the distress of choking to death be preferable to ripped-out nails?

He opens his eyes as the car slows and turns. A bridge looms overhead; Pascual can see long files of parked railway carriages and beyond them apartment blocks, crowding the edges of the vast rail yards. They are creeping along an access road, past loading docks. Here is a hangar of some sort, with broken glass, illegible graffiti in dripping paint on the dull brown brick of the wall. The Mercedes creeps around a corner and, hidden from the road, halts.

Pascual tries stalling, knowing that any move he makes brings him closer to things he will not be able to bear. His companions waste no time cajoling; he is dragged out of the car by his hair. He falls on the concrete, skinning a knee through his expensive twill trousers. *'Debout,'* the wrestler orders him. He climbs slowly to his feet and is shoved toward a broken door with a panel missing, leaving a gap just wide enough for a man to squeeze through. Pascual whirls and takes a wild swing at the first face he can find but misses. The consequences are immediate; Pascual thinks he will die right there on the concrete, in agony from the swift brutal kick to his stomach. As soon as he is able to draw breath again he is hauled up by an arm and pushed through the gap in the door into darkness.

When his eyes adjust he sees detritus of failed industry: carcasses of trucks, rusted machinery of indeterminate purpose. Some light enters through smudged windows. There is a pungent smell of animal waste. Steel beams hold up the roof and Pascual is efficiently immobilized with his back to one of them, his wrists bound behind him with a convenient twist of wire from the concrete floor. He is rapidly searched, Hugo Berger's papers removed, sorted through and pocketed without comment. His four captors are not in suits today and they could be oil roughnecks on leave or cops from some rogue unit. Besides the Turkish wrestler there are three more from a familiar mold, the ex-Soviet military man in mufti, hard-faced Slavs.

The Turkish wrestler steps toward Pascual and gives one brief snort of laughter. He places his hand on Pascual's forehead and bounces his head violently off the beam. 'See how you like it.' Lights flashing, his back scraping painfully against the rusty beam, Pascual slides to a sitting position on the floor.

When he opens his eyes the long beak and the big handlebar mustache loom in his face. 'I can help you,' the man says gently, hooded Asian eyes unblinking.

Pascual has a feeling he knows the script but sees nothing to be gained by refusing to say his lines. 'How?'

'Talk and I kill you quickly. I'll be your best friend. You'll kiss my hand.'

Pascual looks him in the eye. 'You've got a deal,' he says.

The wrestler gives him an affectionate slap on the cheek. 'Now you wait a little. Think about mama. *D'accord?*' He rises and follows his colleagues out through the hole in the door. Through the gap in the boards Pascual can see laundry hung on a distant balcony far across the yards. Step out on the bloody balcony and look what's going on under your noses, he wants to scream.

Pascual has sweated out police sweeps with a cool head and held his own in more than one fair fight, but sitting trussed on the floor waiting to be slaughtered is destroying his manhood. Given a chance he would plead. His heart is knocking painfully in his breast. This I cannot bear, he thinks. This is more than even I deserve.

There is always his tongue, he thinks, and recovers a measure of calm. How long will Djemila wait for his call before she flees? In perhaps ten minutes a second car draws up outside. Doors open and close, there is a murmur of voices, footsteps sound on the concrete. The light coming through the gap in the door is occluded as men slip into the garage, a parade of them. Suddenly the place is crowded. Bodyguards on either side of him, Daoud Najjar paces slowly over the floor toward Pascual.

He halts, hands in the pockets of his trousers. He wears a natty dark blue suit and today he looks less the intellectual than the banker, a sleek Lebanese in the hire of Saudis perhaps, in town to stash oil money where the Shiites will never get it. He peers down at Pascual, letting his eyesight adjust to the gloom. After a time he takes his hands out of his pockets, hitches up his trouser legs and squats gingerly, flexing his fine Gucci shoes, coming down to Pascual's level. 'I know you,' he says. 'I knew I had seen you when you popped up in Paris, but for the life of me I can't think of where.'

Quite irrationally Pascual finds Najjar's presence reassuring. This at least is someone he knows. Voice under control, he says, 'I believe we last saw each other in Sofia, in nineteen eighty-seven. At the Hotel Vitosha.'

A smile stretches Abu Yussef's lips. 'Ah, yes. The old Hotel Vitosha. With that dreadful bar full of drunken Russians. I don't remember what name you went by.'

'I think you called me Jacques that time.'

'Jacques. Yes, Jacques, I remember. You were one of Abu Salim's people from Damascus.'

'Originally. Later detached as special liaison to other groups in Europe.'

'Yes, I remember.' Najjar stands up, grunting gently from the effort. He stands looking down at Pascual with the same look he had in Paris, that look of detached and clinical interest, remote and inhuman. After a moment he says, 'You were the one who betrayed us all, weren't you?'

Pascual runs rapidly through possible responses: excuses, denials, the most craven apologies. Nothing he can say will make any difference. Because Najjar is waiting, he says simply, 'Well, after all, you were nothing but thugs, really.'

Najjar blinks, twice, and his look hardens just perceptibly. There is a frozen silence and then Najjar laughs abruptly. 'And that makes you a hero, does it?'

'It makes me just a little less of a shit than you are.' Pascual has gone light-headed. Is this courage? He knows only that he feels a strange exaltation.

Najjar sticks his hands back in his pockets, paces a couple of steps, head down. 'Hypocrisy is a common trait among informers, I've noticed.' He wheels back toward Pascual. 'So. Why don't you tell me what you're doing here?'

Pascual sags back against the beam. 'I'm a spy.'

'No, really? How thrilling. Who's paying you?'

'The French. They want you for Paris, nineteen eighty-seven.'

Three seconds go by. 'Why now?'

'I couldn't tell you. But it's a French operation. Mediane talked to somebody before he died.'

'Who's that, Mediane?'

'You don't know? Ask your Algerian friends, then.'

'Don't try my patience. Who's Mediane?'

Wearily Pascual says, 'An Algerian who worked at the bank. He had ties to French intelligence. He'd met you once and he recognized you.'

'And now he's dead.'

'Yes, one less for you to worry about. They took care of him for you. It seems he recognized the general as well.'

Najjar's look is faintly puzzled. 'And where do you come in?' he says.

'You know where I come in.'

Najjar nods slowly. 'How did they find you? Or have they been keeping you in reserve all along?'

'I didn't run far enough, I suppose.'

With a thin smile Najjar says, 'Not all you hoped it would be, was it? You should have stayed with us.'

Pascual lets the seconds go by. 'So it seems.'

'What's the setup at the hotel?'

Pascual hesitates, though he has no doubt Morrel would sell him out in a flash in similar circumstances. 'I don't know exactly. My role was to finger you. There are at least three men, more probably. The idea was that we'd spot you when you checked in. I would point you out and be spirited away.'

'How much did they promise you? Or was there more stick than carrot?'

'A little of both. They promised me a hundred thousand dollars.'

'Good God, I'm worth that much to them?'

'Apparently.'

'One wonders why.' Najjar muses, drifting away. His feet crunch on the grit-strewn floor. 'Do they know about Boucherif?' he says over his shoulder.

'They know he's here. They don't know why you're meeting him.'

Najjar stands motionless for a few seconds and then turns. 'You're being very cooperative.'

'What would I gain by resisting?'

'Nothing, you're quite right. I'm just wondering if I can believe you.'

'You want a show of good faith? I'll lead you to them. Let me go, keep a watch on me and I'll blow them sky high. I'll be a double agent for you, plant whatever story you want. I'll lead them on a wild goose chase all the way to Tahiti.'

Crunch, crunch go Najjar's feet on the concrete as he comes closer. 'You're quite desperate, aren't you?'

'Wouldn't you be?'

'No doubt, no doubt.' Najjar is looking down at him with amusement in his eyes. 'I'm sure they saw us take you. If you come back alive they'll never believe another word you say.'

'I'll make up a story for them. A miraculous escape. You were last seen making for the German border, whatever you want me to tell them. I could be quite useful.'

Najjar says nothing for a very long moment, then leans down, hands on his knees, bringing his face close to Pascual's. In a quiet voice he says, 'Or you could betray me again the moment you're free.'

Pascual opens his mouth, feverish schemes for insurance and counterinsurance on the tip of his tongue, but realizes that Najjar will never accept any arrangement that puts Pascual beyond his reach. He closes his mouth, lets out a long breath. 'And I would,' he says finally. 'With pleasure.'

Najjar straightens up with the satisfied look of a man whose judgment has been proved correct. 'Well, then,' he says. 'Nobody likes a *mouchard*. I think I'll fill the boys in on your history before I leave.' He wheels and goes, flanked by his guards.

Pascual feels panic rising; he will be spared nothing, after all. At the same time he is ashamed of his cowardice and as Najjar approaches the door he calls out, 'You know what makes me different from you?'

Najjar pauses, looking over his shoulder. 'What?'

'You sold out for money. Nothing but money. You wouldn't know a principle if it kicked you in the balls.'

Najjar laughs, a puff of contempt. 'You've got your principles, I've got my money. Who would you say got the better deal?'

Total despair, Pascual finds, simplifies life enormously. He has no time for reminiscence, longing, regrets; his only concerns now are how long he has and how bad it is going to be.

His hopes have risen with the departure in Najjar's wake of everyone except the Turkish wrestler, who stands over him smoking a cigarette and regarding him with a look that is almost affectionate. Pascual is grateful; a bullet in the head, he thinks, he can manage. He has left, he estimates, the time it will take to finish the cigarette.

'Don't worry,' says the wrestler. 'They'll be back soon.' The cigarette glows under the mustache.

Pascual's heart sinks. 'Where have they gone?'

'To get gasoline.'

Seconds go by, dominated by the thumping of his heart, before Pascual is able to whisper, 'Why?'

The wrestler squats as Najjar did, though with greater ease, settling on to his heels in true Oriental fashion. He smokes and says, 'No identification. No face, no fingers. Burn everything.'

From a constricted throat Pascual squeezes the words. 'You'll kill me first?'

A smile spreads the mustache. This man is not his friend, Pascual sees. 'You say please.'

'All right, please. I'm begging. Kill me now.'

'No. You say please when fire starts. Very loud.' Holding his cigarette delicately between thumb and forefinger, the wrestler touches it with great deliberation to the side of Pascual's neck. Pascual writhes with the sudden pain, choking off a curse. There is nowhere to go with his hands wired behind the beam, and his arms take a beating against the steel. *'Salaud!'* he screams. Skin on his wrists is tearing as he strains at the wire.

'That's me,' says the wrestler, replacing the cigarette in his mouth. 'I'm the king of the *salauds*.'

Pascual is pushing at his soft palate with his tongue, starting to fear that it is much more difficult than advertised to swallow the thing, when a figure darkens the gap in the door. *'Was machen Sie da?'* it growls. There has been no noise of approach; this is a voice from the heavens.

After a startled silence the wrestler rises, reaching inside his jacket. He whips out an automatic and puts the muzzle to Pascual's temple. Pascual squeezes his eyes shut and then immediately opens them again, looking for the far-off drying laundry, wanting that last glimpse of human presence before the lights go out forever. No shot comes, however, and he realizes this is only a warning; the wrestler is moving away already, finger to his lips, gun still trained on Pascual.

'This is private property,' barks the man at the door, his head silhouetted in the gap. 'You're trespassing.' Divine or not, this intervention has given Pascual's heart a leap of hope, but he quickly tumbles to the fact that this means nothing but two corpses instead of one. The wrestler is sidling toward the door, pistol hidden close to his body, counting on the interior gloom to mask his intentions. The man at the door has not moved. 'Come out of there at once,' he says, peremptory and indignant.

Pascual realizes that in three seconds there will be one less citizen of the free Swiss Confederation. He can see it all happening and he can do nothing; if he speaks he will be the first to die. And yet he cannot watch it. As the wrestler nears the door, gun hand starting to move, Pascual gropes for his German and shouts, *'Achtung, er hat eine Pistole! Polizei bringen!'*

The wrestler spins toward Pascual as the silhouette disappears; his attention is fatally split and rather than take a wild shot at Pascual he opts to go after the man outside. He dives for the gap in the door and gets his head and his gun arm through it before there is a heavy sickening crack and the big body goes rigid; there is another impact and a deep growling moan and the body is sagging, wedged in the gap. Suddenly the wrestler is shoved violently back through the gap to collapse on the floor. He rolls, groans, scrabbles on the concrete; Pascual can see dollops of crimson blood splashing in the dust.

The wrestler has made it to elbows and knees, forehead resting on the floor. Somebody is slipping through the gap, blocking out the light momentarily. The automatic comes first, followed by the figure of a man who looks very much in possession of his nerve. Inside, he ducks away from the doorway immediately and crouches, back to the wall, looking for further opposition as his eyes adjust. When nothing happens but a few messy wheezes from the wrestler's shattered face, the man rises to his full height and tosses a chunk of concrete onto the floor. Pistol trained on the wrestler, he says, 'That's good. Keep praying. Move and you'll eat something worse than concrete.' The wrestler responds with a sound of distress.

Standing over Pascual, the man lowers the gun. He is of ordinary height, bearded, on the lean side, not a man to pick out of a crowd. He wears a look of intense concentration. 'I thought I'd find you dead,' he says, in French.

Pascual is just coming to terms with the prospect of a life span measured in more than seconds and he barely notices the switch in languages. 'Are you a policeman?'

Rather than answer, the man walks behind Pascual and kneels, laying the gun on the floor. The wire tugs painfully at Pascual's wrists as the man works at it. 'Why didn't he shoot you?' he says.

'The others are coming back. They went to get gasoline.'

'Gasoline? They really don't like you, do they?'

'There are at least three more. They've been gone fifteen minutes already.'

'Hold still, will you? I know how many there are because I saw them. And they've been gone about five minutes. Get a grip on yourself.'

Pascual feels the wire come off and brings his hands together, easing the pain in his shoulders. His wrists are raw in a couple of places but not too gruesome. He makes it to his feet with a strong helping grip on his arm. 'Who are you?' he says. His rescuer has brown hair shading to grey at the temples and calm blue eyes.

'Let's move,' the man says, scooping the pistol from the floor. 'I think we'll leave him for his friends.' The wrestler has pushed up to one hand on the floor, the other cupped beneath the dripping wreckage of his face. He says something that sounds like no human language but is intelligible as pure venom.

Outside Pascual follows the man down a long deserted

alley, terrified, listening for the sound of a car wheeling around a corner. At the end of a narrow passage a silver Opel Astra stands by a fence, the railway yard opening out beyond. The man unlocks it and Pascual leaps onto the passenger seat. Through the windshield he can see workmen stepping over tracks, a train moving, distant hills. It is late morning and a glorious day and he is, remarkably, alive.

FIFTEEN

Having stashed the trophy automatic in the glove compartment, the man drives with the ease of a professional, pushing through traffic, the sheds and hangars of the *Industriequartier* flashing past. 'You need a doctor?' he says. 'No broken bones, no internal bleeding? No shock?'

Pascual touches the blister on his neck. 'I think I'll live.'

'That took guts, calling out like that.'

'I thought it was my only chance. I thought he'd get you, too.'

'Not stuck in that hole in the door he wouldn't. My only problem was, I wasn't sure how many were in there. I lost count in all the milling about.'

Perhaps because of the effects of the bump on his head Pascual is having trouble making sense of things. 'You had the place staked out?'

'No. I followed you from town.'

'Why were you following me?'

'Not you specifically. Your friends. What are they, Russian?'

'I think so.'

'Actually it was the Algerians I was interested in. I've been watching them since they flew in yesterday. When they got chummy with the Russians I got interested in them in turn. I saw them throw you in the car and I followed.'

Pascual can make nothing of this. 'Who are you?'

'Before I answer that, where am I taking you?'

Kloten and don't spare the horses, Pascual wants to say, though without papers or money an airport is useless to him. 'Someplace safe. A deep hole in the ground, perhaps.'

The man appears to be mulling this over while parking in a narrow side street. He cuts the ignition and says, 'I can have you at a police station in five minutes. But before we go and spend the rest of our day talking to policemen, a frank talk is all the payment I'm going to ask for saving your hide.'

Pascual is beginning to find his land legs again. 'I didn't thank you yet.'

'All in a day's work. Who are you and what does a crew of Russian thugs have against you?' He has produced cigarettes and offers one to Pascual, who takes it with trembling fingers. 'Start at the top.'

Never has a cigarette tasted so good. Blowing smoke, Pascual says, 'I'll start wherever you want, but it would help to know who I'm talking to. You're not a cop?'

'I was.' He stretches a hand across the seat. 'Didier Couvet, formerly of the Police de sûreté in Geneva.'

'Formerly?'

'That's right.'

'And currently?'

The face is impenetrable above its neatly trimmed beard. Couvet has crow's feet at the corners of his eyes, a brow seamed with cares; his face is a map of travails endured. This is a man who has been around the block several times and learned something on every pass. 'Why don't you just start at the beginning?'

'All right. The beginning would be when the French found me and made me an offer I couldn't refuse.'

'Which French would that be?'

'One of their security agencies, the DGSE I'm assuming but couldn't swear to.'

'And what was the offer?'

'A handsome fee to pick a man out of a lineup, give him the kiss of Judas, choose your metaphor. Identify Daoud Najjar.'

Couvet frowns out of the windshield for a moment. 'The Syrian terrorist? Active in the eighties?'

'That's the man. Now employed by Mirakl, the big Russian company.'

'There you're out of my area of expertise. Russia's a madhouse now. Why you?'

'Because I once worked with Najjar. And survived, which makes me a rarity.'

'I see. Was that Najjar, the fellow in the suit?'

'Yes.'

Couvet works on his cigarette in silence. 'What's he doing in Zurich?'

'Meeting a general named Boucherif.'

Couvet raises an eyebrow. 'What's the meeting about?'

'We don't know. The French don't seem to care much. All they want is Najjar.'

'Well, they seem to have missed him.'

'For the second time. We've been through this already in Paris.'

'Interesting.' Couvet studies Pascual for a few seconds. 'You've told me everything but your name.'

'That's a rather fluid concept, actually. You can call me Pascual.'

'All right, Pascual. Spanish?'

'More or less.'

Couvet smokes and says, 'You'll be wanting to report to your handlers, no doubt.'

Prey in fact to profound doubts on this point, Pascual says, 'I suppose so.'

'If you can put it off for a while, I have a feeling that we would both benefit from a leisurely exchange of views.'

Wondering what garden path he is being led down now, Pascual nods. 'No doubt.'

Couvet tosses his cigarette out of the window. 'Are you hungry?'

Pascual blinks, startled. 'Hungry? God yes, I'm hungry.'

Schnitzel and potatoes, a glass of beer. Pascual eats with reverent pleasure, still dazed to be alive. Around him the lunchtime crowd fills the plain workingman's café with a pleasant tumult of talk and laughter. Pascual has given Couvet the whole sordid history of the campaign against Najjar, deciding that he can think of no better reason to trust a man than that he has saved his life. Couvet has listened with the patient impassive alertness of the policeman, putting in the occasional question.

After a period of silence Pascual says, 'All right then, why is a former policeman from Geneva playing cat and mouse with Algerians?'

Couvet clasps his hands above his plate, frowning. 'Because they pay me,' he says.

'Who pays you?'

Couvet thinks hard before answering. 'Other Algerians.'

'There's a good story here somewhere, I expect.'

'If you like the dirtiest kind of political intrigue.'

'That's something I'm quite familiar with.'

'Then see how you like this.' Couvet drinks beer and hunches down, elbows on the table. 'I was a good cop.'

He says it with such fervor that Pascual feels impelled to respond. 'I can believe it.'

'I was a cop for twenty years. *Inspecteur principal adjoint* in Geneva. Attached eventually to the Special Investigations Group of the federal government. Much like the Renseignements généraux in France.'

'Counterintelligence.'

'That's right. And a merry chase they lead us, too. All the losers in all the factional squabbles all over the world come to Switzerland to set up shop. That's what our neutrality earns us. We've got more thugs and swindlers and wild-eyed fanatics per hectare than any other place in Europe. And we have to see that they stay out of trouble. It keeps us busy.'

'So I imagine.'

'A lot of what we get in Geneva spills over the border from your French friends, of course. And in nineteen ninety-five the DST came to us with a list.' Couvet pulls out his cigarettes and organizes his thoughts while getting two of them up and running. 'They'd narrowly missed nabbing an Algerian doctor in Besançon who they thought was running the show for the GIA in France. Reda Lakhdar by name. They missed him—he ducked across the border and settled in here in the land of eternal hospitality, of course—but they got a gold mine of evidence. Address book, bank documents, the works. The bloke had a list of the killers who did in those Italian sailors back in ninety-four, remember? I mean, it was a treasure trove for an intelligence officer. And they told me to go to it, no holds barred, telephone intercepts authorized, everything, and find out what he was up to. So I did.' Couvet smokes, embittered by the memory. 'I put together a team and for six months we lived with Lakhdar and his pals, day and night. Shot roll after roll of film, brought in translators to transcribe the phone calls, everything. After a month we had enough to reel in most of the GIA networks in three European countries.' Couvet vents a sour laugh.

'And what happened?'

'Not a fucking thing. I sent report after report up to Bern and they sank without a trace.'

'Curious.'

'Yes. So I thought. Particularly since I'd got proof that Lakhdar was running a veritable pipeline of Semtex from Slovakia down into Algeria. Fifty people a week were being blown to shreds in Algiers and I could tell them where the plastic was coming from. But nothing happened. The orders to move in never came.'

'Who the hell's protecting them?'

Couvet smiles. 'Well, who's got the money?'

'In this country? Who doesn't?'

'Among the Arabs, I mean.'

Pascual taps ash onto his plate. 'The people who have the oil, I'd guess.'

'That's right. Lakhdar's a bosom pal of one of the directors of a Saudi-owned bank in Lausanne, and that's all the protection he needs in this country.'

'Even with all that's going on down in Algeria? Aren't your bosses shockable?'

'Ha!' Couvet's eyes take on a strange luminous look. 'If what I sent them didn't do the trick, nothing will. Know what we found with Lakhdar's documents?'

'Tell me.'

'Video cassettes.'

'Ah.'

'Some of the usual propaganda nonsense, bearded imbeciles waving Kalashnikovs and quoting the Koran, and some that were quite riveting.'

'Yes?' Pascual feels suddenly uneasy in his freshly filled stomach.

Couvet is studying him, as if deciding whether he is old enough to hear it. 'They'd gone in with a camera on some of their massacres. Nice close-up shots of throats being cut, skulls knocked in, complete with pleading, screams, splatters on the wall. Plenty of women and children, bewildered looks into the camera as the knife approaches the throat—try getting to sleep with that in your head. The image was a little jittery at times, I imagine it's hard to hold the thing steady when you're excited, but quite vivid. I had to watch them all.'

Pascual sits frozen.

Couvet shakes his head. 'I worked in Vice for a while, long ago, and I thought I knew what obscenity was. *Now* I know.'

A silence follows. Around them people are laughing, drinking, calling for the bill. 'What happened?

'I ran out of patience. I knew a fellow, an Algerian. Translator with some UN outfit in Geneva. I knew he had some connections with the right sort of people in Algiers and I sounded him out. A week later he brought along a friend from Algiers to a meeting and I handed over the list of GIA operatives we'd compiled. I'd become a traitor to my country, handing over intelligence secrets to a foreign power.' Couvet raises his eyebrows, inviting comment.

'Bravo,' says Pascual.

'That's not what the Cour pénale said.'

'They caught you, eh?'

'Not right away. I passed information to Algerian military security for nearly four months. They offered me money but I wouldn't take it. All I felt from the start was outrage. And eventually the outrage caused me to make a stupid mistake. Nothing was moving, Lakhdar was still enjoying the good life in Lausanne and funneling arms to the killers in Algeria. I leaked what we knew about him to a journalist and he published it. All that happened, of course, was that the leak led straight back to me. I was booted out of the police, stripped of my pension, sent off in disgrace. Action injurious to the interests of the state, they said. I was lucky they didn't throw me in jail.'

Pascual nods. 'And the people on the list?'

'One was arrested when he went back to Algeria and wound up dead in one of their torture chambers. That's what really got me in trouble. It became a human rights scandal, you see. I'd helped the nasty Algerians rub out one of their dissidents. As if he were a poor innocent lamb.' Pascual's expression is apparently too noncommittal, for Couvet leans closer and snarls at him. 'Look, I'm not a Gestapo thug. I know what kind of regime they've got down there. You think I'm not aware of the moral ambiguities? But I saw those tapes. There's nothing ambiguous about a man swinging a baby against a brick wall. Sometimes you have to side with bad against worse.'

'Yes.' Pascual lets Couvet settle back again, calmer, and says, 'And what happened to Lakhdar?'

'He brought a suit against me and was allowed to apply for status as a political refugee.' Couvet's smile is grim, the smile of a man who has lost his last illusion.

Pascual shakes his head. 'That's taking neutrality to extremes.'

'You want a fluid concept? Try Swiss neutrality. The only thing we're not neutral about is money.'

Pascual studies the tip of his cigarette. 'So who's paying you to watch Algerians now?'

'Who do you think? The same people who wanted to pay me before. This time I accepted. I've got a family to feed. I get my orders from Algiers via the original man in Geneva. Along with my pay, in a small brown envelope. Not exactly the career trajectory I'd counted on.'

Pascual frowns. 'I'm a little confused. Who are you supposed to be spying on, exactly? The Algerians you saw at the hotel are working for General Boucherif.'

'I know. That's my assignment—find out what he's up to.'

'But Boucherif's part of the regime.'

'Yes. You want moral ambiguity? With the Algerians it's an art form.'

Pascual gives him a suspicious look. 'What's the idea?'

'The idea is, Boucherif himself is in contact with the GIA. Maybe, some say, actually behind the GIA.'

'Good God.'

'Shocked? At this late date?'

'Bewildered. You mean he runs them?'

'I think the idea would be that he's co-opted them, some of them, anyway.'

'What's in it for him?'

'Power. The GIA's the wild card down there. If you can control the violence, turn it on and off like a spigot, you control the pace of events. Every GIA massacre is an argument for more arms, more troops, more power for the general with the best grip on the purse strings. And if you can claim eventually to have tamed them, bring them to the table, get them to cough up some scapegoats and scrap a few rifles, then you're the hero of national reconciliation to boot.'

Slumped on his chair, Pascual says, 'And I thought I was a cynic.'

Almost jauntily, Couvet says, 'Of course, it could all be a foul slander on the part of his jealous rivals on the junta. Who really knows? All I can say is that I was apprised of his visit to Zurich and asked to watch him. And now I find he's meeting with Russians. It's been an interesting day.'

'And it's only half over.' Pascual grinds out his cigarette. 'Thanks for the lunch.'

'Maybe it's time for you to report in. There will be some very worried Frenchmen back at the Baur au Lac.'

'I'm half inclined to let them fret while I head south. But I have no money and they've got my papers.'

Couvet shrugs. 'There's always the police.'

'Yes. And where there are policemen there are court proceedings and journalists close behind. Quite apart from my employers' objections, I have a particular aversion to that sort of thing.'

'Then you don't have many choices, do you?'

Pascual shakes his head, wearily. 'I never have,' he says.

'Gone,' says the landlord, flinging the door open and waving them into the empty flat. 'Not two hours ago. Came rushing back, made a lot of thumping noises and then came barreling down the stairs dragging all their bags and boxes, left the keys on the hall table. The rent's paid up in advance, so I can hardly complain. But I'm beginning to suspect they weren't exactly on the level.' Years of renting shabby rooms to foreigners and other dubious types have left the landlord wizened and glowering.

'It does look a bit peculiar.' Couvet's polished official

manner and excellent German have won the man's confidences. He and Pascual trade a look.

The landlord spreads his hands in appeal. 'They had all the proper papers. How was I to know? They couldn't speak German at all. The wife had just enough French to talk to them. They told her they were from Lausanne and were here to install a new production system at one of the plants across the way. I thought they'd be better than the bloody Bosnians.'

'You never can tell,' says Couvet, making for the door. 'Better luck with the next tenant.'

Unlocking the car, he grins at Pascual. 'You've been orphaned.'

'So it seems.'

'You want the police now? Ready to claim political asylum? Or shall I just give you ten francs and drop you off at the entrance to the autoroute?'

Pascual looks at him across the roof of the car, feeling dazed. 'I'll give it some thought,' he says. 'First, though, I know someone else you should talk to.'

SIXTEEN

Djemila stands at the broad window, looking out over tree-tops to the distant lake. Couvet is making noises in the kitchen; Pascual pokes nervously about the vast, elegantly appointed room. He has not entirely recovered from the exhausted doze he lapsed into while waiting for Djemila in the lobby of her hotel. The hallucinatory nature of the day has continued with their arrival at this large silent house, nestled among firs on a steep shaded street on the side of the Zürichberg, far above the plebeian quarters. 'Somebody I once did a considerable favor for,' Couvet said brusquely by way of explanation as he pulled the Opel into the garage. 'He lives mostly elsewhere now and doesn't use the house. I don't get to Zurich much but when I do I save on hotel bills. All it takes is a phone call.' The house is gloomy, large rooms with little light filtering through the trees outside, but full of solid comfortable furniture, books, unassuming paintings and statuary. From the windows the views are extraordinary.

Djemila seems to have taken things in her stride,

though she was obviously not happy with Couvet dropping from the sky. Today she is dressed up in a linen suit, blue silk blouse beneath; her hair is an unrestrained tangle of black and the merest touch of makeup brings out the deep warm hues of her face. Pascual has given her an account of the morning's doings, heavy with irony and dismissal, that he suspects did not entirely mask his suppressed hysteria. She has been tracking him about the room with a worried look.

The coffee that Couvet produces brings them to a low table in front of a sofa facing an empty fireplace. 'So we share an interest in General Boucherif,' says Couvet.

'Yes,' says Djemila cautiously, stirring. 'Though I'm not sure we *serve* the same interests.'

Couvet shrugs. 'I'm not even sure I could tell you what interests I serve. What I know is that the people who pay me want to know why he's here.'

'And who pays you?'

'Presumably somebody in Algiers. So far I've been assuming that they want the killing to stop. If that's so, I'm their man. If that's not the case I can probably get a paycheck elsewhere. Maybe you can tell me which is more likely.'

Djemila sets down her spoon. After a moment she says, 'How would I know who's paying you? The fact that they want to know the same thing I do doesn't mean we're on the same side.'

'No.'

'And things seem to happen to people who are interested

in Boucherif. So the fact that you are paid to pass information to the regime makes me less eager than I might be to talk to you.'

Couvet nods. 'I'm supposed to report to the regime, yes, some faction of it, anyway. But that's a bit in flux right now. Until recently I thought things were fairly simple. There was black and there was white. Now it's all starting to look a little grey.'

She blinks at him coolly across the table. 'You can see why I might be cautious.'

Couvet smiles. 'You're the first journalist I've met who's more concerned about stopping leaks than starting them.'

'I've seen too many journalists die. It's given me a peculiar view of the profession.'

'Don't get me wrong, I like that. I'm not very fond of leaks myself.'

Djemila toys with her coffee cup and says, 'So what can you tell me about Boucherif?'

Couvet shrugs. 'At the moment, not much. But I can do a lot of legwork for you while he's here. I've got skills and resources you don't have and I'm willing to put them at your service. I won't pass anything to Algiers before I discuss implications with you, and anything that might come the other way I'll share with you. Fair enough?'

'That's fair to me. It sounds like a bad deal for your employers and that makes me a little nervous.'

'It won't be the first time I've given my employers the short end of the stick. At this point my only loyalty is to myself and my only ambition is to find out what these bastards are doing here in my country. It sounds to me like we're the perfect team.'

Pascual lights a cigarette and watches as Djemila makes the decision, staring forthrightly across the table at Couvet. 'Possibly,' she says finally.

'Well, then. What's our next step?'

Djemila sighs. For a moment as she brushes hair from her eyes her control wavers and the stress shows, a tremor just beneath the surface. 'I don't know. I need to find out what Boucherif and Najjar are saying behind closed doors. Usually a journalist can find someone who will talk. I don't know who's going to talk here. I think both parties we're dealing with have a lot of practice not talking.'

'The disgruntled employee is a good one,' says Couvet. 'I can tell you that from personal experience. Find someone who got screwed.'

'I'm not sure either the general or Mirakl lets that sort of person wander about for very long.'

'Maybe not. But there's always a crack somewhere. The first thing to do is establish whether they're still here or whether you've scared them off again. If they're going ahead with the meeting there are ways and means.'

Pascual frowns. 'The hotel will be overrun with security, Mirakl's and Boucherif's. If they decided to stay.'

Couvet shrugs. 'Maybe. But so far there's only one man who can recognize me and I doubt he's going to be on duty tonight. He'll be in a hospital somewhere, drinking soup through a straw.'

'Me, I'm not going near the place.'

'You won't have to. You two stay here and plot strategy. I'll do the legwork.' Couvet looks at Djemila. 'There are plenty of bedrooms here. One of them could be for you, if you're tired of that flophouse downtown.'

Djemila hesitates, her eyes flicking to Pascual's; he can see her making fast assessments of circumstances and people. He gives her the ghost of a shrug. To Couvet she says, 'That would make it easier on the budget.'

Pascual says, 'I have a feeling my own employers haven't just given up. Sooner or later I'm going to have to deal with them. You might keep an eye out for them when you're casing the hotel. They'll be the ones hiding panicked expressions behind French newspapers.'

Couvet rises, smiling. 'I'll do my best not to step on their toes.'

'I had a long talk this morning with the man at UBS,' says Djemila. She has removed the linen jacket and she sits smoking, a sheaf of notes on the table before her. 'He told me some interesting things about Mirakl. Did you know that they own a majority stake in Giuliani now?'

Pascual's eyebrows rise. 'The Milan fashion house? That's a far cry from cruise missiles and Afghan opium. Though it might dovetail nicely with the white slave trade.'

'They're diversified and very well insulated. The Russian laws being what they are, or rather aren't, transparency is not a key feature of their accounting. "Magic realism," was the way my source put it.'

'You could probably hide a few container loads of antitank missiles under petty cash. Boucherif must be salivating.'

Djemila looks up from her notes. 'I'm not sure quite what to make of him. I've been thinking more about the other end of it, actually.'

'Meaning what?'

'Have you wondered yet what Mirakl wants from Boucherif?'

'Money, I'd have guessed,' says Pascual. 'I've been assuming he's buying something from them.'

'With what? Algerian generals are fairly low on the income scale as kleptocrats go. Boucherif especially has a reputation for austerity. I'm not sure how much he could afford out of his own pocket.'

She waits while he works on it. 'Ah,' says Pascual, brow furrowed.

She gives him another three seconds and says, 'What's the foundation of Mirakl's empire? The original base?'

'Oil?'

'That's right. And what does Algeria have a lot of?'

Pascual blinks at her. 'But Russia's swimming in oil. What do they want with yours?'

'We've got more than oil. We've got the largest gas fields in the world. Who do you think keeps the stoves lit in Spain and Italy? The cynically minded might say that's why the EU hasn't been a bit more engaged with our present troubles. Anyway, that's part of what I learned today. Mirakl started out more or less even with a handful of other companies that divided up the Soviet oil fields—Gazprom and Sibneft and that bunch. But in the last year or two they've lost ground. The others have consolidated, signed agreements with the

Asian republics, expanded their fields. Mirakl, for a variety of reasons, lost out. Partly, they've been busy with other things, widening their base. But according to my expert, Kovalenko's worried about being outmuscled on the oil front. He's no fool. He knows his most valuable core asset is all those petroleum engineers he's got on the payroll. And so he's started to look outside Russia. It's been established that in April he spent a week in Jakarta and another in Brunei, talking with Suharto and the sultan. They weren't talking about cloves, my source said.'

'Hang on,' says Pascual after a brief pause. 'Who runs your state oil company, what do they call it, Sonatrach? That's not Boucherif's portfolio, is it?'

'Not in theory. All he's got is the best-trained units of the army.'

'I see. But what about the existing arrangements? Isn't everything in Algeria leased out for the next decade or so? I thought the Americans and the French had things sewed up there.'

'The British are in there too. But leases come up for renewal, new fields get discovered. And after all, a lease is just a piece of paper. A civil war has a way of upsetting the status quo. If you pull your people out because bullets start to fly a little too close, you may find a new government won't let you back in. You can spend years in the Hague trying to get justice. And meanwhile somebody else is pumping your oil.'

For a moment Pascual merely gapes at her. 'What's he hoping for, a split in the junta? A full-scale shooting war?'

'Who knows? There could be other ways of letting Mirakl in. A Russian-style privatization of Sonatrach, with all the bids rigged and Mirakl declared the winner. I'm just bringing out hypotheses. All I'm saying is that Mirakl's on the prowl for oil and Boucherif has the whip hand in a place that has a lot of it.'

Pascual nods. 'So however it goes, Mirakl's betting on Boucherif to come out on top when the dust settles and give them all the oil.'

'With one foot in Asia and the other in Africa, Mirakl could be the next Standard or Shell.'

After another silence Pascual says, 'Proof?'

'Not a shred. Speculation based on circumstance. I have nothing but the fact that Boucherif is talking to Mirakl.'

'You could make a big splash with that alone.'

'I don't want to make a splash. I want to shine a steady light in some dark places.'

Pascual stares into her eyes across the table. He is familiar with fanaticism, which can also illuminate a gaze, but this is something different. Djemila's eyes are too sad for fanaticism. This is something Pascual has spent his life groping for but cannot put a name to. Purpose, perhaps?

'Do you think we're safe here?' says Djemila.

Pascual does not have to ask what she means. He rises and goes to the window. Outside, the sun is declining and the blue of the lake has deepened. 'I think it's a good risk,' he says.

Her footsteps sound behind him, coming to join him. 'Say everything Couvet told us is true except the last bit. Say he's on the payroll of the regime but the part about their mistrusting Boucherif is a lie. Say his real job is to protect Boucherif while he's here. In that case, he's done a good job. Can you think of a better scenario? He's persuaded us to isolate ourselves, no record anywhere of our location. It's a pretty good spot for an ambush.'

Haunted by thoughts of carnage in a Paris basement, Pascual looks for answers in the treetops and church steeples below. The emotional roller coaster he has ridden all day has left him ill-prepared to consider this hypothesis. 'I'd say, if he wanted me out of Boucherif's hair, all he had to do was let them kill me this morning. And you can't fake bashing a man's face in. That was real.'

A couple of seconds go by and Djemila says, 'Notice he didn't bash in any Algerian faces.'

'No, that's true. Still, why wouldn't he just let them kill me?'

'This morning they didn't have me.'

Pascual looks at her in profile. He knows that what is screaming paranoia in some circumstances may be the soberest common sense in others and that if anyone is qualified to judge the circumstances it is Djemila. 'I think,' he says, 'that if Boucherif wanted to draw you out of hiding there are less elaborate ways of doing it, like simply tearing out my fingernails until I cough you up. I also think a man who sacrificed his career because of his outrage over slaughter is not likely to sign on to our slaughter just for an envelope full of cash. In short I think Couvet's telling the truth. But I'm also aware that my judgment has never won any prizes. So if you don't like the setup here, I'm ready to grab our bags and hop on the next tram down the hill. You make the call.'

Djemila turns to him and just now there is nothing in her eyes but the fatigue of a long succession of life-or-death decisions. She opens her mouth but does not speak; when Pascual reaches for her she does not resist. He folds her into his arms and feels her tremble. 'I don't know,' she says. 'I don't know anymore.'

He holds her, waiting for the trembling to stop. He squeezes harder, feeling her arms go round his middle. Her breath is on his neck, her hair in his face. He eases his embrace enough to seek her face with his lips but now she is pulling back, gently, turning away. 'Djemila,' he breathes.

'No,' she whispers. Suddenly she is free of his grasp and hurrying away across the floor toward the kitchen, hands to her face. She turns in the doorway and shoots him a pained look. 'I'm sorry,' she says.

'No, no. I'm sorry. Forgive me.' Pascual turns back to the window and listens as she does nothing elaborately in the kitchen. His chagrin begins to ebb and he wonders what he wants, whether the person or the act. The act, because he looked death in the face this morning and is undergoing the standard psychic and hormonal storms? Simply because he felt her heat next to him?

Or the person, he wonders, looking at the far-off lake and seeing only Djemila's eyes.

SEVENTEEN

Pascual is awakened by the ringing of the telephone. Coming up off the couch in confusion, he sees Djemila rising from the table in a haze of cigarette smoke to answer it. She speaks softly into the phone and turns to him. 'It's Couvet. He wants to talk to you.'

Pascual takes the phone, just beginning to get his bearings. 'Had your supper yet?' says Couvet in his ear.

'What? Yes, we found some things in the kitchen.'

'Good. Then you're ready to come out and lend a hand.'

'Where are you?'

'I'm in Oerlikon, not too far from the airport. Interesting things are happening, and I need another pair of eyes.'

'All right. How do I get there?'

'Call a taxi and have it drop you where the Binzmühlestrasse runs into the Thurgauerstrasse, in Oerlikon. Got that?'

'Hang on. Where's a pen?'

Couvet repeats the directions. 'Look for the car. And wear dark clothing.'

'Fine. I'm on my way.' Pascual rings off and stands bare-foot and dazed, the man of action. Djemila is staring at him.

'What's happening?'

'He wants me to come and help him watch somebody. How do you suppose one calls a taxi in this town?'

Djemila puts out her cigarette. 'You're not leaving me here alone.'

Calling a taxi proves to be a simple matter and in twenty minutes they are on their way. The suburb of Oerlikon lies up the valley beyond the Zürichberg, and the Binzmühlestrasse leads eastward out of town into an area of scattered industrial sites. The taxi driver cannot understand what business they could possibly have out here but he drops them as instructed and speeds off. The lights of a car parked thirty meters ahead flash once and Pascual recognizes Couvet's Opel. He and Djemila hike to the car and get in, Pascual in the front with Couvet.

'I get both of you, do I?' says Couvet.

'What was she supposed to do, sit and watch the telly?'

'Did you tell her there's a certain amount of risk?'

'I think her imagination's as good as mine,' says Pascual.

'Fine.' Couvet starts the car and pulls onto the road. 'On the other hand we may be about to waste an entire night looking at empty warehouses. I hope you're patient.'

He drives for a few hundred meters, as construction thins out on either side of the road. They pass long low sheds, yards full of pallets, a construction site dominated by a crane. Five hundred meters up an intersecting street, a building of ten to fifteen stories looms in the night. Couvet slows and turns left into a narrow lane that runs at right angles to the road with a line of brush and small trees on the left and a vast fenced-in compound on the right. Two hundred meters along he pulls off the lane and parks beneath a gently swaying willow in deep shadow next to a low brick shed with broken windows. He cuts the ignition.

In the distance lights rise into the sky as a jet takes off from Kloten. Beyond the wire fence twenty meters away there is an industrial park, a haphazard collection of sheds, hangars, warehouses spreading out over a half-dozen hectares, intermittently lit by lamps on high posts. 'Guess who owns this showcase of Swiss industry and commerce,' says Couvet.

Djemila comes up with the answer first. 'Mirakl.'

'That's right.' Couvet lowers the window and lights a cigarette. 'Or more precisely ZX Holding, whose headquarters you'll find in that building just up the Leutschenbachstrasse back there. You have to do some rather tedious raking through records to find out that they're ultimately owned by Mirakl.'

'You've been busy,' says Pascual.

'Not really. I have contacts, that's all. There are a few people who will still talk to me. One of them is a fellow in the Federal Office of Justice in Bern who tries to track dirty money coming into this country, a labor of Sisyphus if there ever was one. He's rather a Mirakl enthusiast, actually. He says nobody does it better, nobody's cleverer.'

After a pause Pascual says, 'So what are we doing here?'

'We're waiting for somebody to cut and run.' Couvet blows

smoke out into the cool night air. 'We seem to have alarmed them.'

'It's nice to know it's mutual,' says Pascual.

Couvet makes a grunt of laughter. 'I had an interesting visit to the hotel this afternoon. Quite a nice place. You must have been sorry to leave it, all that luxury.'

'I can't say I paid much attention. Did you get anything incriminating on tape?'

'No, I didn't manage that. But I spent the afternoon with the house detective, which was almost as good. He's an old *flic* from the Stadtpolizei and he was pleased to help, after he checked a reference or two. I was a bit vague about details but he'd heard about me and he had no trouble believing I was still tracking down nasty gun-running Arabs. He had no idea he'd got a member of a foreign government staying in his hotel, and I didn't give him the whole story. But we had a careful look at the registration records.'

Intent, Djemila says, 'Nobody's traveling under his real name, of course.'

'Not the VIPs, at any rate. But it wasn't too hard to figure out. The Algerians all had Algerian passports and the Mirakl people all had Russian ones except for a Mr. Ardabil, who's travelling on Azerbaijani papers.'

'Najjar?'

'That's probably a good guess. A nice confirming factor was that the Russians had booked one of the small conference rooms but canceled it early this morning. Instead they seem to have met in Ardabil's suite, as one of the Algerian gentlemen asked to have calls routed up there to him. Apparently they were still talking when I was there.'

'They would have canceled the conference room after they spotted Pascual.'

'That's right, wanting to make things a little less public, going to earth in a private room. The house detective said the security people had been a bit pushy, a bit demanding. He's dealt with heavyweights and their entourages before but he said he didn't like this bunch much. And today they were particularly edgy, he said.'

'So what's happening tonight?'

'Maybe nothing. All my guesses could be wrong. But there were some funny goings-on at the hotel. While I was sitting there talking to the house dick, somebody came in with an odd report. One of the cooks back in the kitchens had been taking delivery of a load of meat from the butcher's when three men had come slinking out of a corridor and struck up a conversation with the driver of the truck. The cook couldn't hang about to watch, but somebody else told him that some money had changed hands and the three men had climbed in the back of the truck and been driven away.'

'Aha.'

'Yes. The witness thought they looked like Arabs. One of them had a face to give small children nightmares, he said.'

'Boucherif.'

'And Najjar and one of their gorillas, most likely. Well, that made me very curious. Wherever they were going, they wanted to make damn sure nobody who might be watching knew it. It only took me an hour or so to track down the butcher's driver, but of course all he'd done was drop his passengers in a side street back behind the railway station where another car was waiting. They'd given him five hundred francs for the favor, pretty good for fifteen minutes' work.' Couvet taps ash out of the window. 'He thought the car that was waiting for them was a grey Mercedes. There are a lot of those about, but then the car that Najjar arrived in when he came to kiss you good-bye this morning was a grey Mercedes and I did get its number. So I decided it was time to work the phones.

'All it took was a call to an old mate with access to the right computer to find out that the Mercedes is registered to ZX Holding. So then I thought it was worth it just to run out here and take a look. They have a big parking lot back there where you can sit without attracting any notice. And after I'd been there a few minutes, what do I see but my grey Mercedes, pulling into a reserved space? I thought I'd found Najjar and the general, but only the driver got out, the same bloke I'd seen in the morning. He went into the building and I wondered how long to give it. I decided on an hour, but fifteen minutes later he came back out and jumped in, in a hurry. I followed him to a bar back there in Oerlikon, where he went in and came out a few minutes later with three men. I was fifty meters away, but even at that distance they could have been wearing signs that said Bosnian or Albanian, something Balkan anyway. They didn't look too prosperous and they didn't look like the type of men who'd be burdened with a lot of scruples either. They lingered on the pavement just long enough to do a lot of nodding, with the look of men getting final instructions, and then the man in the Mercedes took off. Me, I followed the hired help. They had a beat-up Volkswagen parked nearby and they took me out near the airport to a bloody great freight depot, where as far as I could tell from a distance they rented or stole or otherwise acquired two Volvo FLC seven-and-a-half-ton lorries, blue with no distinguishing markings. They drove off in them, at any rate, the VW following, and stashed them in a yard not too far from here.'

Couvet tosses the fag out into the night. 'Mirakl's moving something. I'd bet it's happening tonight, and I'd bet it's happening here, because this is the only place in Zurich where Mirakl actually owns property. If Mirakl wanted to truck something in, fly it in maybe, and store it for a while, this is where they'd do it. I'd also bet you this is where Boucherif and Najjar came this afternoon. The general would want to get a look at what he's buying before he takes delivery, wouldn't he?'

'I know I would.'

'So. We may be wasting our time, but then again I'm a pretty good guesser, because I've had a lot of experience at guessing. And what would you rather be doing on a lovely summer evening than sitting out here listening to the crickets and waiting for Russian gangsters to move a fortune in illicit and possibly deadly merchandise?'

'I don't know,' says Pascual. 'Drinking myself to sleep, probably.'

Couvet reaches for a pair of binoculars on the dashboard

and raises them to his eyes. 'There'll be time for that later,' he says. 'Right now we've got work to do. Have a look at that.' He hands the binoculars to Pascual. 'See the two lorries just pulling in through the gate from the road there? You can see it through the gap between those buildings. That looks like a grey Mercedes right behind it.'

EIGHTEEN

'I'm starting to get an uneasy feeling,' says Pascual. 'I'm starting to think you want us to go in there.'

Couvet laughs softly. 'Don't tell me you're scared just because they wanted to burn you alive this morning.'

'I find that sort of thing brings out the meek and retiring side of my nature.'

'Can't say I blame you. I wasn't going to ask you to come with me anyway.'

Pascual takes his fear by the throat and shakes it, without notable effect. 'I'll come with you if you want,' he says weakly.

Couvet lowers the binoculars. 'They've gone out of sight, somewhere on the far side of the complex. No, what I want you to do is stay with the car, be ready to come down the lane here and pick me up if need be. Either that or run for help if I don't come back in an hour or so.'

Pascual shakes his head. 'An hour's a long time.'

'It's a big complex and I'll have to go slowly. The main thing is, be ready if I signal. Watch that stretch of fence, by the warehouse there. If you see me flash the light, get down there and wait for me to come over.'

'You can climb that?'

'Didn't you ever scale a fence when you were a kid? You can see there's no razor wire at the top. The fence is there to stop people driving out truckloads of computers, or whatever they store in there. I don't think they're particularly worried about the odd vagrant. The place to get over is in the shadows over there, where there's a bit of a gap between lights. As long as no watchmen come along, it shouldn't be too hard to get in without being seen.'

'Christ, it's lit up like a stage in there.'

'Not right next to the fence. They'd have to be looking to notice me. And once I'm over, there's cover. I'll work my way along between buildings. With the binoculars I don't have to get too close. If I'm spotted, I'll sprint for the fence, right there along the lane. I'll be waving the light like a madman. You just hustle the car down there and we've got a pretty good chance of getting away clean. Otherwise just wait for me here. If all goes well I'll be back in an hour with a good idea of what our friend the general is taking home to Algiers.'

'You really are going in there?'

'You have a better idea, perhaps?'

'Call the police. Call up your famous civilian army. Send in a couple of platoons and round them up.'

Couvet loops the strap of the binoculars over his head. 'On what grounds do we call the police? Mirakl owns this place. Anyway, by the time we got anybody with any authority on the phone they'd be finished and gone. No, I'm afraid the best we can do is get close and watch.'

From the back seat Djemila says, 'It's not worth the risk. I don't need to know what they're up to that badly. Can't you just track the lorries or something?'

'Once they're on the road, who's going to stop them? Who's going to be able to follow them without being detected? How are you going to get a look inside?'

'Surely your former colleagues can find a reason to stop them, given what we know. Did you get the numbers off the lorries?'

'I did. But by the time we get all that mobilized, presuming anyone will listen to me, they're in Budapest or Marseilles or God knows where. No, I'm afraid we've been too clever. We've opened the box and we're the only ones who can get a look at what's inside before it vanishes.'

There is a silence. Pascual says, 'Is that automatic still in the glove compartment?'

'No, it's in my pocket.' Couvet reaches up to flick the switch of the interior light to *off* and then swings open the door. 'I may be mad, but I'm not a fool.'

He gets out and stands for a moment listening, then leans into the car and says, 'If you have to drive, don't switch on the lights. It'll take me five or ten minutes to get inside and at least another ten or so to find them. The tricky bit will probably start twenty minutes to half an hour from now. But don't fall asleep. Surprises have a way of coming up. Watch for my light along the fence.'

'Understood.' Pascual watches through the windshield as

Couvet moves off. Once he crosses the lane he is merely a shifting of shadow in the dark. Gently, Pascual opens the door and gets out. Djemila does the same and they stand together at the front of the car. The night is filled with the murmur of breezes, distant traffic, the hollow roar of a jet engine far away over the airport. Pascual takes an uneasy look up and down the lane, scans the complex beyond the fence.

Djemila speaks in a whisper. 'Just suppose.'

'Suppose what?'

'Suppose he is in their pocket.'

'Whose?'

'The regime's. Somebody in Algiers who may not like Boucherif but likes publicity even less. Somebody who said we'll handle Boucherif and you make sure nothing hits the papers.'

Frozen, Pascual supposes. 'So?'

'So he's done a very good job. We've agreed to sit and wait and all he has to do is go and tell somebody where we are. Or perhaps the site was prearranged.'

Two hundred meters away a figure emerges from shadow and steps to the fence. They watch as Couvet goes up three meters of fence like a spider and rolls over the top to drop on the other side. Once on the ground, he trots to the shadows at the side of the nearest building and disappears around a corner. 'There he goes,' says Pascual. 'Just as he said he would.'

'Is that proof he's telling the truth?'

Pascual is trying to resist the fear that wants to leap across the space between them like a spark. He looks back toward the road, and now he looks at the looming hulk of the derelict shed beside them as well. Black windows stare back at him. What happened to him in the morning has stripped him of resources and the only thing keeping him here now is the memory of Couvet coming through a hole in a door with a chunk of concrete in his hand. 'If it worries you, we'll move.'

'It worries me.'

Pascual nods. 'I think there's a place further down where we could hide the car and still watch the fence. In the trees there.' In silence they get in the car. Pascual eases out onto the lane, no lights showing. He goes in low gear, feeling exposed, the fence passing by on his right, the line of brush to his left. They reach a cluster of three or four trees and Pascual pulls into the shadow beneath them. He cuts the ignition and there is silence. 'Better?' he says.

'Let's hope so.' They get out and close the doors gently. Pascual listens, scans, thinks. 'Let's get away from the car,' he murmurs. 'Just in case.'

They move, hugging the line of brush. Pascual hears a murmur and sees that just beyond the vegetation is a drainage ditch, a steep concrete-lined slope down into a trickle of black water. Where a larger tree erupts from the brush they halt. From behind the trunk the view is good and they are in darkness, and Pascual begins to breathe again.

He leans on the tree trunk and thinks about all the places he would rather be with Djemila on a pleasant summer night. He squirms, shifts his weight; he follows Djemila's example and sinks to a sitting position on the grass, branches clawing at his back. After a time he yawns. From

their right the growl of tires on gravel sounds. Djemila's
fingers dig into his arm.

The grey Mercedes glides ghostly and almost noiseless out
of the night, headlights off, just visible in the light from the
compound. They watch as it draws near. Djemila shifts,
rustling in the grass. 'Run,' she says.

'Wait.' Pascual has been holding his breath. 'They'll hear us.'

They watch, turned to stone, as the headlights come on,
silhouetting Couvet's car beneath the trees. The lights swing
toward them as the Mercedes creeps off the track. Pascual
sinks slowly onto his side, trying to vanish into the earth. He
can hear doors opening; through the grass he can see dark
figures moving in front of the lights. Djemila has followed
his lead and lowered herself on top of him, still grasping his
arm; he can feel her heart beating against his ribs. Steps
sound on the gravel, a low murmur of voices.

The headlights are switched off. In the darkness there are
small noises, someone rooting in a car, and then smaller
lights come on, dancing like fireflies in the dark. Someone
has found flashlights and the tips of the tall grass shine white
as the beams sweep toward them. 'Now,' breathes Djemila.

'No.' Pascual finds her hand and clamps on to it. The
beams sweep closer. Djemila tears free and plunges through
the thin screen of underbrush masking the ditch behind
them. In two seconds the flashlight beams converge on the
spot as Pascual rolls behind the tree. There is a growl in
what sounds like Russian and something flits in front of a
flashlight beam, feet scuffling on gravel and then swishing
through grass. Behind him Pascual can hear Djemila sliding

down the concrete, splashing into water. In front of him two men loom up, backlit.

It takes no thought, merely reflex, for him to rise into the path of the leading man and loose off a wild swing that catches him on the side of the head and knocks him sideways into the tree. Immediately the second man fixes him with the flashlight, a few steps away. Pascual runs, along the line of the ditch but away from the lights, screaming insults in a polyglot logorrhoeic frenzy, his only thought to draw them away from Djemila. There is an appalling CRACK in the night, and a crease in the air next to his head. A madman's *son et lumière* breaks out as the flashlights catch and lose him again and two more shots come. Pascual dives through brush and tumbles through darkness where the ground has fallen away. He hits the concrete and rolls, splashing into cold water that takes his breath away. For a second he panics, stunned and drowning, before finding that on his hands and knees his face is well out of the water. He fights to his feet and thrashes on, water clawing at his feet, hoping Djemila will lie silent behind him.

Pop, crack, bang-bang. Someone is shooting off firecrackers as Pascual stumbles along the stream. He runs until he falls, then claws out of the water onto the slope, exhausted, and waits for the light to find him. Cheek to the concrete, he hears feet scamper above. Someone is shouting. There is a brief lull and then another volley of shots, high snapping pistol reports, but nobody seems to be shooting at him. Bewildered, Pascual can only lie still in the dark. The shots cease.

The silence is torn by a low rapid voice, full of tension, somewhere above. After a moment there is a muffled rush of feet, and tires spin with a grinding of gears and a spray of gravel; the whine of the engine fades quickly away.

Pascual does not dare to move. He could not say how much time has gone by when he hears the rustling in the brush above. 'Pascual,' Couvet calls softly.

Pascual will not believe it until Couvet snarls into the darkness. 'If you're alive, now's the time to move. Look sharp, for Christ's sake.'

'Anybody bleeding?' Couvet manhandles the gearshift, slewing around corners, eyes flicking to the mirrors. Empty streets fly by in the night.

Soaked and shivering, Pascual says only, 'Why did you come back?'

'I saw you move the car and I knew they would, too. They had a guard posted down at the corner and it was just too obvious. What in the name of God possessed you?'

A couple of seconds go by. 'I didn't trust you,' says Djemila from the back.

'Next time perhaps you will,' says Couvet, hunched over the wheel. He drives for a while and then laughs, a low wheezing sound. 'That's the first time I've ever fired a shot in anger. I don't know if I hit anybody or not and I'm not sure which to hope for.'

An hour later Pascual has showered and put on a bathrobe Couvet found in a cupboard. They have gravitated to the kitchen, where Couvet has sucked down one bottle of beer and is opening a second. Pascual is working on a cigarette and Djemila, hair still damp, sits with her arms folded, staring at the tabletop. She has not said a word since they returned.

'Unfortunately, I never got close to the trucks,' Couvet says. 'I'm afraid by now they'll be on the road, long gone.'

'Our fault,' says Pascual. 'We should have stayed put.'

'Yes, what's that story about the fellow who goes to Samarra?'

'All right, all right. What do we do now?'

Couvet takes a long pull on the beer. 'You, you sleep. If you can. Me, I've got phone calls to make. It's time to put out the word. We're on a different level now.'

Pascual's room has a single bed, a chair on which he has thrown his bag, a lamp on a dresser. Nobody lives here; it is as bare as a hotel room. He sits on the bed and waits for bathroom noises to subside, hears doors close. He rises. In the bathroom he looks at himself in the mirror and sees a man who needs sleep, sunshine, peace. A man who needs to go home.

He lies on the bed in the dark in his borrowed robe and finds it impossible to sleep, the images too vivid, the ringing in his ears too persistent. Too often in his life he has been here, in a strange room in a strange city with death in his nostrils, his hair, under his nails. There is a soft, just audible tapping at the door, a mere fingertip drumming gently on wood. Stupidly, Pascual murmurs, 'Who is it?'

The door opens with a creak. 'I'm afraid,' whispers Djemila in the dark.

'Me too,' he breathes, up on one elbow. 'Come in, then.'

She pushes the door shut, softly. There is just enough light that he can see her as she crosses the room. She has put on something black and loose that does not reach her knees; she is a deeper black in the darkness. She sits on the bed, within reach, turned away from him. Pascual moves a hand up her back, feeling nothing under the soft cotton. He finds her neck, gives the gentlest of experimental tugs. 'I need . . .' she says, not yielding.

Pascual waits but no more comes. His hand rests on the nape of her neck, his thumb caressing her hairline. 'Me, too,' he says.

She turns then and he folds her into his arms, sinking back onto the mattress with her on top of him. He cannot believe how thin she is, how lithe, how warm. 'I need . . .' Again she cannot finish, but her arms are around him, her breath on his face, and she shudders as their limbs slide silkily together.

Pascual wonders if it is him she needs, or just the act, and decides tonight it does not matter. 'Sometimes this is all you need,' he says.

'Yes,' says Djemila, and her mouth tastes of cigarettes and a yearning beyond words.

NINETEEN

In the morning she avoids his eyes. Daylight puts such things to the test, and Pascual quickly sees that there will be no nuzzling, no sentimentality. She does not flee him but she does not seek caresses. What happened in the night was mere gravity, inescapable but not to be celebrated. There is a new comfort with proximity but no more.

Couvet is nowhere to be found but has left a note with their freshly dried clothing: *Wait by the phone.* In silence they negotiate a stranger's kitchen, finding coffee, stale bread, spoons. Pascual will not allow himself to think beyond today, beyond this moment. This is something that has no future, a life raft on a tossing ocean. And yet he stands and holds her as water murmurs on the stove, sunlight warming the kitchen tiles, and she seems content to be held.

'They've gone,' says Couvet at the other end of the wire. 'Checked out, all of them.'

Pascual stands with the phone to his ear, looking out of the window at treetops and a glimpse of distant water. 'That was fast,' he says finally.

'First the Algerians and then the Russians, close on their heels. The house detective said they made quite a production of it, lots of milling about and more taxis than they really needed, going off in different directions. It looked to him as if they wanted to confuse anybody that might be watching.'

'At this point somehow I doubt anybody was.'

'It looks as if your Frenchmen have missed him again, then.'

For the first time in days, Pascual finds himself thinking of a hundred thousand dollars. 'Pity,' he says.

'Don't worry. He left some tracks.'

'What do you mean?'

'He used the telephone.'

'Ah, of course.'

'He's careful, I'll give him that. Even though it's all direct dial now, no need to go through a switchboard, he knows there'll be a record of calls from each room, and with computers you have practically instant access. So he had the desk put it through on a house phone, downstairs, and he paid for it in cash. If I hadn't thought to have a chat with the concierge he'd have got away with it.'

'Smart.'

'A little too smart. The concierge is paid to be discreet, but the house dick and I got him to go to the computer and dredge up the number. I didn't recognize the prefix, had to look it up. Turns out Najjar had had a long chat with somebody in Turkish Cyprus.'

'Cyprus. That would make sense. Isn't there a lot of Russian money going there these days?'

'So they say. In any event, I found it hard to contain my curiosity, so I rang the number, simple as that. A woman answered, but we didn't get anywhere, as she spoke nothing but Turkish as far as I could tell. After a moment she handed me to another woman who had pretty passable English, enough to strain mine to its limits in fact. This one sounded a lot younger and had a distinct mistress-of-the-castle tone to her voice. I asked if she was ready to take delivery of the new satellite dish and she told me she didn't know anything about it and asked who ordered it. I took a chance and said it was billed to an outfit called Mirakl, with a signature I couldn't read. She thought about that for a moment, and then just as I was sure I was about to get told off she said it was probably her husband who'd ordered it—she hesitated just a bit at the word *husband*—but I'd have to talk to him about it. He was out of town and getting back tonight and I should call tomorrow. She even gave me his name.'

'Which was?'

'Daoud Halabi.'

'Halabi.'

'That's Arabic, isn't it?'

Pascual feels a small flutter in his lower regions. 'Yes, Syrian to be exact. Quite a common name. It means from Halab. Aleppo that is, which is where Daoud Najjar originally came from.'

After a moment of silence Couvet's rasping laugh comes over the line. 'Well, now we know his weaknesses. Women and sentiment.'

'*Chapeau.* You've found his hideout.'

'I'd say it's a good bet. It shouldn't be too hard to trace the number. Though there's probably a reason he's in Turkish Cyprus. I'd bet he's got good protection there.'

'I'll pass it on to my friends in Paris.'

'And I'm afraid I've got to pass it on to certain people here. After last night I can't go on playing Lone Ranger. I've been on the phone to Bern and started the ball rolling. I don't know if we'll get those lorries, but it's time for somebody here to take an interest in Mirakl.'

'The French won't be happy.'

'I can't worry about them. At any rate, it's probably safe now for you to drop by and collect your things.'

'There's nothing I really want, to tell you the truth. A change of socks, maybe.'

'Well, it wouldn't be a bad idea to check out, if you want to avoid eventual stir about mysterious disappearing guests. Do they know you at the desk?'

'They ought to.'

'Then it should be a simple matter of signing off on a credit slip, turning in your key and so on.'

'Well, that's a bit of a problem. They took everything off me yesterday, key card included.'

'Ah, they'll have searched your room, no doubt. Well, you'll have to give them a story about the lost key. As you're checking out, there shouldn't be too much fuss. They'll reprogram the lock and that will be that.'

Despite the all clear Pascual finds the prospect of returning to the Baur au Lac less than thrilling. It does seem a pity to abandon Hugo Berger's expensive wardrobe, however, and Pascual is inclined to trust Couvet's judgment. In addition, he feels obscurely that Djemila would think him a poor creature if he balked. 'Are you at the hotel?'

'Nearby.'

'You might just keep an eye out for me, if you would. I don't fancy running into any rear-guard actions.'

Couvet says, 'I don't think you have to worry about it, I really don't.'

There is a certain amount of fuss made over Pascual at the desk when he recounts his mugging late in the previous evening at the hands of rough-looking scoundrels with primitive German. The consensus is that Zurich suffers greatly from the presence of so much flotsam from regions to the south and east. As the hotel is in possession of a perfectly acceptable credit card number for Mr. Berger, there is no objection to his collecting his things from the room and departing. It is greatly regretted that he must curtail his stay.

He is escorted to his room and discreetly left alone. If the room has been searched no sign of it remains; the maids have swept through to restore everything to perfection. Pascual stuffs things haphazardly into his bag. There is a knock on the door. Expecting the next higher level of management with futher expressions of concern, Pascual is stunned to open it on Morrel.

The Frenchman slips in and pushes the door closed. 'What are you doing here, making a scene in the lobby?' he says in a stage whisper, looking genuinely astonished. 'We thought you were dead.'

Pascual bristles. 'I damn near was. It's a good thing you were there to protect me, eh?'

'What the hell were we supposed to do? You took off like a shot and we only just caught up in time to see them throw you in the car. What happened?'

'I cut through the chains with the hacksaw I keep up my sleeve and knocked them all out with the concussion grenade from the heel of my shoe. Meanwhile, you were so busy clearing out you forgot to leave a forwarding address.'

Morrel's face clouds, brows clamping down. 'We'll do the postmortem later. Right now you're just in time. We're about to reel him in.'

'Who?'

'Najjar, imbecile. Forgotten what we're here for?'

Pascual gapes. 'Najjar's gone.'

'The hell he is. All that choreography at the front door took you in, did it? If you'd been paying attention you'd have seen that Najjar wasn't even with them.'

'How do you know? You don't even know what he looks like.'

'That was him you took off after yesterday, wasn't it? Now we've seen him once, we can carry on on our own, thanks. But as long as you're here you might as well be there for the clinching identification. Come on, they've got the whole thing set up.' Morrel is reaching for the door.

Baffled, bag in hand, Pascual follows him to the stairwell at the end of the corridor. Trotting down the stairs, Morrel goes on in a rapid undertone. 'It's the classic ruse. Put on a big show, draw off the pursuit, split it up with several vehicles. Then sneak out afterward. He'll be leaving on foot, or maybe be picked up in a private car, but he sure as hell didn't go with the caravan.'

'How do you know he hasn't already left? Maybe he slipped out early.'

'Jacky spotted him in the barber shop, about the time the others were checking out. Getting his hair cut, cool as could be.'

'Getting his hair cut?'

'Clever, eh? The purloined letter principle. Out in the open, no guards, no escort, let the circus at the front desk attract all the attention while you change your appearance and have a look at the lay of the land. He headed back to his room after that but any minute now he'll try and slip out and we'll have him. It'll have to be quick, before he gets to wherever they're picking him up.'

Morrel halts abruptly, Pascual jostling him from behind, and puts his hand to his ear. For the first time, Pascual notices the thin black wire snaking up out of his collar. Looking at the wall, Morrel says, '*Compris*. I've got Paco in tow. We're on our way.'

'Paco?' Pascual strives to keep up as Morrel takes off down the stairs again.

'Your code name. Najjar's just left the building, on foot. What did I tell you?'

At the bottom of the stairs they emerge into a passage and Morrel leads Pascual around corners to a door. They are in regions of the hotel Pascual has never seen; they pass a stout woman pushing a wheeled bin full of towels. Through a door and another turn and here is an exit; outside is bright sunlight and the Börsenstrasse. They have just left the hotel when Morrel slows and touches his earphone again. His eyes widen and he says, 'Super, good work.' He snaps Pascual a feverish look, slaps him hard on the arm and says, 'They've got him.'

Pascual opens his mouth but says nothing; he is being swept along by the current. Morrel is talking into the air again, a madman in the sunshine muttering at no one. 'Sixty seconds,' Pascual hears. Morrel looks at him and says, 'Step lively. Serge is on his way with the car and we don't want to make him wait.'

Morrel is walking briskly, arms swinging. Pascual finds himself thinking of a hundred thousand dollars, his deep-seated fatalism crumbling in the face of what is beginning to look like the first happy ending of his life.

Morrel is murmuring, hand to his throat to help the hidden mike, the very picture of the modern covert operator at the height of his powers, timed to the second and directing action at a distance. They leave the hotel behind, making for the Talstrasse, and Pascual casts a last look at the handsome façade, thinking now he will be able to afford the place on his own. He gives a little puff of laughter at the thought. 'Paco?' he says to Morrel's back. 'You couldn't come up with something a little sexier, like Lancer or Eagle One or something like that?'

'Serge picked the names. Take it up with him.'

A grey Audi careens around the corner from the Talstrasse and pulls to the curb in front of them. Over the steering wheel Pascual sees Serge's oxlike countenance, sunglasses in place. Morrel is clawing at the door before the car has stopped rocking on its springs. Pascual makes it onto the back seat just as Serge tears away again. 'Clockwork,' Serge is crowing. 'Like fucking clockwork. The bastard just froze. They had him in the van before he knew what hit him.'

'No trouble from witnesses?'

'What was there to see? A man with a map stops a stranger to ask for help. Who hangs about to see what happens? Somebody else sees him assisted into the back of a van. I'm telling you, it was fast and smooth, a thing of beauty. Jacky never took the piece out of his pocket.' Serge thrusts his massive chin at Pascual in the mirror. 'You,' he says. 'What happened to you? I thought we'd seen the last of you.'

'Sorry to spoil your party.'

'Don't fret about it. You see, we didn't need you after all.'

Morrel says, 'Still, it's good you turned up. Your identification is the last nail in the coffin. I want to see his face when you finger him. Pierre knows where he's going?'

'He picked the spot, he ought to. The big thing is not to get stopped. You get excited, your foot gets heavy on the pedal. Look at this cretin. Who taught him to drive?'

Pascual delivers a terse account of his morning's misadventure as Serge fights out of the city center and onto the Mythenquai, which leads along the west shore of the lake. His tale is met with a disappointing silence, his audience absorbed in their own escapade. Zurich falls away behind them as sailing boats play and sun dapples the water. Serge drives hunched over the wheel, pushing the limits but not too far, weaving his way smoothly through traffic. 'There they are,' he says.

Ahead Pascual can see a dark blue van cruising sedately in the right-hand lane, a tradesman on his rounds. Serge slows to keep his distance.

In fifteen minutes they are in rolling, open countryside scabbed with clusters of tile-roofed houses and fringed with copses, the lake now vanished behind hills. The van leads them into narrow lanes where they have to slow down; Serge has closed to fifty meters. The road leads into a wood and the van pulls off on to a dirt road that runs into the trees.

Serge draws up beside it. A man Pascual has not seen before steps out of the cab and flashes Morrel a grin. Serge and Morrel pile out and there is a certain amount of handshaking and back-slapping. The driver goes to the rear of the van and grunts with effort as he raises the overhead door. 'There you go,' says Morrel. 'Say hello to your old friend.'

Pascual looks into the gloom in the rear of the van. He can make out three figures, two seated on benches at the sides and one on the floor, hands behind him. One of the seated figures rises; it is Jacky. 'Come on, then. Give him a kiss for old times' sake.'

'Bring him into the light,' says Pascual. The man on the floor wears a suit that is suffering as he is dragged across the floor toward the rear of the van. Light falls on the high forehead, the olive complexion, the long curving nose above the mustache, a Latin intellectual wide-eyed with terror. Pascual has never seen this man in his life. He is thinner than Daoud Najjar, with somewhat less hair and more prominent cheekbones, an Adam's apple working up and down as he tries to find his voice. He resembles Najjar as much as an ass resembles a horse, which is to say only vaguely. Pascual looks into the bulging eyes riveted on his and sees a man frightened to death.

Pascual turns and claps a hand on Morrel's shoulder. Morrel is watching him intently, perhaps having caught a whiff of the truth from his bearing. 'I don't know how to tell you this,' Pascual says.

'*Déconne pas,*' says Morrel. 'No fucking around, eh?'

'You got the wrong man.' Pascual gives him a light, affectionate slap on the cheek. 'Imbecile.'

Morrel does not move but his face darkens and Pascual can see his blood pressure rocketing to crisis levels. Morrel seizes a fistful of Pascual's shirt. 'I said no fucking around.'

'You're the one fucking around. You grabbed the wrong man.'

Morrel's arm shoots out, his index finger stopping a scant two centimeters from the bewildered victim's nose. 'That's the man you followed out of the hotel yesterday. Don't tell me it's not.'

'I'm telling you. Superficially the same type, but not the same. He's thinner, for one thing. Absolutely not our man.'

'*Merde!*' Morrel plants both hands on Pascual's chest and shoves him violently backward. 'You lie to me, I'll tear your heart out. I'll cut your balls off.'

Pascual shoves back; before Morrel can swing his raised fist, Serge is between them. 'You'd fuck that up, too,' says Pascual over Serge's massive shoulder. 'You'd miss and cut off your dick.'

'Shut it.' Serge gives Pascual a more effective shove with one hand than Morrel could produce with two and Pascual finds himself on his ass, two meters back. Serge is leading Morrel away from the van and murmuring in soothing tones. Pascual rises and dusts himself off. Jacky has already dragged the hapless ersatz Najjar back into the van; Pierre is reaching for the overhead door.

'*Je dis merde!*' Morrel shoves away from Serge and circles, approaching Pascual the way the *bandillero* approaches the wary bull. 'He's lying. He made a deal with them. That's all lies, the miraculous rescue, the Swiss cop dropping out of the sky. He made a deal with them. They bought him and all he has to do is fail ever to identify Najjar.'

'It would have been a lot simpler just to kill me,' Pascual says in the wondering tone of a man explaining the obvious to a moron. 'I'm the last one who can identify him. Why would they bother to deal?'

Morrel halts, arms akimbo, steaming. 'Because now I stop looking. Now you've cleared him, so I let him go and he's off my list, permanently. That's one man I'll never bother again. The whole thing's a setup. That's why he was out in the open—he wanted us to see him.'

Serge is looking at Morrel with his head cocked to one side and his eyes narrowed. 'That would be working a bit too hard, wouldn't it?'

'I'm telling you, that man in there is Najjar.'

After a pause of three seconds Pascual says, 'Ah, well. I guess I can't fool you.' He fishes for a cigarette. 'Fine, then. I'll take my money now, shall I? A hundred thousand, wasn't it? Could I possibly have it in cash?'

Morrel rocks back on his heels. '*Putain.*'

'You don't believe it yourself.' Pascual blows smoke at him. 'You got the wrong man.'

Morrel turns on Serge. 'You got a better look at him than I did. How could you pick out the wrong man?'

'Don't you *fucking* blame this on me. You agreed on the ID.'

'He's a bloody double. I'd swear it's the same man.'

Pascual intervenes. 'The general stature and type fooled you. You saw him across a crowded lobby, moving fast. These things happen.'

Morrel shoots him a ferocious glance. 'I don't need *your* fucking comments.'

'Maybe he's the decoy,' says Serge. 'Maybe it's not coincidence.'

Morrel stares at the back of the van, and Pascual fears for the man inside. 'You could rake him over the coals,' he says. 'But while you do, the real Najjar is waiting for a plane. He's traveling on an Azerbaijani passport. Under the name Ardabil.'

Pascual finds the rabbit-from-hat effect immensely gratifying. 'How do you know?' says Morrel, staring.

'My Swiss cop. He's real.'

Morrel gapes for a moment longer and then he and Serge trade one of their soulful looks. *'Merde,'* says Morrel. He shoots Pascual a look. 'Does he know about us?'

'In general terms. I don't think he could have followed us out here without your seeing him, but he might be better than I think.'

'Oh, brilliant. Fucking brilliant,' says Serge, shooting a look back down the road.

Pascual smokes, serene and unruffled. 'I'm not sure what

his attitude toward kidnapping is, but I imagine in general it's frowned upon in this country. If I were you I'd handcuff that poor bastard in there to a fence post and make tracks for the airport.'

Morrel needs only a second to see the wisdom of Pascual's advice. 'You've got a lot of explaining to do,' he says, making for the van.

The recriminations carry them all the way to Kloten, after a half hour of precious time spent playing hide-and-seek in the hills to insure that in fact no rogue Swiss policemen are lurking on their tail. Serge appears to be taking things philosophically but Morrel has sunk into a mood of vicious moroseness. 'An Ecuadorian surgeon, God help us. Here for a medical conference. I didn't know they had enough money in Ecuador to send their doctors to conferences.'

'I didn't even know they had doctors in Ecuador,' says Serge. 'He seemed quite a reasonable fellow, considering.'

'He was just grateful we weren't going to kill him. Don't kid yourself. The minute we were out of sight he'll have started screaming his head off. If we're lucky nobody will find him till we're in the air.'

'I've got no papers,' says Pascual. 'They made off with Hugo Berger's wallet yesterday.'

'We've got your real papers. You'll get them when we're ready to step on the plane.'

'Fair enough.' Pascual looks out of the window as Serge navigates the approach to the terminal. 'You're not interested in talking to my policeman, then?'

A silence ensues while Serge pulls to the curb. 'Why?' says Morrel. 'So he can lecture us on our infringement of the sovereignty of the Swiss Confederation? Arrest us for kidnapping? Think again.'

'So he can tell you what he's learned about Daoud Najjar.'

'And what's he learned, beyond the name, which you've already given us?'

'I don't know. He's got a source at the hotel. Who knows what he might have picked up?'

'Look. You still haven't quite got it, have you? Secrecy is the prime consideration here. We don't want this hitting the papers, we don't want Najjar driven any further underground than he is. We start sharing with other services, soon we've got a continent-wide furor and front-page articles in *Le Monde* and the *Times*. You don't know how these things work.'

'You think Najjar's still blissfully unaware anyone's flushed him, do you?'

'What I think is that if we stop to talk to Swiss cops we'll still be talking to Swiss cops a week from now.'

Pascual shrugs. 'Maybe. On the other hand, this is not your average policeman. You'll notice that nothing of my little adventure yesterday has hit the papers.'

'Forget it. Our only move now is to catch the first flight out. I think we'll go for just about anything heading west. And from now on you *will* keep your mouth shut. This casually dropping Najjar's name to every stranger who gives you the time of day has got to stop.'

Serge goes to drop the rental car while Morrel leads Pascual toward the Air France ticket counter. Jacky and Pierre, charged with disposing of the van, are flying under separate cover. 'One step ahead of the lynch mob,' snarls Morrel under his breath. 'The story of my life.' Pascual trails just behind him, in a reflective mood. He has no desire to step on a plane with Morrel but he wants his papers back. 'You wait there,' Morrel says, pointing at a pillar. 'If you see Najjar go by, do come and tap me on the shoulder, won't you?'

Pascual drifts to the pillar and leans on it. Flight announcements echo through the terminal; people pass, oblivious of him and his concerns. He spots Couvet, sidling through the crowd toward him, a man on an aimless stroll through the airport. Couvet comes to rest two steps from Pascual and stands staring up at the departure board. 'Well, they're predictable,' he says, just audible over the hubbub. 'I thought you might wind up here. Though it took you long enough to get here.'

'How much did you see?' says Pascual, careful not to look at him.

'Very little. They caught me by surprise when they picked you up outside the hotel. But I got the license number, and I thought you might be heading this way. All I had to do was camp across the road and wait. Why the delay?'

'They wanted me to look at a fellow they thought was Najjar. He wasn't, of course. I can't tell you exactly where they left him because I don't know the roads, but he's unharmed. They're expecting me to fly out with them.'

'And you don't want to?'

Pascual gives it a moment's thought. He can see Morrel in the line at the ticket counter, casting glances his way.

'There's nothing in Paris for me but an empty room. And I'm starting to get interested in the parts they're not interested in. Of course, I have no papers and no money.'

'You and ten thousand others in Zurich. Well, I'm not sure if there's anything useful you can do here, either, but the interesting bits are getting more interesting by the minute.' Couvet begins to move away. 'I'm parked outside, down at the far end of the terminal, near the bus stop. Do you think he'll chase you?'

'He's just about reached the counter,' says Pascual, stooping to reach for his bag. 'I don't think he'll want to lose his place in the line. What do you mean about the interesting bits?'

Over his shoulder Couvet says, 'Somebody found a burned-out VW Beetle over toward Dietikon this morning. With three dead men in it.'

TWENTY

The smell still lingers in the copse nestled in a hollow a few hundred meters from the highway, somewhere between Spreitenbach and Neuenhof. Somebody has grilled meat here, none too appetizingly, over a bonfire of tires soaked in gasoline.

The VW is a blistered hulk resting in a blackened circle on the grass. The bodies have been removed, 'a bloody disgusting job' according to the tense Kantonspolizei inspector who appears to be in charge, and three technicians are peering, circling, measuring, probing at the wreck. Another man is on his hands and knees looking at marks on the earth, which bears scars of the movement of vehicles. In the trees above, the birds have recovered from whatever shock they may have sustained and have resumed singing. Couvet has slipped under the tape stretched across the dirt road at the entrance to the hollow, while Pascual and Djemila stand behind it, watching as he and the inspector confer, too softly to be overheard. Behind them on the road three police vehicles are parked and more officers huddle; occasionally a radio crackles with static.

Couvet paces back to them, deep in thought. He ducks under the tape and nods toward his car, down the lane. They follow him and go on past as he stops to take care of protocol, exchanging words with the officers waiting by the cars. There are handshakes; something is said in a jocular tone and there is a rumble of laughter, the universally recognizable laughter of men confronting horror and looking for a way to efface it. Pascual leans on Couvet's car, arms folded, and trades a long look with Djemila.

'No doubt about it,' says Couvet, opening his door. 'That's my Volkswagen.'

On the highway heading back to Zurich, Couvet breaks a long silence. 'Shots were heard about five this morning, a lot of them. There's a farm just over the hill and somebody called the police, even before they saw the flames. By the time they found the road the gas tank had gone up and there wasn't much left to identify. But they found a lot of shell casings on the ground and took a few slugs out of the wreckage.'

Which wreckage, human or mechanical, Pascual does not ask. 'At least they shot them first,' he says.

'Yes. Though probably not for humanitarian reasons. The car's registered to an Albanian national, here legally, who claims he lent it last week to his cousin, who's not. The cousin didn't come home last night, it appears, nor did the two friends with whom he was last seen. Also Albanian.'

'You called it right.'

'They make a wonderful labor pool, these illegals. Cheap, unscrupulous, damn near untraceable. And totally expendable, it would seem. They were probably told to wait in the car to collect their pay.'

'So where are the lorries?' says Djemila from the back seat.

'Ah, good question. A long way from here, probably. Wherever they are, they won't look the same as they did last night.'

'How do you know?'

'There was paint on the grass, flecks of paint from a spray gun. White, as if that's going to help much. All round the depressions left by the tires. They drove them here, gave them a quick paint job, probably slapped new plates on them, and then somebody else drove them away. And they got paid.'

Everybody thinks for a while as Couvet steers back into Zurich traffic. 'Why?' says Pascual. 'Why not keep them on to do the driving? Why hire them just to go a few kilometers?'

'My guess would be that they were hired mainly to load the lorries. And repaint them, of course. Whoever drove them away from here never looked inside, I'd bet. And would be under strict orders not to. They're probably locked up tight, in fact, and Boucherif or somebody he trusts was given the keys. That's the way I'd do it if I wanted to make absolutely sure that no word got out about what was being moved. You compartmentalize. The only fellows who know what's in the back of the truck don't survive to tell anybody.'

'Vicious.'

'Yes. The pirates on the bounding main used to do it that way, didn't they? The poor bastards who buried the treasure got a knife in the back and a shove into the hole to keep them quiet.'

'But that would mean Najjar doesn't even trust his own people.'

'Would you? How do you think he's survived this long? The people who guard him never learn enough about his business to pose a threat. The men who came after you last night were there to stand guard, and to kill the Albanians later, but if we ever pick them up, they won't be able to tell us what Najjar delivered to Boucherif. Nobody knows that but Najjar, Boucherif and whoever's higher up the totem pole than they are.'

Pascual scowls at the dreary streets passing by. 'Well, let's make some guesses. We're talking about two lorry loads, right? What can be loaded on two lorries that's worth enough to an Algerian general to go to all this trouble? I mean, you guessed weaponry. But what can you put on a lorry that will shift the balance of power inside Algeria?'

'These days? They've got some nice little missiles that will turn a skirmish around in a hurry. Shoulder-fired things that will bring down aircraft, blow up tanks. A lorry the size we saw could hold a couple of hundred of them. And what Mirakl could offer wouldn't necessarily be limited to the old Soviet arsenal, either. There are enough American Stingers floating around Afghanistan to neutralize the whole Algerian air force, I would imagine, and I think Mirakl probably has good contacts in Afghanistan. But that's just one guess. There are other possibilities I don't like to think about. Just about everything the Soviets had went up for sale when the Union collapsed, and I mean everything.'

'Christ, don't tell me Boucherif's going nuclear.'

Couvet shrugs. 'As I say, I don't like to think about it. But you have to.'

'But it's absurd,' says Djemila. 'Who does he think he's going to use it on?'

'He doesn't have to use it. Once India and Pakistan went nuclear and got away with it, everybody else who had ever thought about it pulled out the file again. If you're the man who can make your country a nuclear power, you've got instant respect at the next cabinet meeting. All he needs to produce is something they couldn't get legally. Fissile material, even an intact warhead—I don't know, I'm not an expert. And I'm just making wild guesses. But I'd really like to find those lorries.'

'They've got to be traceable. The hire firm will have serial numbers and so forth.'

'Sure. But we can't flag down every truck on every highway in Switzerland. They've had time to get out of the country by now anyway.'

'Won't they have to pass customs somewhere, at some point between here and Algeria?'

'I'd say it's well within Mirakl's capability to arrange for passage across a border, even ours. Actually, with their resources they could probably fly it out. One way or another I don't think we have much time.'

'So what next?'

'Well, I'm afraid I'm done with playing things close to the vest. I've got certain responsibilities as a citizen, even if I'm not a cop any longer. The deal I made to get us admitted to the murder site back there involved sitting down afterward for a frank talk with various concerned officials. Sometime today I'm going to have to tell them everything I know. And then they're going to want to talk to you. I'll give you time to contact your friends in Paris, but then you're going to have to come in and talk.'

Pascual shrugs, seeing a hundred thousand dollars fly out of the window. 'I'll come with you now if you want.'

'No, call Paris first. Professional courtesy. If I'm going to shoot their Najjar operation out of the water, they've got a right to know. You might just tell them that with their help we could actually catch the bastard this time.'

Due to a passion for privacy bred by long years underground, Pascual has always had a pronounced aversion to modern communications. He would rather walk for half an hour to confer face-to-face over a friendly drink than pick up a telephone, and he is always faintly surprised when the apparatus works. True to form, he is startled when the number he has always dialed in Paris to reach Morrel works equally well from a house in Zurich. 'You must have just got in from the airport,' he says.

'I damn near missed my flight because of you,' Morrel snarls. 'What the fuck possessed you?'

'I decided I wasn't quite finished here.'

A strangled curse comes over the wire. 'You're with your friendly Swiss copper, are you?'

'That's right.'

'Look, there's nothing he can do for us but torch the whole business. If you want even a distant chance at that hundred thousand dollars, you'll give him the slip and get back here as fast as you can. What's got into that booze-soaked sponge you call a brain?'

'There are other developments.'

'There always are, with you. What in God's name have you done now?'

'It's what Mirakl's done that might interest you. They killed three people last night.'

A second or two goes by. 'Who?'

'Three men who had just loaded a couple of lorries.'

This time the pause is longer. 'Tell me,' says Morrel finally.

'Mirakl's moving something, probably Boucherif's *quid pro quo.*'

'Where? Where are the lorries?'

'On the road somewhere. What do you care?'

'Najjar's probably with them, imbecile. You mean to tell me nobody's tracking them?'

'Couvet did a hell of a job just to find out they were moving. And he's got a lead on Najjar, too.'

'What kind of lead?'

'He's got a phone number that Najjar called from the hotel here. A residence, Couvet thinks.'

'Have you got the number?'

'Couvet's got it.'

'For Christ's sake. Get it from him.'

'Look, the point is, Couvet has to tell what he knows, and that means bringing me in.'

'Has he got you in custody?'

'No. But I'm going to talk.'

'*What?*' Morrel's shout crackles in Pascual's ear.

'I owe Couvet. Besides, there's been a homicide and I'm going to act like a responsible citizen is supposed to act.'

'When have you ever been a responsible citizen?' Morrel asks blisteringly. 'Listen. If you talk to the police, it's over. I've never heard of you. As far as I'm concerned, you're lying through your teeth, delusional. And there won't be any money, not a fucking cent. *And* I've still got your papers, so you're welcome to see how far your golden tongue will get you with the Swiss.'

Pascual holds the phone to his ear and frowns at the tabletop. 'I understand that secrecy gets to be a habit after a while,' he says. 'But I don't see that a Swiss police investigation poses that much of a threat to your operation. They understand a few things about international crime and they've kept secrets pretty well here for five hundred years.'

'You don't understand. Once you talk, it's an official matter and once it's an official matter the word spreads. Journalists detect movement, questions get asked. And Najjar burrows deeper underground.'

'He's already doing that. Listen, Couvet's not a breathless amateur. He's a professional and he'll be talking to professionals. The smart thing for you to do would be to sign on and try to retain some control. If I were you, I'd hop on the next plane back here and talk to Couvet. He's given me until tomorrow to stay unavailable.'

It seems to Pascual, blinking at Djemila across the room, that Morrel takes an eon to think it through. Somewhere outside where treetops ripple in the breeze, a clock in a tower chimes the hour and falls silent. Pascual is just about to ask if the Frenchman is still on the line when Morrel says, 'Stay by the phone. I'll ring you when I've got a flight. Do you think you can bring your cop to the airport? I don't want to go parading around Zurich if I can help it.'

'I imagine he would agree to that.'

'I'll have to come up with new papers, you realize that? I'm going through resources like water on this fucking operation.'

'They're bringing in the federals, of course,' says Couvet, his hand still resting on the telephone, a thoughtful frown on his face. 'Somebody's decided I was given too free a rein. I told them about your man from Paris coming in and I promised to bring him along if I can. Nobody's very happy with me, but I'm all they've got. If I don't bring you in by midnight they come looking. Though where they think they'll find me, I don't know. You can be sure I never told anyone about this place.'

'Can we keep it out of the papers, do you think?' says Pascual.

'For a while.' Couvet turns to Djemila. 'Though I'm afraid it's about time I gave my paymasters something for their money. I think somebody back in Algiers ought to know what Boucherif's up to. Those lorries are rolling. As for other considerations, I can't sort out good from bad down in Algeria, but I'm being paid to pass on what I learn about Algerians up to no good in Switzerland, and this is an Algerian up to no good, whatever side he's on in the end.'

Djemila looks at it for a while and says, 'Fair enough.'
Couvet turns back to Pascual. 'It will be interesting to see
just how tractable your friend Morrel is.'

'Friend would be stretching it.'

Couvet grunts softly. 'He's DGSE, is he?'

'That was my guess. Though if they want Najjar for the
Paris bombings he could be considered an internal matter
and thus the DST's business.'

'I'm not sure it really matters. The French are famously
informal in their institutional arrangements anyway. Well, it
will be interesting to talk to the man. If we can persuade him
to come with us, we'll all have an easier time in the next
couple of days.'

'Her, too?' says Pascual, nodding at Djemila, sitting in
silence across the table.

Couvet shakes his head. 'I think there's probably no need
for her to come in, unless she wants to.' He looks at Djemila
and says, 'You're our secretary, are you? You're keeping the
records?'

She shrugs. 'I'm writing the story.'

'Then you'll need this.' Couvet pulls a slip of paper from
his pocket and slides it across the table. 'That's the number
of Najjar's little love nest in Cyprus. Keep it safe.'

Djemila reads the number and refolds the paper. 'I'm not
sure I want it.'

'You've got it.' He smiles at her. 'I've got another job for
you, if you want something to do while we're talking to a lot
of suspicious bastards from the Federal Security Service.'

'What's the job?'

'You'd like to know what sort of commodity your General Boucherif just bought?'

'Of course.'

'Well, there may be one possible trail, though it's fairly cold. The inspector in charge of the investigation told me that when he saw the setup this morning, he thought it wasn't the first time he'd seen it. It rang a bell. Six years ago there was another killing that looked a lot like this one. Near Kloten, in fact, not too far from where we were last night.'

'What do you mean, it looked like this one?'

'I mean three immigrants wound up dead in a burned-out car.'

'That does ring a bell.'

'Actually, I should have said two immigrants wound up dead. The third went missing. These were Arabs. Two Lebanese and a Syrian. The Syrian and one of the Lebanese were found in the wreckage and identified. Witnesses said they'd been hired on a job the previous evening, just like our Albanians. And the witnesses said there'd been three of them. The dead Lebanese had a brother named Khaled Marwan who had been part of the party, but he was never found. Disappeared without a trace.'

Pascual works on it. 'You think he helped unload a lorry and somehow managed to escape when it was time to get paid.'

'It's just a guess. But it would fit.'

'And they never found him?'

'Well, that's an open question. The police were told the brothers had relatives in Paris, so they put in a call to the

Quai des Orfèvres, asking them to keep an eye out for Khaled, just in case. Nobody had high hopes of his turning up, but one never knows. Well, according to my contact, the French got in touch fairly quickly, saying they'd knocked on some doors and picked up a Khaled Marwan with a Lebanese passport and did we want to talk to him. But when somebody rang back to say yes, the word was, it was all a mistake. A case of impersonation, a different Lebanese who'd admitted buying the passport off the real Khaled Marwan in Besançon three days before. The story was, the real Marwan was anxious to disappear and the impostor needed new papers because he'd run into trouble with the law. And that was how it was left, with the French apologizing and promising to follow up the Besançon angle. And nothing ever happened.'

Djemila thinks it over, lighting a cigarette. 'What don't you like about it?' she says.

Couvet smiles. 'The logic. How did the French find their *faux* Khaled Marwan? The only lead we gave them was the relatives in Paris. Now, if you're not Khaled Marwan but you've just bought his papers, how is it that the police are able to find you by knocking up Khaled Marwan's cousin? Are you trying to tell me this total stranger just happened to take up with the real Khaled Marwan's family upon arriving in Paris? That's too much coincidence for me.'

Pascual scrabbles for a cigarette while everyone thinks. 'So they had the real one,' he says, shaking out the match.

'That would be my guess.'

'So what happened?'

'Probably Khaled Marwan lied. I have no doubt he was anxious to disappear, with Mirakl on his trail. He'd have told the police the first thing that came into his head, to avoid going back to Switzerland and appearing in court.'

Djemila frowns. 'But surely his passport picture would have established whether he was the real one or not.'

Couvet shrugs. 'Maybe not. Passport photos are notoriously unreliable, particularly if they're a few years out of date. I can see Marwan sticking to his story and letting them deport him or even doing a little time in jail rather than let them take him back to Zurich.'

'So where is he now?'

'Who knows? But it would be interesting to talk to him, because there's at least a chance he knows what's in the back of that truck. It would be worth a little digging. I don't know if anybody has the resources to track him down in Lebanon, but he could still be in Paris.'

'I'd call that a fairly long shot,' says Pascual.

'That's all we have,' says Couvet. 'The longest of long shots. Whatever's in that truck, it could be in Algiers by now.'

Djemila nods. 'I'll try to get a message to Rachid.'

Couvet checks his watch. 'Your man's due in in half an hour. Who's for a trip to the airport?'

Morrel comes off the 6:05 Air France flight from Paris looking like a man whose vacation has gone on three days too long. Under his sports jacket he wears a shirt open at the neck and he has a pair of sunglasses perched on top of his head. There is a distinctly haggard cast to his face.

'They've got to have a bar here somewhere,' he says. 'Let's go have a talk.'

The bar at the end of the concourse is comfortingly deserted. 'You have no official standing,' says Morrel as soon as they are seated with drinks in front of them. 'We looked you up. In fact, you're a bit of an outlaw.'

Undaunted, Couvet nods. 'I'm not claiming any official status. I'm a citizen of the Swiss Confederation who's assisting the police in an inquiry.'

'Agreed. What we're wondering is how we can persuade you that nobody benefits if you go on assisting them.'

'The law benefits. Justice even, maybe. In any event it's my duty, and that's one thing I ought to know about, if anybody does.'

Morrel nods heavily. 'Fine. I'm here to say one thing—this is the best chance we've had to rope in Daoud Najjar and it would be a pity to have it go up in smoke because a disgraced Swiss police inspector wanted to make some headlines.'

Couvet seems to have a faint smile on his face as he studies Morrel across the table. 'It's not going to go up in smoke because of that. If anything, you need more resources and this is one way to get them. What I'm wondering is why you're so keen not to have anyone else get to Najjar first.'

'You think that's what it's about, do you?'

Couvet nods. 'You're obviously desperate to get him before anyone else even finds out you're looking.'

It is Morrel's turn to smile. 'Oh? That's obvious, is it?'

'Yes. I'm wondering if Najjar is really ever intended to see the inside of a French jail.'

Soft music meanders behind the hum of conversation; a cooing voice cuts in on the loudspeaker to invite passengers to board a flight to Rome. Morrel's smile fades and he says, 'It is good fun to speculate, isn't it?'

'Great fun.'

'And who would weep for him?'

Couvet shrugs. 'Not me. But the point is, I can't hide what I know any longer. An inquiry has to take place. Even an intelligence officer has to understand what it is to be subject to the laws of a country, right?'

Morrel stares at him across the table, and then begins to nod, just perceptibly. He looks wrung out and almost comically sad, a man admitting he has lost all his money at the poker table. 'Who are we dealing with?' he says.

'Some federal cloak-and-dagger types from Bern. It should all be nice and civil. A collegial atmosphere. And if you can make a good case for it they'll play it very close to the vest. They're good at that.'

Morrel nods finally. 'Well, then. Let's go talk to your cloak-and-dagger men.' He looks at Pascual and reaches inside his jacket. 'Here. You'll be needing this if we're going legitimate. I'm certainly not going to lie for you.' He slides Pascual's Spanish passport across the table, the one that was handed to him as a reward for his betrayal in 1989.

Pascual hefts the comfortably bulky leather case, the emblem of the Spanish state embossed in gold on the cover, with more enthusiasm than he would have ever thought a legitimate passport could elicit. He opens it, sees his familiar morose visage in the photo, sees the name Pascual March inscribed. He feels as if someone has handed him back his life. He meets Morrel's gaze and says, 'The play acting's over then, is it?'

'Don't worry, you'll still be in demand. You're still the only one who can fill the role.' Morrel drains his glass.

Couvet's car is in the multilevel parking garage across the road from the terminal. He slows as he approaches the automatic barrier at the exit, fishing for coins in his shirt pocket. From the rear seat Pascual has an excellent view of the back of Couvet's head, and he sees it fly into crimson fragments as the point-blank shots shatter the driver's side window; the noise is atrocious. Pascual is aware too late that the movement in the corner of his eye was a figure approaching the car much too fast; after a half second of shock, watching what is left of Couvet's head loll sideways, he pitches over on the seat to his right, scrabbling for the handle of the door. He will not be shot sitting helpless in a car. The car has rolled through the barrier, the wooden arm giving way with a crack; now it drifts into a column and jolts to a halt. Pascual is frozen by the sound of steps running around the back of the car, running toward the door he is reaching for. He jerks back across to the left side of the car, as far as his convulsing muscles will take him from that gun. He can see the man now, a black ski mask covering his face, and as he finds the handle of this door he can see Morrel with his own door open but no place to go, blocked by Couvet's body from going left and able only to watch as the masked man arrives. Pascual's door gives and he seems to be falling backward in slow motion as Morrel raises his hands and has time to say

'*Salaud*!' before the automatic kicks him back across the seat on to Couvet, flecking the windshield red.

Pascual lands hard on a shoulder but flies, skims birdlike and weightless over the concrete; he will never be able to say just how he got so far from the car so fast. All he knows is that he finds himself belly to the ground, looking past tires at feet that are running away from him, disappearing toward the far side of the multistory. When Pascual finally tumbles to the fact that he is not going to die like Couvet, like Morrel, he is up and running himself, up the exit ramp and out into the night.

TWENTY-ONE

'Who knew?' says Pascual. He steers Djemila by an elbow, hustling her from the tram stop toward the escalator down to the shopping complex beneath the Bahnhofplatz. Trams and autos ply the square; the pavements are crowded, the populace hitting the streets as the light fades. 'Who knew Couvet was going to the airport?'

At the bottom of the escalator, jostled by the crowd, Djemila halts, pulling her arm free. So far she has done just what he told her to do in his breathless phone call from the airport: grab what you can and get out. Now, recovering from shock, she is beginning to resist his panic. 'Besides you, Couvet and Morrel?' she says. 'I did.'

'And I don't think you set us up. So who's left?'

'I don't know.'

'I'll tell you who's left. The police.'

He can feel the tremor that runs through her. 'Good God. Not here. Don't tell me the Swiss police kill, too, don't tell me that.'

Pascual shakes his head, pulling her on. He scans the

brightly lit underground mall, looking for policemen, looking for gunmen in ski masks, looking for something to erase the vision of Couvet's head bursting all over the car. 'I don't think the police killed them. I think some policeman talked to somebody he shouldn't have. I think Mirakl's better connected in this town than we thought. Either that or somebody knew about the house and followed us. Either way, it's time to run. There will be trains to Basel at least, if not all the way to Paris. You're better off stranded in Basel than here.'

'I'm not sure I have enough money to buy you a ticket.'

'I'm not going with you. The station would be the first place I'd cover if I were a cop. And they may be looking for both of us. So we separate. They shouldn't have anything more than a description. I don't think Couvet would have given them your name. In any event there's not much in the way of frontier controls at Basel.'

'But what about you?'

'I'll hitch.'

'At this hour of the night?'

'In the morning. Tonight I find someplace to hide. I've slept in parks before.'

They are approaching the escalator that leads up to the station hall. Djemila pulls him aside, gripping his arm. He gapes at her. 'You're a wreck,' she says. 'Get a grip on yourself.'

'It was bloody awful. You can't imagine.'

'Yes, I can.'

Pascual stares at her and gropes for control, ashamed. 'All right.' He exhales, becomes conscious of the pounding of his heart. 'All right, I'm fine.' Her eyes hold his; he can see that she is shaken herself; yet where does she find this composure?

'So what happens in Paris?' she says quietly.

Pascual straightens, scans, takes a deep breath. There is a bar over there, cheerfully lit and full of people who have never seen men die by gunfire; he wants a drink desperately. 'I don't know,' he says. 'First I see who answers the telephone, I suppose.'

'Do you think there's going to be any operation left?'

'Who the hell knows?'

'You could get out now. I'm not going to tell anyone where to look for you.'

'Get out?'

'Go home. It never was your fight, was it?'

Pascual studies her face, looking for a sign. Djemila's gaze is habitually so sad that nuances are difficult to see. 'You want me to go?'

'No.'

'Then I'll see you in Paris.'

She nods. `You want that phone number in Cyprus?'

It takes him a second to think what she is talking about. 'I don't want to know anything anyone else might want. If I were you I'd throw it away.'

'Too late. I've already memorized it.'

He sighs. 'Do us all a favor. Do your best to forget it.'

Pascual creeps into the Parisian *banlieue* with the setting sun in his face, clothes clinging nastily to greasy skin and head throbbing in sympathy with the ill-tuned engine. The driver of the van has lapsed into a sullen silence, all conversational avenues exhausted. Pascual has been only intermittently conscious on the long succession of rides across the plains of northeastern France, finally dozing after his sleepless night on the streets of Zurich. 'Hop out, then,' says the driver abruptly. 'I've got to get on the *Périphérique* up ahead. There's the Métro round about here somewhere.'

Pascual drifts along crowded pavements. The heat is easing and lights are coming on, shops closing and a more tractable Paris beginning to stir as evening descends. Pascual is dazed, not quite connecting. The days in Zurich could be a hallucination. He finds a telephone.

This time the magic number conjures up Serge. 'Where are you?' he growls, skipping the niceties.

'In Paris. You've heard about Morrel?'

'Heard? It's turned this fucking place upside down. Were you there?'

'I was there. I damn near died with the others.'

'Where are you now?'

'Métro Porte de Montreuil. Boulevard Davout.'

'Don't move. I'll be there in half an hour. Which side of the street?'

Serge listens as he drives, shoving through the traffic like a man through a crowded barroom, hunched over the wheel as always. Periodic grunts, an occasional question show he is listening. 'Could you give a description of the shooter?' he says, wrestling with the gearshift. Pascual watches faces drift by on the pavement.

'He was tall. He had a mask on. He was quick on his feet. Do you think that's going to help?'

Serge snorts with laughter. 'I think the shooter's probably back in Russia by now. But you never know. If you could describe him we might get a shot at him someday.'

'I could describe the gun. I got a good look at that.'

'The word is, they've already found the gun, in the parking garage. No prints, of course. A Glock. They're trying to trace it but they won't have any luck. Did he suffer?'

'Who, Morrel? I don't think he had time. He had a bad couple of seconds seeing it coming and then it was over.'

Serge waits a beat or two and says, 'And why didn't you die, too?'

'Sheer luck, I think. I think Couvet was the priority, which is why he went first. After that, I went for the right-hand door, which brought the bastard around to that side. When he got there Morrel was the obvious target because he'd gotten his door open. And he just didn't have time to get me because I went back out the other side. If I'd gotten my door open first maybe Morrel would have survived.'

Serge grunts again, a sound of disgust. 'Fifteen years we worked together.' Pascual waits; he has no condolences to offer. 'Listen,' says Serge. 'Morrel told me before he left that you had a lead.'

'Yes. Najjar made a call to Cyprus.'

'You've got the number?'

Pascual does not answer immediately. Deny it and he will only send Serge in other directions, he sees in time. 'I've got it.'

'We've got to have it, *mon gar*. They've brought the big guns in on this. Now that Morrel's dead the powers that be want blood. You help us bag Najjar and they'll throw in a medal or two on top of the money.'

Pascual muses. 'They want blood, do they?'

'Wouldn't you?'

After a pause Pascual says, 'There's not going to be any trial, is there?'

Serge gives him a sharp sideways glance. 'I was speaking figuratively.'

'Were you? I wonder. Couvet practically accused Morrel of wanting Najjar dead and didn't get what I'd call a denial. Couvet thought perhaps Najjar knew too much about certain areas of French foreign policy that are better left unexamined.'

Serge drives for a time in silence. 'And what do you care?' he says finally.

An excellent question, thinks Pascual. 'If Najjar simply disappears, who's going to explain what the deal with Boucherif is all about? Or do you plan to arrest Boucherif next?'

Serge bullies his way through an intersection and says, '*Écoute*. You know what I am? I'm a fucking mechanic, that's all. Morrel was the brains of the outfit. I don't know Najjar from fucking Napoleon myself. I just do what I'm told. If they want Najjar, I go and get Najjar. If they tell me dead or alive, I figure that just makes my job easier. Boucherif, nobody mentioned him. That's where I stand. I've been told to find Najjar and that's why you're going to bring that number in to the people that give me my orders.'

Pascual shrugs. 'Now here's where I stand. If I thought I was performing a public service I might be willing to go back and give Najjar's support staff another shot at me. But a public service would be putting him on trial and pasting details of his deal with Boucherif and whatever other deals he's swung on the front page of every paper in Europe. And I don't think that's what your bosses have in mind.'

'You, perform a public service? That's a pretty good one, I have to say. Why don't you think about the money? Not enough for you? I could probably get them to toss in a little more.'

Pascual takes a deep breath; here is the edge of the cliff, the Rubicon, the end of the gangplank, all in the guise of the red light that even Serge must halt for. '*Désolé*. I think I'm going to find somebody who shares my enthusiasm for a public trial, thank you very much.' The car slows, the rear end of a BMW looming ahead.

Serge gives him a look and shakes his head. 'I've got a sneaking feeling this is your Arab *nana* talking. She's really got her hooks into you, hasn't she?'

'She's not involved, not anymore.'

'I hope not. I'd stay clear of her if I were you. Look, personally I don't care. You're just a portable object to me. Next week they give me another job. But I don't think you'll have much fun debating ethics with the people I report to. Pick a fight with those people? You've got to be out of your mind.'

'No doubt,' says Pascual, one hand on the door lever and the other on the grip of his bag. 'That's what everyone tells me. *Adieu*.' He has one foot on the pavement before Serge's mouth can open.

The evening air is a faceful of fetid breath after the air-conditioned interior of the car. 'They'll kill you,' he hears Serge call as he slams the door and trots away.

There is a wait before Djemila comes to the phone. Pascual can hear voices, faintly: television and querulous children, too many people in a small apartment. 'I told them to go fuck themselves,' Pascual says. 'Or words to that effect.'

'Why?'

'Because if the French get him it ends there. They don't give a damn about Boucherif.'

There is a brief silence and she says, 'What about your money?'

'I never quite believed in it anyway.'

Another few seconds pass. 'So are we ready to talk to the police?'

'The French police? I have a feeling that that's just a conduit right back to Morrel's people, and that's the end of the story. I've been warned off you, by the way. This might be a good time to keep your head down. They don't want their intentions showing up in the press.'

'So what now?'

'Well, there's one party that will go after Najjar in earnest. And take a shot at finding out what Boucherif's up to as well.'

'Who's that?'

'The Israelis.'

Silence. Djemila is not happy and Pascual cannot blame her. *Évoluée* or not, for an Arab the Israelis come with a lot of baggage. 'Why the Israelis?' she says.

'Because they're the ones who will work hardest to get him. Because they have long memories and they don't fool around with the niceties. That's what we need now.'

Silence. 'They'll kill him just as fast as the French would.'

'Not until they get to the bottom of the Boucherif deal. That, they have to take seriously.'

'Maybe.'

'And I'll set conditions. You'll be my insurance. If Najjar dies, or me for that matter, you publish the whole story. You'll be the equivalent of a sealed letter to my lawyer.'

'How fast does all this happen?'

'As soon as I can convince them I have the goods. I don't know how long it will take. They'll need time to trace the number, do reconnaissance, set things up. But I think they'll move fast.'

At the other end of the wire Pascual hears a child crying, somebody scolding in Arabic. Time passes, eons of it, and Djemila says, 'All right, then. You'll need the number. Have you got a pencil with you?'

Pascual knows the location of the Embassy of Israel well; it was in demonstrations here in the Avenue Matignon that he began to work his sense of outrage to the pitch that finally sent him off on his six-year sojourn in hell. In the fading light of a Paris evening the embassy squats silent and innocuous behind its concrete blast barriers.

He wants neither to be shot nor to attract much attention, but he has no time for telephones and business hours. Having made sure on Métro and on foot that nobody is following him he crosses the avenue and approaches the black-uniformed French police guards clustered at the barricaded entrance to the side street where the entrance lies. They stiffen professionally as he nears. 'I need to talk to the Mossad,' he says.

This sergeant in his *képi* has heard it all before; his chin rises as he examines Pascual from the ground up. 'The embassy is closed,' he says.

'The Mossad never closes. What I have to say, they'll want to hear. All you have to do is take in a message.'

The sergeant looks at it from every angle as his men, roused from boredom, put thumbs to safeties and shift their feet, jackals spotting a wounded antelope. 'Identification,' he says.

Pascual's Spanish passport absorbs him for a full minute before he hands it back. 'And the message?' he says.

'Tell them,' Pascual says, 'I can take them to Daoud Najjar.'

Pascual awakes confused, with light coming in around the shutters and voices in the flat. He has slept badly, bathed in sweat, and for a moment he thinks he is still deep underground, with nothing but the road ahead and policemen close behind. Then he remembers the ride from the embassy, bracketed by two sturdy Israelis in the back seat of a Renault sedan. He was driven swiftly up the rue Saint-Lazare past the station and into the streets behind it, a catalogue of European cities: Londres, Athènes, Milan, Liège. He thinks it was the rue de Bucarest where the car halted. The flat is small, nearly bare, with few signs of occupancy.

His interrogation takes place at the same table where he is given coffee and bread, his hair still wet from a shower, uncomfortable in yesterday's clothes, his bag having disappeared at the embassy last night. The man who put him through the wringer last night at the embassy is there, a hard-eyed man with tightly waved brown hair, thick forearms and bad French. This morning he has brought someone new, a pit bull of a man with iron-grey hair and slightly better French. 'The Spanish appear to find you rather tiresome,' the new man says, sliding Pascual's passport across the table. 'They claim you were foisted on them by the Americans.'

'That's about what happened,' says Pascual. 'A Spanish passport was my reward for talking. What the Spanish got out of it I don't know.'

'And where does Daoud Najjar come in?'

'The French want him. They came to me because I worked with him.'

'The French?' Incredulous, the Israeli vents a laugh. 'The French let him go. Twice.'

'Well, they want him now. That's why I was brought in. Apparently I'm the last man on earth who can identify him.'

A look is exchanged between the two Israelis. 'If they want him now,' says the pit bull thoughtfully, 'something has changed.'

'I think they want to kill him,' says Pascual.

The pit bull nods and says, 'That would make sense. Najjar would know far too much about certain episodes. Somebody's tying up loose ends.'

The man from the embassy is looking puzzled. 'Why did you come to us?'

'Because I thought you might just possibly want to put Najjar on trial for the killing of those two Israelis in Malta in nineteen eighty-five. Or maybe the bombing in Buenos Aires. Most of all, though, because there's a good possibility he's supplying advanced weaponry to the Algerians, and the last time I looked, Algeria hadn't exactly gotten on board the peace process.'

The looks passing between the two Mossad officers are becoming more skeptical. 'What kind of advanced weaponry?'

'I don't know. Something that came out of Russia and can be loaded on a lorry. Najjar works for a Russian outfit called Mirakl that's run by a man named Kovalenko. It has—'

'I know Mirakl. How do you know it can be loaded on a lorry?'

'I saw the lorry. Two of them in fact.'

'But not the contents?'

'No, I don't think they'd have stood for that. A glimpse of the lorries nearly got me killed. You heard about the two men killed at Zurich airport yesterday? One of them was a Swiss cop who was interested in the Algerians and the other was a French intelligence officer who was interested in Najjar. I was the third man in the car and I was lucky to get away.'

'There was no mention of a third man.'

'Fear gives you wings.'

The Israeli makes a skeptical noise and studies him for a few seconds. 'You didn't really answer my question,' he says. 'Why didn't you go on cooperating with the French?'

'Besides the fact that they're hopeless incompetents?

Because they want Najjar dead and buried. They're not interested in the deal with the Algerians or anything else except shutting him up. I'd rather see him in a courtroom, answering questions.'

This, Pascual sees, evokes the same incredulity as the news of renewed French zeal. 'You've gone very public-spirited in your old age,' says the pit bull.

Pascual has long since resigned himself to the fact that people will believe in fairies before they will believe in a genuine change of heart. Dispirited, he says, 'What do you care what my motives are? For you the only question is whether I'm telling the truth. Step number one might be to check out the lead I'm offering you.'

The Israeli peers at him. 'I *always* care about motivation because in my business there are a lot of professional liars.' He waits a beat. 'How much did the French offer you for your cooperation?'

Pascual sees where things are heading. 'That's your take on it, is it? Tell you what, I'll settle for expenses. Feed me, lodge me for the duration of the operation, get me back to Spain. Throw in a thousand dollars if it gratifies your cynicism. I'm trying to give you Najjar because I don't like him. I never did, and I like him even less now that I'm out of the business.'

There is a slightly embarrassed silence. 'Just out of curiosity,' says the embassy man, with an amused light in his eye, 'How do you know we're not going to kill him ourselves?'

'I thought about that. You've got a pretty solid track record in that regard. But this time I think you'll have to talk to the man first. If he and Kovalenko have swung something big with Algeria, that's got to make you nervous. I don't care if the country's a mess right now. Whoever wins, ask yourself if you want to take chances with somebody over there getting his hands on, say, a couple of warheads you could slap on a cut-rate North Korean rocket.'

After a moment the pit bull says, 'A phone number and a likely sounding name make a lead but they don't make a case. It's going to take time to check all this out and more time to mount an operation if we decide to. I'm afraid we can't have you running around Paris while all that's going on.'

'Fair enough.'

'I don't think at this stage we'd go as far as flying you out to our part of the world. For now we'll just keep you on ice. We'll probably move you somewhere a little more comfortable, but you should be prepared to be immobile and incommunicado for a while.'

With a sinking feeling Pascual says, 'What's awhile?'

'As long as it takes.'

Pascual nods once. 'Of course. Forgive me, stupid question.'

TWENTY-TWO

Pascual is well-suited to leisure by temperament and long habit, but even he has reached his limits. There is only so much a man can read, television is excruciating and the solitary consumption of alcohol has never appealed to him. After six days he has begun to wish for turmoil and disruption. Instead he gets a daily ramble in the Bois de Boulogne, under carefully disguised supervision. Once he mastered the art of waiting out confinement, but now the thought of Djemila at the other end of a telephone wire he is not allowed to approach troubles his sleep. From the second-floor window of this gloomy house in Neuilly he can see the Eiffel Tower beyond treetops, no more real than a print on the wall.

'You know what those things are doing to your lungs?'

'No.' Pascual blows smoke over his shoulder at the pretty girl who somebody decided would make better company for him than the usual cauliflower-eared toughs. 'Why don't you tell me?'

'They're turning them black. Does that sound like a good idea to you?' Her name is Rachel and she speaks voluble

French with the faintest undertone of something else, Hebrew perhaps. She has glowing brown skin, much in evidence in her shorts and sleeveless top, and raven hair. Pascual suspects that her true role, more than keeping him supplied with reading matter and fresh fruit, is to collect stray confidences.

'It sounds like idiocy to me. Maybe you can tell me why I do it.'

'Because you saw too many Bogart movies as a child.' She jerks a thumb toward the door. 'There's somebody to see you downstairs.'

Pascual has been questioned so often and so thoroughly this week that it has ceased to offer any hope of novelty. He flips the cigarette out of the open window into a flower bed. 'Somebody new? Or are they lining up for a second look at the prize catch?'

'This one, I think, has seen you before,' Rachel says.

Dan has not changed. Past a certain point further aging is not possible, it seems; only death can follow. And yet Dan looks as if death could not touch him; he looks as if he were carved from oak and well seasoned, impervious to weather and time.

'I have good news for you,' he says.

'What's that?'

'They've decided you're telling the truth.'

Pascual stares back at him. 'I'm honored.'

'There was some lively discussion when you popped up, you know. Opinion was evenly split between those who think you earned your thirty pieces of silver back in eighty-nine and those who think you ought to be rotting in jail right now.' Somewhere early on Dan was taught the Queen's English, but certain of his vowels still hint at an origin east of the Oder.

Pascual shrugs. He is obscurely glad to see the old terrorist hunter, intimidating though he finds him. Rachel has brought them tea and gone away again, and they sit facing each other across a table in a room with a parquet floor. 'Funny, I never got the silver.'

'I think maybe your freedom was supposed to suffice.'

'I've never complained.'

'No, and you certainly delivered the goods. But it does raise the question, what makes a man turn like that? How does a man who plotted with Abu Yussef to kill Jews wind up here, offering to identify him for us? There are those who wonder if there couldn't be more turns in store.'

'All they have to do is take nothing I say on faith and keep me on a very short leash. I'm a very simple proposition, really.'

'That's what I told them. And now it seems they've corroborated your story.'

'They've found him?'

'Maybe.' Black eyes glint deep in the seamed face. 'You know where Kyrenia is?'

'On the north coast somewhere, isn't it?'

'That's right.'

'Is that where Najjar is?'

'So it seems. The telephone number belongs to a villa on the coast just to the west of Kyrenia. There's a sizeable house with the terrace overlooking the sea, a couple of out-buildings. He's got some fancy cars in a big garage and a small staff, housekeeper and gardener and people like that. Mr. Halabi apparently values his privacy. It's taken some very sharp work to come up with this. There were several layers of people to bribe, and bribe discreetly.'

'No cooperation from the locals?'

Dan laughs, a brief rumble. 'The locals are the Turkish mini-state, which nobody but their big brothers in Ankara recognizes. Najjar knows nobody's going to extradite him from there. He's probably bought himself some pretty good protection. But we've got some resources, too. Take a look at these.' He slides a half dozen or so large-format black-and-white photographs across the table.

The photos are evidently taken from a great distance, with the grainy quality of blow-ups. In the first one a man is lounging on a faraway terrace, feet up and cell phone to his ear. He wears a bathing suit and slippers and sunglasses and he could be Daoud Najjar or he could be any of a million men on earth. In another picture a woman in a short dress with long blond hair has joined him and sits on the side of a chaise longue holding a drink and leaning toward him. In a third the man appears without sunglasses, in sports shirt and slacks, making for a car parked on a gravel drive, with two other men in tow. This profile is familiar but the image too indistinct for certainty. Pascual goes slowly through the stack of photos and slides them back toward Dan. 'I'd say it's him, but I wouldn't send the Phantoms in on the strength of these photos. I'd have to get a lot closer to be sure.'

'Oh, you will, don't worry,' says Dan. 'And there won't be any bombers involved.'

Pascual nods. 'So what's the drill? Parachute? Submarine? I never was much of a swimmer.'

'You're not going near the place. Once we've got him we'll fly you in to have a look at him.'

Pascual's heart sinks. There will be no quick end to this, he sees. 'He's likely to be well guarded.'

'Oh, we're aware of that. We'll do our best to get the drop on them, but you never can tell. It's always a bit sticky with civilians about. The boys on the ground are understandably concerned about the young lady, for example. From what they could see through their fancy optical devices, she's young and blond and very satisfactory in all respects. They'll do their best not to damage her.'

Pascual feels things knotting in his belly; not for the first time he wonders if he has started something he will regret. He can hear Djemila, softly saying *they'll kill him*. 'When do you go?' he says.

'In a couple of days. It takes time to set these things up properly. There are a lot of logistics involved.'

Pascual sits nodding slowly. 'So I just sit and wait.'

'That's right.' Dan peers at him across the table. 'Have you been keeping up with events in Switzerland?'

'As much as I can. The press reports are sketchy.'

'Yes, aren't they? The Swiss are good at keeping their cards hidden. But they're clearly desperate to find you, the mysterious third man. Your ex-policeman had told them all about you, apparently.'

'I'm surprised they haven't come up with a name for Morrel yet.'

'They always know more than they say. And I'd bet your cop told them all about Mirakl and Najjar as well, though so far it hasn't come out in the press. Speculation is leaning heavily toward Algeria.'

'Ultimately that's what it's all about, I think. That's what you have to sweat out of Najjar when you get him.'

'We'll do our best.' The old man sips tea. 'You could disappear, you know,' Dan says. 'You're asking for trouble if you go back to Barcelona.'

Pascual muses. 'It's my home. You reach a point where you need an anchorage.'

'This is the second time someone's come to get you.'

Pascual considers. 'I'm not running.'

A smile strains all the creases in the old leathery face. 'Because, of course, they have to find you in order for you to have a chance to atone.'

Time passes. 'Maybe.'

'This will count, you know.'

'What do you mean?'

'I mean, if we get Daoud Najjar, you will have done a good thing.'

Pascual shoves his teacup away, feeling for satisfaction and not finding any. 'Well, it's a start, maybe,' he says.

'One good thing,' Dan says. 'That's one more than a lot of people can claim.'

'That's a living legend that just walked out of here,' says

Rachel. 'Did you see where he was missing those fingers? He lost them in hand-to-hand combat with the Arab Legion in nineteen forty-eight. A walking history lesson, that old man.'

'He's a character,' says Pascual absently, pacing across the room. He wants to hit something, smash glass, run screaming down the street. Instead he winds up standing face-to-face with Rachel, who leans in the doorway with her arms folded, long brown limbs ending in bare feet.

'Bored?' she says. Her lips are parted just enough to show perfect shining teeth; her eyes are huge and very dark. Her stance, her voice, her face are suddenly blinking the word 'available' in bright red neon. Pascual has been wondering when it would come to this.

Stray confidences, yes, but also a test, he thinks. A man who hates Jews will be troubled by Jewish beauty. Pascual knows this from experience; his conception of Israel as the seat of evil was always most vulnerable to an Israeli girl with a nice laugh or a short skirt. One step on his long recovery, he recalls, was the dawning of an innocent lust for a dark-eyed corporal who manned the desk at the military institute where much of his debriefing took place. He runs the back of a finger down Rachel's cheek. 'You're very pretty,' he says.

She slides her arms about his waist. 'Everybody's gone out for the evening,' she murmurs.

Pascual has lived in close proximity to Rachel for a week without once wondering what it would be like to bed her. Instead he has wondered who Rachel is, what a girl this young has done to reach this position in the security services, what kind of life a pretty girl like this wants and can expect. Now the pretty girl is presenting him with a dilemma. His hand drops away from her face.

'I have two problems,' he says.

Her face clouds slightly. 'What?'

'One, I have a feeling this is part of your job, and two, there's somebody else.'

She releases him and sags away. The look she gives him is utterly frank but not unfriendly. 'I'll forgive you for the first suggestion if you'll tell me who the somebody else is,' she says.

Pascual has not stopped thinking of Djemila for an hour. He finds he wants badly to tell Rachel all about her and realizes that the people who are running this show know exactly what they are doing.

'Just a woman,' he says, moving away.

Pascual is awakened early after a poor night's sleep by unaccustomed commotion. He props himself up on an elbow, listening to voices and the creaking of distant doors. When the knock sounds he is already sitting on the side of the bed, feet on the tiles. 'You're wanted downstairs,' says Rachel through the door. 'Things are happening.'

Downstairs, Dan and the pit bull from the embassy are standing with heads close together, in conference. When Pascual pads in barefoot they wave him to a chair. 'What's going on?' he says.

Dan wanders toward him, hands in his pockets. 'There's been a little hitch in the plans.'

Pascual rubs sleep out of his eyes. 'Somebody got caught?'

'Oh, no. We're too careful for that.' Dan halts a couple of steps away. 'They're all dead,' he says, rocking on his heels. The look he gives Pascual is grim but somehow amused.

'Who's dead?'

'Everybody in the place. That's the word anyway. Turkish Cypriot radio is calling it a slaughterhouse.'

Pascual stares at him for a long moment. 'Najjar, too?' he says.

'Nothing is confirmed. The radio says four men and two women are dead, all shot.'

Pascual sinks into an armchair. 'When?'

'Last night. What little we've got so far from our people said the place was overrun with police vehicles and ambulances, lit up like a circus. It's going to take us some time to get solid information.'

From the kitchen comes the sound of running water. 'Who?' says Pascual.

Dan vents a brief laugh. 'We were hoping you could enlighten us.'

'Why me?'

Dan looms over him, a faint detached smile in place. 'Somebody talked, didn't they? Had to.'

Pascual peers up at him. 'It wasn't me.'

'Never said it was.' Dan shakes his head, making for the kitchen. 'Can I get you some coffee? We've got things to talk about.'

Dan sits smoking at the far end of the table, watching the proceedings without comment, the elder statesman. 'These

are hot off the fax,' says the pit bull. 'Our people in Kyrenia
got them from the police, God knows how. The latest word
is there were at least three shooters, and they came and
went by boat because there are no traces of strange cars.
Shots were heard by a neighbor down the road about one in
the morning. By the time the first officers got there the
bodies were cooling.'

The pictures get passed down the table to Pascual.
Mercifully they are black-and-white, the vast pools of blood
only dark blotches on shades of grey. There are bodies
everywhere, sprawling half out of bed, face up on a tile floor
with ankles haphazardly crossed, crumpled at the bottom of
a stairway. An old woman sits in the closet where the killers
found her, eyes closed, mouth open, the front of her night-
dress soaked with blood. Everybody but the blond is in night
attire, pajama bottoms only on the athletic young man
whose automatic lies ten centimeters from his inert hand,
old-fashioned flannels on this round little man at the foot of
the stairs. The blond, it seems, slept in the nude. The head-
board of the double bed shows holes and splotches from the
exit wounds in her back; there are smear marks where she
slid along it to topple on to the floor. The long blond hair
hides her face. Pascual tosses the photos into the middle of
the table. 'Najjar's not there.'

'You're absolutely sure? This fellow with the jaw shot
away couldn't be him?'

'Too much hair. And muscle. That's a much younger man.'

The pit bull gathers the photos and squares the edges carefully. 'Well, then. Somebody got in and killed two bodyguards,

the mistress, the cook and her husband, even the poor god-damn gardener, but they didn't get Najjar.'

'Maybe they did,' Pascual ventures.

'Ah. Bravo. You're on the same page with the rest of us. Maybe they did.'

'But who?' says Dan.

'And why?'

'And where is he now?'

Pascual guesses that this sudden collegial give-and-take is staged for his benefit. He waits a beat or two and says, 'And how did they find him?'

Dan is smiling. 'That's the real question, isn't it?'

'And you're waiting for me to answer it, aren't you?'

'Any thoughts you may have would be greatly appreciated.'

'The only thoughts I had I've already given you.'

'All right, I'm inclined to agree with you. It wasn't her.' Dan flaps a hand in dismissal. 'I think you're right. If they'd got to her, she wouldn't be around to answer the phone.'

Pascual can still hear Djemila's voice in his ear, surprise and then alarm coming through the sleep-thickened tones, the grumbling of her long-suffering brother receding in the background. No, she said. Nothing. Nobody has bothered me. Of course not, who would I have given it to? And where the hell are you anyway?

'Of course,' says the pit bull, 'if she's cooperating with them, would she admit it?'

'Why the hell would she cooperate with them?' Pascual snaps. 'The whole point is that they want to cover the whole thing up and she wants it out in the open. They're on opposite sides. And in any event they have no reason to think she has the number. They don't even know she was in Switzerland with me.'

Silence reigns while looks are traded between the professionals. 'So who?' Dan says finally.

'My money would be on the Swiss,' says Pascual. 'Couvet must have given them everything. Somebody in Bern talked to somebody in Paris.'

'Hang on, you've been telling us the Swiss sold Couvet and Morrel out to the Russians. Now they're in bed with the French? I don't get it.'

'I don't get it either. I'm just trying to trace how word got out. The only place for a leak that I can see is in Switzerland. Couvet gave the whole thing to somebody there. What happened after that, I don't know. Frankly, I'd never count out Najjar's employers. Shooting everyone from the girlfriend down to the cook sounds like their style, and they'd know where he lived. Maybe he broke a rule or two, or maybe he was holding out on them. That's never appreciated in an organization like that.'

'No,' says Dan. 'They'd just summon him to a meeting and he'd never be seen again. They wouldn't need to take the risk of hitting him at home.'

'All right, I'm out of ideas.' Pascual retreats into his headache, kneading his brow.

'Motivation,' says the pit bull. 'Who wanted Couvet and Morrel dead and who wanted Najjar? And are they the same party? There would seem to be opposite interests at work here.'

'Factions,' says Dan. 'That's the word that leaps to mind.

Are we looking at a war between factions in the Algerian government? Let's remember how this all started, and who was paying Couvet.'

'Of course,' says his colleague, 'factional strife is not limited to Arab dictatorships. I can recall some famous dustups among the French.'

A thick silence follows and then Dan says, with an air of finality, 'In any event, I think "cut and run" is our governing principle here. The last thing we need is an accusation that *we're* running around knocking off Arab businessmen and their household staff in Cyprus. Everybody's been told to bail out.'

'Leaving us where?'

'Leaving us without mandate or budget to pursue things any further at this point. I think it's time to sit back and watch. I think now we let factional warfare run its course and see where we stand. I have a feeling that nothing we could do at this point is any more likely to turn up those two truckloads of Russian contraband than this kind of horseplay. I think we keep the feelers out but sit on our hands for a while.'

When the pit bull and his colleagues have departed Dan sits smoking and looking at Pascual. 'Well, that's that, then. I'm sorry there won't be any medals or even a bottle of champagne, but that's the nature of the business. I think we can spring for a small honorarium and air fare back to Barcelona.'

A little stunned by the pace of events, Pascual can only blink at him for a moment. 'I'm staying here,' he manages finally.

'I'm not sure that's wise,' Dan says. 'In fact if I were you I'd skip Barcelona, too, try somewhere completely different for a while. You're the classic case of the man who knows too much.'

Pascual pushes away from the table. 'I'm sure you're right,' he says. 'All the same, I've still got a couple of things to do in Paris.'

The cigarette smolders in the old man's good hand. 'You've thought this through, have you?' he says.

'It's not over,' says Pascual. 'Not by a long shot.'

'No,' says Dan. 'I don't think it is.' He takes a long drag on the cigarette and stubs it out. 'I'll be going back. But I'm going to give you a telephone number. And a code word. Don't pester me with trivialities, but if you really need help, I might be able to organize some. Understood?'

Startled, Pascual stares at him. 'Understood.'

TWENTY-THREE

'I'm free,' says Pascual into the phone. Outside the cabin a Paris evening is gearing up, tires squealing about the Étoile and a café waiter sneaking a cigarette on the pavement, tray in hand and scowl in place. Pascual waits for a response.

'It's good to hear your voice,' says Djemila finally.

Pascual's spirits rise. 'We have a lot to talk about.'

'Yes. Where are you?'

'Now, nowhere. I need to find a place to go to ground and then I'll ring you. Later tonight?'

She hesitates. 'I'll be here,' she says.

M. Gilbert looks if anything closer to death, but with a violin in his hands he has found a place to make his last stand; only something tenaciously, ferociously alive could produce this sound. He keeps on playing as Pascual steps softly down the long room and sinks onto a chair. The old man's eyes remain fixed on the music in front of him, the spidery fingers stepping with precision along the neck of the instrument, the bow moving with assurance; the room resonates with the ethereal tracery of a Bach partita. Pascual watches as the old man coaxes it into resolution and then takes the instrument from his shoulder and sits panting very slightly. At length he raises his eyes to Pascual's. 'The Allemande from Number I in B minor,' he says. 'About all I can manage these days.'

'My mother used to play it quite often.'

Gilbert rises and goes to lay the violin and bow in their case. 'Yes. Why do you think I hauled it out?' He closes the case and turns, smiling. 'So you're still about, are you?'

'I need your help. I'm going to ask you a great favor.' Pascual has decided that there is no better approach than the truth. He has lied skilfully and intensively throughout his adult life and found it often highly useful, but he has come to recognize its corrosive effect. If Gilbert has an ounce of sense he will send him packing, but the truth at least has the merit of sounding too wildly implausible to be a confidence trick.

'Whatever I can do,' says Gilbert, with a gracious nod and a look of surprise.

'I need a place to hide for a few days. I've got some business I have to finish and I've got on the wrong side of some very nasty people. I have no money and no other recourse. I was hoping I might lie low in one of your flats upstairs. For a week, perhaps two. Perhaps until the wreckers come.'

Gilbert stands looking at him blankly and Pascual can see all the reflexes of the solid bourgeois kicking in. Seconds go by and Gilbert does what Pascual least expects: he laughs. He quivers silently for a moment and then sounds emerge, brief juddering exhalations that shake his frame. He says,

'Your mother did worry about you so. You're quite serious, aren't you?'

'I am. I won't blame you if you throw me out. In your shoes I probably would, too.'

Gilbert stands looking at him until the light of amusement begins to fade. 'The estate agent is coming to collect the keys tomorrow and I'm leaving Paris for good. But I don't think they plan to start construction until the autumn. If I were to leave you an extra key for the garret I don't think anyone would notice, if you were discreet. It's not my building any-more, so what do I care?'

'I'm in your debt.'

'I've stored a lot of old furniture and things up there. Perhaps even some old sheets. You could make it quite cozy if you don't mind a little dust.'

'It will bring back old times,' says Pascual.

'They haven't identified him yet,' Djemila says. 'They've estab-lished that his passport was a forgery. The French are denying any knowledge of him, but nobody believes them. The inves-tigation is focusing on Couvet. The Islamists are the prime suspects, of course, given his recent history. The idea seems to be that the French had teamed up with the Swiss to root out the GIA networks in Switzerland, and this is a counterstrike. Meanwhile, Algerians keep on turning up dead.'

'What, here?'

'Three of them. Shot and dumped in the Canal de l'Ourcq northeast of the city, in classic underworld style. They were found this morning. The interesting thing is that they had papers saying they were with military intelligence. Whether that has anything to do with us, I don't know. The Algerians aren't saying much but the speculation is that this was a team sent here to go after the people who did the massacre in the *dix-huitième* and they got ambushed. Who knows? It's the sort of thing the generals in Algiers might do. With such an abundance of dead Algerians, it would be a mistake to assume all of them are involved in the business we're interested in.'

Pascual can find no response and he takes a long swallow of beer. 'I can't sort it out. I'm through trying. What I'm thinking is, if the French have Najjar, they won't be interested in us anymore.' Tonight Pascual is finding the little bar in the rue de Belleville a welcoming place, crowded and cheerful and unpolluted by death. In the elation of easing stress and reunion with Djemila he has no energy for intrigues.

She gives him a penetrating look. 'Is there nobody you would trust enough to talk to? You're a key witness.'

He shrugs. 'So are you for that matter. What can I tell them at this point? *I* don't know who the hell he was. Najjar's vanished and Morrel's dead and those lorries are God knows where.' He wants her to answer his shrug with her own, but her look is demanding and he makes an effort. 'I think we're waiting on events at this point. If there's anything left we can do, it sounds like the trail of Khaled Marwan may be it.'

She nods. 'I haven't talked to Rachid in a couple of days. He said he had a contact or two. I've just been trying to follow the pack on the Zurich killing. Everybody's looking for you, you know.'

'I know. It's lucky I never gave Couvet my real name.'

'I think you were lucky in several ways.'

'No doubt.' Pascual drains his beer and looks Djemila in the face, leaping headlong into those bottomless eyes. 'Let's hope my luck holds.'

She gazes back, running a finger around the rim of her glass. 'What's your stake in all this at this point?' she says.

The truest answer is on the tip of his tongue but he is not ready to give it, not directly. 'We made a deal,' he says.

Something passes across Djemila's face for an instant, no more, and her eyes fall to the countertop. She places a hand on Pascual's arm, and that is all he needs to know.

On the promenade running down the middle of the Boulevard de Rochechouart there is a carnival in progress: a carousel whirls; street vendors offer roasted maize and miscellaneous trinkets, possibly stolen. Opposite the entrance to the rue Seveste, a wiry busker with the face of a gutter tough is thrashing at the strings of a guitar, trying with indifferent success to beat music out of it. A sign taped to the lining of his battered guitar case pleads for help but the dark red velvet is notably free of coins. Pascual and Djemila cut across the flow of the crowd toward the rue Seveste.

'What have I learned?' says Rachid, shutting the window to keep out the noise from the street. 'I've learned that Algerian press credentials mean nothing to a Paris *flic*. I've learned that I was never cut out to be a reporter. I'm not stubborn enough. I don't know how you do it.' He sits at the table, looking limp and wilted in the heat.

Djemila smiles. 'Me, I'd rather talk to people than stick a camera in their faces.'

'You can hide behind a camera.' Rachid reaches for a paper. 'I found some interesting things, though. First of all I confirmed that a Khaled Marwan, a Lebanese, was arrested on May seventeenth, nineteen ninety-two, 1992 and taken to the Santé in the Boulevard Arago. I also confirmed that he was the real Khaled Marwan. I found his cousins, one of them, anyway. There used to be a whole clan of them apparently but some have gone back. I got the impression that relations between the family and the police were not always the best. Anyway, this fellow told me that Khaled and his brother had gone to Switzerland months before to work for a branch of the family there but Khaled had come back unexpectedly with a horror story about his brother's killing and a tale that somebody was after him. He was extremely tight-lipped about why but he was frightened half to death. He was more or less lying low at his flat when the police came around and grabbed him. The cousin heard nothing for a few days and when he went to the *préfecture* to inquire, he was told Khaled had been released. As indeed the record shows.'

'Released to whom?'

'Ah. That's the interesting part. On the nineteenth of May he was released to two Swiss police officers. That's what the PJ records show.'

Djemila's mouth hangs open for a moment. 'To the Swiss? But Couvet said they were told it was the wrong man.'

'I know. I'm telling you what the records here say. Two men from something called the Ministère public de la Confédération signed for him and took him away. Presumably they had credentials. I don't think you could walk out of the Santé with a prisoner without showing some ID.'

Djemila is peering at him, incredulous. 'Did you follow up with the Swiss? The names of the officers must be in the record.'

'Yes, the names are there. Brossard and Kohl, for what that's worth. I did get on to the Swiss, and what a joy that was, talking my way through five or six layers of bureaucracy, half of which admit to speaking only German. It took two days to establish that nobody in Bern would admit to knowing anyone named Brossard or Kohl. Whether that's conclusive, I don't know. I knew it had happened near Zurich, so I finally had the idea of calling the cantonal police there and hoping somebody spoke French. I got lucky and found someone who remembered Khaled Marwan, but when he rang back after checking the files he just repeated what Couvet told you. The French had said they got the wrong man. Brossard and Kohl, *connais pas*. Phantoms, both of them.'

Djemila sags on her chair. '*Bon dieu.* Somebody pulled a fast one.'

Rachid tosses the paper on the desk. 'Somebody made Khaled Marwan vanish in a puff of smoke.'

A long silence ensues. Djemila says, 'So who told the Swiss Marwan was an impostor?'

'There's no mention of that in the records, nothing about

his being an impostor. The reason for the arrest is given as wanted for questioning and then there's simply an annotation that he was questioned and released.'

'Couvet thought Marwan himself might have claimed to be somebody else, to avoid being sent back to Switzerland.'

Rachid shrugs. 'Could be. But you'd think then they would have held him until they knew who he was. Charged him for having used someone else's papers, certainly.'

'True. There's no record of who questioned him?'

'Not in the arrest record. But I had a thought. If he was questioned at the Santé there might be a record of who came to see him. So I've got one more possibility. A lawyer I know who works for the CFDT has a contact at the Santé, a clerk or something who's leaked things to him before and might be able to do some delving in the records. He's promised to put me in touch. I'm waiting for him to ring.'

In the silence they exchange looks. 'Somebody sprang him,' says Pascual. 'From above.'

'Why?' says Djemila.

'He said the magic word to someone. He knew something that somebody didn't want the Swiss to know.'

'Somebody French.'

'Yes. The word I've heard is that Najjar had French protection for a long time. If Marwan was in a position to give him up to the Swiss, that could have made someone here nervous.'

'So what happened to Marwan?'

Pascual gives a shake of the head. 'On an optimistic scenario, they packed him off somewhere and paid him off. If you're inclined to think the worst, he probably didn't last long after he was released. If no one's ever found a body, the first scenario is probably what happened.'

For a few seconds there is no sound but the hubbub from the boulevard. Djemila reaches across the desk to grasp Rachid's hand. 'You've done incredible work. Not bad at all for a mere shutterbug.'

Rachid returns the smile, a bitter twist of the lips. 'I much prefer taking pictures, actually. Aim and click, and the film never lies to you.'

No one has heard the approach and the three of them start as the door handle rattles, a shadow looming through the pebbled glass. A key clicks in the lock and the door swings open. Pascual has caught his breath but Rachid's *salut* tells him there is nothing to be alarmed about; this man bursting into the room belongs here. He is Arab, tall and grey-haired, moving briskly and wide-eyed with excitement. 'They've caught them,' he says. 'The ones who did the restaurant massacre.'

'They got signed confessions from all three. I've just come from the press conference and I've got a story to write.' Tariq Abdelatif, founder and editor-in-chief of *La Voix du Maghreb*, jabs at the keyboard of his computer, hair in disarray and notes spilling out of his briefcase onto the desktop. 'Three poor dumb *beurs* from La Courneuve. The usual story, shiftless alienated delinquents, looking for identity, fertile ground for the first smooth-talking fake in a turban who lures them into the mosque. They sent them off to Afghanistan and they came back killers.'

Abdelatif speaks in rapid bursts, simultaneously bullying his computer into writing mode. 'There's no doubt, then?' says Djemila.

Abdelatif pauses, hands over the keyboard. 'None at all. They laid it all out for the police, how they staked the place out, which of them shot and which of them hacked, where they ditched the guns and the knives and burned the bloody clothes. They're proud of themselves, the *salauds*. They'll try to turn the trial into a circus, of course. Rachid, we've completely missed the boat on pictures. How would you feel about spending the rest of your day at the Cité, waiting for a photo op? They're going to move them sooner or later and there's always an inspector or two anxious to get his face in the paper.'

Djemila leans on the desk. 'Who ran them? Who chose the target?'

'That's the big question, isn't it? The *flics* were a little coy on that point. But the word is, there are more arrests coming. They're going to roll up the whole network, squeeze the pipeline back to Peshawar, or wherever it is they go.'

'How did they choose the victims? Why that particular restaurant?'

Abdelatif leans back in his chair and fixes her with his gaze. 'The Islamists hate us as much as they hate the regime, you know that. The place was a rendezvous for the type of Algerian who wants a country with a few modern conveniences, like secularism and the rule of law. I'd gone to some of those meetings there myself.' For a moment the horror flickers in his eyes. 'This time, I don't think it was the regime. I think it was just what it seemed to be. And I hope they throw away the fucking key.'

Pascual and Djemila leave Rachid festooned with photo gear at the Métro entrance on the boulevard. 'We'll talk,' says Rachid, hurrying down the steps. Djemila looks dazed, wandering back along the promenade. 'So Mediane was just unlucky,' she says. 'The old story, the wrong place and the wrong time.'

Pascual says nothing. He is wondering if he is imagining this, this feeling of giddy relief in the streets. Only the carnival, perhaps, and yet he is seeing smiles on haunted African faces, hearing laughter. Surely he is projecting and yet these are people who have been living with horror for weeks and have finally had a face put on it, a name put to it.

'Word's getting around,' says Djemila. 'People are happy.'

'I thought so.'

A few paces further she says, 'Where are we going?'

'I don't know. Want a drink?'

'I don't think so. I want . . . I just want to think about nothing for a while.'

Pascual takes a deep breath. 'You haven't seen my hide-away yet.'

'No,' she says a few steps on, 'I haven't.'

Up here at the top of the building the hot air has collected, trapped beneath the eaves with rays of sunshine lighting up the dust motes in it. Pascual has opened a window and found an old electric fan that sounds like a Junkers 88 revving for takeoff, but the cooling effect is laughably slight.

He has wrestled furniture into a liveable configuration and thrown a sheet across the mattress on the sagging spring bed in the corner. To use the toilet they must go one floor down, but rusty water, blessedly cool, comes out of the tap in the corner. From the window he can see the towers of Notre Dame rising above rooftops near at hand; to the left a slice of the river and the façade of the Palais de Justice on the Quai des Orfèvres and the limitless sprawl of the metropolis beyond.

Djemila paces, *clip clop* across the bare planks, looking distracted and vague. She stands at the window, a shock of black hair above bare brown shoulders in the light sheath of blue cotton that catches at hips with just the right curve, the perfect swell to complement the slender limbs. Pascual has been watching her move and trying to remember how it felt to hold her in the dark in Zurich. Since bringing her here he has begun to wonder if the whole thing is not a mistake. Sitting on the edge of a chair, Pascual wipes sweat from his forehead with his hand, watches the play of light on moist fingers.

Clip clop, clip clop. There is a clattering noise as she kicks her sandals off. She is standing by the bed and now there is the hiss of cloth sliding over skin. Pascual looks up to see the blue cotton sheath land in a heap. He suddenly needs more air and breathes in sharply through his nostrils. Djemila is standing with her back to him and the sight of this much rich brown skin is overwhelming. Her thumbs are hooked in the waistband of the red bikini panties she has been wearing beneath the dress; who could have suspected these? The artless way in which Djemila pushes down and steps out of her panties stirs Pascual's loins with something approaching violence. The black of her hair, the deep coffee brown of her skin, the perfect darkness where the curves of her bottom converge: Pascual cannot move. She turns toward him now, running her hands through her hair, and the look she gives him is one of utter frankness, complete trusting simplicity in the ebony-black eyes. Her breasts are small and high with nipples as dark as teak, her delta as black as the night. Pascual has risen, he finds, riveted by her look, by the sight of her; he begins to move as she sits on the bed, swings her legs up, lies back and watches him approach.

She lies with one hand palm up on the sheet, the other across her belly, one leg straight and the other bent. She blinks a few times as Pascual stands over her, not yet daring to fumble at his belt, and then a wonderful thing occurs: Djemila smiles. It is a smile of simple relief, peace, welcome; Djemila has recovered something. 'Don't say anything,' she whispers. 'Think later.'

Pascual has the presence of mind to take his time with his clothing; nothing spoils the mood like hopping about with a foot caught in one's trousers. She receives him on the bed with frail arms sliding around his ribs, hands moving down his back. Belly to belly, mouth to mouth, the sweating begins. Pascual has her tongue in his mouth; she has found his sex with her warm firm hand. Pascual wants to taste all of her, every curve and hollow of her flesh. This stubbled armpit, tasting of salt; this nipple, hard and dark, growing in his mouth. This yielding mound pressing itself into the palm of his hand, begging for his tongue; what is this but perfection, completion?

Djemila's cry sounds across the garret and out of the window into the restless city, full of anguish and release.

TWENTY - FOUR

When Djemila pulls open the door, Pascual can tell immediately that something is afoot. Pen in hand, she hurries back to the desk where the phone receiver lies off its cradle to resume her conversation. Pascual locks the door and dumps the sandwiches and a bottle of water on the desk. Djemila scrawls on the pad in front of her, murmurs a few words into the phone, rings off. She looks up and says, 'They've identified him.'

It takes Pascual a second or two to catch up. 'Morrel?'

Djemila nods. 'Rumor has it the Swiss have known for days but there has been some resistance here to releasing the information. The consensus now seems to be that this was part of some extralegal joint Franco-Swiss dirty war on the Islamists. There's going to be a good deal of outraged editorializing.'

For a moment Pascual can see and hear him: the man who wooed him, ran him, died in front of him. 'Who was he?'

'His real name was Albert Nogent. At least that's what my source at the Ministry of the Interior tells me.' She looks up at Pascual. 'He was a DST man. An *ex*-DST man.'

Pascual stands trying to work out implications. His eyes widen. 'Ex since when?'

'Since nineteen ninety-five.'

Pascual hauls a chair to the corner of the desk and sits. *'Putain,'* he breathes.

'Provided they're telling the truth, of course. They're admitting he was once an officer but insisting he resigned in nineteen ninety-five. To enter private employment, they're saying.'

Pascual's eyes narrow. 'With whom?'

'That, they're not saying.'

'He certainly seemed to have some resources.'

Djemila stares out of the window. 'Let's try the cynical view. Maybe he wasn't *officially* working for the government, but that doesn't mean he wasn't. This dirty war idea doesn't sound too far off to me. It just wasn't aimed at the Islamists. It was aimed at Najjar.'

'He was called back as a sort of independent contractor, you mean.'

'The greatest asset an ex-officer could offer would be his deniability.'

Pascual peels paper off a sandwich. 'The DST, eh?'

'You had the impression he was what, the other one, the DG whatever?'

'I would have guessed DGSE because they've got a reputation as the cowboys, the fellows who go about the world pulling off the type of thing Morrel was in fact planning. But then it's the DST that would be in charge of counterterrorism here in France, and Najjar was active here at one time. But what difference does it make? The question is, what the hell was he up to?'

A period of thought ensues, Pascual feverishly reviewing his brief and unprofitable association with Morrel *né* Albert Nogent. Djemila says, 'Let's not lose sight of the key question. What's the deal between Mirakl and Boucherif? Anything else, like who Morrel was working for, is useful only in so far as it gets us closer to the truth about that. Whoever was behind him, he apparently didn't know about the deal.' She starts to take a bite but freezes with the sandwich in midair. 'Or did he?'

Pascual takes a swig out of the bottle of water and sits shaking his head. 'I'm getting an impression of great yawning gaps in our knowledge here.'

'Never forget,' says Djemila, 'these are professional liars. They're masters.'

They convene the *conseil de guerre* in a *brasserie* opposite the Gare de l'Est and Rachid looks healthier and happier for the fresh air, hair combed, his pendulous lip glistening with the cheerful sheen of a refreshing *demi* at the long bar. 'Nothing yet,' he says, shaking his head. 'But I'm optimistic. Over the phone the *mec* seemed quite a decent sort, not your usual functionary. The only question is whether he can actually get access to the records. But anyway, that's where we stand. Waiting for our mole in the Santé to find out who sprang Khaled Marwan. He's promised to ring me later this afternoon at the office.'

Djemila nods, toying with her glass. The post-lunchtime crowd is cheerful, the noise covering their conversation. 'And Mirakl? Anything new on that score?'

'Mirakl?' Rachid vents a laugh. 'Miracle's the word, all right. How to make billions vanish with a snap of the fingers. They've mastered the art.' He pulls a thick file from his briefcase, pushes it down the bar. 'Here's the Mirakl file. There is a lot of material out there, but it has to be sifted carefully and some of it's probably bunk. I did manage two real interviews as well. There's a man in Brussels whose job it is to keep an eye on cross-border criminal activity, and he gave me half an hour on the phone. And I had a talk with a Russian who owns a bar down in the *quatorzième* and claims to be an ex-MVD investigator run out of Moscow by Kovalenko in ninety-four. He had lots to say but most of it would have to be called hearsay. Anyway, a picture emerges. Kovalenko and his pals have stolen more money than most nations have in their budgets. Gold, cash, oil, minerals, you name it—if it wasn't bolted down they took it out of the country themselves or sold it and stuck the money in accounts all over the globe. They rigged the privatizations, they drew up the property titles, they confiscated the facto- ries. Who was going to stop them? They were the state. Miracle, indeed. What's miraculous is that there's anything left they don't own.' Rachid waves off depressing thoughts with a flick of the hand. 'Anyway. What I found is here in this folder.'

Djemila riffles through the stack, eyebrows raised. Pascual has been silent, nursing his beer, watching the pro- fessionals at work. Now he says, 'Mirakl. A Russian outfit with an Arab element. *Mir* is Russian for *world*. And we know what the A-K-L root in Arabic means.'

'Eat.' Djemila blinks at him. 'The world devourer? Coincidence, surely.'

'Perhaps.' Pascual drinks beer as his companions gape at him. 'Let's hope.'

We will lie here until the wrecking ball comes smashing through the brick, thinks Pascual; then we will worry about where to hide next. Djemila is asleep with her head in the crook of his arm; the light has gone golden as the sun reaches the rooftops. Outside, the city stirs, murmurs, roars like a distant ocean.

If this is now a little more seaworthy than a raft tossing on an ocean, there is still no shore in sight. Pascual has made an art of living for the moment and he will not allow himself illusions, but here and now, her breath on his neck, he would almost claim to be at peace.

He dozes off himself and when he awakes she is at the window, looking down into the rue Git le Coeur. *Ci-gît mon Coeur*, Pascual hears, his inner ear transforming the name. Here lies my heart, and it is almost enough to make one believe in fate that he has wound up here with Djemila. As he approaches on bare feet she turns her face to him and he sees the tears. He embraces her gently from behind. She sniffs, seeks his hand with hers. He has no need to ask; she is crying for a husband perhaps, for her country or because she does not have one; crying because nothing lasts, because everything dies like the day that is expiring in the street below.

Her voice is barely audible. 'In Algiers, when I was a child,

I loved the early evening. It began to get cool as the sun went down and suddenly the streets were full of people. There was a feeling of release, from work, from school, from the heat. Lights came on, you met your friends on the corner, you went down to the square to gossip and play and look at the light dying out over the sea.' Her eyes close. 'Now, when night falls the streets are empty. Deserted, a ruined city. People sit at home and listen. That's all, just listen. A shot, a scream, a troop carrier rumbling by. You turn down the volume on the TV and listen. You listen and wonder who's going to die tonight.'

Pascual turns her to face him. 'Not you. Not tonight.'

She searches his face. She is calm but her eyes are bottomless and there is no joy there. 'No. Not tonight.' She blinks at him for a few seconds. 'I don't even remember my father. I was a baby when he died. But they made sure I grew up with the story. He was killed by French paras at a roadblock along with two of his friends. They had a bomb in the car with them and they were on their way to plant it in a café in the rue d'Isly. For a long time I was proud of my father, but now I wonder. Did my father help to plant the seeds of what we have now? Was savagery the only thing he contributed to our national tradition? You'll have to help me, I'm confused.'

Pascual holds her and has no answers. After a time he says, 'I made the same calculations as your father did, and with less provocation. You can always find reasons to call murder by another name. Me, I lived to repudiate all that. Your father didn't, so you have to do it for him. And I'd say you've made a pretty good start.'

'That's a bitter consolation.'

'Sometimes that's the only kind you get.'

Their rendezvous with Rachid is for eight o'clock, at the newspaper office, dinner and discussion to follow. The carnival on the Boulevard de Rochechouart is in full swing and Djemila's spirits seem to rise; with the local demography she could almost be in Algiers in the early evening here, reclaiming the streets. The rue Seveste is lively tonight, tourists on their way to and from Montmartre contesting the passage with Arab families on a stroll.

Pascual looks up as they approach the entrance to the courtyard. The light is on in the newspaper office, the window closed; something has spotted the panes. Rachid has brewed one cup of tea too many and flung it against the window, perhaps. Pascual peers upward until they pass into the cool of the entrance. He halts Djemila with a hand on her arm. 'Wait for me here.'

'Why?' Her eyes are immense.

'I don't know. A feeling. Wait here until I come to get you.'

'What? What is it?'

'Precautions, that's all.'

Her eyes narrow. 'I'm coming with you.'

'I tell you, wait here.' She hears the steel in his voice and freezes. She nods, rigid now, and he goes up the stairs. Pascual does not pray but he is pleading with somebody that this is mere skittishness, imagination run wild.

Tea was never so viscous as that, Pascual knows. Here is the corridor, in darkness. He cannot find a light switch but he can see the light behind the pebbled glass. Here is the door and Pascual's step slows; he raises his hand and knocks, the sound echoing down the landing. He waits, hearing noises from the street. He knocks again and continues to plead with the deity he will never acknowledge. Rachid has not answered, and as clearly as speech Pascual can hear someone telling him: do not open the door. Praying that the handle will not cede, that the door is safely locked and Rachid long gone, Pascual grasps the handle, feeling it begin to turn.

Do not open the door, and he stands with the sound of the nearby carnival in his ears and the peal of a car horn on the boulevard, inadequate speakers somewhere distorting an Arab melody and the evening deepening to night: do not open the door. Somebody must, thinks Pascual. His hand cannot rest on the door handle forever; he must choose forward or back. He chooses forward and opens the door.

Pascual cannot stop trembling; Djemila holds him but cannot stop the shaking; it only passes to her. They have found a dark place under the Métro tracks on the Boulevard de la Chapelle, Pascual dragging her away from the rue Seveste by the hand; he had no need of words. He stands with his back to a pillar and holds on to Djemila for dear life, watching the few passers-by with terror. 'Only Rachid?' whispers Djemila, rigid against him, and Pascual nods, a brief muscular spasm, though he cannot be certain; he did not stop to count limbs.

He opened the door and it took his breath away, took away

something else as well, his peace of mind for ever. He had seen carnage before but nothing like that; the splatter on the window was only a sideshow. Walls, desks, the glistening smears on the floor: someone had done great evil in that room and then walked in it. 'He didn't suffer,' says Pascual, exerting great willpower to get the words out. Djemila gives way to a sob and he squeezes her tighter, hanging on to the notion that decapitation is necessarily quick, hanging tight to the idea as a bulwark against the image of Rachid's head perched on a chair.

TWENTY-FIVE

'I need help.' Pascual cannot quite believe that a phone card borrowed from Djemila and slipped into a telephone at the Gare du Nord can put him, after two minutes of code-word horseplay with an intermediary, in contact with Dan three thousand kilometers away, but the old man's voice in his ear is unmistakable.

'Where are you?'

'In Paris.'

'Paris, fine, I know that. Where in Paris? Are you safe for an hour?'

I will never be safe again, Pascual thinks, looking wildly about the station concourse, seeing only late-evening travelers but feeling the breath of the devil on his neck. 'I'm at the Gare du Nord. Yes, we might live for an hour. She's with me. We need to talk to somebody we can trust. They're killing everybody.'

In fifty years Dan has talked more than one panicked field agent through a crisis; he could be a grandfather calming a six-year-old who has skinned his knee. 'Give me a rendezvous and I'll have somebody there within the hour. The Gare du Nord, where? Is there a bar open, somewhere you can wait?'

Pascual scans. Things are closing down, but knots of idlers remain. 'We'll be opposite the departure board. As if we're waiting for a train to be posted. How will we know your people?'

'I'll send somebody who knows you. He'll ask you for a light and tell you what to do. Simple enough?'

Backs to a wall, they slide to the floor and wait. Djemila is crying mutely again, arms wrapped around her knees, in control except for the tears tracking down her cheeks. Pascual has finally stopped trembling but nausea and a primal scream are not far beneath the surface. He is marginally reassured by the sight of two soldiers coming through the hall, too young to shave but sporting the regulation FAMAS rifle that just might, if deftly handled, stop a madman with an axe. So much blood, dear Jesus, he will never rest again.

'I'm ready to go to the police,' says Djemila. 'They can't all be crooked.'

'The man Rachid was waiting for was with the PJ. The word is out. We go and talk to them, how long can we expect to last? Marwan, now Rachid. We talk to the police, we die. Sooner or later.'

'If it was Rachid's questions that set off the trip wires, they might not know about us.'

'Morrel told them all about us. All about you. He had you followed, remember?'

She hides her face in her hands. 'I'm ready to give up, then. It's over.'

Pascual puts an arm around her and it is still there when the man from the Israeli embassy pops up in front of him, complete with kinky brown hair and bad French, brandishing a cigarette. Handing back the lighter, he says, 'You look half dead. If you can walk, you'll find a silver Peugeot out front. Give me a thirty-second lead.'

It is past midnight but sleep will never come again, another casualty. Pascual has seen too much death now, too vividly; it has fouled the world forever. From the window of the flat in the rue de Bucarest he can see nothing but Rachid's half-closed eyes, utterly dead. 'Is there anything to drink?' he says.

'I don't know. There may be something in the kitchen. You're sure you touched nothing, left no prints?' The Israeli has made a few notes, sitting at the table, taking him through it. Djemila has gone into the bedroom, unable to listen.

'Only on the door handle. And that will only be my palm, maybe part of my thumb. Of course, they'll find our prints inside from previous visits. One way or another they'll look for us. Abdelatif will tell them. Everybody will want us. And I'd be happy to tell them what we know, provided we have some protection. The question is, can one group of policemen keep us safe from another and how do we tell which group is which?'

The Israeli shoves the notebook away. 'I certainly can't tell you that. And it's none of my business anyway. We don't go fucking with the French police. I'm not sure why I got the word to come haul you out of the soup, but ours is not to reason why and all that. You'll have to take it up with your friend from Tel Aviv tomorrow.'

Pascual looks up sharply. 'He's coming back?'

'That's what I'm told. You must have some clout. That man's a living legend.'

Pascual awakes, stiff-necked on a chair. He reels into the bedroom; when last he saw Djemila she was motionless in her clothes on the bed. Now she is gone. Out in the flat the watcher who replaced the embassy man sometime in the night shrugs. 'I cleared it by phone. Nobody told me to hold her.'

Pascual rings her brother's number in a fever. 'I couldn't take it any longer,' she says. 'I won't be held prisoner.'

Pascual has no desire to hold her anywhere against her will but his confidence in any bureau, faction or manifestation of French law or security organizations is gone. 'They'll kill you.'

'I've lived with that risk for years. Listen, they've found him already, it's all over the radio. I've got to talk to Tariq, maybe talk to the police. I know the risks, I'll take my chances.'

'You might not be safe there. They could be watching your brother's place.'

'I've learned a lot over the past few weeks. I got here unobserved.'

'Djemila, they're a lot better than you are. It's their profession, remember.'

'It's time to speak,' she says. 'Silence won't protect us any longer.'

Pascual exhales. 'Then write your story, give it all to Tariq, give it to the United Nations if you want. But stay away from the police. Go to our hideaway. Just make sure nobody follows you.'

He can hear her thinking about it. 'I don't have a key. Or the door code.'

'Come by here and get it.'

Behind him the Israeli says, 'No.'

'Hang on.' Pascual wheels, exasperated.

Coolly the Israeli says, 'If somebody's picked her up, she's not bringing them back here. You can forget that.'

'All right, all right.' Pascual rubs his brow and lifts the phone. 'I'll come and meet you someplace.'

The Israeli is shaking his head. 'Not if she's contaminated. If she's not a pro, I don't trust her to stay clean. And I have orders to keep you out of trouble.'

Pascual glares, his hand over the mouthpiece. 'How about a third party? Can I go and leave the key where she can pick it up?'

The Israeli gives it three or four seconds' thought and says, 'I think we can have somebody take care of that for you. You, we take no chances with.'

He dozes, dreams, awakes; he prowls from kitchen to bedroom and back again, fleeing images of frenzy in a blood-spattered room. He told Djemila that Rachid did not suffer, but before the end there was panic and struggle. Pascual knows that the head was not the first to come off; he saw the evidence. Fearing madness, he paces until his minder snarls at him to sit down. He has no appetite but drinks coffee until his stomach will take no more and then stands over the toilet throwing it up again. Finally he winds up at the window looking down into the street.

Factions, he thinks. How many hands are at work here? And to what end? Something so dirty that a government security agency has to bring back a departed officer in secret to run it. The French wanted Najjar dead, but where is his corpse? And why now? Who wanted Couvet dead, and Morrel? The Russians? The Algerians? Which ones? Somebody with an eye to a Swiss keyhole, in any event. Mediane was only unlucky, but Rachid stirred deep waters. And where is Khaled Marwan?

Pascual is dizzied and exhausted. He sinks onto the couch with a final question thrumming in his ears like the aftermath of an explosion: who benefits?

For a man so universally esteemed, Dan arrives with remarkably little fanfare, slipping in with an escort of two, looking like a retired laborer on holiday shepherded by two robust nephews perhaps. The nephews murmur in Hebrew and move warily about the room while Dan shakes Pascual's hand and takes his measure. 'You've seen it up close again, haven't you?' the old man says.

'Too close.' There is no one on earth who can shame Pascual the way Dan can, but no one else, he feels, who comes as close to understanding him. 'Thanks for coming.'

'I didn't come to comfort you,' Dan says brutally, turning away. 'I hope you're in the mood to talk, because I want to hear it all again. Can we arrange for a bottle of water and an ashtray, do you think?'

They begin at the table but after an hour they move to the single creaking sofa in the front room, traffic noises coming up from the street through the partly open windows. The support staff has slipped away quietly to other rooms. Dan makes no notes, seldom interrupts, grunts at intervals, nods. He smokes, sharing his strong cigarettes with Pascual; the ashtray on the sofa between them fills up. There are periods of silence in which Pascual almost drifts off to sleep; at other moments Dan pushes him to the point of irritation, forcing him to recall, sharpen his account, confirm, repeat, reconstruct. A slatted pattern of sunlight moves across the floor.

'I don't remember,' says Pascual, hands to his face. 'I can't remember everything.' He expects to be challenged, but Dan only rises, takes the ashtray, leaves the room. Pascual listens to the noises the old man makes in the kitchen, the quiet exchange of words with a minder whose job is never to be far away. When Dan comes back he goes to the window and looks out at Paris in the late afternoon with the caution of long habit, standing three steps back so as not to be seen. 'You know where we're going, don't you?' he says.

Pascual has been seeing the road signs for some time but will not admit it. 'Impossible,' he says.

Dan paces back to the sofa and sinks onto it with a creak and a sigh. 'It's the only possibility left.'

Pascual sits paralyzed, unable to move his eyes from the

floor or his mind any further along this path. 'But it makes no sense.'

'It makes perfect sense.' Pascual knows this tone in the old man's voice: the ominous purr of ineluctable logic. 'She's the only one who was in a position every time to know the movements of all concerned. Every time.'

With the spoken thought hanging in the air Pascual is forced to confront it. It is a tsunami on his psychic horizon, gathering force. He takes a deep breath, groping for energy to dispute it. 'Why? Who would she be taking orders from?'

'You know the answer to that. Who are the interested parties?'

'You tell me. You're the fucking expert. I'm just the guy who finds the bodies.'

'All right, I'll tell you. The key to the whole thing is in Algeria, of course. That's where those lorries are headed, that's where the oil and the gas are. The French, all that's just a distraction. What we have is the chance intersection of a French intrigue with the main one, the deal between General Boucherif and Mirakl. A deal that is going to make or break Boucherif, put him at the top of the food chain or get him killed. Now, if you're trying to pull off a deal like that, in secret, concealing it from your colleagues and your constituents, you'd take some precautions, wouldn't you? You'd deploy a lot of resources to make sure word didn't get out. Wouldn't you?'

Pascual shakes his head with a puff of laughter. 'Sure. But you're just speculating.'

'Of course I'm speculating. That's my job. Speculate,

excavate, until a guess turns into a verdict. That's what this is, an educated guess. But it's a guess with a very distinguished academic record.'

'No.'

Dan leans toward him, his voice hardening, now almost a snarl. 'She forced herself on you, like a magician forcing a card. You really believe she was fool enough to let herself be caught like that at the bus stop?'

'She's an amateur. She didn't know what she was doing.'

'Or she knew very well. How did she know about Boucherif's movements?'

'She had a source in Algiers.'

'Yes, a convenient source that she had good reason never to reveal. Of course she had a source. His name was Boucherif.'

'No, it's fantastic. It's ludicrous.'

'It's the only hypothesis that covers everything.'

'What about Rachid? You're saying he was in on it?'

'No. She used him, too.' Pascual makes a sound of disgust but Dan bores onward. 'Who is it that the owner of the newspaper can vouch for, him or her? Who showed up out of the blue three months ago?'

'Hang on. Why would she even bring up the story if she was working for Boucherif? If her task was to keep things quiet, why was she pretending to investigate it? It's absurd.'

'Perhaps she didn't bring it up. Maybe Rachid had caught a whiff of it and Boucherif knew there had been a leak. Somebody in Algiers talked and got caught. Boucherif sent her to monitor things. He'd need to know how far he was compromised. Did she tell you the details of how she got onto the story? Did she give a satisfactory account of how her collaboration with Rachid began?'

'But it's preposterous. You're trying to tell me she's a trained agent?'

'Algerian military intelligence, I'd guess. Some bureau under Boucherif's control. Agencies tend to splinter and pro-liferate in a place like that.'

'They don't *let* women do that down there.'

'Women did their share of the heavy lifting against the French. And they've certainly used women since then. Come now, you've trained with Arab women yourself.'

'She's got family here, roots.'

'Have you ever met her brother? Was he ever more than a voice on the phone?'

Pascual is up off the sofa, looking for something to kick. 'I heard children crying in the background.'

'Perhaps you did. Perhaps her brother's even real. He wouldn't have to know why she was really here. The point is, she knew everything. And she had some convenient escapes. Didn't you ever wonder how she made it out of the bank that day?'

'She was going to publish the story. I saw her work on it. It was a real collaboration with Rachid, a real effort to gather information. She wanted to trumpet the story across the world.'

'I have no doubt it was a genuine collaboration. She needed to know what he knew.' Dan stabs a finger at him. '*And* what you knew.' Pascual whirls, scowls, freezes, hands in his pockets. 'She knew all about Morrel, all about Couvet, all about everything from the time you took up with her. Even though Morrel warned you about her.'

'Why would she have Morrel killed? He didn't care about Boucherif.'

'She didn't have him killed. She had Couvet killed because he was reporting back to Boucherif's enemies. Morrel was just there. As, I remind you, were you.'

A chill sinks slowly through Pascual but he shivers, stiffens, resists. 'What about Najjar? The killings on Cyprus. What's that all about? Who would she give his hideout to and why?'

Calmly Dan lights another cigarette, crosses his legs. 'Again I'm only speculating, but it would fit with other things we've seen. I think maybe Boucherif got cheated. The Russians do not exactly have a reputation for fair business dealings. And I can see Najjar trying to palm off some second-rate stuff on an inexpert customer. Only, Boucherif got his toys home and had his experts take a look at them and found he hadn't got quite what he paid for. Something like that, I'd guess. Fortunately, he had a phone number to trace, thanks to his invaluable agent in place at the center of the pursuit of Najjar. That, I think, really was fortuitous—it all dovetailed nicely for Boucherif.'

'No, it's madness. What about this business with Khaled Marwan? That's why Rachid got killed, and that doesn't fit anywhere.'

'Is that really why Rachid got killed? Or was it only his time to go, finally? An old scandal like the disappearance of

Khaled Marwan would be a wonderful distraction to anyone investigating his death.'

'So what happened to Marwan?'

'The Swiss came and got him, just as the record says.'

'Then why was Couvet told they had been put off the trail? Why did Marwan never show up in Switzerland?'

Dan shrugs. 'The Swiss have a wonderfully clean reputation. But they have their intrigues, too. I think Mirakl had to have Swiss cooperation to get the goods into the country back in ninety-two, and Marwan could throw too much light on that. So somebody was sent to get him, quietly. It's a bloody dirty business, start to finish. And my only consolation is that it seems to have gone sour, judging by what happened in Kyrenia. I take a certain amount of satisfaction in thinking of Daoud Najjar in the hands of a disgruntled customer.' Dan smokes, exhales and watches Pascual through the rising tendrils.

'There's something wrong with your picture,' says Pascual, in despair, swaying a bit from fatigue and the excess of nicotine in his blood. 'I don't know what it is, but I'm going to find it.'

'I would welcome any new interpretation. As long as it fits the facts.'

Pascual shakes his head, slowly. 'I know her,' he says. 'I've been with her, we've been intimate. And nobody could be that good an actress.'

The look Dan is giving him now is almost pitying, as close to pity as an old Mossad man can get for a man who once ran with Syrian wolves. 'That's what they all say. Every one of them. Every man who's ever been honey-trapped. I've caught them myself. And let me tell you, we use only the finest actresses.'

'You don't know her.' Pascual is shaking his head.

'There's an objective test, you know,' says Dan, the faintest hint of amusement in his ancient eyes.

'What?'

'You're planning to see her again?'

'Of course.'

'Then the test would be whether or not you survive,' says Dan.

TWENTY-SIX

Pascual walks: down the rue d'Amsterdam past the great hulking station, along the boulevards to the Porte Saint-Denis and then down toward the river, sidestepping tourists and hustlers and a few early whores. He walks light-headed and bemused, revived by the open air after a night and a day in the cramped smoky flat, but estranged from these turbulent cheerful streets by his intimacy with murder and treachery. The newspaper placards speak of the *tuerie* in the rue Seveste but no one is lining up to buy the papers; Pascual wants to grab people by the collar and shake them.

He wants to walk for hours; at the end of the walk the test awaits. He took his leave of Dan in a hair-trigger state of resentment, a word or two away from an explosion. Nothing aggrieves him like the old man's calm, his disinterested certainty. Pascual cannot refute him but there are things he knows and one of them is that Djemila is true. What he needs now is a clear head and the space to find his refutation.

An objective test. The streets may have the answer, but they distract Pascual from finding it; his pace slows as he grows footsore and he stops for a *demi* in a bar on Sébastopol. Standing at the counter, he smokes and despairs. If Dan is right there is no safe haven, no shore, no rest ever again.

But Dan is wrong. Pascual slogs on, across the river, across the Cité past the brooding façades that mask the mean, sordid workings of the law, the river again and the Place Saint-Michel, a crowd watching a man juggle fire. Pascual turns toward the rue Git le Coeur.

There is another objective test: if Djemila has gone to the police, if she has shouted her story to the world, then Dan is wrong and Pascual's heart is saved, even if she has put them both in peril by doing so. Before Pascual despairs he will speak to her. His certainty grows as he turns into the street. Gilbert's shop window is empty, the business vanished. He punches in the door code, pushes into the dark hallway. He finds the light switch and mounts the stairs.

Djemila was to pick up the key to the flat upstairs at the bar in the rue de Belleville; he gave her the code to the street door over the phone. If all has gone well he will find her at the top of the stairs, sweating a little in the heat perhaps, calm, focused, full of purpose. She will tell him the steps she has taken to shine light into dark places and they will plan how to stay alive. If she is not there he will wait for her on the final narrow flight of steps up to the garret, until midnight if he has to.

His trek has exhausted him. He rests halfway up the dark stairwell, listening for signs of her presence but hearing none. The light clicks off, leaving him in darkness relieved only by the skylight high above. He toils on. The beer he drank in Sébastopol is beginning to cycle through and when he reaches the last floor before the garret he takes the few steps down the landing to the tiny water closet.

He pisses, eyes closed, swaying a bit; weeks of stress and troubled sleep are taking their toll. Tonight he will sleep in Djemila's arms, hidden and safe in a hazardous world, and tomorrow he will tell Dan to take his jealous fantasies, half lechery no doubt, back to Israel.

Pascual turns away from the toilet, zipping up, and for the first time notices the object that slightly obstructed the door when he pushed it open. A black guitar case leans against the wall behind the door. Pascual stares at it for a very long time.

His heart has begun to accelerate even before anything has been consciously formulated. He has been looking at the case for what might be seconds or minutes, and now it is time to reach out and open it. His hand is steady as he bends slightly to undo the clasp and pull the case open.

The case is empty but the sign is there, taped to the maroon velvet: *Aidez-moi SVP—Chômeur et père de famille.* Pascual has seen this before, but for a long moment he cannot say where.

When recollection comes he nearly dies from the shock of it. Pascual has undergone adrenaline surges before, but this one is the mother of all of them; he nearly shouts from the mere mechanics of breathing. For an instant he is frozen in panic and then he becomes coherent enough to fear that retreat is cut off. His hearing has become preternatural and for agonizing seconds he awaits the telltale creak of floor-boards, the squeak of an ill-oiled hinge too close at hand.

When he is still alive after five seconds he is able to recognize that the danger will be above him, up in the garret, where a gutter tough will be lying in wait, blade gleaming. The clarity with which Pascual can remember the face helps to calm him; a man with a face is only a man after all. If Pascual can cover the four meters to the head of the stairs he might live. He is afraid to open the door but more afraid to wait here to be slaughtered; as panic probes at his defenses the decision is made somehow and he reaches for the handle.

The landing is empty and nothing has stirred. With his pulse throbbing in his ears Pascual takes slow, careful steps toward the stairs, listening for movement overhead. There is none; the butcher will be waiting for him to mount the garret stairs at the end of the short landing. Pascual reaches the main stairs and begins to trot downward, spiraling into darkness, straining the ancient banister as he wheels around the turns. He is not yet capable of drawing conclusions.

That comes at the bottom, where he tears open the street door and pitches out into a quiet street where nothing has changed except that his heart has been torn out: everything Dan said is true. As Pascual staggers away, hugging the wall of the building, afraid to be seen from above, he knows that he has failed the objective test. He cannot yet trace out the logic explicitly, but one thing is clear: only he and Djemila knew both the code and the location.

Pascual breaks into a run, trots a few steps, slows again;

his instincts are taking him toward the river, where he can cross the bridge to the Quai des Orfèvres and pound on doors, raise the alarm. Not yet; he will not accept this conclusion that is being forced on him. He cuts across the street into the rue de l'Hirondelle and finds a doorway to duck into; looking back he can just see the entrance to Gilbert's building and high above it the garret window, closed. Pascual shrinks back into shadow, his breath rasping in his throat.

He can hear himself reciting the door code to Djemila over the phone. He can hear her repeating it, the better to pass it on to a man who will slip into the building and climb the stairs, guitar case in hand. No—he will never admit it. The Israeli heard it, too, eavesdropping behind him. Is it Dan who has betrayed him? Horror is everywhere.

But the Israelis could not know the location. He never spoke it in their hearing. Gazing at nothing, Pascual confronts the brutal syllogism. Steps sound in the street; people pass, glancing warily at a man suffering wide-eyed in a doorway.

He looks up at the window of the garret where Djemila made love to him. Nobody ever believes it, he can hear Dan saying. No, thinks Pascual, I don't believe it, not yet, not quite; when I do, the night will be long and black. He remembers Djemila's caress on his cheek and something dies inside him.

He is still standing, unable to move, when Djemila strides up the rue Git le Coeur from the direction of the river, passing within a few meters of him, black hair tossing with her familiar stride. She is an apparition and each step she takes is a blow to his heart. Suddenly he is overcome with rage; he wants to dash after her, grab a handful of that hair and throw her to the ground, put his hands on her throat and watch those deep black eyes dilate with terror. Instead he watches, paralyzed, as she arrives at the door of Gilbert's building. She turns, stooping a bit to bring her face close to the panel in the fading light, and carefully punches in the door code. The sight of her face shakes him; even now he wants to love her. The mechanism works and she pushes the door open and disappears.

Pascual is nauseous; this is beyond appalling, that she would come here to gloat over his corpse, to climb the stairs through the gloom and . . . and what? Wallow in his blood? Shake his killer's bloody hand? Pascual's head is spinning; he understands nothing at all.

As he comes out of the doorway with the first hurried steps, Pascual has not yet begun to make what could be called deductions; he is moving on intuition, sensing that whatever her sins the picture of Djemila coming to stand over his body is wrong. Trotting now, he is striving to grasp the principle here, not yet quite coalesced: if it was Djemila who betrayed him, the last place on earth she would come to would be the rue Git le Coeur. By this time he is sprinting.

If Djemila betrayed him, she would be long gone; her task would have ended with his death. Pascual fetches up with a crash against the solid wooden door and grabs for the number panel, frantically summoning the code. He gasps the six digits as he punches them, misses the last one, stabs again, hits it wrong. He curses, clears and begins again, speaking each number distinctly, forcing himself to hit it right; he can feel Djemila ascending the stairs inside. She has had time enough nearly to reach the top. The soft electronic tone goes and he shoulders into the entryway.

'DJEMILA!' Pascual screams her name, leaping for the stairs. *'Don't go up there!'* The light has not yet expired but he has no time to look up the shaft. He screams as he runs: *'He's waiting in the garret! He's going to kill you!'* Pascual is taking the steps three at a time, hauling himself up by the banister, fighting gravity and time, and he will never make it; it is too far, she has gone too high. As he turns about the second landing his mind is working with terrifying clarity and he knows it is worse even than he thought: the killer has no key and thus cannot be in the garret; he must be on the garret stairs, even now beginning to move with no doors between him and Djemila. *'Run, Djemila! He's just above you!'*

The electric light clicks off, leaving the stairwell in half-light. Above him now Pascual can hear movement, someone coming down with quick light steps; he flings himself around another landing and there she is, his Djemila, eyes wide in the gloom, key in hand, one flight above him.

There are too many footsteps now, and Djemila's face snaps upward; Pascual sees the shock run through her. She screams, a single harsh cry of terror, as something comes flying through the gloom from the floor above and thuds onto the landing next to her; a vast rustling bird with wings spread and a metallic flash tracing its path.

'Jump!' The bird of prey has resolved itself into a man in a hooded plastic poncho with a machete in his hand, steadying

himself against the wall after his hard landing, arm drawn back for the killer stroke at Djemila's neck. *Whoosh-crack*, the slash misses, chopping plaster out of the wall as Djemila leaps, sailing down the entire flight of steps on to Pascual's outstretched arm, staggering him. Above them the wings are spread again and the blade raised and as the bird comes skipping down the stairs Pascual pitches Djemila bodily over the banister into the stairwell, knowing her chances are better with a broken leg two stories down than here on the landing with a severed artery. The motion carries him half over the rail himself and he just has time to heave himself sideways as the machete descends with a thunk, embedding itself in the wood. The second it takes to tug the blade free gives Pascual time to deliver a roundhouse kick that does no damage, the poncho absorbing the blow, and then as the arm is cocked Pascual drives forward, ducking inside the slash and ramming his head into the man's face. They fall against the steps and Pascual butts him again, twice and three times, feeling nose cartilage crack under the solid bone of his forehead, but before he can deliver another blow a hand is clamped over his face, fingers seeking his eyes and the heel finding leverage at the base of his nose, forcing his head back.

Pascual knows that to allow the right arm room to operate is to die; he knocks the hand away from his face and tries for an embrace as fervent as a lover's, but it is too late. The man has twisted free and rolled Pascual onto his side; if not for the fact that his sword arm is needed for support the fight would be over. It takes one more convulsive effort, the man ramming Pascual's head into the steps, for him to regain the upper hand and raise the machete high enough for a quick chop.

Pascual raises his forearm, hoping its bones will be barrier enough to keep the blade from slicing half through his neck, and only peripherally does he see a shape come out of the darkness to knock the man into the wall. The blade never falls because suddenly the man has his own eyes to worry about; Djemila is snarling as she claws at him. He hacks at her but she is inside his radius and he screams as her thumbs go into his eyes. Pascual grabs for the wrist and for his pains receives a lip-splitting blow from the butt of the machete; the man twists again and his face is free but now Pascual has clamped onto the sword arm. As the man hauls himself erect, both feet planted, all he does is to bring Pascual up with him. Pascual drives him against the wall with a shoulder, the machete pinned against his side; he takes a blow to the ear. He hangs on for dear life as the man thrashes, roaring now, pulling away from the wall. Pascual plants his feet and drives him backward toward the banister. He hits it and the frail construction shudders but holds; a fist falls on Pascual's neck, stunning him.

The man's strength is appalling; he forces Pascual away from him and has begun to wrench his arm free when Djemila grabs hold of his leg and lifts. The motion rotates the man backward, out over nothingness; he grabs for the rail with his free hand but it is too late. His weight carries him over and Pascual has the sense to let go of his arm. As he falls, twisting, the man lashes out with the machete and Pascual feels a sharp blow on his hand caught resting on the banister. He watches the shrouded figure tumble as it falls, much further than two stories, it seems, to land with a thump, just visible below.

Djemila is sobbing beside him, leaning over the rail. Pascual stalks slowly down the stairs, watching for signs of life. He passes a light switch and hits it. In the stark electric glare he sees the poncho spread out on the tiles of the foyer, motionless bare legs sticking out, the first ghoulish tongues of blood beginning to seep out from beneath the green plastic. At the bottom of the stairs Pascual approaches, still feeling a suspicious dread, and lifts a corner of the poncho to see that an awkward fall with machete in hand can do nasty things to a man's groin; it will be, Pascual believes, the femoral artery that is dispensing this considerable volume of blood onto the floor.

Djemila has come to join him, reeling but alive. How she reappeared he can only surmise; he must have thrown her too far, onto the next flight down. He reaches for her but she gasps as she sees his hand; only now does Pascual realize that much of this blood must be his, as it seems to be dripping wherever he moves. He looks down to see that something is missing; he is a match for old Dan now.

They have given him drugs and put a blanket over him; he can feel the drugs beginning to work and knows that not only will the pain in his head and his phantom digits be dulled but that he will sleep as well, finally. His left hand is bandaged so heavily he could box a couple of rounds with it. A light is shining in his eyes and he wishes someone would turn it off.

He rolls his head to look at Djemila, watching him with her look of mute patient suffering and holding his good hand. Pale, exhausted, running on willpower, Djemila has her own injuries, a rib cracked, an ankle sprained, but after treatment she has insisted on staying here at his bedside. In the long corridor outside, voices echo. A PJ inspector has come and gone, promising to return; Pascual can still see the impassive skeptical look on his face. There is no keeping them out of it now; like it or not he is going to spend hours, days of his convalescence with policemen. 'I doubted you,' Pascual says.

Djemila brushes hair from his eyes, gives a slow shake of the head. 'You saved my life.'

'And you mine.'

Djemila raises his hand to her lips and then lays it gently on the blanket. She takes her bag from the floor, wincing with the movement, and reaches inside. She pulls out an envelope and holds it for Pascual to see. 'Rachid gave this to Tariq yesterday, about an hour before he was killed. Apparently he also put a copy in the mail to me and e-mailed others to various people.'

'What is it?'

With a note of pride nearly drowned by infinite sadness, she says, 'He solved it. He knows what's on those lorries.'

Pascual blinks at her, finding it hard to summon the energy to respond. Before he slips away he must give her his own news. While waiting on doctors he has had time to put the pieces together. 'And me,' he says, 'I know who killed them all.'

TWENTY-SEVEN

Pascual has learned to get a cigarette lit one-handed, no mean feat with matches. Tonight there is no one about to watch his newly acquired skill. From where he stands in a doorway he can look a long way up three streets without seeing a soul. Gennevilliers has closed down for the night and the only movement is the occasional rush of a car passing by, in a hurry to find brighter lights and brighter prospects. Pascual would flee with them if he could; the longer he stands in this forlorn corner of the far *banlieue,* the tighter the knot in his stomach is pulled.

Pascual knows this car has come for him the moment it appears at the end of the street; instead of fleeing it is cruising. As it eases to the curb he pitches the butt of the cigarette into its path. The men who get out of the car are familiar and Pascual comes out of his doorway. The men cut him off before he can get to the car and propel him gently back against the wall of the building; first there are ceremonies to be gone through.

'Hello, Jacky,' says Pascual. 'Hello, Pierre.'

'What the fuck happened to you?' says Jacky, wiry and intent as ever.

'I got bitten by a nasty little animal,' Pascual says, smiling as Pierre begins to search him.

'Maybe you should keep your hands to yourself,' Jacky says. Pierre freezes as he feels the gun in Pascual's waistband at the small of his back. He tugs the wicked-looking black automatic free and hands it to Jacky with a raise of the eyebrows. Jacky peers at it, turns it over, hefts it, shakes his head and finally lets out a contemptuous laugh. 'It's an air gun. A fucking toy gun. Fires little round pellets, for Christ's sake.' He slips it into his pocket. 'Now what the hell were you going to do with that, put somebody's eye out?'

'Frighten somebody, maybe. It was the best I could do.'

'You'll get yourself shot just for being stupid,' says Jacky. To Pierre he says, 'Check for a wire. That's the type of thing I'd expect from this one.'

The search is thorough, involving a certain amount of indignity. 'He's clean,' says Pierre. Pascual lowers his hands as Pierre steps back. Jacky says, 'Get in the car. No, the front.'

With Pierre behind him, Pascual is careful to avoid sudden moves on the ensuing drive. Past dismal houses and failed bistros they roll, and by the third or fourth turn they are in a wasteland. Oil tanks, vast yards full of scrap, endless brick walls. Jacky pulls over in the shadow of a warehouse and parks, engine running. Pascual is in no mood for banter and there is no conversation. Five minutes later the headlights of a second car wash over them through the rear window. The car pulls up five meters behind them and Jacky opens his door, saying, 'Out you get. Your ride's here.'

Pascual climbs out and follows Jacky toward the second car, squinting into the headlights. The car is a Renault, a common make. Jacky leans down at the driver's window, offering the confiscated pistol. 'He had this on him.' The driver takes the gun as Pascual opens the passenger door and slides onto the seat.

'What the hell is this for?' says Serge, hefting the pellet gun. He is without sunglasses tonight and Pascual can just make out his hazel eyes in the dim light.

'I don't know. Take it if you want.'

Serge points the gun out of the window at a blank wall across the street and squeezes the trigger. Nothing happens.

'I couldn't get any pellets for it,' says Pascual.

Serge shakes his head in wonder and tosses the gun into Pascual's lap. He puts the car in gear. 'What the fuck happened to you?'

'He cocked it up,' says Pascual, stowing the gun. 'Your errand boy blew his big chance.'

Serge sighs. 'It's hard to get good help these days.'

'The police know who he was. They had his prints on file, of course.'

'Of course. He was a common delinquent. And a fucking head case to boot. But don't worry, they won't trace him to me.'

'I should hope not.'

Serge steers through the industrial moonscape with one hand, free arm resting on the windowsill. He could be picking up a weekend guest at a country railway station. 'Found us all right, did you? The directions were clear?'

'Perfectly clear.'

'You've impressed me, I have to say. You found the one weak point in my defenses and went straight for it.'

'Well, after all. Once I knew you and Morrel weren't on official business, it was obvious you'd had to cobble things together a bit, using your own private resources. And the *quincaillerie* had the feel of a place where you were known.'

'Yes. Old Christian is a relative of my mother's. Cousin or something. Old bastard, he's run minor scams of one sort or another out of that back room for years. If I'd ever thought you'd live long enough to get curious, I wouldn't have used him.'

'Nice to know the high regard in which you held me.'

Serge grunts. 'So. How the hell did you smoke me?'

With a wary eye on the massive taurine profile Pascual orders his thoughts. 'Information. The whole thing was about information control.'

'It usually is.'

'The last piece was the door code. It was all pretty confusing until I fixed on that. Your killer had to know the door code. And there weren't too many possibilities for how he could have gotten it. Old Gilbert was gone and the only time the number was spoken aloud was over the phone. The only people who heard it were the Israelis and Djemila. If the Israelis wanted me dead I'd have been dead a week ago and Djemila was a target herself. That left nothing but the phone line. And I finally remembered Morrel telling me about you and that room at the George V.'

'Ah, yes. Bugging the African potentate. My masterwork, if I do say so myself.'

'So then I remembered other things. Like Djemila giving me Najjar's number in Cyprus over the phone.'

'That was lucky. I was in a bit of a panic when you jumped out of the car, I have to say. I'd have got it one way or another, but your fondness for chatting over the wire made it a lot easier.'

'I should have known, I suppose, considering whom we were dealing with. How many taps were there?'

'Just two, the brother's flat in Belleville and the newspaper office. The two key ones. And both as easy as some faked credentials and a box full of tools. Who's going to be suspicious? In these old apartment blocks it's always somebody else's phone that's being worked on. And it's a simple matter to slip in and pick up the cassettes every twenty-four hours or so.'

'And for the rest, you must have tailed us. From the Boulevard de Rochechouart to the rue Git le Coeur. I have to say, you were pretty good. I thought I was being damned careful, taking all the precautions.'

'You were. I cheated a little.'

'How?'

Serge creeps around a corner, steering one-handed. 'Have you had a look at your passport recently? A good close look?'

Pascual thinks; he remembers Morrel sliding the passport across the table to him in the Zurich airport. 'Don't tell me.'

'Yes. They've got clever little transmitters smaller than a one-franc piece these days. And those nice sturdy leather-bound passports the Spanish used to issue can be tampered with, if you're careful. We knew you'd take good care of it. After that you were never off our screen.'

'Brilliant.'

Serge flaps a hand, modestly. 'So you put two and two together.'

'Finally, yes. Once I had the idea, other things fell into place. I remembered that the first time I'd seen your killer guitarist was before Rachid had even got onto the man at the Santé, so he couldn't have set off alarms that way. You'd already got wind of it somehow. The phone, of course. He'd discussed Khaled Marwan with Djemila.'

'At considerable length. I couldn't let that go by.'

Pascual nods. 'Because Albert Nogent was on record as having come to question Marwan at the Santé.'

'Ah, you did finally get that, did you?'

'Rachid got the word from his contact and immediately wrote it all down and posted it. He just had time before your man got to him.'

'The imbecile waited too long. I told him quick and dirty was the way to go, but he said he knew how to get a key and set up a quiet ambush. I deferred to his expertise. He was good at that sort of thing.'

Pascual shakes his head slowly. 'So who were the two Swiss who came to pick up Marwan? You and Nogent?'

'Of course. And that's why I couldn't let the inquiry go on. If anybody checked, they'd find that those Swiss credentials had been used in a little caper we'd run together with the DGSE a couple of years before, over in Lausanne. And I was on record as having signed for them.'

'Phone taps, phony papers. Is there anything you don't do?'

With a laconic shrug Serge says, 'Everyone has his talents. Me, I'm the technician.'

'So what happened to Marwan?'

'What do you think happened? He's fertilizing a nice leafy glade out in the Ardennes somewhere. I couldn't find the place again if I had to.'

'Why did Nogent go and talk to him in the first place?'

'The PJ called us in when Marwan started babbling about terrorists. He knew who Najjar was and thought he could swing a trade.'

'He should have kept his mouth shut, the poor trusting bastard.'

'Save your tears. He was another delinquent. Here we are.' Serge turns, and suddenly the river opens out before them, a vast sheet of brooding unquiet blackness reflecting the lights on the far bank. A skyline of smokestacks, cranes and massive piles of indeterminate matter crowds a shore broken by a jumble of docks. Nothing is moving on the water, but the long, dark shapes of barges huddle along its edge. Serge parks and he and Pascual get out as Jacky, who has been trailing, pulls up a short distance away.

'Le Port Autonome de Paris,' says Serge, sauntering toward the water's edge. A night breeze comes over the water, ruffling Pascual's hair and making him shiver. 'Most people don't even know it's here. The tourist boats don't come this far. And it handles thousands of tons of shipping, imagine.' At the water's edge he turns, at arm's length from Pascual. There is just enough light for Pascual to see the narrowed eyes in the broad butcher's face. 'And Zurich?' says Serge quietly. 'You figured that out, too, did you?'

'Don't worry, I won't tell Jacky and the others.' Serge nods very slightly and Pascual goes on. 'It was easy, once I started thinking of you as the protagonist. I realized that there was no reason to think you'd gone back to Paris except that Morrel said so. I remembered that the shooter was a big man, about your size in fact. I remembered Morrel saying *salaud,* and that somehow sounded more personal than a man dying in a professional hit. That started to sound a lot like a man protesting betrayal. And the more I thought about it, the more I started to think there was a reason I'd survived. A good hit man would not have left me alive. But you still needed me.'

Serge nods. 'Until I got Najjar.'

'It was just supposed to be Couvet, wasn't it? Morrel planned it that way but you decided to take him out as well. A man you'd worked with for fifteen years.'

Inscrutable in the gloom, Serge says, 'Worked *for* would be more like it. Albert could be a real prick when he wanted to. And he never liked the concept of equal partners. If I hadn't done him first, he'd have done me.'

'That'll do for a justification, I suppose.'

Serge grunts with what might be laughter or contempt. 'It's all I need. Now tell me what you want.'

Pascual spreads his arms in an extravagant shrug. 'I want my share. I want my hundred thousand dollars. As promised. That's all I want and I think you'll agree it's only fair.'

Serge gives him a long look. 'And what's to stop me from cracking your skull and tossing you into the water right here?'

'Information control, again. If Djemila doesn't hear from me tonight, the story goes out in the morning. And I guarantee you, she's well out of your reach. You'll never stop her.'

Serge shakes his head, a smile spreading. 'The power of the press, eh? Your faith is touching.'

Pascual leans into Serge's space, jaw jutting. 'Who's talking about the press? The story goes to Mirakl in the morning. Direct line to Kovalenko, chapter and verse. You want to run from *them* for the rest of your life?'

The smile does not fade immediately but Serge has the look of a man making rapid reassessments. He finishes his sums and says, 'I'll be able to buy a lot of privacy, a lot of distance.'

'You'll be able to buy *me* for a hundred thousand dollars and never have to worry about Mirakl. I'd call that a fucking bargain, wouldn't you?' Pascual holds the stare as seconds crawl by. Finally Serge shrugs.

'All right. You'd better come aboard.' He turns and beckons. Moored beneath them is a barge, the classic Seine *péniche*, forty meters long with a wheelhouse at the rear. Serge goes down a ladder to the narrow walkway along the gently humped deck and Pascual follows him aft as Jacky and Pierre descend behind them. There is a third man on the deck in the shadows near the wheelhouse, another hard type Pascual believes he last saw in the back of a van in a meadow near Zurich. Serge exchanges a quiet greeting in passing and leads Pascual into the dimly lit wheelhouse and down a companionway to surprisingly spacious quarters below.

There is a short corridor with two doors on either side;

Serge goes through the first door on the right. Pascual follows and finds himself in a small cabin reeking of tobacco smoke with a porthole, a long narrow table with a padded bench on either side, and some shelves bearing a jumble of crockery, books, a small television, miscellaneous clutter. Sitting at the table with ashtray and playing cards between them are two men: a gaunt middle-aged hawk of a man in a brown jacket and a blue baseball cap with the name and number of an American naval ship on it and a very haggard Daoud Najjar.

Pascual can do nothing but stare. At a look from Serge the gaunt man tosses down his cards, stands and shuffles past Pascual out of the cabin. Serge stands with his hands in his pockets looking like an amateur magician who has just amazed a room full of dinner guests. 'You may recognize an old friend,' he says.

Pascual sinks to the bench opposite Najjar. 'You didn't kill him,' he says.

'I didn't have to. I didn't even have to pressure him in the slightest. Once he recognized the parameters of the situation, he was more than willing to help. Mr. Najjar is a realist. Eh, Najjar?'

Najjar has lost weight and his eyes have hollowed out. He has not shaved recently and his glasses have gone missing; the suit coat he is wearing is too big for him and several years past its prime. He draws on a cigarette and gives Serge a completely impenetrable look. 'We've reached an accommodation,' he says.

Serge inclines his head, graciously. 'Mr. Najjar's help has

been invaluable but his participation is nearly completed. We'll be setting him ashore once the transfer is made at Le Havre, as agreed. He'll even make a substantial fee on the deal.'

Pascual scrambles to catch up and says, 'And what's to stop him sending Mirakl after you?'

'Guarantees.' Serge is looking down his nose at Najjar. 'He's got a pretty daughter in school in Berlin. He doesn't care much for the mother anymore, but even a bastard like Najjar can be a doting father.' Serge turns to Pascual. 'It always pays to do the research.'

Pascual looks at Najjar and remembers all the times Najjar has wielded the stick. He shakes his head and rises to his feet. To Serge he says, 'I'd like to have a look at your cargo if I could. It's not something you see every day.'

Serge smiles and jerks his head toward the door. 'Follow me.'

As Pascual steps to the door Najjar speaks. *'Istanna.'* The Arabic word for *wait* halts Pascual in his tracks. 'He's going to kill us both,' says Najjar in his native tongue. 'You know that, don't you? If you believe a word he says you're a fool.'

Pascual stares at him and in the same language says, 'You, maybe. It's all you deserve.'

'We've got to cooperate,' says Najjar to Pascual's back. 'You and me, it's our only chance.'

'What's that all about, then?' says Serge, leading him back up the companionway.

'He thinks you're going to kill him.'

'Not as long as there's any chance of Mirakl picking up a trail,' says Serge. 'He's got a certain value as a hostage. But as soon as we're in open water I could be persuaded to reconsider the position.'

He leads Pascual through the wheelhouse out onto the deck, where Jacky and Pierre and their colleague are smoking and murmuring in the darkness. Serge takes a flashlight from Jacky and leads Pascual along the side of the deck to a hatch at the bow. He lifts the hatch, shines the light onto the steps of a ladder, and lowers his considerable bulk onto it with a grunt of effort. Pascual follows him down.

At the bottom of the ladder the light sweeps about a vast empty hold. 'This thing can hold two hundred and fifty tons,' says Serge. 'Those two great lorries Najjar scared up were creaking on their springs, but this thing's got room to spare. We're going to take on a hundred tons of sand tomorrow as cover and then we'll be on our way.' He is leading Pascual aft and the light is already flicking over a shrouded mass sitting roughly amidships; the hold is not empty after all. Serge lifts a corner of the tarpaulin that covers the shoulder-high pile. Beneath is wood: four layers of wooden crates sitting on wooden pallets. The crates are small, the size used to transport oranges or bananas, and they are unmarked. With his fingers Serge pries up a slat on a crate in the topmost layer. 'The nails were gone from this one when we got hold of the stuff. I guess everyone just has to have a look.' Pascual leans forward.

The light plays lovingly over the neatly aligned bars glowing with the rich heart-stopping hue that nothing else in the world besides gold can ever quite match. Pascual can see the hammer and sickle, the serial numbers and assay marks stamped in the metal.

'How many tons?' he says reverently.

'There were fifty to start out with. Kovalenko got them out of Russia in ninety-one when you could do just about anything you pleased if you knew a few key people, but when he got them to Zurich he found out it wasn't as easy as he thought to get a Swiss bank to just stash them and give him a receipt. There would have been a lot of awkward questions and sooner or later somebody would have come out of Russia after them. The state had collapsed but nobody just lets fifty tons of gold walk away. Kovalenko didn't want to answer the questions and he didn't want his name bandied about, so he just hid it and decided to wait for the fuss to die down.'

'Fifty tons of gold,' Pascual breathes.

'Very roughly half a billion dollars,' says Serge. 'Just lying there for anyone with the initiative to take it.'

Pascual can just make out Serge in the reflected light from the flashlight. 'So Khaled Marwan told your pal Nogent that day at the Santé that Daoud Najjar had fifty tons of gold stashed near Zurich. And going after it became your life's work.'

'Albert's, anyway. That was why he left the service. I always thought it was a bit of a wild goose chase until the name Najjar came up in the report from that Arab at the bank. Suddenly it all started to look possible. I rang up Albert and resigned the next day. How did you figure out it was the gold?'

'Rachid guessed. He'd found an ex-MVD man who knew what Kovalenko had gotten up to, and he put it together with Zurich, the lorries and the deal with Boucherif. But he didn't know where it had gone.'

Serge looses a chuckle into the dark. 'Here, of course. Why do you think they wanted the Banque Villefort?'

Pascual nods. 'It's got a vault large enough, has it?'

'And no upright Swiss deacons to stand on ceremony. Just their own pet banker to fiddle the papers. But the best part was that they couldn't lose on the deal with Boucherif. If he reneged, they had his gold right there in their bank.'

'And what is Mirakl receiving for this princely sum?'

'Oil. Gas. The works. A virtual Mirakl monopoly, when Boucherif takes power. With half a billion dollars in a legiti-mate Paris bank he would be in a position to buy himself two or three private armies. For Mirakl and the general it was what the Americans call a win-win proposition. You have to admire them both.'

Pascual shakes his head in admiration. 'How did you get it back out of the bank?'

'Most of it never made it into the bank. You don't just back up the lorries and start unloading. If you want to get the stuff discreetly stashed away, you have to bring it in in small amounts, over time, using the same armored car firm that you usually use. Fifty tons of gold will raise a lot of eye-brows. So they stashed the lorries at the big depot up in Aulnay-sous-Bois and went to work. In the week it took me to track down Najjar in Cyprus, they moved about five tons into the bank. The rest is right here.'

Pascual frowns. 'Aulnay-sous-Bois, that's not too far from the Canal de l'Ourcq, is it? Those three Algerians they pulled out of the canal, would they have anything to do with this?'

'Bravo. They were Boucherif's people, left to stand guard

over the load. With Najjar to get us in, it was child's play for Jacky and his boys to take them out. Fast and quiet. Jacky learned his trade in a rough school, you know. He spent a lot of years in Africa.'

Pascual runs his fingers over the smooth, hard surface of a gold bar. 'If Kovalenko had trouble turning this into cash, what makes you think you can?'

'Kovalenko was an amateur. He thought he could drop fifty tons of gold off at the back door of Crédit Suisse like a man depositing his paycheck. Me, I'm more realistic. And I'm patient. I know it's going to take time. I figure five years at least to turn this pile of metal into safe discreet bank accounts with names on them that no one will ever trace to me. And there will be a lot of expenses. I've got staff to pay, palms to grease all along the way, high transport costs, and a big commission to the people in Beirut who are going to re-smelt all this so nobody ever questions its provenance. It's a major enterprise and if I pull it off I'll have earned my retirement.'

'You're not worried about Jacky getting ideas like you did, about the wisdom of sharing?'

'Ah, no. Jacky knows his limits. He's not a manager, he's a foot soldier. A very highly paid one. That's the secret, you keep people happy. That's where all the expense money's going.' He plays the light over the pile of gold. 'But even if half of this goes out in expenses, a couple of hundred million dollars ought to be enough to retire on, don't you think?' Serge replaces the pried up slat, gives it a tender pat.

'It would last me for a while. But all I want is my hundred

thousand. And not a check on some fictional bank in the Caribbean, either.'

Serge laughs again, a rumbling wheeze. 'The bank was real. It would have been a hell of an overdraft, though. You've got a lot of balls, you know, walking in here like this.'

'I'm a realist. You won't kill me as long as Djemila's got the goods on you.'

'No, I suppose I can't.' Serge pulls the tarp back over the cargo and seeks the ladder with the flashlight beam. 'Shall we go and talk terms?'

'The terms are very simple.'

'I don't have a hundred thousand in cash on me, if that's what you're thinking. We'll have to reach an accommodation.'

Pascual laughs softly, following him up the ladder. 'Why don't I like the sound of that word?'

They make their way aft under the shadow of the dock. The smoking party is still there, silent now, cigarettes glowing in the dark. Serge hands the flashlight back to Jacky and he and Pascual go into the wheelhouse. The man in the brown jacket is rummaging in a corner, pulling things out of a locker, his back turned. Serge and Pascual go down the companionway. In the corridor Serge says quietly, 'Poor Captain Lagrange, he's not too happy with the class of person using his precious boat. But he's a realist, too. The barges are dying, killed by road and rail. He hadn't had a load in months and now he'll be able to pay off all his debts.' Serge pushes into the cabin.

He pauses, looking at the empty benches, a cigarette smoldering in the ashtray. He turns, pushes back past Pascual, goes to the next door down and opens it, then crosses to the door on the opposite side of the corridor. He pushes on the door, meets resistance, looks around the edge of the door, toward the floor. He curses and comes tearing back past Pascual to the companionway. He goes up at speed.

Pascual does not see the blow but he hears it; it sounds like a flowerpot dropping on cement. Serge slides back down the ladder feet first and crumples at its foot. He is not quite out; he is able to make it on to his hands and knees and crawl two or three baby steps down the corridor toward Pascual, eyes squeezed shut, as Daoud Najjar comes down the steps, dressed in the captain's brown jacket and blue cap.

Najjar tosses the wrench into a corner and reaches into the right-hand pocket of the jacket. He pulls out a short-bladed wooden-handled kitchen knife. As Serge begins to growl, pain forcing animal sounds out of his throat, Najjar straddles him and takes a handful of his hair.

'This is for Lisette,' he says, pulling Serge's head back and cutting his throat with a swift savage jerk of the arm. Blood rains onto the planking with a soft splattering sound. Najjar releases his grip and stumbles against the wall, regaining his balance. He tosses the knife to the floor. He pushes Serge's corpse over onto its side and stoops to tug the automatic from the holster on the dead man's belt, taking pains to avoid the creeping blood. Straightening he looks at Pascual.

'Are you with me?' he says.

'I'm with you,' Pascual says without hesitation, amazed to find his voice. He cannot take his eyes off Serge's face, already drained of color.

'Then we can take them all,' says Najjar. 'You go first, ask them for a light, chat them up. That will occupy them and give me a chance to get close enough for three sure shots.'

Pascual gapes at him but his mind is working with a supernatural calm. 'They won't see us if we just slip over the stern. Can you swim?'

'Swim? In this muck? You're out of your mind. Three quick shots and we're quit of the whole rabble.'

'Give me the gun, then. I'll go first and do the shooting, you can bring up the rear.'

Najjar smiles, the jovial butcher. 'You don't trust me? The man who kept you in funds and out of jail for six years?'

'I know you won't fire down here because it would alert them. So for now I trust you. Up there, no. I won't trust you because I know you.'

Najjar gives one impatient shake of the head. 'All right, stay here then. I'll go and do the dirty business.' He starts to turn away and then halts and says, 'You never had any fucking nerve, did you? The first time they gave you a real assignment you ran and sold us all out.'

'I'm a coward to my toes,' Pascual says. 'Always have been.'

'Then stay here and keep him company.' He wheels and makes for the companionway.

Pascual watches him disappear and then begins to move. He steps carefully around the wreckage of Serge and reaches the bottom of the ladder as, above him, the door giving on to the deck opens. He climbs up into the wheelhouse and raises his head cautiously high enough to see through the windows. At first he cannot see Najjar but then the figure in cap and jacket shambles into view, going forward along the walkway. Jacky and his companions are just visible at the foot of the ladder up to the dock, two of them seated on the curved deck covering and one standing. The glow of a cigarette traces a path from waist to mouth. Three heads turn as Najjar approaches, hands in the pocket of the jacket. Pascual is ill, teeth clenched. Now is the moment, he thinks, nip out the door and over the stern and take my chances with the bacteria in the Seine. Instead he watches Najjar approach the three men on the deck; he sees the hand with the cigarette rise, sees the standing man reach into a shirt pocket, sees the first stiffening of alarm, recognition, and then sees and hears the shots, flashes in the dark CRACK CRACK CRACK, men twisting, dying and a pause and then CRACK CRACK and silence. Pascual watches Najjar lean over for a *coup de grâce* CRACK.

He watches Najjar come quickly back along the walkway, knowing that his chance to run is lost forever. He can hear somebody, he cannot remember who, saying *you've gone very public-spirited in your old age*. He can also hear the shots, all five of them, no, six. He watches as Najjar returns, Najjar watching him as he stands in the lighted wheelhouse as good as on display, waiting. As Najjar pushes open the door Pascual brings the harmless pellet gun out of his pocket and points it at Najjar's face. 'Don't even think about it.'

Najjar halts, hands in the jacket pockets, a look of wary intensity on his face. 'What the hell's the matter with you? I just cleared the way for us.'

Pascual sees him looking at the pellet gun and knows it

will not stand much examination, even at a distance of two meters. 'And if all you wanted was to run, you'd have gone straight on up the ladder. Now take the gun out *slowly,* by the muzzle, and toss it to me. Gently.' This is the role of his life, Pascual knows; he has pulled off myriad impersonations and crossed half of Europe on false papers and lied his way out of imbroglios large and small, but if he cannot pull off this deception he dies. 'Toss me the gun and you're free. Simple terms. Your gun for your freedom.'

Najjar considers everything, eyes going back and forth between the muzzle of the pellet gun and Pascual's face, and his tried and tested capacity for risk analysis produces a decision. He pulls Serge's automatic out of the pocket, slowly, and tosses it across the wheelhouse to Pascual, who tries to pin it against his body with his bandaged hand, drops it on the deck with a solid clunk, stoops to hook his thumb through the trigger guard, and rises again, never taking the muzzle of the pellet gun off Najjar. 'All right?' says Najjar.

'All right.' Pascual slips the pellet gun into his pocket and shifts the automatic to his right hand.

Najjar begins to turn away, glaring. '*Adieu, donc.* That's twice. I don't recommend you try your luck with me a third time.'

The gun is a Glock 17, a state-of-the-art weapon, so named for the seventeen rounds it can hold in the magazine; Najjar could have fired twice as many shots and had some to spare. 'One more thing,' says Pascual.

'Eh?' Najjar freezes, but the supercilious look of the man who always manages to walk away has returned to his face.

Pascual has memorable lines on the tip of his tongue but this is not the time to use them. He fires, twice into the torso and then, stepping forward, once more as Najjar's terrified eyes gleam at him from the deck where he has fallen, half out of the wheelhouse, clutching the doorframe, and then finally the *coup de grâce* through the high forehead. Pascual steps over the body and stands in the freshening river breeze, listening as the distant sirens draw nearer.

TWENTY-EIGHT

'It was self-defense. He had a knife.' Pascual runs a hand over his face. He has not slept in forty-eight hours and it is beginning to tell on him.

The burly inspector from the police judiciaire raises an eyebrow. 'The one we found on the floor belowdecks? That knife?'

'I don't know. It was dark, there was a lot of confusion, I was under a lot of stress. I may have got a few things wrong.'

'You sound remarkably calm on that,' the inspector says, gesturing at the tiny voice-operated digital recorder on the table between them.

'That wasn't calm, it was terror.'

The inspector scowls at Pascual for another half minute before deciding that he has wrung all he is going to get out of this damp rag. He trades a look with the silent pale man at the end of the table, the DST *éminence grise* who is the mastermind of this whole bloody fiasco. 'I've got to take this thing before a judge, you know,' the inspector says.

The pale man makes a faint sound of amusement. 'I think

everything's clear, don't you? I don't see any problem with self-defense. You can't tell from the recording where the knife wound up.' He reaches for the pellet gun, hefts it admiringly, peers into the cavity in the grip where the recorder was hidden. 'That was a hell of an idea the tech boys came up with, eh? Even if they'd taken it from you, it would still have been there to record things.'

Pascual has closed his eyes, resting his head on his hand. He is acutely aware of alternate pathways down which the cleverness of the tech boys could have taken him and all he wants is to sleep.

The inspector is looking at the DST man with distaste. 'I'll admit, you got some remarkable evidence on that tape. It seems to clear up a lot of obscure matters.' He pushes away from the table, gathering papers. 'It's just too bad there's nobody left to prosecute.'

'Save you all a lot of trouble,' Pascual murmurs. 'Call it a public service.'

'The news out of Algiers is that Boucherif has been arrested. There are rumors of tanks in the streets but then there are always tanks in the streets.' Djemila looks somehow softer today, some of the angles smoothed, some of the knife-edge wariness gone. Perhaps some of the tension has eased, or perhaps she is only tired. Pascual thinks she is the loveliest woman on earth.

'Your work?' he says.

'Couvet's, more likely. His employers got their money's worth.'

For a moment they are silent, shades of the dead passing like a cold breath across the heart. Pascual feels a hundred years old. He takes a drink of tea made thick and sweet, as in her martyred homeland. In the next room Djemila's brother is watching football, dandling a child on his knee. From the kitchen come clanging and sizzling sounds along with smells that remind Pascual how long it has been since he has eaten well. 'When does the story run?'

'Tomorrow. Tariq's doubling the press run and I've been fielding offers from papers from here to Moscow.'

'You're not worried about your name being on the story?'

She shrugs. 'It's my story. What other name am I going to put on it? I may even get a job out of it. I've had some calls.'

Pascual reaches for her hand. 'Be careful.'

She shrugs. 'When are you going?'

'As soon as the *juge d'instruction* is finished with me. A matter of days, I'm told. And before any of your professional colleagues catch up with me, I hope. Thanks for leaving my name out.'

The melancholy is there in her eyes again. 'We made a good team, didn't we?'

Pascual nods, noting the verb tense. He knows as he says them that his words are futile; he is a bad bet for any woman and this is not just any woman. 'You could come with me.'

Djemila appears to give it some thought, gazing at him with those eyes full of knowledge. 'I'll know where to find you,' she says. 'Let's leave it at that for the moment.'

It is raining again in Paris, a thick vengeful downpour in the night, drumming on roofs and windows, driving people to shelter, blurring, splintering and multiplying lights in the City of Light, washing the dirt and the waste into the river that will carry it away. Under their awning Pascual and Djemila stand in an embrace, silent for long minutes now, unable to compete with the pounding of the rain just above their heads. Across the square the coach stands rumbling, a cluster of umbrellas at its door. 'They're loading,' says Pascual.

Djemila eases away and takes his face in her hands. 'Tomorrow you'll be in Barcelona.'

The thought lifts his spirits for a moment: France passing in the night, the southbound Rhône shining at dawn, mountains and the sea. 'It's not too late. There are empty seats, the driver said so.'

She smiles, tears just beginning to gather at the corners of her eyes. 'What about my things?'

'Have your brother send them.'

'No. It's a pretty idea, but no.'

'You'd like Barcelona. We can live cheap, you'll find work. It's a good place to be poor and happy.'

Shaking her head, she says, 'No. I'm going back to Algiers.'

Pascual has seen it coming but it takes the bone from his legs, the breath from his voice nonetheless. 'You can't. They'll kill you.'

'They can try. They can't kill us all.'

Pascual feels panic rising; Paris is one thing, but Algiers is the belly of the beast. 'Don't go. This is where your work is, your family.'

'Algeria is my family. My brothers and sisters are dying.'

This is a fight he will not win, Pascual knows. There are people whose strength is beyond measure. He opens his mouth to say the things that have never been said, but Djemila places a hand over it. 'Don't say it. Me, too, believe it. We had it longer than some people do.'

'Listen . . .'

'Adieu, donc,' she says, and then she is gone, running away into the rain, sodden coils of black hair flying, raising splashes as she goes.

We'll always have Paris, Pascual thinks bitterly, watching the shimmering city slide away from him through the window of the coach. But he knows that he has never had it, never will, any more than he can have Djemila. A city, a human heart; who can know all the byways?

Rain falls on Paris in the night and in the morning it will be gone.

About the Author

Dominic Martell was born in the United States but has spent a considerable period of his life abroad. He has lived in Spain and France and made extended journeys in Latin America, Europe, and the Middle East. He studied philosophy and languages and has worked as a translator and a teacher. *The Republic of Night* is his second novel featuring Pascual Rose (*Lying Crying Dying,* also published by Carroll & Graf, was the first). He is currently working on his third. Mr. Martell is married and has a son and a daughter.